The SHOESTRING CLUB

Sarah Webb worked as a children's bookseller for many years before becoming a full-time writer. Writing is her dream job as she can travel, read magazines and books, watch movies, and quiz her friends and family – all in the name of research.

She is the author of nine novels, the most recent being *Anything for Love* and *The Loving Kind*. She also writes the Ask Amy Green series for young teenagers, and her books have been published in many different countries including Italy, Poland, Indonesia and the United States. Sarah lives in Dublin with her partner and young family.

Find out more and read Sarah's Yours in Writing blog at
www.sarahwebb.ie

Or connect with Sarah on Facebook:
www.facebook.com/sarahwebbauthor

or Twitter: @sarahwebbishere

The
SHOESTRING
• CLUB •

Sarah Webb

MACMILLAN

First published 2012 by Macmillan
an imprint of Pan Macmillan, a division of Macmillan Publishers Limited
Pan Macmillan, 20 New Wharf Road, London N1 9RR
Basingstoke and Oxford
Associated companies throughout the world
www.panmacmillan.com

ISBN 978-0-230-74871-2

A CIP catalogue record for this book is available from
the British Library.

Typeset by CPI Typesetters
Printed and bound by CPI Group (UK) Ltd, Croydon, CR0 4YY

Visit www.panmacmillan.com to read more about all our books
and to buy them. You will also find features, author interviews and
news of any author events, and you can sign up for e-newsletters
so that you're always first to hear about our new releases.

*This book is dedicated to my dear friend
and fellow writer, Martina Devlin*

The credit belongs to the man who is actually in the arena, whose face is marred by dust and sweat and blood; who strives valiantly; who errs, who comes short again and again, because there is no effort without error and short-coming; but who does actually strive to do the deeds; who knows great enthusiasms, the great devotions; who spends himself in a worthy cause; who at the best knows in the end the triumph of high achievement, and who at the worst, if he fails, at least fails while daring greatly, so that his place shall never be with those cold and timid souls who neither know victory nor defeat.

The Man in the Arena, from a speech by
Theodore Roosevelt, 23 April 1910

Prologue

In June I screamed for two days solid.

It all started on a quiet Sunday morning. I was standing behind the till at Shoestring, my sister Pandora's designer swap shop, flicking through a copy of *i-D* magazine and minding my own business, when Pandora handed me a cream envelope.

'This was in the postbox outside,' she said. 'Must have been delivered last night.'

I looked at the envelope suspiciously. Plush, expensive looking, my name – *Julia Schuster* – carefully handwritten in sky-blue ink across the middle.

I relaxed a little. A final warning from my credit card company was unlikely to come in such smart packaging. Then I peered at it closely. The script looked familiar but I couldn't quite place it. Wish I had. I would have thrown the whole wretched thing in the bin unopened. Or burned it.

'Take it.' Pandora thrust the envelope into my hands. 'Some of us have work to do,' she added with a sniff and then walked off. I rolled my eyes behind her back. Pandora was in one of her moods and I'd spent most of the morning trying to avoid her.

Curious, I ripped open the envelope and pulled out the letter which had been wrapped around an invitation card. I unfolded it and read the Dear Jules at the top. Only then did it come to me – of course – it was Lainey's neat, prissy handwriting. Bloody nerve. My stomach clenched at the mere thought of Lainey Anderson. But being terminally nosey, I had to read on.

Dear Jules,

I know we haven't spoken since the morning after the party and I'm still SO sorry about all that. I hope your head is OK. Those stitches must have hurt.

You're totally right, I should have told you about me and Ed beforehand. The night of his birthday do was a rubbish time to announce it. But when you got back from New Zealand, Ed made me promise to keep quiet for a few weeks, said you needed time to process everything. I guess after that the right opportunity never came along and, to be honest, I was a bit scared of what you'd say. And the longer I left it, the harder it got.

I hated sneaking around behind your back, Jules, believe me. And I feel even worse now that you're so upset. But at least there was no one in the toilet to hear you screaming at me that night. I genuinely had no idea you'd take it so badly. You told me you were completely over Ed, that you had no idea what you'd ever seen in him.

OK, I understand how you must have felt, being the last person to know, and I swear the proposal came as a complete shock to me too – I genuinely had no idea he was going to fall on his knee like that, in front of everyone! But you know Ed, he loves a bit of drama. At least Kia was there to catch you when you fainted and take you to the hospital.

Please answer your mobile, Jules, I really need to talk to you. I rang the shop but Bird went all funny and refused to put you on the line, said you were distraught and that she'd shoot me with her air rifle if I went near the shop or ever tried contacting you again. (Does she actually own one by the way? Or any sort of gun? I wouldn't put it past her!)

I rang back loads of times and eventually managed to get Pandora who said you were shaken but as well as could be expected in the circumstances; that the scar on your head would heal even if the scar on your heart would be there for all eternity. (Everyone in your family's so melodramatic, Jules, but I do love them for it!)

Look, I know you and Ed have oceans of history – I was the one who picked up the pieces every time you guys argued. But that was a long time ago, things change, people move on.

Anyway, I guess you need some space right now, but we've been best friends for ever and I really want you there at the wedding. And Ed feels the same way too. I know you're unlikely to want to be a bridesmaid after everything that's happened, but if you change your mind the offer's still there.

Please, please, please say you'll come! It won't be the same without you. I'll try calling in to the shop again. I'm not giving up, we've been friends for too long and I don't want to lose you. Besides, who's going to help me find the perfect wedding dress? My sisters will probably put me in some sort of hideous meringue.

Please forgive me! I miss you, Jules.
Love always,
Lainey XXX

There was a smiley face over the 'i' of her name and I stared at it, practically growling. I pulled the thick cream invitation and RSVP card out of the envelope and ran my fingers over the embossed gold writing. Classy.

MR AND MRS NIGEL ANDERSON
REQUEST THE PLEASURE OF THE COMPANY OF

Julia Schuster + guest

AT THE MARRIAGE OF THEIR DAUGHTER
ELAINE MILDRED ANDERSON TO
EDMUND PATRICK POWERS

AT ST JUDE'S CHURCH, DALKEY

ON SATURDAY 27TH OCTOBER AT 2.00 P.M.

AND AFTERWARDS AT
THE ROYAL ST GEORGE YACHT CLUB,
DUN LAOGHAIRE

RSVP SEA VIEW, VICO ROAD, DALKEY

My eyes started to well up and I blinked the tears back furiously, grabbed a pen and scribbled across the RSVP card:

Never! I'd rather die. You have got to be kidding me, Lainey!

Then I ripped the invitation in half, which wasn't easy as the card was ultra thick, threw it on the floor and stamped on it. Lainey and Ed. My best friend and the love of my life – together, for ever. It was really happening.

And that's when I started screaming.

4

Chapter 1

By August, Lainey had eventually stopped ringing my mobile several times a day, leaving contrite messages. So I was caught out on Saturday evening when I snatched up my iPhone and gave a cheery 'Yello?' before checking the number first.

'Jules!' she said. 'Finally. Please don't hang up.'

'Too late,' I yelled, my hands shaking so much it took me a second to click the end call button.

I sat on the edge of my bed, quivering with rage. My phone rang again but I let it go straight to messages. Then . . . silence. I picked it up, willing myself to delete the message without listening, but it was no use. I had to torture myself.

'Hi, Jules.' Lainey gave a nervous laugh. 'Look, you have every right to put the phone down on me. But I just wanted to tell you that I'm seeing my sisters tonight, to talk about my hen night. Karen and Kia are organizing it. Maybe you'll think about coming – the date hasn't been set yet, but it won't be for a while. I know I'm not your favourite person right now, but I hope you'll get in touch soon. Um, well, I guess that's it then. I miss you, Jules. Bye, love you . . .'

Hen party. If things were different, I'd be the one organizing Lainey's hen for her. I knew I had no right to feel annoyed, I was the one not speaking to *her*, but it still hurt. I erased the message, stood up and checked myself out in the mirror, determined to block Lainey from my mind. I stared at my reflection. Vintage black, blue and green 70s Missoni minidress I'd found in Pandora's shop, teamed with a pair of pale blue Meadham Kirchhoff beaded platforms. I threw my favourite black biker jacket over the dress and smiled. Perfect. I grabbed my bag and went downstairs for a swift glass or two of wine before Rowie collected me in a taxi. My nerves were still jangling from Lainey's call but I wasn't going to let it spoil my night.

Rowie is actually one of Pandora's friends from fashion college. Now she owns her own boutique in Sandycove, Baroque, where I also work. She used to be a real party girl, but now only goes on the razz when her Danish boyfriend, Olaf, is at some car rally or other in the bog lands. He's decent enough and I guess attractive in that clean, blond Nordic way that does nothing for me, but very intense and rather boring.

But even after many, many drinks I still couldn't get Lainey's niggling voice out of my head.

'I miss you, Jules.' 'Love you.'

Really, Lainey? If you love me, why did you betray me? Answer that.

Now it's Sunday and I'm standing behind the till at Shoestring again, head dipped, elbows resting on the wood, trying not to think about my raging hangover or Lainey Anderson.

'Julia, what are you doing? If you're reading magazines on my time again, I'm docking your wages, understand?'

I look up and groan. Pandora is striding towards me, a stark white dress-carrier the size of a body bag clutched against her chest.

'I was massaging my temples. I have a headache.'

She scowls at me. 'Shouldn't have drunk so much last night then, should you?'

'I forgot I was working today, OK?'

'You always forget, Jules, that's your problem. You should keep a diary. What happened to that Filofax I gave you last Christmas? The pink leather one.'

6

I rack my brains and stare at her blankly. I have no idea. To be honest, I was a bit of a mess on Christmas Day. Ed and I had done our usual Christmas Eve thing – Finnegan's pub in Dalkey to catch up with all our ex-pat friends who were home for Christmas. It was a tradition.

We'd officially broken up in early December, just after I'd returned to Dublin after six months working and travelling in New Zealand, but Ed and I were always breaking up and making up, so I figured that after a bit of Christmas cheer everything would be back to normal.

Over the past five years I'd lived in Paris, Rome, Budapest, Wellington, Christchurch and Auckland, travelling until I ran out of money, then working in bars and shops until I got homesick for Ireland and, pining for Ed, flew back to Dublin. It had become a bit of a pattern – I spent spring working at whatever temporary jobs I could find at home, saving and organizing myself to go away; summer in another country; and autumn, and most especially Christmas, back home again. And then I'd get bored of Ireland and its parochialism, my itchy feet would kick in and the cycle would start all over again.

But last Christmas Eve, something had changed. I'd spent all night willing Ed to make a move, hoping that he'd had time to come to his senses, every molecule of my being begging him to want me again. But when our usual snog under the mistletoe morphed into an awkward hug and cheek kiss, followed by a firm goodbye and I staggered home from the pub alone, I slowly came to the crushing realization that the clock was not going to turn back in a magical *Dr Who* manner, and that Ed Powers no longer loved me.

'I'm sure it's around somewhere,' I mumble. I think I gave it to my niece, Iris, and God knows what she's done with it.

Thankfully Pandora lets it go. 'Guess where I've just been?' she asks, her voice uncharacteristically upbeat.

7

I study her face with interest. Yep, she's actually smiling. Pandora is the biggest grump in the universe and it takes a lot to animate her, especially on a Sunday afternoon. She hates opening Shoestring on Sundays, but with all the competition from Dundrum Shopping Centre, which is pretty much open 24/7, she feels she has to. The shop's not exactly setting the fashion world on fire, and even with Pandora working flat-out, and Bird, our sprightley but slightly barking seventy-nine-year-old granny, helping out when she can, the takings are pretty abysmal at the moment.

The only thing that's keeping the place open is the café, run by two Slovakian sisters, Klaudia and Lenka Ková, and their mum, Draza – who doesn't have a word of English but is an amazing cook. Klaudia's built like a navvy and works incredibly hard. Even Bird's a bit frightened of Klaudia, and that's saying a lot. Lenka's completely different: elfin, with white-blonde hair to her bum, and an easy, laid-back manner. She helps out on the shop floor when the café's quiet.

Pandora's still standing in front of me, clearly expecting an actual answer. I look at her in surprise. Largely, she pretty much ignores me at work due to:

a.) my general lack of interest in most of the clothes she peddles. I just don't understand why so many women want to look like identikit Barbies. The rails are bulging with nondescript, overpriced 'designer' jeans and boring black tops. Unlike Pandora, I have no real interest in what's fashionable or 'in'; for me true style has nothing to do with how much money you've dropped on the latest it bag, and all to do with imagination and flair. Which is why many of Shoestring's customers, who can't see past the Gucci double Gs, drive me to distraction.

And b.) the fact that I spend most of my time checking out my favourite fashion and art blogs on the shop's computer, or flicking through back editions of Paris and Italian *Vogue*, *Pop*, *Wallpaper* and *i-D* under the desk. I buy them for next to nothing at a secondhand bookshop in Sandycove and I adore their sumptuous fashion spreads, even if I can't understand a word of some of them. Good design makes me happy – clothes, jewellery, furniture, anything really. Bad design simply irritates me.

I'm Pandora's occasional Sunday girl, employed purely to allow her to visit some of her well-heeled clients – high-powered career women who work all week, and play golf or sail yachts all day Saturday, and are only available to flog their cast-offs to Pandora on certain Sundays.

I told her I'd only work for the pittance she offered if I could drink coffee at the till and didn't have to tidy the rails or clear out the changing rooms, which I hate since I always end up walking in on someone in their knickers and bra. The worst offenders are the thong women who try and engage me in conversation whilst bending over to hand me shoes or a top they've thrown on the floor – Pandora's pet hate – she reckons most people must have maids at home to pick up for them. Not normal behaviour, people! I do not want to see anyone's bum crack on a Sunday, or any other day for that matter, thanks very much.

A lot of our sell-in clients – people who bring us their designer clothes to flog on their behalf – are D4s, named after the post-code of a posh area of Dublin. They're wives of barristers, CEOs, accountants. The developers' wives tend to keep a low profile these days and most have sold their Dublin trophy houses and have slunk back into their more modest country piles. They're all desperately trying to hide their well-honed retail habit from their hubbies. Compared to the rest of the country, they're well off but still seem to get a kick out of haggling with Pandora to try and increase their cut of the sale, even though the shop's terms are set in stone. We offer our sell-ins 50 per cent net. So if we sell a dress for a hundred euro, they get fifty. It's all pretty simple, but the D4s aren't the sharpest knives in the drawer and it takes them a while to take it all in. Plus some of them have no idea how much they paid for particular items and claim their simple Issa wrap dress cost thousands, when Pandora knows every item Issa have ever produced, in every season, including each piece's list price. Her mind is like an elaborate fashion spreadsheet. For a country in the middle of a recession, there are a lot of expensive frocks out there, all just waiting for Pandora to whisk them away after their solo charity lunch outing, so they don't linger incriminatingly in already bulging wardrobes.

'Go on, guess,' Pandora says again.

'Not Sissy Arbuckle's place?' I ask. Pandora's been itching to visit her house for weeks on account of our bet. Sissy is one of RTÉ's *Red Carpet* girls, a telly programme dedicated to the lives of the rich and famous, but for all the glossy front Pandora is convinced she's living way above her means, her expensive designer frock fetish funded largely by her dentist boyfriend. Nice guy called Ian, small, with strangely wonky teeth for a dentist, who drops clothes into the shop for her sometimes, but I'm still not convinced. Surely telly presenters get paid a fortune? Pandora is so confident that she's right she has ten euro on Chez Arbuckle being a semi-d in a pretty average estate; I'm banking on it being Bling Castle, mock Georgian, with lots of white pillars and sweeping silk curtains.

Pandora shakes her head. 'Nope. Try again.'

I'm already tiring of this game but I humour her. Otherwise she might ask me to take the out-of-date stock off the rails and mark it down – yikes! We only keep items for three weeks, after that the pieces get reduced by 25 per cent. If they still don't sell, we give customers three weeks to collect their items or they get donated to charity. You'd be amazed how lazy some people are – our local Oxfam loves us! Or even worse, Pandora might make me iron fresh stock. A lot of the clothes come in clean but wrinkled and we charge the clients a 'pressing' fee. We also have a deal with the local dry cleaners and also Mrs Snips, the local repair and alteration shop, run by a friend of Klaudia and Lenka's. Both give Shoestring a small commission for any work we pass on to them. Pandora has it all sorted, she's like a mini Mafia don.

The original shop, Schuster's Department Store, was set up and run by my grandpa, Derek Schuster. When he died – years ago, I never knew him – Bird took over. During the boom – the 'Celtic Tiger' – she leased it out to a beautician as there wasn't much call for a Ma and Pa shop that sold thermal underwear, net curtains and knitting wool, but last year the beautician's went bust and Bird couldn't find another tenant. The shop was just sitting there, empty, so after a few months, with Bird's encouragement, Pandora packed in her job at Brown Thomas's, where she'd been running the designer rooms, and set up Shoestring, a designer swap shop. Perfect for the current recessionary times, she said. She cannily took her Brown Thomas address book with her and now many of our clients are her old BT customers. She's smart that way, Pandora. Has a proper degree in fashion and everything. Unlike me, the college dropout.

I shrug. 'I don't know, Jillian Soodman?' Another of our top clients, a Dalkey lawyer with a passion for snappy Italian suits.

'Wrong again.' She leans in towards me conspiratorially. 'Kathleen Ireland.'

I scrunch up my nose. 'Hang on why does that name sound familiar?'

Pandora tut-tuts. 'Don't you read the papers?'

'Yeah, the cinema reviews and fashion pages, not the boring stuff.'

She rolls her eyes. 'She's the American Ambassador, Jules. Had a fashion show in her residence last month showcasing up-and-coming Irish and American designers, followed by a fashion ball to rival anything in London or New York. It was in all the papers. And as for her own dress. Ooh, la, la. She looked stunning, like Princess Grace.' Pandora sighs dreamily. She's clothes obsessed, always has been. When she was tiny she used to shuffle around the house in Mum's high heels. There's a photo of her standing on a kitchen chair wearing Mum's wedding dress at the age of six, the fitted silk bodice swimming on her tiny frame, head flung back proudly like a Russian ballet dancer.

When Mum died, she left Pandora most of her wardrobe, apart from two things I'd always loved – her fake leopard-skin box jacket, and her favourite 'coat', a pink tweed 70s cape with a hood attached that I used to use as a tepee when I was little, buttoning it up and sitting inside it like a wee squaw.

I wore the leopard-skin jacket so much the lining ripped around the armpits and the ends of the sleeves frayed. The year before last, Pandora dropped it into Mrs Snips and they did a stellar job, making the sleeves three-quarter length and carefully sewing in new scarlet lining. Of course, then I went and ripped the side seam climbing over a fence at a music festival and bundled it into the back of my wardrobe before Pandora had the chance to have a go at me. It's been sitting there ever since.

The cape is also hidden at the back of the wardrobe in a thick plastic bag. Sometimes I take it out, press it against my face and breathe in Mum's smell – warm and musky. I close my eyes and imagine she's holding me tight against her chest. Then I fold it up, put it back in the bag and seal it up carefully again with thick elastic bands. I try not to take it out too often these days. After fifteen years Mum's scent is faint, so slight I wonder if I'm imagining it, as if there's some part of my brain that now associates pink tweed with musk. Maybe the mere sight of the cape triggers a scent memory. Tears and musk, for ever mingled.

'And guess what's in here,' she says tantalizingly, stroking the dress carrier.

'Are you actually going to unzip that thing, Pandora?' I ask. 'I could really use a coffee break.'

'You poor doll. Run off your feet all morning from the look of things.' Pandora sweeps her hand around the completely empty shop. 'Eager bargain hunters throwing themselves at you, begging to be shown our secret stashes of Chanel and Versace. Mayhem was it?'

I'm not in the mood. 'Just get on with it. Show me the dress and then let me grab some caffeine. And please tell me it's not another Coast number. We're up to our eyes in safe mother-of-the-bride-dresses already.'

'It's not Coast, I can promise you that. And is it caffeine you need, or a handful of painkillers?' Pandora raises one carefully filled-in eyebrow. She over-plucked during her teens and is still suffering. 'You shouldn't drink so much, Jules, it can't be good for you. And if it puts you in such a bad mood the next day I really do think—'

'Jesus, sis, stop with the lecture. I don't need this, not today. In fact, you know something? You can stuff your stupid job. I'm not that broke.' Total lie, I really am Stony Broke McBroke. I yank open the drawer under the computer, pull out my bag and sling it over my shoulder huffily. 'I'm going home.'

Pandora is strangely unmoved by my outburst. 'Calm down, Jules, don't be so tetchy. I'll show you the dress and then you can take an extra long break, say twenty minutes, OK?'

Then she quickly zips open the carrier and pulls out the most exquisite thing I've ever seen. It's a lush dark pink, with layers of silk chiffon floating towards the floor.

'Holy moly,' I murmur, immediately transfixed. I chuck my bag back in the drawer and put my hand out to touch the delicate material. 'You're right, it's extraordinary. Almost too perfect. It needs . . . something.'

I stare at the dress for a second, then tilt my head, thinking. 'You know those Joe Faircrux pieces?' I say. 'They'd look amazing with it. Wait there.'

I fetch a jewelled belt and necklace from one of the glass covered display tables and lay them down carefully on the cash desk. Both have large, irregularly cut semi-precious stones in muted shades of pink, red and purple, set in gold plate. They're real statement pieces, and so OTT we've had trouble shifting them, even to Sissy who loves a bit of bling.

Pandora smiles. 'You've a good eye, Jules. The colours are perfect together and the belt will make it a bit more edgy. Here, take it for a second while I find some heels to go with it.'

She hands me the dress, which is as light as a feather, and while she looks for shoes, I hold it up against me. It's a little long, hitting my leg just above the ankle bone – it would look best mid-calf. A faint smell wafts up, delicate perfume, fresh, like a summer meadow.

Pandora walks back with a pair of gold Jimmy Choo sandals.

'I don't think it's been cleaned, Pandora,' I say.

She looks around, then satisfied there's nobody looking, sniffs under the armpits, and then down the bodice.

'You really are some sort of bloodhound, Jules, I can't smell a thing. And dry cleaning will only stiffen the material. It's perfect.'

'It is beautiful all right,' I say, playing the material through my fingers like water.

She smiles back; it's so rare we agree on anything.

'Will you try it on for me, Jules? So I can see how the material falls. Slip your feet into the heels so you don't stand on the hem. Go on, humour me.'

Normally I'd tell her where to go. I'm not some sort of human mannequin. But there's something magical about the dress that makes me nod wordlessly and toddle off to the changing rooms, the chiffon laid out over my outstretched arms like a bale of precious material, the slim straps of the barely worn Choos hooked over my fingers.

I untie my tassel belt, peel off my top, wiggle out of my skinny jeans and carefully lower the dress over my head. There it is again, the subtle summery scent. The chiffon drifts down over my hips and pools slightly on the wooden floor. The matching pink zip is carefully hidden to one side and I pull it up gently, making sure not to catch any of the delicate material in its teeth; Pandora would murder me. I slide my feet into the sandals; they are at least a size too small and my toes poke out over the sole but it's only for Pandora. I take a deep breath, and turn around.

I stare in the mirror, my mouth falling open in a wow. Then I start giggling to myself. Is that really me? The glamour puss in the drop dead gorgeous dress, the deep pink zinging colour into her pale, hung-over face – surely it can't be me? I put one hand behind my head and wrap my long curly hair into a messy chignon.

'Va va voom!' I whisper, sticking my hip out and kicking up my back foot. I pout and say 'Happy Birthday, Mr President,' in a breathy Marilyn Monroe voice. 'Like to give me one, Mr President?' I wink at myself in the mirror and catch Pandora's face staring back at me. I swish around.

'What are you playing at, Jules?' She's stuck her head through the grey silk curtain and her face is a picture.

My cheeks flame. 'Nothing.'

She stands beside me. 'You forgot these.' She fastens the necklace around my neck, hooks the heavy belt around my waist, and then rearranges the material, gliding her hands down my hips. 'Come outside so I can get a better look at you.'

I protest but she grasps both of my hands and guides me out towards the large gilt-framed mirror propped against the wall. Then she positions me in front of it, stands back and whistles. The belt has made the skirt the perfect length and the belt and necklace glitter in the shop lights like wet pebbles on the beach.

'Where have you been hiding those curves, Julia Boolia?' She shakes her head. 'You look a million dollars. Grecian goddess meets Hollywood.'

I grin. Pandora isn't one for compliments.

'Who designed it?' I ask, unable to tear my eyes away from my own image. 'I forgot to check the label. And how much are we selling it for?'

15

'It's by Faith Farenze. She's from Chicago originally, used to work for Prada; set up on her own two years ago in New York. Jennifer Aniston wore one of her dresses at the Oscars last year. No one sells them over here – Kathleen bought it in Barney's. It's worth three grand, but she's happy to sell it for twelve hundred. She's donating the proceeds to the Red Cross; her brother works as a field doctor in Ethiopia and I've promised her we won't charge any commission.'

She stands back and looks me up and down again. 'Could you do a window, Jules? Use this as the centrepiece. Maybe it will tempt people in.' She sighs. 'If we could find more dresses like this, I'm sure it would make a difference. Show-stoppers in the window always bring people in. Remember those Louboutin courts we dangled on a fishing line? The red ones? They went in a flash –'

She breaks off and looks at me closely. 'What is it? Are you OK? You've gone very pale. You're not going to puke, are you? If you are, take the dress off first.'

There's a very real chance that I might do just that. Because framed in the shop's doorway is Lainey Anderson. A ball of pain and anger careers around my stomach like a Catherine wheel. I can barely look at the girl, let alone speak to her. Luckily she doesn't seem to have spotted me yet. She's doing that ring twisting thing she does when she's nervous, only this time it's an engagement ring she's playing with.

'Cover for me,' I say in a low voice. 'Tell her I'm not here.'

Pandora's face darkens. 'Don't you worry, I'll happily give Miss Anderson a piece of my mind. But for God's sake, don't get sick on the Farenze.'

Chapter 2

I dash into the staffroom and close the door firmly behind me. Burnt toast lingers in the air and I wrinkle up my nose. My feet are already hurting from the sandals. I'm a size six and none of the posh secondhand shoes ever fit me. Rich women must have their feet bound to keep them under a size five, like they used to do to Chinese girls.

I flip off the heels and they clatter onto the tiles. Then I unzip the dress, step out of it, and stand there in my knickers and bra, holding the chiffon carefully in my arms, looking around for somewhere safe to rest it. That would not be the crumb-splattered table with the knife resting across the Bon Maman pot, a blob of pink strawberry jam dripping off its blade. Which immediately strikes me as strange.

Although she does like her toast practically cremated, Bird is anally tidy. And then I feel something, or someone behind me and I swing around. And there he is, sitting on the small sofa tucked between the fridge and the door leading to the office, looking up at me through his dark shaggy fringe, an amused look on his face. I shriek and clutch the chiffon against my practically naked body.

'Jamie Clear, what the hell are you doing in here?'

I've known Jamie pretty much all my life. The house where he grew up, Sorrento Lodge, is slap bang next to Bird's, and his mum, Daphne, despite the twenty-year age gap, is Bird's best friend.

Jamie takes a last mouthful of what looks suspiciously like burnt toast with strawberry jam and wipes the edges of his lips with his fingers.

'Long time no see, Jules,' he says easily. 'Actually I'm waiting for Bird. She said to make myself at home. I reset your toaster by the way, some eejit had left it on the highest setting.'

I stare at him in confusion. 'Bird? Why?'

'I'm setting up electronic loyalty cards for your customers. And redesigning your very sad and dated-looking website.'

'I thought you were living in Galway, working in that animation place.'

He gives an exaggerated shrug, his blue Superman T-shirt lifting towards his ears, showing a good inch of surprisingly toned belly above his black jeans. In fact he's bulked up a lot since the last time I saw him; no longer the weedy computer nerd of old.

'That didn't work out,' he says. 'I'm living with Mum until I can find a place in Dublin.'

'I'm surprised I haven't bumped into you yet.'

'Only moved back last week. I was going to call in but, well, you know.' He pauses for a beat. 'Mum told me about Ed and Lainey, the engagement and everything. For what it's worth, I'm sorry.'

'You hate Ed,' I remind him. In fact Ed is the reason Jamie and I haven't spoken for years.

'I know. And he's just proved that he's an even bigger dickhead than I thought.' His eyes rest on mine. They're gentle, sympathetic. I can feel tears welling up so I look away.

'You OK, Jules?'

'Fine. They're welcome to each other.' I quickly change the subject before I start crying. 'Why you? To do the techie stuff I mean.'

'I can design websites in my sleep and Mum promised Bird I'd help her out seeing as I'm not working at the moment. Plus I'm damn good.'

18

'Says who?' I say with a smile, glad the conversation's moved away from Ed and Lainey. But Jamie's not being big headed, he really is a computer genius. He was almost arrested when he was eleven for hacking into a bank's computer system and trying to shift money around. He'd read about it in some book and wanted to see if it was actually possible. It was.

He looks at me, a bemused expression on his face. 'Are you going to stand there arguing with me, woman, or are you going to throw on some clothes? Don't get me wrong, I'm enjoying the view, but your ass must be cold.'

I blush deeply, remembering I'm wearing black knickers that I'd rescued from the depths of my underwear drawer this morning – see-through Myla ones with ribbon ties at both sides. A present from Ed. I was in a rush and they were the only clean pair I could find. I would have gone commando if I'd been wearing a skirt but with jeans, it's never a good idea unless you're a sadomasochist.

'It's August, Jamie. I'm fine, thanks very much.'

I consider my options, then turn my head and spot some new stock hanging on the back of the door, waiting to be priced, so I back towards it and grab the first thing that comes to hand.

'Close your eyes,' I say firmly. We used to be like brother and sister, but even so.

He grins, then clamps down his eyelids. I hang the chiffon dress carefully over the hook and wriggle the new one over my head and down my hips.

'OK, you can open them now,' I say.

'Kickin' outfit.' He's smiling at me again, his green eyes twinkling.

I've chosen a red lycra number that's at least a size too small for me and looks more like your average swimsuit than a dress. It just about covers my bum and looks exactly like something Sissy would wear and she's all of a size zero. In fact it probably is Sissy's. I hope it's bloody clean. I don't want Sissy's dead skin-cells anywhere near me, her idiocy might rub off.

I grab a white shirt, throw it over the dress and knot it at the waist.

'Very *Pretty Woman*,' he adds.

'What do you mean?'

'*Pretty Woman*. Julia Roberts borrows one of Richard Gere's shirts to make her outfit look less, well, less hookery.'

'Hookery? Is that an actual word?'

The door swings open and Bird bustles in wearing a shell-pink Chanel jacket over skinny jeans (which look surprisingly good on her) and black ballet pumps. There's a white silk scarf looped through the top of her jeans as a belt and tied in a jaunty bow over her left hip. I smile to myself. It's an outfit I styled for her two weeks ago when the shop was quiet.

Bird looks at me, Jamie, and then back at me. 'What *are* you two talking about?' she says in her distinctive clipped, cut-glass voice. Bird has lived in Ireland all her life, but retains the Anglo-Irish accent that her parents had before her. Bird scandalized her family by marrying a Roman Catholic, although her new hus-band wasn't in the least bit bothered about religion – said it had caused quite enough nonsense in Ireland already – and gave her his blessing to bring Mum up as Church of Ireland, even though it wasn't the done thing at the time.

I can't really remember Mum's voice, but Pandora says she sounded like a softer, watered-down version of Bird. In fact, Pan-dora can sound a bit marbles in the mouth at times, but I've made it my business to make my voice sound as Irish as I possibly can.

'Hookers,' I admit.

She tut-tuts. 'I do hope you're not being rude about our cli-ents again, Julia.'

I laugh. 'No, Bird. Jamie was making charming comments about my clothes.'

She looks me up and down. 'He's right, my darling. I'm not

sure it's quite you. Unless you add some cowboy boots and call it ironic trailer trash. And even then, you'd be stretching it. But aren't you supposed to be out on the floor, not testing new outfits out on Jamie?'

She turns to Jamie. 'And as for you, come along, dear boy. We have work to do, *n'est-ce pas*? You and Jules should catch up later. She'd love to see you, wouldn't you, darling? She's been feeling a little—'

'Bird!' I snap.

'I'm just saying,' she continues, unabashed. 'You have been rather a misery guts the past few weeks . . .'

I scowl at her. The woman is impossible. 'Stop!'

'And she could do with a friend.'

'I mean it, Bird.'

She's unrepentant. 'It's all right, darling, I've finished what I was trying to say.'

Jamie is smiling. He's well used to Bird, and his own mum's just as bad. They can't seem to help interfering.

Jamie and I exchange a look and I suddenly realize how much I've missed him. He's so easy-going, so uncomplicated and, most importantly, after everything that happened, he's still talking to me. I feel a stinging surge of regret that he's not in my life any more. I know for a fact that the past is best left alone but, for a split second, I wish things could be different.

He gets to his feet, still beaming at me. 'Later, Jules. Bird's right, we should catch up. I'll call in sometime, yeah?'

I feel so grateful, so utterly pathetically grateful, that tears prick the back of my eyes and I have to stare at the wall for a second and blink them back.

'I'd like that,' I say, trying not to sound too needy. But 'Tonight?' is out before I can stop it.

He's looking at me, an expression I can't quite make out on his face.

'Sure,' he says finally, then follows Bird out the door.

I watch them leave. Then I stand there for a second, lost in thought, the memories flooding back. For some reason I suddenly remember Jamie's sandpit. His dad built it before he did a runner with a woman from work, and it was huge, with a thick wooden ledge around all four sides to sit on. We used to spend hours building our own little world in the sand, complete with roads, houses, and 'people' (my Sylvanian Family animals who were permanently dripping sand out of their arm and leg cracks because of it). We progressed to playing Superman saves Lois Lane, and Indiana Jones versus the Nazis, and Jamie sometimes let me be Indiana, even though I was a girl. When my family moved into Sorrento House with Bird, Jamie and I became inseparable, and stayed that way until a certain Ed Powers came into the picture.

The last time I saw Jamie was Christmas two years ago, when Ed and I were still together. Jamie was back from Galway for the holidays and we'd bumped into each other in Finnegan's pub while Ed was talking to someone at the far end of the bar. We said hi to each other politely and exchanged a few words about the weather, about Bird and Daphne being as mad as ever, and how frantic Christmas was, but we hadn't mentioned the elephant in the room: the fight when Ed had nearly killed him.

Then Ed came back, glared at Jamie wordlessly, slipped his arm around my waist proprietorially, and guided me away.

Jamie is a year younger than me, and two years younger than Ed. When I'd started college – Business Studies in Dublin City College, more because I couldn't think of anything else I wanted to do and DCC was rumoured to have the best social life, including the busiest student bar – Jamie was still in school. I'd met Ed in the DCC bar during Freshers' Week. It was surprising we hadn't already met. He was a Glenageary boy, lived in Silchester Park, a ten-minute cycle from my house.

He'd taken a year off to travel before college – a gap year – and was dripping with self-confidence. I was instantly drawn to him. He'd been travelling around Europe for the past few months in a camper van and was full of stories of his exploits. Quickly we became a couple, and I admit that at first I was a little obsessed.

It was Jamie's Leaving Cert year. He hated exams but was determined to get onto a cutting-edge computer course in Galway, one of the best in Europe, so he made himself study. And I hate to admit it but I pretty much abandoned him during my first term at college. I didn't answer his calls, stopped dropping in, and when he arrived on the doorstep, wondering what was happening, worried about me, I just turned him away saying I was busy studying, which was a total lie . . . I wasn't doing a thing. What I was busy with was partying with Ed, Monday to Friday, and collapsing at the weekends, exhausted.

That first Christmas Ed and I were together, something happened. On Christmas Eve, Ed and I had spent all day and night in Finnegan's and were high as kites on Christmas spirit and spirits. Ed had been flirting with this girl we both knew from college all evening and on the way home I gave him a hard time about it.

'What?' he'd demanded. 'It was a drinking game, Jules.'

'Ed, when I got back from the loo you had your tongue stuck down her throat. And when I slapped you, you just pulled away and grinned and wiped your mouth on the sleeve of your hoody. Nice.'

'Don't take it so seriously, babes. Honestly, it didn't mean anything.'

'It was insulting, Ed. I was mortified.'

We stopped outside my house and then went around the side. He grabbed his bike from where he'd left it against the oak tree in the garden, under my tree house, and made to leave.

'Are you not coming up? I left a bottle up there like we planned.' The tree house had become our den. It was perfect, no one bothered us there, and when I pulled up the ladder and

23

closed all the hatches and doors it was like our own special kingdom. Years ago I'd dragged up an old rug, a cot mattress I'd found in the shed, plus blankets and cushions and had created a really comfy seating area. It was my haven, my escape.

I used to share it with Jamie; we pretended to be prince and princess of Treelandia, and had all our own laws and everything. We used to spend hours up there, inventing our own fantasy world. Jamie drew up this amazing map of our kingdom, and we had 'subjects' – we were the Tree Dwellers, the royalty of Treelandia. Then there were the Dalkey elven folk who made all our leather and gold clothes and shoes, the Animalati, an animal army who could talk. They kept the kingdom safe from the evil Dalkey Islanders, bloodthirsty vampire Vikings, who were always trying to invade Treelandia and enslave our subjects. Jamie's drawings were incredible and we had books and books of them, kept in an old wooden box Bird gave us that smelt of tea.

But I was eighteen by then, too old for all that stuff, and now Ed was my tree-house prince.

Ed snorted. 'No way, babes. Not with you in this mood.'

'Ed! It's Christmas Eve. Come on. It's not even twelve yet. I thought we were going to see in Christmas Day together.'

He shrugged. 'Changed my mind.'

I grabbed his arm. 'Please. I'm sorry. I'll forget all about it, I promise. Just come up.'

He shook off my arm and pushed me away. I don't think he intended to be rough, but I tripped on a root and fell backwards, hitting my head on the tree trunk. The next thing I knew Jamie scrambled down the rope ladder and stood glaring at Ed.

'You hit her,' he said. I think he'd been laying into my vodka, because his eyes were glassy and he didn't seem himself.

Ed just looked at him and laughed. 'Shut up, squirt.'

'What were you doing up there, Jamie?' I stood up straighter and stopped rubbing my skull. It hurt like hell, but I didn't want Jamie to see it.

'Waiting for you. It's Christmas Eve, remember? We always see Christmas Eve in together, Jules.'

'I haven't seen you in weeks,' I said, confused. Did he really think I'd want to spend Christmas Eve with him instead of Ed now. Was he deranged?

'Just get lost, Clear,' Ed said, putting his arm around my shoulders. 'Julia's with me now. Find someone your own age to play with.' He looked at Jamie and started to smile nastily. 'I get it, you're jealous. You'd love to get into Jules's knickers, but I got there first, and man she's hot, really—'

Bang. Jamie landed a punch across Ed's nose, making it bleed instantly.

Ed put a hand up to his face, took it away and stared at it, blood dripping down his fingers.

'You little fucker,' Ed muttered. And then they started laying into each other, pulling, kicking and punching. Ed was a good six inches taller than Jamie and within minutes had him pinned to the ground, and was pounding his face, over and over again, as I screamed and tried frantically to pull him off but it was no use.

Suddenly Bird appeared out of nowhere in a billowing white nightie and threw a basin of water over the pair of them, making Ed stop mid-punch. But then he shook off the water and threw another one.

'Get off him for God's sake, Ed.' Bird hit Ed over the head with the basin, hard, and then raised it again.

Ed put up his hand to protect himself. 'Jesus, what the fuck?' He stopped hitting Jamie and twisted his head to stare at Bird.

'Watch your language, young man,' Bird snapped, her eyes flinty.

While Ed was distracted, Jamie landed a thump on the side of Ed's face. We could all hear the crack. Ed climbed off Jamie, and hopped around the garden, holding his nose.

'Shit, shit, shit. I think you've fucking broken it, you moron.'

25

Jamie crawled to his hands and knees, his face dripping blood. 'That's what you get for pushing women around and being an arrogant prick, you, you, fucker.'

'Jamie Clear!' Bird thundered. 'While your sentiments are admirable, brawling is never acceptable. And for pity's sake, language! Now, Julia, go and fetch my car keys. We'd better take your sorry excuse for a boyfriend to casualty. Oh and happy Christmas everyone. It's just turned midnight.'

I stood staring at her.

'You heard me, Julia,' she ordered.

I opened my mouth to apologize but she cut me off. 'I don't want to know. Not another word from any of you until you're sober, understand? Now get my keys. And Jamie, that cut on your eyebrow looks bad. You'd better come with us. And I want utter silence in the car, understand, or there'll be hell to pay.'

We all nodded silently. Ed was staring at Bird, a dark look on his face, but he kept his mouth firmly shut. At that moment I felt about an inch tall. From that night on I refused to speak to Jamie Clear, mortified at what he'd done, furious at him for breaking Ed's nose, angry at him for picking a fight in the first place. If Bird hadn't intervened, who knows what might have happened.

Ed and I broke up later that day over the phone. He said I hadn't defended him in front of Bird, had let her fawn over Jamie in the hospital, like he was some sort of hero. I was distraught. For months I couldn't eat, couldn't sleep, everything seemed pointless. I didn't bother taking most of my first year summer exams, knew I'd fail. Which I did. In spectacular form.

The following Christmas Eve we got back together, in Finnegan's ironically enough, although that night Jamie was conspicuously absent.

That punch up marked the end of my friendship with Jamie. The summer after the fight, as soon as he'd finished his Leaving Cert exams he went to America to intern with Pixar and, when he returned, went straight to Galway to start college. It's only now, after years of reflection, that I finally appreciate what he tried to do for me.

I shake off the memories, rub my damp eyes with my knuckles and then concentrate on flicking through the rest of the clothes hanging on the back of the door, hoping to find something more suitable to wear. My head throb now taking on epic proportions. The door suddenly flings against me, the wood smacking against my temple, exactly where the throbbing is at its worst. It's really not my day.

'Ow!' I yell, rubbing my skull. 'That hurt.'

Pandora sticks her head around. 'It took me ages to get rid of Lainey. She's bloody stubborn sometimes, but she's finally gone. You owe me one, Jules. And where's the Farenze dress? I don't trust you with it.'

'Charming.' I hand it to her. She gives it a quick once-over and, satisfied, leaves.

The door opens a second time. It's Pandora again. 'Sorry, forgot to ask. You all right?'

I nod silently and, satisfied with that, she disappears again. I stand there and sigh. I've a good mind to sneak out the back way, jump on my bike and skedaddle, if it wasn't for the fact that I have no shoes, unless you count the Choos and Pandora would kill me if I scuffed the heels from cycling in them. I'm also wearing what Jamie so delightfully referred to as a 'hookery' outfit. Instead I decide to sneak back to the changing room, grab my jeans and *then* hotfoot it home. Yes, Pandora will probably sack me, again, but at this stage I just don't care.

I open the door, check there's no one around and then sprint to the changing room, where my jeans, shoes and top are still on the floor where I left them. I whip the curtain across and start untying the knot in the shirt. I hear a familiar voice outside and my back stiffens.

'Pandora Schuster, you had no right to make my sister cry.'

It's Karen Anderson, Lainey's oldest sister, in full swing. Karen prides herself on being direct and is always, always right; Lainey hates it and tends to avoid all confrontation with her because of it. And from the sound of things, Karen's on the war path. I pull the curtains open a crack and peek out. There she is, leaning over the cash desk, in a purple Juicy tracksuit and runners, her hair pulled back into its usual face-lift ponytail. When she's not minding her perfect blonde (perfectly ghastly) children, she spends her life at the gym or playing tennis.

Pandora is standing her ground. 'After what she did to Jules, she deserves it.'

Karen plants her fists on her waist. 'Says who? Lainey and Ed are in love and now they're making a proper commitment. Jules shouldn't be acting like such a child. Anyone would think she's still in love with him. Maybe she wants him back.' She cocks her head and gives Pandora a 'what do you say to that?' look.

But she's underestimating Pandora, who, like Bird, is always calm under pressure. My sister narrows her eyes. 'Karen, Jules is no fool, she knew Ed saw other people while she was away, they had an understanding. But while she was avoiding the rain in Wellington, your darling sister had her beady eye on Ed, and once she seduced him, she stuck to him like a limpet. And didn't even have the decency to tell Jules about it until months later. Jules got shafted by both Ed *and* Lainey, and we both know it. Ed, well, OK he's a man, but you don't betray your best friend like that, Karen. You just don't. And you're wrong, Jules has no interest in that worm, not after everything he's done to her. Now kindly leave my shop. None of your family is welcome here.'

Karen's lip curls up. 'Don't worry, I'm leaving. Your shop is shite, Pandora. No one wants to wear stinky secondhand clothes. And you're wrong, Jules does want Ed back. But he's marrying Lainey and there's nothing you or your freako family can do about it. They're off to Paris the weekend after next to collect her wedding dress. And you can tell Jules from me, if she arrives at the ceremony and throws herself at Ed, like something out of *The Graduate*, she'll have me to deal with. I know Lainey has invited her,' she breaks off and sniffs. 'Purely out of guilt if you ask me, but Jules is hardly going to turn up now, is she. She couldn't bear to see Lainey get something she wants so badly.'

'Get out.' Pandora flicks Karen's face with a silk scarf she's grabbed from the dummy behind her.

Karen puts her hand to her face, like she's been stung. Her eyes are wide. 'I could sue you for that.'

'Out!' Pandora flicks her again. 'And you're lucky it's not a belt.'

'Jesus, Pandora, no wonder Jules is so weird.' And with that Karen scarpers.

Seconds later Pandora walks into my cubicle, closes the curtain behind her and collapses onto the chair. 'I saw your mad dash into the changing rooms. I guess you caught all that?'

I nod, anger pumping through my veins. I hate the whole bloody family.

'What a wagon,' she says. 'As if you'd go near her sister's poxy wedding.'

I stare at her. 'Are you mad? I have to go now. If I don't make an appearance everyone will think Karen's right, that I want Ed back, that I can't bear seeing the two of them together.'

Pandora's eyes are soft. 'But it's true, isn't it? You *do* want him back.'

I say nothing, just stare down at the floor. Of course it's true, but I'm not admitting it to anyone, especially not Pandora.

'I don't want to be poor old Julia, the girl whose best friend stole her boyfriend, for the rest of my life,' I say in a rush. 'No, I'm going to find a really cute guy, wear a knockout dress and spend the whole night snogging the face off him in front of everyone. Then no one will feel sorry for me and I'll be able to

29

hold my head up high and forget all about Lainey bitch-face Anderson and Ed bastard-features Powers.'

Pandora looks doubtful. 'Are you sure? Hearing them exchanging their vows might tip you over the edge.'

I nod vigorously. 'Positive. It'll be my Ed swansong. But I have to look amazing.' An image floats in front of my eyes – me wafting into the church in the Faith Farenze dress and everyone gasping at how stunning I look. 'And I have to wear the Farenze. I just have to.'

Pandora sighs. 'Don't be daft, Jules. Where are you going to find twelve hundred euro? You already owe Dad a grand from your New Zealand trip.'

Trust old elephant memory to bring that up. Ancient history. I'm hoping Dad's forgotten all about it. 'Please, Pandora? I'm begging you, hold the dress for me until I think of something.'

She throws her eyes to heaven. 'You're living in cloud cuckoo land, Jules, but I'm willing to humour you for exactly one week, otherwise it goes back on the floor. But I'm really not sure you're strong enough for the wedding. Even in the Farenze, with Johnny Depp himself on your arm, it will still be difficult.'

'In that dress I can cope with anything,' I say with more confidence than I feel.

She strokes my head and for once I don't pull away. 'Just think it through properly, Boolie, that's all I'm saying.' I look at her. She hasn't used Mum's pet name for me – Boolie, short for Julia Boolia – for a long time. We lock eyes for a second and then I pull mine away.

'I'll put it on the rail in the office in case you think of something, OK?'

I smile at her. 'Thanks, Pandora.'

While she takes the dress to the office, I sit down on the velvet-covered chair in the changing room and put my head in my hands. Seven days to come up with twelve hundred euro. Pandora's right, I do need to think. Think, Jules, think!

When I get back from lunch Pandora is twirling in front of one of the shop's mirrors, in the Faith Farenze.

'What are you doing in my dress?' I demand. 'I have it on hold, remember?'

She sighs. 'Don't get your knickers in a twist, Jules, I'm just trying it on.'

Lenka is slouched over the desk, gazing at Pandora admiringly. 'You look a million dollars,' Lenka says. 'The colour really suits you.' She walks towards Pandora and pulls at the front of the dress. 'But maybe a padded bra, yes? Or chicken fillets?' Lenka thinks you're not properly dressed unless you're showing a cleavage worthy of Dolly Parton. As soon as she's saved up the money, or can cajole her latest boyfriend into paying for it, she's straight off for a boob job.

'It's irrelevant,' Pandora says glumly, slapping Lenka's hand away. 'Someone like Sissy will end up owning it. Besides, I'd have nothing to wear it to.' She runs her fingers over the chiffon. 'But it is stunning,' she adds wistfully.

'When Jules buys the dress, you can borrow it, Pandora,' Lenka says brightly. 'Is good idea, yes?'

Pandora smiles in an annoyingly condescending way. 'Like that's going to happen. I'm just humouring her, Lenka. There's no way she'll come up with the money in a week.'

I scowl at my sister. Great to see she has so much faith in me. After a brief show of sisterly support, I guess it's back to business as usual in the Schuster household.

Chapter 3

Six o'clock, closing time can't come quickly enough. Because the more I think about it, the more convinced I become that I have to have the Faith Farenze. It's not rational or logical, I just have this feeling in the pit of my stomach that if the dress is mine not only will I be able to attend the wedding with my head held high, but my whole life will change, will be magically transformed overnight, like Cinderella's. The dress will hang in my wardrobe, no, on the wall, like a valuable Impressionist painting, so I can gaze at it all the time; and the very same day I'll win the lotto, meaning I'll never have to get up early for work ever again. Then I'll meet Prince Charming, or else I'll manage to convince Ed that Lainey is all wrong for him and that he should marry me instead.

As soon as the final customers have left – there are always one or two stragglers – I leave Pandora and Bird to close up, grab my bike and cycle home slowly, feeling completely out of energy. Once inside the house, I dump my bag on the floor at the bottom of the stairs. It's strangely quiet. Then I remember that Dad's away working in Kilkenny, and Iris is staying overnight with one of her little friends. Iris is Pandora's eight-year-old daughter, very bright and a right little chatterbox. And as Pandora and Bird are off to some sort of boring choral thing tonight, I have the place to myself for a change – perfect. Once Jamie arrives I'll crack open a bottle of wine, grab some beers for him and we can settle down on the sofa in the living room. After a few drinks we'll be able to talk about the past without any recrimination or regrets, clear the air properly. I feel warm just thinking about it. Now that Jamie's back everything will be different, I just know it.

I wander into the living room and slump down on the sofa to wait for him. I switch on the telly and flick through the programmes I've saved on the Sky box. *America's Next Top Model*, that will do, nice and mindless, and the idiocy of some of the girls always makes me laugh. They make walking up and down a room without falling over your own two feet sound as difficult as brain surgery sometimes. I sit back and start watching.

Every few minutes I check the time, wondering when Jamie will appear. I miss having someone to confide in so much at times it physically stings. Before the whole Ed and Lainey debacle, I talked to Lainey several times a day, especially when I was feeling a bit low. She understood me better than anyone, always knew exactly what to say to make me feel better. In turn I was able to cheer her up when one of her sisters – Karen usually – had been teasing her or picking on her. Lainey is the quietest of the sisters and the most easy-going, but sometimes this means they take advantage of her good nature. I used to pull them up on this, but she has nobody to stick up for her now. I hope they aren't bossing her around too much. I shouldn't care, not after everything that's happened, but she was part of my life for so many years it's hard not to worry about her, even now.

It's amazing we ever became close. She's the polar opposite of me – calm, patient, always sees things through. At school she always handed in her essays and projects on time and made sure I remembered too. While I was off travelling, Lainey was plodding through her accountancy exams, steady as she goes.

She was brilliant at keeping in touch – always dropping me newsy emails about her course and what all her sisters were up to. There's five of them in total and they're all pretty close. There's Karen of course, at thirty she's the eldest, with a 'going places' barrister husband and two straight-out-of-a-Ralph Lauren-catalogue children; Tilly, twenty-nine, who runs her own company, Hot Cakes, making bespoke cakes and cupcakes with logos on them for things like launches and festivals. Tilly's married to a banker but doesn't have children as yet; she's too busy building up her company. Then there's Kia, who's twenty-seven, single and great fun, a physio and probably my favourite of the clan apart from Lainey, who at twenty-four like me slots in next; and finally, Chloe, who at twenty-one is the baby of the family and is about to start her first job as a primary school teacher. If I ever felt lonely or sad, sitting in the Andersons' kitchen with the bread maker almost permanently on the go and the daily cries of 'who nicked my black tights/earphones/charger?' always managed to banish my woes and make me feel part of something bigger than myself.

Lainey and I met on the very first day of senior school and bonded over our mutual passion for Robbie Williams and Keanu Reeves – but only in black leather in the Matrix films. Over the years she weathered many storms with me, including the many Ed Powers hurricanes and tornadoes. I never once considered her lack of boyfriends strange – she always said she was waiting for the perfect man and, knowing what Lainey was like and how much patience she had, I believed her. It never occurred to me that Ed was her very own Robbie/Keanu.

I've never admitted how kicked in the head, crucified and utterly stupid and blind I feel about the whole damn Ed and Lainey thing to anyone, not to Pandora and certainly not to Bird – and believe me, they've tried to drag it out of me. It's all too overwhelming. I'm afraid if I start digging around, letting every-thing come bubbling up to the surface, I'll start crying and I won't be able to stop, ever. Or I'll work myself into such a state, I'll slip up and say something I'll regret, let the past slither out and spread around my feet like an ugly oil slick.

I'm hoping talking to Jamie will be different. He'll understand when to push and when to just listen. He'll understand because he knows – everything. He knows what it's like to blame yourself when things go belly up. Because he's been there too. But right now it looks as if he's stood me up.

I sit there for a few minutes, staring into space, feeling itchy with anger and disappointment, before pushing myself off the sofa and marching through the kitchen and into the pantry. I grab one of Dad's bottles of wine and a glass, stomp back into the living room, pour myself a large drink, and settle back in front of the telly, grumpy to my bones. As one of the models talks about her brush with breast cancer, I try to zone out, to think about something else, anything, but my mind is determined to rake up old memories today.

I was eight, and Pandora was fourteen when Mum and Dad sat us down in the living room and told us the news. Our beautiful, vibrant, clever Mum had breast cancer, Dad said, but we weren't to be worrying, the doctors had caught it nice and early and there was every chance that with treatment she'd be absolutely fine.

'Of course I will,' Mum had said brightly, her hands clasped tightly in her lap. 'I'm not going anywhere. And that's a promise, girls.' But there was sadness behind her big china-blue eyes. Mum looked like a model but had a razor-sharp mind, which confused people no end. When she opened her rosebud mouth, they always expected her to witter on about shopping or shoes, but she was more interested in the details of the latest budget. As Economics Editor at RTÉ, she was on the telly and radio almost every day, presenting her carefully researched news pieces on the current state of the nation. Mum was invincible, or so I thought.

It was the 'every chance' that got me; I didn't say anything at the time of course, didn't want to say it out loud, make my worries real. But even at eight I knew 'every chance' meant there was also a possibility that she wouldn't make it, that she would in fact die.

Later that night I crept into Pandora's bed. She was also wide awake. 'Is Mum really going to be OK?' I whispered.

'I don't know, Boolie. But you know Mum, she's pretty determined.'

I fell asleep there, warm and comforted beside my big sister.

And Mum fought it all the way, until eventually, after a gruelling operation, and an intense bout of chemotherapy and radiotherapy she was given the all-clear. And life slowly went back to normal. Until almost a year later when Mum started getting crippling headaches and was rushed into hospital. Eventually, after a lot of tests, the doctors found cancer cells in her spine. This time the diagnosis was not so good.

Mum insisted on telling us herself. Dad and Bird brought us into her hospital room and then Dad left. I don't think he could bear to stay.

'My darlings,' Mum said, then broke off, her eyes welling up. She started sobbing, which set me and Pandora off. After a few minutes, Bird stepped in.

'Kirsten, would you like me to tell them?'

Mum nodded. 'I can't . . . I just can't.'

'I understand,' Bird said gently. She turned to me and Pandora. 'Your mum is very sick, girls. She'll be coming out of hospital tomorrow, but to Sorrento House, not your own house, where your Dad and I will look after her. We'll all live there, together, until, until . . .' Bird stopped abruptly and pressed her lips together.

'Until it's my time,' Mum added. 'And we can spend lots of time together, as a family.'

I looked at Pandora. She was biting the inside of her cheek, hard, trying not to cry. Our eyes met and I could see she was as scared as I was, which made me even more frightened. She blinked and then gave me a sad smile.

'That sounds like a great idea, Mum,' I said firmly. 'I'll help Dad and Pandora pack everything we need. Don't worry. You need all your energy for getting better.'

36

Mum and Bird exchanged a look. Pandora stared out of the window.

'Boolie,' Mum said gently. 'I'm not going to get better.'

I forced out a smile. ''Course you are, Mum. Don't be silly. You're always saying you won't let a stupid thing like cancer stop you, you're Kirsten Schuster. You nearly brought the government down.'

Mum just sat there, looking at me, tears streaming down her pale, waxy face. 'Oh, my darling girl,' she whispered. 'My poor, darling girl. Come here.'

She held out her arms and although it must have hurt her, hugged me tightly to her chest.

Eleven days after being discharged, Mum died. Dad did his best but he was in pieces, overwhelmed by grief. He'd been devoted to Mum, she was his world. He was the only dad I'd ever heard of who had allowed his children to take their mum's surname. Mum, an only child, was so determined not to be the 'last' Schuster in Ireland after Bird died that she made it a condition of their marriage. Ironic that. Fifteen years later, Bird's still going strong.

Dad was bad, but I was worse. I went catatonic, couldn't eat or speak, let alone cry. I was afraid to sleep because of the terrifying nightmares involving being lost in black caves, or finding myself shut in tiny dark rooms. Bird was so worried about me she called Daphne in to try and talk to me. Jamie came along with her and the minute I saw him, I threw my arms around him and started to sob, finally able to let it all out. After that I started talking and eating again, but the nightmares lingered. Bird held us all together, fed us, and, after exactly one week of grieving, made sure Pandora and I went back to school. At the time I thought she was heartless, but now I see that getting us back into some kind of normal routine, surrounded by our friends, who didn't know quite what to say but were all being very kind to us, sharing their lunches and having us over to play, was vital.

After six months we were still living with Bird, and Dad seemed reluctant to move back to our empty house in Deansgrange. He said without Kirsten he just couldn't face it. So with the help of some of his builder friends, he converted Sorrento House into two living spaces, creating a comfy apartment for Bird in the basement. He left his job making posh bespoke D4 kitchens, and with some of the proceeds from the house sale set up his own company – Wooden Monkey – selling and setting up climbing frames and swing sets, imported from Germany. It meant he could work from home and be around when we got in from school and Bird was out running the shop.

To compensate for moving and as our Christmas presents – plus I think money was tight that year; Mum had been the main wage earner in the family – Dad offered to build me and Pandora something special. Pandora, ever practical, chose a walk-in wardrobe for her new bedroom, complete with state of the art lighting, but I had other plans. The main reason I was upset about moving from Deansgrange to Bird's house in Dalkey, was because it meant leaving my beloved tree house behind. So Dad let me design a new one, even bigger, with real glass windows, a trap door and a fireman's pole. And boy did he work hard, every evening, in the dark, to make sure it was ready for Christmas.

On Christmas morning Bird put a big white ribbon on the door and made me cut it with pinking shears. And I spent most of the day up there, happy in my new palace for one.

Exactly one year later, I climbed up the rope ladder, my arms filled with red damask curtains – Bird's Christmas present to me that year, made from one of her old ball dresses – dying to hang them on the bamboo curtain rails Dad had rigged up. I found Jamie sitting on the makeshift sofa in the corner, his arms wrapped around his skinny legs, crying his heart out.

'They're at it again, Jules. Shouting.'

I dropped the curtains on the floor and stared at him. 'On Christmas Day?'

He nodded and wiped his eyes with the back of his hands. 'Do you think they'll get a divorce?'

I sat down beside him. 'No! They're always arguing. It doesn't mean anything.'

'Suppose.' He sniffed but the tears had stopped.

'Do you want to see my Christmas presents? I could go and get them. I got a Selection Box. You can have the Crunchie, I know it's your favourite. And any time they're shouting you can hide in here, OK? You can even sleep here if you like. I don't mind.'

He smiled, his eyes still blurry. 'Thanks, Jules.'

And so it began. Jules and Jamie. Jamie and Jules. We shared everything, we had no secrets. I thought we'd be friends for ever, but I guess I was wrong.

That night I fall quickly into a groggy sleep, helped by the second bottle of wine and a vodka nightcap. There's always wine in the house. Mum used to be in this wine club that sent her a mixture of different bottles to try every month. Mum always swore by a few glasses of red at dinner, when she was actually home that is; her job was horribly busy. Dad has never quite got around to cancelling the subscription, even though Bird reminds him the odd time, and the pantry is stacked with wine boxes. I've never really liked drinking alone, especially not at home, it's always seemed wrong somehow, but the way the last few months have gone, I think I'm entitled to enjoy myself a little, even if it is on my own. And at the moment I don't exactly have any friends to hang out with – Olaf takes up a lot of Rowie's time and Pandora is a dead loss, she puts far too much energy into Shoestring to have any time for socializing or having fun – so drinking solo is the only option.

In New Zealand, things were different. I was out pretty much every night. The bars close unreasonably early over there, so afterwards we'd always head to a club or back to someone's house to continue drinking. I guess it's different when you're away, even if you have a full-time, proper nine to five job it's not like 'real' work; you're in permanent ex-pat party mode, whatever day of the week. And in Auckland, if you knew the right people – musicians, artists, the fashion pack, hairdressers (who love a good party on a Sunday) – you could pretty much party your way through the week, Monday to Sunday. So I did. When I got back to Ireland I guess the habit just stuck. And before all the Ed and Lainey hoo-ha, I had no problem persuading Lainey or one of her younger sisters to join me – Kia in particular loves a good night out. And if they weren't free, they knew someone who was. But now I'm reduced to dancing with myself.

In the middle of the night I wake up, my heart pounding and my body slick with sweat. Another nightmare. The image of a baby floats in front of my eyes. It's lying face down at the bottom of what looks like an empty lift shaft, its tiny body grey and lifeless, blood seeping out of a gaping wound on its back and spreading slowly outwards, like ink on blotting paper. I rub my eyes with the heel of my hands and take a few deep breaths.

Think of something else, I tell myself. Anything! So I focus on the beautiful Farenze dress, then I think about Jamie catching me in my underwear in the staffroom, Jamie lying about calling in, leaving me sitting there all night on my own. The back of my neck prickles. How dare he? Was he trying to prove a point? Or get back at me?

And then I remember Karen's challenge – 'But Jules is hardly going to turn up. She couldn't bear to see Lainey get something she wants so badly' – and I'm filled with so much anger and remorse I can taste it. Karen was right. I can't stomach the fact that Ed is marrying Lainey and not me.

On and on my mind races. If only Jamie's Dad hadn't been

such an idiot, and Mum hadn't got sick, then I would never have got so close to Jamie in the first place; then Jamie wouldn't have punched Ed on the nose, Ed and I would never have broken up that first, crucial time, then I wouldn't have failed my exams and dropped out of college and gone travelling because I was so heartbroken, we wouldn't have had our damn stupid on-off relationship, Lainey wouldn't have had the chance to jump his bones, and *I'd* be the one planning my wedding right now. It's all Jamie's fault. I hate him!

In my heart, I know it's not logical, that I'm just lashing out because I'm hurt and lonely, but it's a hell of a lot easier than blaming myself. I stare at the ceiling and will my mind and heart to stop racing. And eventually, hours later, light dappling through my shutters and birds warming up outside, my eyelids become unbearably heavy and I finally fall asleep again.

Chapter 4

The following morning my alarm clock shrills, waking me up with a start and I groan, slap the snooze button, roll over and go straight back to sleep. Next thing I know, I hear my mobile ringing and vibrating around my bedside table. It's playing the theme song from *The Addams Family*, meaning it's Pandora. I ignore it and, after a few more rings, there's blissful silence. Until it starts up again.

I roll onto my side, press answer and hold it to my ear. 'This had better be good, Pandora,' I mutter.

'I just drove past Baroque and the door's closed. Is everything all right? You sound funny. You're not in casualty again, are you, Jules?'

'I'm in bed! And what's with the *again*? I've only been in hospital once recently. And it was hardly my fault someone dropped a pint glass on my foot, Miss Snarky Pants.'

'You sound groggy. Are you hungover?'

I do feel a little groggy and my brain is hammering against my skull, but I'm not admitting it to Pandora.

'No!'

'Are you sick?'

'No!'

'Then why the hell aren't you in work?'

'What time is it?'

'Ten to eleven. What happened to the alarm clock I gave you?'

I look at said clock. She's right, it's 10.52. I must have hit off instead of snooze.

Pandora says, 'Hang on, Rowie's just pulled her jeep up outside . . . She doesn't look happy . . . She's getting out . . . She's peering in the window . . . She's taking out her mobile.'

'And she's trying to ring me,' I add as Rowie's call comes through. 'Thanks for the running commentary. I'd better get going.'

Pandora sighs. 'Do you want me to say something to Rowie?'

'Like what? Tell her I'm ill you mean?'

She makes a noise, halfway between a snort and a growl. 'You're not ill, you're just lazy; I'm not lying for you again. And I think you've run out of relations to kill off at this stage. I'll tell her you're on your way. Invent your own excuse, keep me out of it. But it had better be good. I don't know why she still puts up with you.'

'She likes me, Pandora, that's why. And Rowie's cool, she won't mind me being a bit late.'

Pandora makes another huffy noise. God, she's annoying sometimes.

'She's not stressy about timekeeping like you,' I say, 'she's far more laid back. She's a great boss and her shop's doing really well. Last week we took in over six grand and she's talking about expanding, opening shops in Cork and Galway.'

Pandora says something very rude and then mutters, 'Bully for her.' And with that she's gone.

I stare at the phone. It's not like Pandora to be quite so tetchy. And she rarely swears. I must have really hit a nerve. To be honest I have no idea how much money Baroque made last week, I made that bit up to annoy her. And I don't think Rowie has any intention of expanding. Maybe I went a bit overboard, but she drove me to it.

I don't have time to decide what to wear, so I throw on yesterday's clothes. I can't find my brush so I give my hair a quick run through with my hands, then tie back my curls with one of Iris's hair bobbins: green, with red plastic cherries hanging off it.

My own raincoat seems to have disappeared and the sky is looking decidedly grey, so I grab Pandora's secondhand Burberry, knot it around my waist, and grab my bike from the hall, ignoring the handwritten notice Sellotaped to the wall above it:

DO NOT LEAVE YOUR BIKE IN THE HALL, JULES. HOW MANY TIMES? YOUR FATHER

Ten minutes later, I'm puffing and panting outside Baroque. The lights are on now and the door's wide open. I can hear Rowie's hippy-dippy Indian music drifting out, along with wafts of incense – not a good sign. She only breaks out the incense when she's seriously stressed.

I lock my bike against the usual lamp post, take a few deep breaths – almost knocking myself out with the smell of patchouli – and walk rather nervously inside, humming Wagner's funeral march to myself.

Rowie is standing behind the till, frowning at the computer screen. She's channelling French peasant meets Riverdance today, in a billowing white shirt, black waistcoat with green piping and grey dirndl skirt, teamed with odd-looking, baby-pink Cuban heeled sandals. Her dark-pink hair is in two plaits, each finished with a piece of black ribbon. Rowie is scarily directional. And she dresses *down* for work, doesn't like to scare the customers.

'Hi, Rowie,' I say, trying not to sound too nervous.

She lifts her head. She doesn't look pleased.

'Did Pandora give you my message?' I add quickly. 'I'm so sorry, what a nightmare. I hate punctures. I got oil all over my clothes so I had to dash home and change.' I hold up my black, greasy fingers – swiped across the chain outside – to make my excuse sound more authentic.

'Jules, Jules, Jules.' Rowie sighs so deeply I almost expect to be blown out of the door. 'Don't get me wrong, as a person I adore you,' she continues. 'You're funny and you make me laugh. And Lord knows I could do with a good laugh most days. But it's not enough any more, I'm gonna have to let you go.'

I'm genuinely shocked. I thought this job was a safe bet. Rowie is the most laid-back boss I've ever worked for. I thought we got each other – we certainly have fun when we're out together. OK, it's only when Olaf is away, but still.

'*What*? Why? Rowie we're friends.'

'I know and it's killing me but the shop's not doing so well, sweets. The figures are way down. People just aren't buying as many clothes as they used to. And to be honest, this whole Sissy business is the last straw.'

'What Sissy business?'

Rowie stares at me. 'Jules! She called in at ten to collect her dress for the telly awards tonight – the electric-blue one we sent off to be altered for her, remember – but you weren't bloody well here. So she rang me and yelled down the phone. Threatened to sue if I didn't get the dress to her place by eleven. Said she wasn't interested in featuring our evening dresses on *Red Carpet* any more.' She rubs her hands over her face and moans into them. 'After weeks of meetings with her production team, streams of phone calls and emails, it all comes to nothing. That show could have made a difference.'

I hit my forehead. Shoot! I knew there was some reason I had to be punctual this morning. 'I'll courier it over on my bike, right now,' I say. 'And I'll try talking her around about the show.'

She taps her watch face. 'It's too late. It's ten past eleven, Jules.'

'I'll ring her, explain,' I add a little frantically. 'She'll listen to me, we're great mates.'

Rowie looks at me doubtfully.

'Honest,' I say. 'She offloads all her old gear in Shoestring, she's in and out like a yo-yo. Please, Rowie, let me ring her. I can hardly make things any worse now, can I?'

She sighs. 'I guess not.'

She walks behind the cash desk, finds Sissy's number in the customer address book, keys it into the shop phone and hands me the receiver.

Sissy answers immediately.

'Yes?' she snaps.

'Sissy, it's Jules.'

'Jules who?'

'From Baroque.'

'*You*! What have you done with my dress?'

'I'm going to deliver it personally. I'm leaving right this minute.'

'I said eleven sharp. You're out of time. I've decided to wear something else.'

'But it looked so amazing on you, Sissy,' I say quickly. 'And it's been taken up especially.' The off-one-shoulder dress is now micro short. 'And if you don't wear it, how can you justify those Jimmy Choos to Ian? You had them dyed especially to match it, remember? You can't wear something you've worn before, not to an awards ceremony. Everyone will think you can't afford a new dress.'

There's an icy silence for a second.

'Fine,' she snaps eventually. 'But you'd better be quick.' And then she gives me her address in Killiney.

'We're on,' I tell Rowie, handing her back the phone. 'I'll throw the dress in a zip up, you can tape it across my back and I'll have it over to her in a jiffy. Problem solved. And maybe the *Red Carpet* thing will still go ahead after all.' I give her a hopeful smile.

Rowie nods and smiles back, but it doesn't reach her eyes. 'We'll talk later, Jules.'

I pedal furiously to Sissy's place and am utterly dismayed to find a rather ordinary looking semi-d. I swear under my breath.

Now I owe Pandora a tenner. Unless I don't tell her immediately of course. I'll come clean when I can afford it.

Ian pulls open the door and gives a warm smile. 'Hiya, Jules. How goes it?'

'Grand thanks,' I puff. If Ian's in, why couldn't Sissy have asked *him* to fetch the dress, I think crossly.

'Thanks for doing this,' he says, helping me pull the duct tape off my T-shirt.

When I'm free of tape he takes the black dress carrier off my back. There's a sheen of condensation on it from my body heat but he doesn't seem to notice.

'I wanted to collect it but Sissy wouldn't let me,' he says. 'Says she needs me by her side all day. She's a bit stressed right now but I know she really appreciates all the extra effort you've made.'

Sissy's voice hammers down the stairs. 'Is that the Baroque girl? Tell her she's lucky I'm not going to sue.'

Ian winces. 'You'll have to excuse her. Big day. She's up for the best dressed gong and I know she's terrified she'll lose out to one of the other *Red Carpet* girls or, even worse, one of the TV3 presenters. I have a whole day of taxi driving ahead of me. From the hairdressers, to the beauticians for her make-up, then on to another beauticians for her nails. At least she had her spray tan done last night.'

'Is your tux all spruced up, Ian?' I ask him.

He looks a bit embarrassed. 'I'm not actually going. She's bringing Albert Dock, the sports presenter. Says he'll look more showbizzy on her arm. Dentist doesn't quite cut it in telly land.'

He leans in towards me and lowers his voice. 'Air kissing isn't really my thing to be honest. And I find the whole TV world a bit intimidating. Everyone's so tanned and glamorous looking. And that's just the men.'

I laugh.

'The dress, Ian?' Sissy shrieks again. 'I'm waiting.'

He smiles at me apologetically and hooks a thumb up the stairs. 'Madame calls.'

Now's my only chance. 'Ian, Sissy was supposed to be doing a *Red Carpet* slot using dresses from Baroque. Retail is difficult at the moment and it would really help. But I think she's changed her mind.'

'I'll have a word with her,' he says kindly. 'See what I can do.'

'Thanks, I'd appreciate that.'

'Ian!' Sissy bellows.

He rolls his eyes dramatically, making me smile. 'I'd better go.'

After saying goodbye I jump back on my bike and pedal up Killiney Hill, my heart nearly thumping out of my chest. It didn't seem this steep on the way down. The climb nearly kills me, but twenty minutes later I'm outside Baroque. I lock my bike, then walk in, peeling my damp T-shirt off my back and flapping it up and down to air my sweaty skin.

Rowie looks up from the desk. 'Jules, must you?'

'What? It's like a ghost town in here.' The shop is still deathly quiet, the only sound the plink-plonk of water dripping, another of Rowie's 'calming' CDs. At least it's not the whale song.

'Jules, listen.' She starts fiddling with the end of one of her pigtails.

Uh-oh. From the grave tone and the deep sigh, I know Rowie's about to give me one of her 'you must be at one with the universe to be truly happy' speeches. Olaf's a Buddhist and some of it rubs off on her.

'I can't go on like this,' she continues.

'Is it Olaf? Has he crashed his rally car again?' My eyes widen. 'Is he all right?'

'Olaf is fine. This is about you. I feel your relationship with Baroque has become completely dysfunctional. You're permanently late, you borrow dresses without asking me, you come in all sweaty from your racer—'

'Road bike.'

'Whatever. Just look at you. Hardly a great advertisement for the shop.'

I check out my reflection in the shop mirror: nice raincoat (even if it is Pandora's and still wrapped around my waist); navy, cropped wide-legged trousers, teamed with a Breton striped long-sleeved T-shirt. OK, so my top is a little wrinkled, and yes, sweaty, but it will dry off. I've nipped it in at the waist with a red tasselled belt I found in Shoestring.

Rowie shakes her head. 'You just don't get it, Jules. You've got all the smarts up here.' She taps her head. 'When you're in good form, the customers love you, but when you're in one of your moods' – she gives a low whistle – 'even *I* have to steer well clear. Apparently you told Sissy she looked like a pregnant hippo in the Debussy Universe dress.'

'It was the truth, the boxy shape did nothing for her curves. I recommended a Hope and Glory dress instead. Suited her much better. She bought it too and it was much more expensive than the Debussy.' I rub my fingers together and say, 'Cha-ching.'

Rowie opens up a paper clip. She pokes dust from the cracks in the desk with it and blows the scud away.

'Look, sweets,' she says finally, 'there are ways of telling customers these things. Calling someone a pregnant hippo is not one of them. She also said you stank of vodka. Is that true?'

'No! She was lying. Vodka doesn't smell. And I'd never come to work drunk.'

Rowie stops scraping the cracks and raises her eyebrows at me.

'Once, Rowie! And it wasn't my fault. I was at a gig the previous night and I hadn't quite made it to bed. What did you want me to do, skip work?'

She shakes her head. 'You shouldn't get smashed when you have work the next day.'

My back stiffens. 'Come on, I get enough of this from Pandora. You like going out on the razz. Who was I out with on Saturday night? Let me think?' I tap my finger against my lip. 'And you had far more to drink than I did.'

'I absolutely did not!' she says. 'I had to drag you into a taxi at two. You wanted to go back to that English guy's hotel room and carry on drinking.'

'He was cute.'

Rowie gives me a knowing smile. 'Jules, he was bald as a coot. If he hadn't kept buying us cocktails, we would have been so out of there.'

I set my chin stubbornly. 'He was funny. All those stories about air hostesses.'

She sniffs. 'I bet he wasn't a pilot at all, I bet he cleans the toilets at Heathrow.'

'Rowie!'

'I'm just saying. Pilots don't generally have neck tattoos. Anyway, it's irrelevant. Yes, I was out with you on Saturday night, but unlike your good self, I didn't have work the next day. You must have been in tatters in Shoestring yesterday.'

'I managed.'

'But that's just it. You never take anything seriously. If Baroque fails I'll be in serious debt for the rest of my life. I took a huge risk opening this place, and the rent is crippling me. I can't play Russian Roulette with my future, I've worked too hard.' She stops, plays with the end of her pigtail again. 'Look, I'm sorry,' she says, 'but I can't afford a full-time member of staff any more. I'll have to run the place on my own.'

I gasp. 'You're really firing me? This isn't just one of those pull your socks up talks?'

From the look on Rowie's face I know the answer. She looks genuinely upset and embarrassed, blood ebbing in and out of her cheeks.

'I'm so sorry, really I am,' she says, faltering. 'I hate doing this . . .' She tails off, then shrugs. 'But I have to let you go.'

I stand there, in shock. 'Please let me stay. I'll make a really big effort to look all neat and tidy, I'll borrow some of Pandora's clothes if I have to. And I'll cycle in slowly so I don't get all sweaty. And I'll be extra nice to the customers, lie to them so they buy the most expensive pieces in the shop; and I'll never, ever, come in hungover again, I swear, and—'

'Jules, stop. I've made up my mind. It's nothing personal, it's just business. If I keep you on, Baroque may go under. I can't risk it.'

'Please, Rowie. Please don't do this to me.' My eyes well up and before I know what's happening I'm pulling at both arms of her shirt. 'I'm begging you. I love working here, I'm sorry for being so crap.'

'Stop, sweetie. You're going to make me cry too. You have so much to give, Jules. You're an amazing person. And I hope we can still be friends.' She takes my hands in hers and squeezes them.

I pull away and wipe my eyes with my fingertips. 'But you're not going to give me my job back?'

She shakes her head wordlessly, her eyes sliding towards the floor.

'I guess this is goodbye then,' I say in a small voice, trying to keep it together. I know it's not Rowie's fault, I know she's only trying to save her shop. I admit I've been a pretty rubbish employee and probably haven't helped the situation, but it still feels like I've been dumped from a great height and then mashed into the ground under her Cuban heels.

I add, 'Unless you need me to stay—'

'No, it's fine. Go home. And I'll drop two weeks' wages into your house on Friday.'

'Thanks. And I never meant to be so useless.'

'You're not useless. You're just—'

A customer walks in the door and Rowie stops mid-sentence and then says, 'Go home, Jules, take a rest. You looked wrecked. But keep in touch, you hear?'

I nod. I take one last look around and then walk out. As soon as I've taken a few steps away from the door, I burst into tears again.

Chapter 5

Bird leaves it until Thursday before she strides into my room, whips back the curtains and clatters open the shutters.

'Up you get, darling,' she says. 'No point in moping in bed. You need to work on your CV. Chop, chop.'

'Leave me alone,' I mutter, rolling over and pulling the duvet over my head. Next thing I know she's yanked it off the bed and is holding it out in front of her like a matador's cloak.

'I've left you alone for three whole days. You know how I feel about self-pity, Julia dear.'

She sniffs the air.

'It's very musty in here. Were you drinking last night?'

'I had a couple of glasses of wine in front of the telly, it's not a crime.' OK, I finished the bottle, but I'm not telling her that, she'll only overreact.

'With Pandora?' she asks.

'No, on my own.'

Bird says nothing for a moment, just looks at me, her bright blue eyes piercing my very soul. Then, without losing eye contact, she sits down on the side of my bed and strokes the side of my head.

'I know you think the world's out to crush you, darling, but it's really not. And drinking's not going to make you feel any better about yourself. You get out of life what you put in. Rowie was quite right to sack you in the circumstances. It might be just the wake up call you need. You were always running late for work, and often hungover to boot.'

53

I open my mouth to protest but she gets in first.

'Don't deny it,' she says. 'I've seen you popping the pain-killers every Sunday in Shoestring, and I can only presume it happens on Fridays and Saturdays too.'

Don't forget Wednesdays and Thursdays, I feel like adding, but I don't. I'm not stupid. Honestly, what is it with everyone these days? Don't they know how to enjoy themselves?

'Occasionally,' I say mildly. 'But what's the big problem? I'm twenty-four, I'm supposed to be out having a good time.'

'Does it always have to involve drink, darling?'

Is she mad?

'Yes!' I say.

Bird sighs. 'Pandora is quite able to go out and enjoy herself without feeling the need to come home legless.'

'Enjoy herself?' I give a wry laugh. 'The last time Pandora kicked up her heels was in Paris. And look what happened then – Iris.'

Bird winces. 'Julia! Please!'

'Sorry.' Sometimes I forget Bird is nearly eighty. 'But it's true. She never goes out these days, except to that stupid karaoke bar and choir practice.' Pandora and Bird are both in the same choir. Dad calls it the Proddy lady choir as it's affiliated to the local church and mainly consists of old biddies – he calls them strong ladies of a certain age, but I know he means old biddies. Pandora fits in beautifully.

'Your sister enjoys a good sing-song, nothing wrong with that. Helps her unwind. And she has a lovely voice.'

'Belting out hymns helps her unwind?'

'Choral pieces, and stop being so sniffy, young lady. Your sister works very hard . . .' I zone out for the work ethic lecture, my heart sinking. No job, no friends, and my family all think I'm a worthless layabout. Fantastic! I press my head against the pillow.

'Are you listening to me, Julia? Unless you get a job by the end of the month you'll have to move out. I'm sorry, but it's for your own good. And before you get it in your head to go off gallivanting around the world again, you'll pay back every penny you owe both me and your father before you leave the country, understand? I have your passport under lock and key, plus all the copies of your birth certificate in case you go getting any ideas about replacing it.'

I feel faint with shock.

'You can't do that,' I protest. 'It's illegal. I'll get a lawyer.'

'Oh, don't be ridiculous, you couldn't afford one. No, you've been coasting for years and it's time to stand on your own two feet. And while you live under my roof, you'll do what I say, understand?'

Her eyes are cool and unflinching. God, she can be scary sometimes. It's not the first time she's threatened to throw me out. But this time she sounds serious. I sit up, fold my legs against my chest and wrap my arms around them. I guess she does have a point, it is her house and it's not as if I pay rent or anything. And to be honest I am getting rather sick of my own company.

I sigh. 'I want to work, Bird, I'm just not sure what I want to *do* exactly. I liked working in Baroque but most of the boutiques are closing down, not hiring. Maybe I should try something different. I did find it a bit boring sometimes.'

Bird stares down at her hands, then lifts her head again. 'You just clocked in, did your time and clocked out again. No wonder you found it boring. You have so much potential, darling, you just need to apply yourself. Make more of an effort. Show people how clever you are.'

'But I'm not clever. I got kicked out of college, remember?'

'You got in in the first place though, didn't you?'

'After repeating in that grind school. And it was only a Business Diploma.'

'Nothing wrong with that. But I am sorry that your father

didn't encourage the whole Art College thing. He should never have left it up to you to finish that portfolio on your own. Pandora offered to help you get organized, remember? But you pushed her away as usual, and then wouldn't let any of us help you after that.'

I wait for it.

'And then you missed the deadline.' She shakes her head. 'Crying shame. Such a talented artist.'

'Even if I had gone to Art College, I still wouldn't have a job now,' I point out. 'Ireland's unemployment figures are at an all-time high, and emigration figures are through the roof.'

She looks at me delightedly. 'You've been reading the papers?'

'Got it from a taxi driver on Saturday night,' I say a little sheepishly. 'He was having a bit of a rant.'

'Ah.' Bird pauses and looks around my room, taking in the heaving pile of clothes on my chair, the mountain of dirty washing spilling out of my wash basket, my dressing table heaped with magazines.

'Julia, dear, you must treat your clothes with more respect. And please tell me that's not my jacket?' She runs towards the chair and pulls a pink tweedy jacket from the middle.

Oops.

'Julia, what were you thinking? This is Chanel, darling. Chanel!'

She brushes out the creases with her hand.

'I didn't wear it, honest, I was just trying it on.'

'What am I going to do with you?' She hangs it over the bed knob and grabs my arm.

'Come on, up!'

She pulls, hard. She's surprisingly strong for someone so tiny.

'Out of that bed, right now, young lady,' she says, 'and into the shower. I'm not too old to spank your spoilt behind.'

I give a horrified laugh. 'You wouldn't dare.'

She raises one slim wrinkled hand, her eyes glittering. 'Try me.'

Ten minutes later, I smell bacon frying and my stomach lurches. I haven't eaten since yesterday lunchtime – the Pringles I washed down with wine hardly count – and I'm ravenous. I run downstairs in my dressing gown, damp hair tied back with another of Iris's hair elastics.

'Dad?'

But it's Bird, standing beside the hob, wearing a black apron (she's allergic to gingham, flowers or polka dots), a Hermès scarf tied over her hair.

'Your father's still in Kilkenny, finishing off that playground,' she says. 'Said he'd see us for dinner this evening. Have you told him about Baroque?'

'No, I'll talk to him later. What's with the Queen Mother's head gear?' I ask, changing the subject. She'd asked me to ring Dad on Tuesday to break the news, but I'm in no rush. I know he'll only be disappointed and make me feel even worse about it.

She touches the silk gently. 'Don't want my hair smelling of grease, do I, darling? Now how many rashers? Do you want them in a sandwich or with an egg?'

I look at her suspiciously. A few minutes ago she was threatening to spank me. What's with the change of heart?

'In a sandwich, please.'

She nods, slaps bacon between two slices of bread and hands me the plate. I drizzle the meat with ketchup and start eating.

'I've been thinking,' she begins.

Ah, here it goes, round two.

'You just need to find your vocation, and I'd like to help.'

I swallow and wrinkle up my nose. 'You want me to be a nun?'

She gives a tinkling laugh, like glass breaking.

'Hardly, darling. No. A *raison d'être*, a reason to live. Something you're passionate about, something to make you bounce out of bed in the morning with a spring in your step, just itching to get back to it. For me, it's the shop. And the news, obviously. I can't wait to find out what's happened in the world while I've been sleeping. I find the news endlessly fascinating. And the choir, the shop, and my bees, obviously.' Bird keeps two hives at the end of the garden.

I look at her doubtfully. Bees, news, work and choir? None of them sound appealing.

'Come on, darling,' she says to my blank face. 'There must be something you adore.'

I think for a minute.

'I like music,' I begin slowly. 'And I like art, but I wouldn't say I'm passionate about it. I know – origami! I love origami.'

'Good, that's a start. But I can't really see there being many job opportunities in the origami field.' She gives me a gentle smile.

'And cycling,' I say, warming to the theme. 'I love bikes. Maybe I could design cool bike frames.'

'Maybe,' Bird says slowly. She doesn't look convinced. 'What about working in a bike shop; isn't there one in Dun Laoghaire?'

I nod. 'Rick's Rides. But Rick seems to spend most of his time fixing punctures. Not very creative.'

Bird cocks her head. 'Creative? So you'd like a job where you could be creative?'

I consider this for a second. 'I guess. I like making things. And don't let on to Pandora, but I love doing the windows in Shoestring.'

Bird smiles encouragingly. 'That's it, a window designer.'

I sigh. 'It's a closed shop, Bird. I did try all the department stores a few years ago but they all have their own in-house teams. And there are only two window-design companies in Ireland. I approached them both but they were looking for people with Art degrees or at least five years' experience.' I stare down at the table glumly and roll some crumbs around under my fingers.

Bird walks behind me and starts to massage my shoulders with her strong hands. 'You're very tense, darling. You should really get more exercise. I do find yoga wonderful for tension. And your posture is slipping. All those years of expensive ballet classes practically wasted.'

She takes her hands away, and props her bum against the kitchen counter. 'Now, back to your job hunt,' she continues. 'What about staying in fashion, but trying to stretch yourself a bit? You have acres of experience, Boolie. And even though some of the outfits you wear are rather odd, you are rather gifted at throwing clothes together for other people. And you spend hours studying all those French and Italian magazines you can't even read.'

I decide to ignore the 'rather odd' insult.

I shrug. 'I do like dressing people I suppose.'

Bird tilts her head. 'And it makes you happy, doesn't it, darling? Seeing their faces light up when you've made them look stunning. Even idiotic creatures like that Sissy girl.'

'Sometimes.' I get the feeling this is leading somewhere.

'I've got it!' Bird says, clapping her hands together. 'A stylist. Lots of the stylists who come into Shoestring look just as strange as you do. One of them has dreadlocks for goodness' sake.'

This is getting out of hand. 'Bird you can't just *be* a stylist. You have to have clients or work for a shop or something. And let's face it, who'd hire me? I have zilch experience.'

'You've been working in boutiques for years.'

'As a sales assistant, not a stylist. Thanks, Bird, I know you're only trying to help, but I'll find something. Maybe I could work in a shoe shop for a change.'

She takes my chin in her hand, her fingers thin and dotted with age spots.

'You listen to me, Julia Schuster, and you listen good. Work in a shoe shop if it makes you happy. But I want you to be the best sales woman in Dublin, understand? Life is short, darling. One day you'll wake up and look in the mirror and see nothing but wrinkles.' She takes her hand away. 'I don't care what you do, just put your heart into it, girl. Stop coasting.'

'I could always find myself a rich husband,' I suggest, only half joking.

'And what happens if he dies or leaves you? No, you must have your own career, Boolie. It's vital. Now go and wash your hair again. Can't have it stinking of sizzling pig, can we? And then we'll work on your CV together.'

Just before seven that evening I hear voices in the hall and Iris squealing. I peer out of my bedroom door. Dad's throwing Iris up in the air and catching her and she's shrieking with delight. I step out and stand watching them for a moment over the banisters. He used to do the same to me – he's always been as strong as an ox from all the timber he lifts.

I close my eyes and recall what he used to look like. The same thick curls as mine, his a little darker brown, tied back in a ponytail, tight goatee, pirate earrings in both ears. He still has the earrings, but his beard and hair are now silver – when Mum died it went grey practically overnight – and his skin is tanned and leathery from years working outdoors. He always refuses to wear sun cream. Whenever Bird or Pandora lecture him about skin cancer, he always says, 'It's in the lap of the gods anyway.'

He puts Iris down and, sensing me, looks up.

'Hey, Boolie,' he says with a grin.

I smile at him.

'Hey, Dad.'

'Hi, Auntie Jules.' Iris beams up at me. 'Don't forget me.'

'How could I forget you?' I say. 'Especially in that lovely outfit.' She's wearing a blue cotton sailor's dress, teamed with a

60

red cardigan and red ballet pumps and her long, straight brown hair is in two neat plaits. Pandora always has her beautifully turned out.

'Come on down and tell us about your week, Boolie,' Dad says. 'I've missed all my girls. Including this wee scallywag here.' He lunges towards Iris and starts to tickle her under both arms.

'Stop, Grandpa Greg,' Iris says through fits of giggles.

He picks her up and throws her over one shoulder in a fireman's lift.

'I'm starving,' he says. 'Let's eat. To the kitchen.'

'I have to wash my hands, Grandpa,' Iris insists. 'I was out collecting honey with Bird. I've got germs.' She waves her little palms in his face. She's so like Pandora sometimes.

He lets her down gently.

'Off you go, pet.'

She runs off and we're left alone. I look at Dad. I know I have to tell him about Baroque but I'd really rather not.

'What is it, Boolie? You look worried. Spit it out.'

I sigh. He knows me backwards.

'Rowie can't afford to keep me on any more,' I say, coming straight out with it. 'The shop's not doing so well and she's had to let me go.'

'Completely?' he asks. 'She can't even keep you on part-time?'

'Completely.'

He sucks his teeth then says, 'Maybe Pandora could have a word with her, ask her to reconsider. A few days a week would be better than nothing. She'd be mad to lose such a good employee.'

I look at him, my sweet, kind, loyal Dad and my eyes start to well up.

'Ah, Boolie, don't cry. Come here to me.' He holds out his arms and I fall into them, wood shavings from his checked work shirt tickling my cheek. I dissolve into tears, engulfed in the smell of fresh sap.

He strokes my head.

'It'll be OK, Boolie. Pandora will fix it. I'm sure you'll have your job back by this evening. And if not, we'll think of something else. It'll all work out, you'll see.'

'Thanks, Dad.' I sniff, and he pulls the end of his sleeve so that it's in front of my face.

'Dad! I'm not wiping my nose on your shirt, I'm not three.'

He laughs. 'Sorry, I forget sometimes. Go and get a tissue. There's the dinner gong. Bird's really going for it tonight.'

We both listen to the hollow bongs together, smiling. Although Bird has her own apartment in the basement, she spends practically all her time up here. She and Pandora take turns to cook dinner every evening, unless Dad is around. Or in Bird's case, reheating dinner. She hates cooking, swears by M&S ready meals. I grab a tissue from the hall table, dab at my eyes and then follow Dad into the kitchen. Iris skips back in to join us.

'So tell me about *your* week, Pandora,' Dad says from his seat at the head of the table while Bird and Iris dish up – Iris carefully spooning rice onto each plate, Bird sloshing Thai Green Curry across them haphazardly.

'Not much to say really.' Pandora reaches across me for the water jug.

'Water anyone?' she says, looking at me pointedly.

'What?' I ask.

'You poured yourself a glass and then ignored the rest of us, Jules.'

'Sorry, I have things on my mind.'

'Like Baroque you mean? Have you told Dad yet?'

I stare at her. She's such a busybody sometimes. Luckily, yes, I have told him. But she wasn't to know that.

There's a long silence while Bird plonks a plate in front of me, and then Pandora. Iris carries Dad's over with two hands and places it squarely on his table mat.

Bird puts a plate out for herself and Iris, smoothes down her skirt and takes her seat. Then she says, 'Pandora's right, Boolie, he does need to know.'

'I've just told him.' I raise my eyebrows at Pandora. 'Satisfied?'

Dad looks at Pandora. 'And I'm sure Rowie will reconsider if you ring her and explain that Julia would be happy to work part-time. Or even take a slight pay cut if that helps. She just wants to keep her job; isn't that right, pet?'

He turns and pats my hand and I nod.

Pandora sits back in her seat and folds her arms across her chest. 'No way, Dad. I'm not ringing Rowie. She must have had her reasons for firing Jules and I'm not getting involved.'

He frowns at her. 'But she's your sister, Pandora. And she needs your help.'

'Can we talk about this after dinner, please? I missed lunch and I'm starving.' She picks up her fork and starts shovelling rice into her mouth.

'Pandora,' Bird says, a warning tone in her voice.

Pandora doesn't look up. 'I'm tired, Bird. And I need to eat.' Pandora gets even rattier if she hasn't eaten. It's something to do with her blood-sugar levels apparently.

'Let's all eat,' Dad says quickly. 'Pandora's right, we can talk about it later. So Iris, what did you get up to this week?'

Iris pushes back her dark-brown fringe with her hand. It's a little long and is falling over her eyes.

'Science camp,' she says. 'We made crystals and bath bombs and stuff. It was cool.' Her face drops a little. 'But a bit messy. I got blue food colouring down my white dress yesterday.'

'It did say to wear old clothes, Iris,' Pandora says. 'And I gave you that old shirt of Grandpa's to put over your dress.'

'But I wanted to look nice.' Iris's cheeks go a little pink.

'To impress the cute science nerd,' I say, wiggling my eyebrows. 'What's his name again?'

She kicks me under the table. 'Shut up.'

Bird hits her glass with her fork. 'Language, Iris, please.'

'Sorry, Bird. But Auntie Jules was teasing me.'

Bird frowns at me. 'Julia.'

I try not to laugh. 'Only because I love you, Iris, honest. I'm sorry, I didn't mean to upset you. Any boy would be lucky to have you as his friend.'

'Thanks, Auntie Jules.' Iris smiles brightly at me.

'And there's this cool exploding bread soda and vinegar trick I could show you later if you like,' I add.

'Cool!'

Pandora looks less impressed. 'Don't expect me to clear up after you both,' she grumbles.

'We'd never do anything like that,' I say, throwing Iris a wink. 'Would we, Iris?'

Iris just giggles.

After apple pie and ice cream (the pie a little cold in the middle but I'm not complaining), Dad bravely opens the Rowie subject again over coffee. 'Pandora,' he says. 'I want you to consider, just consider, ringing Rowie.'

'Dad!'

He puts his hands up. 'Let me finish. I think Boolie has learnt her lesson, haven't you, pet?'

I nod enthusiastically. 'Yes, absolutely. Tell Rowie I'll never come in late again.'

'I'm just asking you to think about it, Pandora, that's all,' he adds finally. 'Subject closed.'

Pandora's jaw is stiff. 'I know you, Dad. You'll go on and on at me every day, making me feel bad until I do it. Why can't Jules ring Rowie herself?'

Dad sighs. 'Because Rowie is your friend. And Jules is your sister. I'm asking you to do this for me.'

'OK, fine, I'll do it right now if it makes you happy. But for the record I don't think it will do any good.'

Pandora pushes her chair back, the legs screeching against the tiles, and stands up.

'Thank you, Pandora,' Bird says. 'I know Jules really appreciates it, don't you darling?'

I nod again, keeping quiet. Pandora's giving me an I'm-going-to-kill-someone-and-it-might-just-be-you look.

While she's out of the room, Iris pipes up, 'Do you have any old perfume bottles, Bird? We're making rose petal perfume in camp tomorrow.'

'Are you dear, how lovely. I'll certainly have a look.'

'I used to do that,' I say. 'With Mum, remember, Dad? We used to collect all the flowers and steep them in this special glycerine stuff she bought from the chemist, and then strain the petals away. It actually smelt pretty good.'

Dad stands up and starts collecting the dessert bowls, clattering them into each other loudly.

'Greg, darling, sit down, I'll do that,' Bird smiles gently at him.

He's still ignoring me. There's an awkward atmosphere in the room.

'Dad?' I say again softly.

Bird looks at him. 'I'm sure you do remember, don't you, Greg? Kirsten and Boolie making perfume?'

Dad just mumbles, 'Yeah,' under his breath. But he still won't meet my eyes.

Bird's about to say something else when Pandora storms back into the room, all guns blazing.

'I can't believe you held a rave in Baroque, Julia. Are you deranged?'

Yikes. I shift in my seat. 'It wasn't a rave. It was just a small get-together thing. To celebrate The Leaf Doctor's debut album. And I cleaned up afterwards. We only lost one T-shirt and I paid for it out of my wages.'

It was Ed's idea. He's a researcher on the *Danny Delaney Morning Show* on 2FM and knows all the up-and-coming Dublin bands. I think they befriend him in the hope that their music will get a spin on the radio. But I keep Ed's involvement to myself; Bird has a limbo low opinion of him as it is.

Pandora shakes her head. 'You're such an idiot. Rowie says there's no way she's taking you back, ever. She loves you as a friend but she says it's too stressful being your boss.' Pandora turns to Dad. 'I told you it was a bad idea. Rowie was very nice about it, but she's not going to change her mind. In fact she's already replaced Jules.'

I feel a tiny stab to the heart. Replaced me? Rowie said she couldn't afford to employ anyone else; I guess she was just trying to spare my feelings. My spirits sink even lower.

'Thanks for trying, love,' Dad says.

Pandora stares at him. 'What about the rave? If I did something like that, you'd murder me.'

Dad smiles gently. 'I'm sure Boolie has learnt her lesson, haven't you, chicken?'

I nod, keeping my mouth shut. I know what's coming next.

Pandora's eyes are flashing. 'This is exactly why she can't hold down a job, Dad. You have to stop treating her like a child. She keeps taking advantage of everyone, doing stupid things and getting away with it. She's twenty-four and she's living at home, scrounging off you. I'm sorry, Jules, but it's the truth.'

Bird slaps her palms down onto the table, making us all jump. 'Pandora, your father is only doing his best. We all need to support Julia in her job hunt, build up her confidence.' She gives Pandora a loaded look.

'Bird's right,' Dad says. 'There's no point worrying about

things that happened in the past, we all need to look forwards, not backwards. I'm sure Boolie will be snapped up in no time.' He smiles at me. 'Employers will be dying to hire a beautiful, smart girl like you. And if the worst comes to the worst, you can always go full-time at Shoestring.'

Pandora snorts loudly. 'Hello? Whose shop is it exactly?'

'Mine,' Bird says firmly. 'But I don't think it's come to that yet.' She pats Dad's hand. 'Let's wait and see what happens. Boolie may surprise us all yet.'

But no one around the table looks very convinced. I feel about an inch tall. 'Can I be excused, Bird?' I say. 'I have something to do upstairs. Job hunting stuff.'

She nods. 'Of course, darling.'

I walk quickly out the door, run upstairs to my room, and flop down on my duvet, completely fed up.

A little later, Bird walks in the door and sits down on the side of my bed. 'Is anything wrong, Boolie? You seemed a little upset after dinner.'

I sit up and shuffle down the bed, away from her.

'I'm fine,' I say, willing her to leave me alone.

'You're clearly not. What's bothering you? Is it your sister? I know she can be a little sharp sometimes, but she only has your best interests at heart. She's devoted to you, darling, you know that.'

I snort. 'Really? Because she sure as hell doesn't show it. Blabbing to Dad about Baroque like that. Calling me a scrounger.'

Bird sighs. 'Yes, I agree, sometimes her timing's a little off. But she's tired, she has a lot on her shoulders.'

She pauses, as if considering her words.

'Your sister doesn't find life easy,' she adds. 'She wasn't blessed with your dogged self-confidence.'

I give a laugh. 'Self-confidence? You're joking, right?'

Bird looks surprised. 'You have oodles of it, darling, too much sometimes. And you can be remarkably charming and sweet when you want to be. Your sister on the other hand obsesses far too much about the shop. At the moment it's her whole life, along with Iris of course, but I do worry about her. And I do wish the two of you were closer. You were like peas in a pod for years. I really don't know what happened.'

She looks at me. 'You used to follow her around like a stray dog, remember? Pandora's little shadow we called you. And then you started pushing her away, just after you turned twelve. I remember it vividly. What happened, darling? Can you recall?'

I blow out my breath. 'Not really.' Which is a total lie. 'I guess we just overdosed on each other. After Mum, well, you know, Pandora was amazing. Did everything for me. Tidied my room, put out my clothes for me, helped me with my homework, plaited my hair . . .'

Bird sighed. 'Too much for a young teenager to take on, looking back. But she insisted.'

I shrug. 'I guess after a while it started to get annoying; she was making me feel like a child.'

Bird gives me a reassuring smile. 'You were a child, darling.'

'No, I wasn't! I was perfectly able to look after myself.'

Suddenly it all comes flooding back to me: the anger and frustration I felt at being treated like a baby, the need to show them all that I didn't need help, that I could happily stand on my own two feet. Three days after I turned twelve I woke up and my pyjamas felt a little damp. I looked down and found spots of fresh blood. I knew what it was, Mum had given me 'the talk' a few years ago when Pandora got her period, but it still came as a shock. I sat on my bed and cried my heart out, desperate for Mum. I couldn't face telling Bird or Pandora, so I hid the pyjamas at the back of my wardrobe and used rolled up loo paper in my knickers instead of a sanitary pad. For two days I hid what had happened, until Bird changed the bed linen and saw faint red stains. I'd tried to rub the evidence away with a wash cloth, but there were still traces left.

During those two days of my very first period, something changed inside me; it was like a switch flicked from off to on. I knew everything was going to be different. I was grown up now. I had to stop relying on Bird and Pandora so much, I had to take charge of my life.

From that point on, I started to do everything myself. I started choosing what I wanted to wear every morning, pushing aside what Pandora had put out. I refused to let her help with my homework, struggled though it all by myself (unlike Pandora, I found school work difficult), and I fixed my own hair.

Then one day I got it into my head to travel home from school alone. I didn't wait for Pandora like I was supposed to; I got the train back to Dalkey all by myself, arriving home an hour earlier than usual.

By the time I got there and Bird realized what had happened, Pandora was already racing around the school in a state, convinced something terrible had happened to me. She was so upset, Bird had to go and collect her. Bird brought me with her in the car, and as soon as Pandora climbed in, she slapped me across the face, hard, shocking both me and Bird. Boy did it sting.

'Pandora!' Bird cried.

'I hate her,' Pandora said. 'I thought she'd been abducted or something.' And then she burst into tears.

She cried the whole way home. I just stared out the window, ignoring her.

Bird sighs now. She's clearly on my wavelength. 'After all that train business, you started locking her out of your bedroom, didn't you, darling?' she says gently.

I nod, feeling ashamed. Not only did I lock Pandora out of my room, I also refused to speak to her for several weeks.

'Can we not talk about this any more? I really do have to write some job application letters.'

She strokes the side of my cheek. 'I understand. But give your sister a chance, Boolie. You two need each other.'

I watch Bird walk out and close the door behind her, then flop down again. As I lie there, staring at the ceiling, I can almost feel Pandora brushing my thick hair, trying to gently tease the knots out of it, one hand on my crown. I used to press my head into the cup of her palm, liking the firm, warm pressure against my scalp. It made me feel safe.

Chapter 6

By the following Friday, I'm seriously depressed. Job hunting is such hard work and so demoralizing. All my previous jobs have been set up by Dad, Pandora or Bird, pulling in favours with friends. But this time Dad's run out of people to try, most of Bird's friends in the drapery business are sadly dead, and Pandora says there's no way she's contacting any of her mates in retail, not after the Baroque debacle. And then she had the cheek to ask me to mind Iris twice this week: on Wednesday night (choir practice) and Thursday night while she visited the local karaoke bar with Rowie. And no, I wasn't invited. I did ask Pandora if I could tag along but she said absolutely not, she desperately needed a night out and she didn't want Rowie to feel awkward.

I've spent every morning this week crawling out of bed and into one of Pandora's boring black suits – the skirt is far too long and makes me look like a civil servant. I've tried rolling the top of it, like I used to do with my school skirt, but then I can't tuck my shirt in, and as my boobs are much bigger than Pandora's, the jacket won't close to hide the shirt flaps. So midi-skirt it is.

Once suited and booted (well ballet-pumped to be strictly accurate), I've walked into each carefully chosen shop with a friendly look on my face and asked to speak to the manager, only to be practically sniffed at when I enquire if there are any openings in their poxy store that I don't really want to

71

work in anyway. Of course I don't actually use the word 'poxy', I'm ultra polite. Bird would be proud of me. But I can't take much more of it. Surely someone, somewhere, will give me a break.

At lunchtime, after dozens of shop managers looking down their noses at me in Dundrum Shopping Centre, I've had enough so I call it a day. Whatever happens I'm going out tonight and I'm going to forget all about my pathetic out-of-work status. I'm gagging for a drink, actually a whole wine lake of it. I've been looking forward to it all week, in fact the only thing that's kept me going is the thought of getting pleasantly hammered tonight. I managed to wangle some cash out of Dad yesterday – told him I needed it for smart job-hunting shoes – and I'm raring to go. I just need someone to join me now.

It takes me hours to get home. I can't cycle in my suit – well technically I could but the skirt would rip and Pandora would not be happy – and the buses to Dun Laoghaire only run about once every hour, and then I have to catch a train to Dalkey.

Once in the door, I climb up the stairs, kick off my ballet flats (freshly polished so they look vaguely new in case Dad asks) and flop down on my bed. I lie there, feeling utterly deflated. Right, I'm going out before I'm too depressed to even walk, I tell myself. I roll over, pull my mobile out of my bag and key in Rowie's number. Two rings and Rowie answers.

'Hi, Jules, everything OK?' She sounds a little nervous.

'Great. But I've been out job hunting all week and I'm pretty wrecked. What are you up to tonight? Fancy going out?'

'Sorry, Olaf's booked theatre tickets. Something about a doll's house, by a Nordic guy, sounds very dark. Not really my bag but he's pathetically keen to share a bit of his culture with me, so I'd better show willing.'

'What about tomorrow night?'

There's a long pause. 'I'd better not, Jules. You know what he's like about me rolling in drunk.'

'We don't have to drink. We could go to the cinema or something.'

Rowie laughs loudly. 'Yeah, right. The last time we went to the cinema we ended up at the dodgy nightclub on Leeson Street afterwards, remember? Fingertons. With those Nokia guys. Look, I'd better go, there are customers in. Are you sure you're OK, Jules? You sound a bit funny.'

I gulp back what I really want to say: 'You fired me, remember, Rowie? It's a job wasteland out there. Please, please, please take me back. And I'm begging you, come out tonight, I really need to talk to someone who isn't eight,' but I bite my lip and say, 'I'm fine, honestly, just tired,' instead.

'Good. Olaf's away again in a few weeks, I'll give you a ring.' And then she's gone.

I don't blame her for being a bit hesitant about seeing me, I don't suppose I'd want to spend time with an employee I'd just fired either, even if we were supposed to be friends.

I stare down at my phone for a second and think. Then I reach over to my bedside drawer, open it and pull out the sticky note Bird had pressed into my hand yesterday. Jamie's mobile number.

'Here,' she'd said after dinner. 'This is for you.'

I looked down at the yellow square of paper and for a second my heart lifted. 'JAMIE' it read. And then his number. I lifted my head and smiled at Bird.

'He dropped it in?' I asked.

She smiled back at me, over-brightly.

'No, Daphne did. I was over there yesterday. We both think you should give him a ring. You're both single and—'

'Bird! If Jamie wants to see me, he knows where I am. And stop with the matchmaking, it's embarrassing.'

Bird and Daphne are obviously back to their old tricks. They've been trying to push the two of us together for years. They could never get to grips with our platonic relationship.

Daphne doesn't think men and women can be friends, and Bird's undecided. I know they mean well, but Jamie is clearly not interested in so much as talking to me and there's nothing they or I can do to change that.

But right now, even though he still hasn't called in, I'm so desperate for company I ring him regardless. I feel tingly with nerves as I wait for an answer. But it clicks straight to messages. I say in a garbled rush, 'Hi, Jamie, it's me, Jules. If you get this ring me back. If you want to that is. But not tonight – I'll be out with my friends. Friday night, you know how it is. Anyway, I just wanted to make sure you weren't lonely and sitting over there all on your—' Beep. The time has run out. Damn. I've always envied people who can leave short, succinct, normal messages. I screw my eyes closed and then open them again. If Jamie does call around this evening, and I'm sitting in front of the telly, he's going to think I'm such a loser. Great! I have to go out now.

And then it comes to me: Clara – Clara Sugars. Clara is one of the researchers on the Danny Delaney team and we've always got on really well. We've even gone to a couple of fashion shows together when she's had free tickets. Every Friday night the Danny gang meet in Dicey Reilly's pub in Ballsbridge to dissect the week, slag off other radio shows and their pathetic ratings, and to get mouldy drunk of course. And as Karen said, Lainey and Ed are away in Paris this weekend so he won't be there. Perfect.

As soon as Clara's voice wings down the line I start to feel a whole lot better. For a start she sounds genuinely delighted to hear from me.

'Jules!' she says, in her sing-song Cork accent. 'It's been an age, girl. What have you been up to?'

'Job hunting mainly. Thrilling stuff – not.'

'What happened? I thought you liked Baroque.'

Self-preservation kicks in. I don't want Lainey to find out via

Ed that I've been fired. 'Didn't work out. I'd like to try something that stretches me a bit, something more creative.'

'I understand. Look, I'm just finishing up here and then we're all heading over to Dicey's. Why don't you join us? It would be great to catch up, yeah, and I always hate being the only female.' She pauses for a second. 'And I'm sorry about Ed and everything. He's away at the moment so you're safe there. How's the head by the way? I heard you had to get stitches, you poor creature.' Clara was at the birthday party, along with the rest of the team.

'Three stitches, and mild concussion. It was just the shock, you know. I've known Ed and Lainey a long time and—'

She cuts me off. 'I'm dying to hear all the details, Jules, but right now I'd better get motoring or I'll never make the pub. See you at seven, yeah?'

At ten past seven I walk into the snug at Dicey Reilly's and feel a wave of nostalgia. For years this used to be my weekly Friday-night haunt. When Ed and I were together I was an honorary member of the Danny Delaney Crew. At first I thought it was weird that they all wanted to spend even more time together – they're practically joined at the hip from seven in the morning until six in the evening Monday to Friday as it is. But they seem to genuinely enjoy each other's company, plus they're all completely paranoid. If you aren't there, you might get talked about, and Noel Hegarty, the producer, has a barbed tongue. You can never tell when he's going to give someone's reputation a lashing.

Tonight, most of Danny's team are already sitting on the curved, green leather seat in the snug, listening as Danny holds court: Noel, Clara, Mickey Darton, who's another researcher like Ed, and a couple of other familiar faces. Plus the ghost of Ed himself, ever the clown, eyes closed, hands out in front of him singing ,'Hello, is it me you're looking for?', making the whole team laugh. I shake myself out of it and try to remember what I'd decided to say.

I wave at everyone and give them all a big, friendly, I've-got-no-issues-whatsoever-and-I'm-totally-over-the-whole-Ed-and-Lainey-thing smile. 'Hey, gang. Great to see you. Clara invited me, hope you don't mind. I'm over my concussion, young, free and single and ready to party.'

'Hey, girl,' Clara says. 'Glad you could make it. Squeeze in beside me.'

Danny grins. 'Aren't you a sight for sore eyes. We've missed you, babes. Thought you'd become a recluse after all that Ed and Lainey business.' He gives a dramatic wince, complete with hissing sound effect. 'Gotta hurt, your best mate shacking up with your man like that.'

'It was a bit of a kick in the teeth all right,' I say, trying to keep my voice light. I'd expected this. 'But hey, life goes on, doesn't it?'

Danny nods. 'Good attitude, babes. Guess you'll be giving the wedding a wide berth?'

'And miss out on all that free booze?' I say, again carefully rehearsed. 'Course I'll be there. Despite everything, they're both old friends.'

'Excellent, we're all invited too. It'll be a blast.' Danny pats the seat beside him. 'Sit right here beside Daddy.'

I sigh inwardly with relief. I've obviously passed the so-over-Ed-it's-unreal test. I wiggle past Noel and squeeze in between Danny and Clara, smiling at her apologetically. I know she likes him but he seems utterly oblivious to the fact.

'You look great,' I tell her, gently bumping her shoulder with mine. The Danny crew make a point of slagging cheek kissers, so I wouldn't dare. And I mean it, she looks stunning – dramatic marine-blue eyeshadow making her hazel eyes pop, black skinny jeans, sparkly midnight-blue top – she's made a real effort and I'm glad I've borrowed one of Pandora's silk skirts.

'Thanks.' Clara smiles. 'Now tell me all the goss. How's Pandora? And little Iris?' I turn my body towards Clara, ready to get stuck into a proper catch-up conversation, when Danny slaps my thigh. He's pretty much just a toddler in a rock god's body – he has to be the centre of attention at all times otherwise he sulks.

'Drink, Jules?' he asks.

'Jager bomb, please.'

'Good woman yerself.'

Danny knocks on the wooden wall of the snug and after a few seconds a young lounge boy walks in and blushes deeply when he recognises Danny. Sunglasses propped on his head, black leather jacket over black jeans and band T-shirt, he's hardly inconspicuous. Danny's show is currently number one in the radio ratings, and he's a regular face in the Irish papers and magazines. At the moment, Mr Delaney can do no wrong.

'Jager bomb,' he tells the lounge boy, 'and another round of the same for the rest of us. Ask Paddy, he'll tell you what we're drinking.' Paddy's the head barman and a bit of an institution in Dicey's.

The boy nods, backs out of the snug, reappears a few minutes later and unloads his groaning tray.

I pick up my drink, knock it back in one and slam the glass down on the table. Danny's wide mouth slits into a grin. 'And we're off,' he says, gabbling like a horse-racing commentator. 'And in the inside lane is Jules and her rocket fuel, middle lane we have Grumpy Noel and his pints, not one mind, two. Tricky Mickey's on a pint and a JD chaser, rare man, Mickey! And on the outside lane, we have Boring Clara. And what's that? A Coke? Surely not. You'll never win the Grand National on a Coke, missy.'

Clara blushes and plays with her glass. 'Sorry, Danny. Driving tonight. Have to drop the babysitter home later.' Clara's a single mum but she always tries to make it out on a Friday, says it's good for team morale, but I think it has more to do with spending time with Danny.

Danny shakes his head. 'Clara, Clara, Clara. What will I do with you? I'll let you off just this once, 'cause you're so easy on the eye.'

She blushes again. Ed thinks Clara's a bit boring, but in fact she's far from it, she's just quiet and a little shy. But once you get talking to her, one on one, she's fascinating – incredibly well read, with her finger on the pulse of every cutting-edge news blog or website out there. She's also one of those rare people who actually listens to what you have to say, and seems genuinely interested in learning how *you* see the world, which is pretty rare.

Clara's also the brains behind the show. She books the 'talent', researches most of the items and types up all Danny's notes, plus she generates most of the weekly slots: Danny's Dish of the Day (celebrity gossip), Danny's Dodos – stupid things celebrities or politicians say. Even the Danny Delaney house band – House – was her idea. Noel always takes credit for the band, but she came up with the concept first. I know 'cause I was right here in Dicey's snug when she suggested it. They're very lucky to have her.

She's pretty too, petite with cropped dark hair, like a little pixie, which is why they call her Tink, short for Tinkerbell, but she hates it, so they don't use it to her face. Everyone on the team has a nickname, even Ed the Head. All a bit childish and prep school, if you ask me.

'Don't worry, Jules will make up for your intoxication inadequacies, won't you, babes?' Danny grins at me.

'Absolutely.' I beam, wondering when my next drink's going to arrive. You need to be a few drinks down to cope in Danny's company – you have to be 'on' all the time, totally engaged in the conversation and in what Danny in particular is saying.

Ed explained it all carefully after my inaugural night in

Dicey's. 'Working for Danny is like selling your soul to the devil, Jules,' he'd said. 'He's the driving force behind the whole bloody radio station, and he knows it. And once you accept that and roll with it, life becomes a hell of a lot easier.'

'So pandering to Danny's ego is part of the job?' I'd asked.

He laughed. 'Exactly! Along with keeping Grumpy Noel fully caffeinated up, and holding Clara's hand when she's having one of her "Noel's picking on me" wobbles. All part of the game.'

Another drink arrives and I down it in one, to the team's cheers. Seconds later the familiar alcohol tingle hits my system and the week's frustrations begin to melt away.

Later that night, I hear voices floating above me.

'I don't know if we can bring her. She's pretty out if it and the bouncers at Champers hate drunks.' Noel.

'We should make sure she gets home OK. Feck, where's Tink when you need her?' Mickey.

I open my eyes. Noel and Mickey are staring down at me. I smile and wave up at them.

'Hi, boys. Where am I?' My head's spinning and my body feels heavy.

'In the beer garden at Dicey's,' Noel says. 'You fell asleep, so we carried you out to get some fresh air. Listen, we're off to Champers but Tink's gone home and it's a boys-only thing, you know how it is.'

''s OK,' I reply. I want to say more but I can't find the words. I push myself up a little but for some reason my legs don't seem to work.

Noel grabs me rather roughly by the arm and pulls me to my feet. 'You go inside, Mickey, order a taxi. I'll look after Jules for a second.'

Mickey walks off and Noel props me up against the wall.

''s very quiet out here,' I say, then hiccup. 'Oops, sorry.' I put my hand over my mouth and giggle.

Noel strokes the side of my face. 'It's after one, Jules. We're the only soldiers left standing.' His hand moves down, onto my shoulder and brushes my breast. 'You look hot tonight. Look what you're doing to me.' He presses his body against mine, rubs his crotch against the top of my leg.

Is he out of his mind? I think groggily: he's married for Christ's sake. And where did all this come from? He's never shown any interest in me before.

'What are you doing?' I say.

'Oh, no, you don't get out of it that easily. Giving me those fuck me looks all night. Skirt riding up your bare legs.' He moves his hand down and starts dragging up my skirt.

'Noel, stop!' I try to push him away but he's too strong. He puts an arm across my throat.

'Shut up, you little slut,' he hisses, a fleck of spit hitting my cheek. His breath smells of stale beer and cigarettes. 'You know you want it.'

His hand paws at my knickers and I'm terrified, my heart pounding in my chest. He presses his arm against my neck again, harder, almost choking me, and I manage a strangled scream.

'I said shut up,' he snaps. His eyes are stony, dead.

'Taxi's here.' It's Mickey.

I look over and Mickey's just standing there, staring at us.

'Ah, right, sorry,' he says, looking awkward. 'Didn't mean to interrupt anything.'

Noel backs away a little and drops his arm. 'No problem, man. We're nearly done here. See you outside in a minute.'

'Sure thing.' And then Noel watches as Mickey turns to leave, and while he's distracted I draw up my leg and knee him in the groin, with as much force as I can. He jumps away and presses his hands against his balls.

'Jesus! You little bitch. Come here.' He throws his other hand out to catch me but I'm too fast for him. I run across the patio, fling open the door and stagger inside. It's completely empty, apart from Paddy, who's putting away glasses behind the bar, his shirt as crumpled as his tired face.

'You OK, Jules?' he calls over.

'Not really,' I say, straightening down my skirt, feeling sick to the stomach and suddenly a lot more sober. I must look a state. I'm about to tell him what happened when Noel comes crashing through the door. His face is an angry red, his flabby jaw set rigid.

Paddy looks from Noel to me, and then back at Noel.

Noel strides towards the bar and slaps his hands down on the wood.

'What did she tell you?' he demands.

Paddy looks confused.

'Nothing. But she doesn't look the best. Mickey's holding a taxi for you outside. Are you taking her with you?'

I manage to force out a 'No!' which sounds more like a wail than anything else.

'You heard the lady,' Noel says. 'She can make her own way home.'

He gives me an icy look, and I want to scream at him, tell him to get the hell away from me, but my throat is constricted and I can't seem to get the words out. I'm stuck to the spot, terrified he'll drag me out with him, insisting to Paddy that I'm drunk and he has to take me home in person.

But instead he says, 'See ya, Paddy. Make sure she gets a cab soon. She's completely wasted,' before walking out, making sure to keep his distance from me. And as soon as the door shuts behind him, I'm so relieved I burst into tears and collapse against a table.

Paddy comes out from behind the bar and steadies me with his arm. 'Ah, here, love, it's all right. Told you he was married, did he? I've seen it all before, believe me. You'll be grand. You'll get over him.'

This makes me sob even louder.

*

'Here, you're not going to puke, are you?' The taxi driver eyes me suspiciously in the rear-view mirror. 'You're looking that way.'

I press my lips together and shake my head. Unfortunately he doesn't believe me. The car screeches to a halt.

'Out!' he says. 'I'm not cleaning this damn car for the second time tonight.'

'No, please, I won't puke, I'm OK.' But even to my own ears the words sound a little slurred.

'I said out.' He jumps out, opens the passenger door, grabs my arm and pulls me out, his rough fingers digging into the bare flesh of my upper arm. I stagger towards the footpath.

As he accelerates away and the cold air hits my skin, I realize I've left my jacket on the back seat. At least I'm still clutching my bag. I look around. And where the hell am I anyway? The run from Ballsbridge to Dalkey is pretty straightforward, but I seem to be in the middle of an industrial estate. I sit down on the edge of the pavement and start to cry. And then my stomach lurches and I vomit its contents onto the road, managing to splatter both my shoes and the bottom of Pandora's skirt. I wipe my mouth with my hand and then look up and down the street for a taxi, but it's deathly quiet.

I peer in my bag for my mobile, half expecting to have lost it again. But no, it's there. I hold it in my hand and think for a second, staggering a little, my head still fuzzy. I right myself and I consider ringing Jamie, before remembering he hasn't replied to my message. Then I get the overwhelming urge to ring Ed. I must talk to Ed – right now. Everything that has happened between us melts away. Ed will know what to do; he'll make me feel safe.

The rings sound funny but eventually he answers.

'Hello?' he says, his voice groggy with sleep. 'Who is this?'

'Ed!' I wail. I'm so overwhelmed to hear his voice I start to cry again. 'I just had the most horrible night. And I'm lost. Can you come and get me?'

'Jules, it's the middle of the night. I thought someone had died. Where are you?'

'I don't know! I told you, I'm lost.'

'Are you drunk?'

''Course I'm drunk, 's Friday. I was in Dicey's.' I stop. Shit, Noel. What do I tell Ed? Noel's pretty much his boss. But Ed's my friend. He'll understand.

'And Noel tried to rape me. You know, Noel Hegarty.'

There's silence for a second.

'Jules, you can't say things like that.' He sighs. 'What really happened?'

'But it's true. He was choking me, and then Mickey came out and—'

'Jules, hang on a second.'

I hear a noise in the background, and a voice, and he's gone.

'Ed!' I yell, slightly hysterically. 'Don't leave me! Ed!'

'I'm here, all right. Calm down.'

'Who's with you?' I ask when he comes back on the line.

'Lainey. We're in Paris.'

'But I need you, Ed,' I wail. 'Can you come and get me?'

'Didn't you hear me? I'm in Paris, Jules, *Paris*. You'll have to ring your dad or Pandora.'

'Noooo! They'll kill me. And I've lost my jacket.'

'You're not making much sense. And rewind, what happened with Noel?'

'I was outside in the beer garden with Noel and Mickey, and Mickey went inside and Noel pulled up my skirt and called me a slut and tried to . . .' I stop and start to cry. 'He was pinning me up against the wall and everything. Then I kneed him in the balls and Paddy rang me a taxi. But the stupid man made me get out. I'm on the side of the road and it's freezing.' I sniff and rub my tears away with my hand.

There's a deathly silence. I hear Ed say, 'Shit,' under his breath.

83

'Do you believe me?' I ask him in a small voice. 'About Noel. Ed? Are you there?'

'Yeah, yeah, I'm here. Are you sure about all this, Jules?'

'Yes! I've had a few drinks, but I'm not that out of it.'

'But nothing actually happened in the end? He didn't – you know?'

'No. But he wasn't messing, Ed, I swear. I was so scared—' I break off and start sobbing again.

'The fecker. His poor wife. Jules, calm down, I'll talk to him, OK? Tell him to keep the hell away from you. Did you call the guards? Jules, can you hear me?'

'Sorry.' I take a deep breath, and try to speak. 'No. I told you, Paddy got me a taxi and now I'm in the middle of nowhere.'

'You'll have to ring your dad or Pandora, understand? Will you do that? Jules, say something.'

'OK,' I manage. 'I'll ring Pandora.'

'Good. And from now on, don't go near Dicey's or any of the team, understand? I'll sort it out when I get back. And don't tell anyone what you told me.'

'When are you back, Ed? I need to talk to you. Will you call in? And why can't I tell anyone?'

'Monday, and yeah, I'll try. But swear to me you won't say a word. If you do, it might only make things worse. Last thing you need is someone like that idiot Jamie or your dad taking Noel on and getting an assault charge for their trouble. Noel's a tricky one, but I know how to deal with him. Now ring Pandora. We'll talk when I get back, Jules, OK.' And with that he's gone.

I click off the phone, feeling a bit better. I don't know what's going to happen exactly, but I trust Ed, I know he'll do the right thing. And he's right, although Jamie wouldn't care what had happened to me, Dad might just punch Noel's lights out. I must admit the thought is very tempting, but I don't want Dad landing in jail over me.

I sit on the edge of the pavement for a few more minutes,

taking deep breaths and trying to calm down before I ring Pandora. She's not exactly thrilled to hear from me but after I beg for several minutes she agrees to come and collect me.

It seems like forever but eventually I hear her Golf spluttering down the street. I stand up and start waving at her. She pulls up beside me and waits as I open the passenger door and climb in.

The first thing she says is, 'What is that disgusting smell? Have you been sick again? And is that my Erdem skirt? Ah, no, you haven't. That skirt is new, I haven't even worn it yet.'

'I'm sorry, Pandora. I'll replace it, OK? And I'm sorry for dragging you out. Like I told you, the taxi driver dumped me on the side of the road. And I don't know where I am, so I couldn't ring another one.'

'*I* managed to find you,' she says grimly.

'Only because you recognized the names of some of the clothing warehouses.'

She sighs dramatically. 'I don't want to hear your excuses, Jules. And not a word while I'm driving, understand? It's late, let's just get home.' She pulls out and we drive back to Dalkey in icy silence.

Once she's marched up the path and opened the front door, she stops and rounds on me. 'You need to sort yourself out, Jules. What were you doing in the middle of an industrial estate like that? It's dangerous. You could have been raped or even murdered. And you have some sort of love bite on the front of your neck.'

When I start laughing manically, which quickly turns into gulping sobs, she groans and says, 'Just go to bed, Jules. It'll all be fine in the morning. You probably won't remember a thing.' With that she leaves me, standing on the doorstep on my own, still crying my heart out.

Chapter 7

I still haven't heard from Ed a week and a half later. I've rung him every day, and first thing every morning I've grabbed my iPhone from my bedside table and checked for messages, but . . . nothing. Until today.

Jules, check your email. Ed

I push myself up in bed, suddenly very awake. I click into my gmail account, which takes longer than usual as my hands are shaking so much, and check through my messages. There it is: From Ed Powers.

> Dear Jules,
> Please stop ringing me. Lainey is under a lot of pre-wedding stress; if she finds out we've been in contact it might push her over the edge.

I stare down at the screen, disgusted. *Lainey's* under a lot of stress? Bully for her. What about *me*? He continues:

> I've cut and pasted a message from Noel. As you'll read, he's very sorry for what happened and he has also agreed to undergo counselling – my suggestion – I think it would really help with his anger issues.
> At this stage it's probably best to accept his apology and move

on, Jules. Noel says he's surprised you can remember a thing. His version of events is a little different to yours, as you can imagine.

I also spoke to Mickey and Paddy who both agreed that you were pretty wasted. Clara said she tried taking you home with her just after midnight, but you were having none of it.

And before you ask, yes, I DO believe you, Jules. But I don't think it's in anyone's interest to take this any further.

Please take care of yourself.
Ed

Tears pour down my cheeks. That's it? Ed has made Noel apologize? That's what he calls sorting it out? Noel probably won't even bother going to counselling; he probably just agreed to get Ed off his back. And even though Ed says he believes me, he obviously thinks I was too drunk to remember things clearly.

Well, Ed Powers, how about this for remembering – I haven't had a full night's sleep since it happened. I keep feeling a heavy weight on my neck and wake up gulping for air. I can't get Noel's leer out of my mind. Sometimes I think I can feel his spit on my cheek. How are you supposed to forget about something like that? I even woke up one night in a panic, with the horrible sensation that some kind of slimy animal was crawling down my face, to find I'd been crying in my sleep. And the nightmares – I don't even want to go there. Move on, you say?

I want to delete Noel's message without reading it, but I know I must look. I have to try and get some sort of closure, stop imagining Noel's still out to attack me, stop jumping every time I hear a branch rubbing against my window, birds in the bushes, or a twig snapping behind me. So I force my eyes back to the screen.

Dear Julia,
I have spoken to Ed and explained the situation. I'm sorry if I came on a bit strong the other night, it wasn't my intention to upset you. You can rest assured that it will never happen again. My marriage is back on track and I'm getting counselling. Your discretion over the whole affair is greatly appreciated.

Yours sincerely,
Noel Hegarty

That's it? Five bloody lines, basically asking me to keep my mouth shut. I feel like screaming.

That's it. I've had enough. I have to keep busy, I have to get out of the house, right now, I have to find some sort of job that will stop me going over and over what happened in my head on a loop, even if it's sorting out garbage, or gutting chickens – at this stage I'll do anything.

Over the last two weeks I've dropped my CV into pretty much every boutique and shoe shop in Dublin city and county with no joy. Some of them refused to take a copy, said I'd be wasting my time. I decide to try one final place before I call it a day – a designer shoe shop in Malahide called Sole Sisters. I've read about it a couple of times in magazines and it's my last hope.

After my shower – I skip breakfast, I don't have any appetite this morning – I try ringing them, but they aren't answering their phone, so I decide to show a bit of initiative and travel over there on the train. Malahide is miles away from Dalkey, but it's on the DART line. And at the very least it will get me out of the house and give me something to do. Bird has already caught me in the hallway and suggested if I wasn't busy this afternoon I might take Iris out to the park after school. Don't get me wrong, I love Iris, but I'm not sure I can deal with her today.

*

When I walk in the door of Sole Sisters, the assistant doesn't even raise her head from her knitting. I stand in front of the desk for a second before she finally notices me.

'Excuse me,' I say politely. 'I was wondering if I could drop in my CV?'

'Hello, deary. Sorry, didn't see you there.' She puts her knitting down on the messy desk and smiles though coral-pink lips. There's a fleck of lipstick on one of her top teeth. 'CV you say? Of course, if you want to. Not much point though. Sales are so slow I doubt if the shop will be open much longer.' She holds out her hand. 'But I'll give it to the owner, you never know. She's my daughter. I just do the odd afternoon for her so she can pop to the bank.'

'Thanks. I'd appreciate that.'

'Have a browse while you're here. Everything is marked down.'

I have a quick look around and frankly I'm not surprised sales are slow. The black shelving is chipped, the mirrors dusty and smeared, and the stock is appalling – from the outdated styles and colours, the shoes and boots look at least two seasons old. There's a small rail of random clothes – badly cut wrap dresses, ripped, grunge-style T-shirts, multi-coloured beach throws – and a shelf of fake-leather clutch bags.

They are even offering a free manicure with every pair of shoes bought, which smacks of desperation. Even I know it's no way to succeed in retail. Customers want to feel pampered and special the moment they enter a shop. Appropriate music (and not seagulls or whale song, no matter what Rowie thinks); a fresh, clean smell; and brand new, just out of the wrapper stock. Some even like colour co-ordinated rails to make browsing easier. Most of the customers are snatching a few precious minutes for themselves before going back to work or collecting the kids from school. Shopping should be a treat. Whoever owns Sole Sisters doesn't have a clue.

After a few minutes I murmur, 'Thanks' and I leave, happy to get out of the place.

After trying all the other clothes and shoe shops in Malahide, I give it one final push – getting the train back to Dun Laoghaire, and dropping my CV into some of the local bookshops (Dad's idea – he's a huge reader). Then I go home and ring some of the bigger book stores in town – Waterstone's, Eason's, Hodges Figgis, and Dubray. They're all very nice, but not one is hiring until Christmas. Then I try both delis in Dalkey, all the restaurants, and all the pubs – but again, nothing.

And then finally I give up, drained and exhausted.

That evening Dad is out at one of his book clubs (he's in two, plus a theatre club), Bird and Pandora are at choir practice, and I'm on Iris duty. We sit down on the sofa together to watch an old episode of *Glee*. Pandora doesn't let her watch it, says it's too teenage, so she's delighted with herself.

Just before it starts I turn to Iris, who is playing her Nintendo while the ads are on. 'Iris?'

She doesn't look up but she does say, 'Yeah?'

'I'll watch it with you on two conditions. One, you turn down the sound on that thing. And two, no questions. In fact, no talking at all, understand?'

She lifts her head and gives me a smile. 'No problem, Auntie Jules.'

'Just Jules, remember? Auntie makes me sound ancient.'

'But Mum says—'

'Your mum's not here this evening, is she? Otherwise you wouldn't be watching *Glee* or staying up so late.'

'OK, *Jules*.' She giggles a little, like she's done something naughty. The opening music rings out and she dumps her Nintendo and snuggles in beside me.

'Who's that boy?' she asks as soon as Finn Hudson, the quarterback, comes on the screen. 'Is he a rugby player?'

'American football. They don't play much rugby in America.'

'What about her?' She points at one of the cheerleaders, Quinn Fabray. 'Why is she wearing her gym gear in class?'

I press my head against the back of the sofa. 'Iris! You promised, no questions.'

'Sorry, Auntie Jules.'

I sigh. I give up on the whole 'just Jules' thing. Pandora has her brainwashed and it will never stick.

By the end of the episode I'm drained from answering and deflecting questions, so I send Iris straight to bed.

'No story?' she says. 'Mum always reads me a story.'

'Iris, it's ten past nine. And I honestly don't have the energy. You can put yourself to bed, you're a big girl.'

'OK, Auntie Jules. But don't forget the pet farm on Saturday.'

'What?'

'The pet farm. You promised weeks ago you'd take me to Glenroe Pet Farm. But it kept raining, remember? I want to play with their rabbits and guinea pigs. I need to decide what to get.'

I look at her. Pandora has been promising her a pet for years, but it's never going to happen. She's just procrastinating until Iris loses interest, says she has enough on her plate as it is. I used to have rabbits – Loopy Lou and Ginger – in the old house, before Mum got sick. Dad made this amazing two-storey hutch. But Pandora refused to so much as touch them, and if she did – mainly because I'd dared her – she insisted on washing her hands immediately afterwards, saying she'd get worms.

Iris has an impressive insect collection in the shed and it's as close as she's going to get to owning a pet, poor moo.

'If it's dry on Saturday, I'll think about it. But now bed, young lady.'

She gives me a huge grin. 'Thanks, Auntie Jules. I'll get my clothes ready for Saturday and then go straight to bed.' With that she skips away.

At least I've made someone happy. I flick through the

channels until I find a rerun of *Come Dine with Me*. That will do. I watch the contestants slating someone's potato and leek soup starter ('common', 'boring', 'a child could make it'), one flush-faced woman pouring red wine down her gullet in the kitchen when she thinks no one is looking. I get an itching for a glass myself, so I fetch a bottle from Dad's boxes, and settle in to watch telly for the night. With my feet on the coffee table and a full glass in my hand, I start to feel calm and almost together. At least, after a few glasses, I just might be able to sleep tonight without Noel's face leering at me in my nightmares.

Chapter 8

On Friday morning my alarm rings at 9 a.m.; I ignore it and roll over. But Bird has other ideas. She walks in and flicks on the lights.

'Bird,' I groan. 'Must you? I've been getting up every morning for the last few weeks and tramping around all the shops like you told me to. But it's hopeless. I may as well stay in bed for the rest of my life.'

'Don't be silly, Julia. I left you alone all day yesterday and you spent the morning asleep and the entire afternoon and evening lying on the sofa in front of the goggle-box. I know you've done your best to find a job, my darling, but enough. I've spoken to Pandora and she's agreed to let you go full-time at Shoestring, on a trial basis. Lenka wants to concentrate on the café, so we'll need an extra pair of hands. The timing is perfect. But what did Pandora say?' She pauses and taps her finger against her lip. 'Ah yes, one false move and you're out on your butt.'

I frown. 'Sounds like Pandora all right. But she wasn't keen, Bird. Did you threaten her?'

'Don't worry about that, my darling.' She pats my arm. 'You just get yourself up.'

I whimper. 'Tell me I'm not starting today. I'm wrecked.'

'No, Monday. You're minding Iris this weekend, remember? But I thought we could put a new window in this morning while it's quiet. No time like the present. The Monkstown Book Festival starts next week and they dropped in posters and asked if we'd do a display. I told them we'd be delighted. Always good to show a bit of community spirit and all that. And in return they'll let us put Shoestring flyers in all their programmes.'

I smile. Bird's no fool. And I know when she says 'we' she means 'me'. She's not keen on ladders and last time she 'helped', she pulled all the clear display line off the spool and it got into a right tangle, making her swear like a sailor.

'You can supervise,' I tell her. 'With a cup of coffee in your mitt.'

She beams. 'Sounds perfect, my darling. Chop, chop.'

Bird drives us to Shoestring in her eggshell-blue two-seater Mercedes. It's ancient and just about holding together, but the classic car insurance costs her next to nothing. She parks in the loading bay outside the shop, and I wait in my seat as she climbs out slowly, ready to give her a push if she needs one as the car is pretty low slung. But today she doesn't.

'Come along, darling,' she says. 'Do stop dawdling.'

I follow her inside. Pandora is standing behind the long wooden cash desk, studying some items a client has just dropped in. The dark-haired woman leaning over the desk is wearing nicely cut black peg-leg trousers and a neat, cream cropped jacket. Well-dressed clients are always a positive sign, although often some of the best and most unusual clothes are brought in by women who look like bag ladies – silk tea dresses they picked up in a tiny boutique in Nice, vintage Hermès scarves, original 1970s hats; we've even had fantastic old naval uniforms and army coats from people's attics.

'Here's your docket, Patty,' Pandora tells the woman. 'All your pieces are itemized. I'll start taking in autumn/winter stock at the end of August, so if you have any jumpers, heavier dresses, boots – especially anything black, grey or brown – do bring them in then.'

'Excellent, I'll have a root in my wardrobe. Thanks, Pandora, pleasure doing business with you.'

Pandora smiles. 'And you, see you soon.'

The woman marches towards the door, nodding at me and Bird as she passes us in a cloud of subtle rose scent. I watch her leave, thinking brogues would work better with the trousers than the loafers she's currently wearing.

Pandora walks towards us, her face head-teacher stern. She's been on my case since collecting me from Sandyford Industrial Estate the Friday before last.

'Any messing and you're out, Julia, understand?' she says. 'I'm only doing this for Dad and Bird's sake. At least this way they might actually get some of their money back. Have you explained the terms, Bird?'

'What terms?' I ask. This doesn't sound good. Am I about to turn myself into some sort of indentured slave?

Bird looks at Pandora. She's equally wary of Pandora when my dear sister is in one of her moods. 'Not yet, darling. Tomorrow's time enough. I'll leave you pair to talk windows. Back in a jiffy.' She waggles her fingers at us and toddles off to the café for her hourly caffeine fix.

Pandora looks at me, her eyes hard. 'Make sure you actually use some clothes and shoes in the window this time,' she says. 'No papier-mâché skyscrapers. Or plastic traffic lights. Or yellow toy taxis. Lots of stock, get it? And for God's sake don't scrape off the Shoestring window stickers again.'

'That New York window was a triumph, admit it,' I say huffily. I'd put a lot of work into those skyscrapers. 'They even used a photo of it in the *Irish Times*.'

'But there were no actual clothes in it. It could have been any old shop. The caption read: 'Shop celebrates new *Sex and the City* movie.' And those window stickers cost a fortune to replace.'

'I'd used copies of the *New York Times* to make the skyscrapers, Pandora. I wanted people to be able to see that.'

Pandora just rolls her eyes. 'Less of the arty-fartiness. Think sales, right? Shifting stock. Speaking of which, why don't you use the Faith Farenze dress as the centrepiece?'

I stare at her. 'But that's *my* dress. It's still on hold, isn't it?'

'Yes, it's still in the office. I know you adore it, but it's been there far too long and you have to be sensible. You're in serious debt and buying an expensive dress would be stupid even for you. Besides, you don't exactly have anything to wear it to.'

'Yes, I do. Ed and Lainey's wedding.'

Pandora's eyes widen. 'You're not still seriously thinking of going? Please tell me you're joking.'

'I have to go,' I say simply.

She shakes her head. 'I really don't get you sometimes, Jules. I thought you were devastated by the whole Ed and Lainey thing. Don't tell me you're over it already. You have such a hard heart sometimes.'

Before I know what's happening my eyes fill.

Pandora sighs. 'I'm sorry. Of course you're not over it. But why on earth would you want to put yourself through that?'

I blink away my tears.

'I know it probably sounds mad, but I want to walk into the church with my head held high, looking amazing. I want everyone to see me there, Pandora. Everyone. Ed and Lainey, and all our so-called friends. Since I got back from New Zealand not one person has rung to see if I'm all right. They've all taken Ed and Lainey's side.'

'It's not that simple, Jules You've been away a lot, and you've never been the best at keeping in contact.'

'I spoke to Ed and Lainey every week. Fat lot of good that did me.'

'Look, I don't think you're strong enough to go to the wedding. I'm just being honest, Jules. And I don't think being there would do you any good.'

'I think it would,' I say stubbornly.

96

She sighs again. 'I guess we'll just have to agree to differ. But I'm sorry, the Farenze will have to go back into stock.'

'Just give me one more day, please? Humour me.'

Pandora sighs. 'One more day, Jules, OK? Tomorrow it goes back on sale. Now I have to get back to work. And you have a window to dress. And I mean *dress*, Jules. With clothes this time.'

I work on the window all day. By four o'clock I'm ready to put the grey-blue elephants I've created from the book festival posters in place. I'm pretty proud of them to be honest. I used origami techniques to fold the paper into seven different elephant shapes – the largest one is the size of a beach ball, the smallest is as small as an egg. I made the ears from cut-out paper triangles, and added black beads for eyes, and tiny plastic tooth-pick tusks. The trunks are paper wrapped around curled spirals of florist's wire. Bird suggested nipping home to collect some of Iris's toys to sit on their backs – Barbies and Bratz dolls – but it's a horrible idea and I managed to dissuade her.

The elephants are in honour of the key-note speaker at the festival, a Booker prize winning Indian author called Asha Bhandari. The festival posters feature one of her book covers – a family of elephants marching over a misty range of hills – and I've brought this image to life in the Shoestring window.

At lunchtime Pandora came over to see what I was up to. 'Elephants?' she said, looking at me sideways. 'Jules—'

'I know you said to put lots of clothes in,' I got in quickly, cutting her off. 'And I'm going to add loads in the background. The hills and fields will be made from coloured tops and dresses, draped over these special chicken-wire frames I've made. Then I'm going to add a blue satin shirt lake, with ballet pumps to represent 'boats' bobbing on the water.' I grinned at my own master plan.

To my surprise she smiled back. 'What am I going to do with

you? It's not quite what I had in mind but it'll certainly attract attention. Good work.'

'Thanks. And Pandora?'

'Yes?'

'Thanks for the job.'

She leaned in towards me to say something, then decided against it. 'You're welcome,' she said instead.

I had a funny feeling she was about to say, 'Don't screw it up' or words to that effect. But she didn't. And at least that was something.

I place the elephants in the landscape and walk outside to check they're marching in a straight line, when I hear a voice behind me.

'What breed of elephants are they supposed to be?' There's a girl standing there, staring down at my models. She's wearing a practical but shapeless navy jacket with lots of pockets over jeans, and she's tall, at least six foot. I have to tilt my head up slightly to talk to her.

'What do you mean?' I ask.

'African or Indian?'

'I don't actually know. I just copied them from a book cover.'

She crouches down and peers in at the paper animals. 'From the size of their ears and curve of their back, I'd say Asian.' She frowns slightly. 'But their tusks are wrong.'

'That may be my fault. I couldn't get the toothpicks to sit quite right.'

'They shouldn't have tusks at all,' the girl says, slightly accusingly. 'There are baby elephants in the group, which means the adults are female. And Asian cows don't normally have tusks. Family groups are always female, bull elephants have nothing to do with their offspring once they're born.' She says it in a matter of fact way, as if this is the kind of conversation she has every day.

I pull a crumpled book festival flyer from my back pocket and hand it over. 'I copied this,' I explain.

'See,' she says, stabbing the picture with her finger. 'No babies. They're bulls, not cows. It's a bachelor herd.'

I look at the picture. She's right. The 'babies' aren't babies at all, they're just smaller elephants. I shrug. 'I thought babies would look cuter.'

'But it's not accurate.'

Now I'm starting to get a little annoyed.

'Look, I've spent the whole day making those elephants. My fingers are full of paper cuts.' I hold them out to show her. 'And I don't think anyone will notice.' I pause. 'How come you know so much about elephants anyway?'

She shrugs. 'I work with them.'

'In a circus?'

She doesn't look too impressed. 'No! Dublin Zoo.'

'*You're* a zookeeper?' I try not to smile.

'Yes. What's so funny about that?'

'But you're so gorgeous. I presumed you were a model.'

She gives a dry laugh. 'You're funny.'

'No seriously.'

Finally she smiles, her teeth tiny white pearls against her dark pink gums. She really is extraordinary looking and she obviously has no idea. Glossy dark hair pulled back off her oval face, perfect black skin, a mouth as wide as Julia Roberts's, and the kind of body most of us would die for; tall and slim, yet not too skinny.

'How many black models have you seen in the Irish magazines recently?' she says, her south-Dublin accent tinged with something more exotic.

'Pretty much none,' I admit. I am rather an expert on magazines. 'Point taken.' She smiles again. 'Anyway modelling would bore me rigid. All that standing around. I have no interest in clothes, or working with people for that matter. I love working with animals, especially elephants. You know where you are with elephants.'

I don't know quite what to say to this; luckily I don't have to. Pandora appears with the Farenze in her arms.

'Jules, this has to go back into stock tomorrow, I'm so sorry. Will you put it on a mannequin for me?'

Then she notices the girl.

'Oops, sorry, didn't mean to interrupt.'

The girl's eyes are glued to the dress. 'Is that for sale?' she asks.

Pandora ignores my glare.

'It will be in the morning,' she says. 'Would you like to try it on?'

The girl nods, her eyes twinkling.

'Please.'

'No problem. Your hands clean, Jules?'

I nod and Pandora hands me the dress, the chiffon melting into my outstretched arms, my heart sinking with it.

'Jules will find you a dressing room, won't you, Jules?' she says pointedly.

I nod again wordlessly. I know I have to say goodbye to the dress eventually, but it still hurts.

'Follow me,' I say.

'I'm sorry,' Pandora whispers in my ear as I walk past her. 'But a dress like that deserves a good home.'

I hang the Farenze in a vacant changing room, turn around and flash the girl a smile. None of this is her fault and at least she seems to appreciate the dress, even if she is a bit odd.

'I'll get you some heels, and a belt maybe,' I say.

She squirms a little. 'What about a little jacket or something? It's quite revealing.'

I smile gently. I can't believe she wants to cover up that amazing body. 'Sure, back in a sec.'

Several minutes later the girl sweeps out of the changing room. Out of her jacket and jeans, she looks a different person, and in fact she's so tall she doesn't need heels, the chiffon hits her long legs just under her knees. The dark pink is incredible against her skin; the soft material hugs her slim figure but the layers make her hips look curvier, more womanly. I realize that she's older than I thought, twenty-two or twenty-three maybe.

'What do you think?' she asks nervously. She has no idea what to do with her arms, so she twists them in front of her, like she's doing yoga practice.

I give a low whistle.

'Stunning. Looks like it's made for you. Try this over your shoulders.'

I help her arms into a green sequined shrug and tie a green sash-style belt around her waist. I stand back and take a look.

'Perfect,' I say.

'Is it really only a hundred and twenty euro?' She pirouettes, the material following her like a ballerina's skirt. 'It's beautiful.'

'Add a nought,' I say. 'Twelve hundred.'

She stops twirling and her face falls.

'I must have read the tag wrong. I'd better take it off. It's just I have this school reunion thing coming up and I've been saving for something special since Christmas, but that's silly money.'

'How much do you have?' I ask. Maybe Pandora will reduce the price a little. Doubtful, but you never know with Pandora.

'Three hundred tops.'

'Sorry,' I say, meaning it. Pandora's right, if the dress has to go, it should be to someone who loves it as much as I do. 'It's being sold for charity.'

'It's all right. I understand. I'll have to face the school witches in something else. Maybe I won't go after all.'

She takes one last, lingering look in the mirror and then turns back to get changed, her shoulders hunched with disappointment. Before closing the curtain behind her, she goes quiet for a second. Then she blows out all her breath.

'Don't you wish you were stinking rich sometimes?' she says

wistfully. 'So you could just walk into a shop and buy any old dress you wanted.'

I give her a sad smile.

'I know. That dress is one in a million. I tried it on as soon as it came in, had my eye on it for a special event too. I think it's magic or something, it seems to suit everyone. Unfortunately like you, I can't afford it.'

'If we had six hundred each, we could share it,' she jokes.

I stare at her. 'Hang on, what did you just say?'

'If we had six hundred each, we could share it.' She stops, looking worried. 'I'm sorry, was that a really strange thing to say? Sometimes I honestly can't tell.'

'Not at all. Would you seriously consider sharing a dress with a complete stranger?'

She shrugs. 'Normally, no. But for this dress, yes, I definitely would.'

I stare at her. 'You have three hundred euro, right now?'

'Correct.'

'That's plenty for a deposit. And if I can find another three hundred, we're halfway there. Then we just need to find two more takers to time share it.'

Her face breaks into the most amazing sun-splitting smile. '*We*? Are you serious? You'd really share it with me?'

'Yes!'

'I guess I should introduce myself in that case. I'm Arietty, Arietty Pilgrim.'

She doesn't offer her hand, just smiles at me. I smile back.

'And I'm Julia Schuster, Jules. And it was your idea, even if you were only joking. When's your school reunion?'

'Twentieth of October,' she says instantly. 'It's a Saturday.'

'And my wedding's the twenty-seventh, also a Saturday, excellent, it gives us oodles of time to find two more dress partners in crime.'

Arietty's eyes light up. 'Wedding? It's going to be your wedding dress?'

'Not exactly. Believe me, it's a long story. But first, we need a plan. What are you doing tomorrow?'

Chapter 9

'Where are we going, Auntie Jules?' Iris stops dead on the pavement. 'I'm not walking any more until you tell me. I'm exhausted.' She leans her back against the metal railings and crosses her arms stubbornly.

I smile to myself. With her jaw set like that she looks the image of her mum. 'We're nearly there, Iris. Two more minutes, I promise.'

'You keep saying that, two more minutes, two more minutes. I'm not moving.'

'Suit yourself.' I walk away from her, slowly, hoping she'll follow me. It starts spitting rain and for once I thank Pandora's Girl Guide streak. Before we left this morning, she'd insisted on filling a rucksack with a packed lunch for Iris and an umbrella. I pause, pull out the umbrella and put it up. One of the spokes is broken, but it still keeps off the worst of the drizzle.

'If you keep dilly-dallying you'll miss all the animals,' I say loudly without turning around, twirling the umbrella like Mary Poppins.

'Animals?' I hear Iris's trainers slapping on the ground behind me. Her small hand grabs my arm. 'Did you say animals?'

I nod, try not to smile. 'This is Phoenix Park, Iris. What's in Phoenix Park?'

Her eyes bug open and her lips spring into a wide grin.

'The zoo! Are we really going to the zoo?'

'Yep.'

She throws her arms around my waist and hugs me tight.

'Thanks, Auntie Jules. I haven't been since my school trip last year.'

I feel bad for Iris. She adores the zoo, she's always asking for someone, anyone to take her, but Pandora works so hard she's always exhausted on her days off, and the zoo is the last thing on her mind. Bird doesn't like to park the Mercedes in the city and hates public transport, so she's a dead loss as the zoo is a bit tricky to get to unless you drive, which only leaves Dad, and he's often working at the weekends. To be honest, I'm only going today because Arietty invited me to meet her at work to discuss our Farenze scheme, an offer I just couldn't refuse, which makes me feel even more guilty.

I pick up her plaits and pile them on top of her head, like Heidi. 'Sorry, Iris, I'll take you more from now on.'

She looks at me solemnly. 'Do you swear?'

'Cross my heart and hope to die, stick a needle in my eye.'

She seems satisfied with this. She takes my hand and pulls hard.

'Come on, Auntie Jules, you're such a slow coach.'

'Thought you were tired, you minx.'

She just giggles.

Arietty has left our names with one of the security guards at the gate, and Iris is delighted with herself.

'We didn't even have to pay,' she says. 'We're like celebs. Your friend must be very important.'

'She is,' I say, shaking the umbrella and folding it away. The rain has stopped, but the sky is still grey and threatening.

Iris skips up the right-hand slope towards the Kaziranga Forest Trail, against the pedestrian traffic as Arietty suggested, and I follow her. Crowds make Iris nervous. She's always convinced she's going to get lost. She did once, in Tesco in Dun

Laoghaire when she was just three, and the fear seems to have stayed with her.

We pass the low-slung Reptile House and continue down the path, avoiding the peacocks. I've never liked peacocks, they have beady, dead looking eyes, and their sharp wail gives me the heebie-jeebies.

I halt beside the leafy entrance to the trail. 'Here we go. This is where Arietty works. We're a little early but we can check out her elephant friends while we wait.'

Iris stares at me. 'Your friend works with the animals?'

I smile back; her eyes are nearly popping out of their sockets again. 'Yes. She's the elephant keeper. Didn't I say?'

She slaps my arm. 'No! You said she worked in the zoo. I thought you meant in the office or something.'

I chuckle. 'I wanted to surprise you. Now are we going in or what?'

Iris runs along the twisting concrete path and I follow her. Every now and then she stops at a bend and checks that I'm behind her. The wind is making the tall bamboo plants swish and there's a waterfall splashing over some rocks. I close my eyes and try to imagine a forest in deepest India. A little hard with the excited shrieks coming from up ahead.

I turn the corner and there they are, Arietty's elephants, four of them, two babies and two larger ones, all playing at the edge of the concrete pool. As we watch, the babies duck under the water and use their trunks as snorkels.

Iris giggles, her eyes glued to the scene. 'Look, Auntie Jules, they're swimming. They're so cute.' I sit down in the stepped visitor's viewing area and watch Iris. She's in her element, pupils wide, face lit up, totally absorbed in the elephant babies' antics, her little body straining against the wooden fence to get as close as she possibly can. She's so engrossed she doesn't seem to notice the gaggle of children building up either side of her.

I take out my mobile and text Arietty:

Bit early. Watching the elephants. Jules X

A second later a message beeps back:

Stay there. AX

Minutes later Arietty appears. I almost didn't recognize her. She's wearing a green Dublin Zoo sweatshirt, black work boots, green combats, a yellow walkie-talkie and keys hanging off her belt. She looks very official.

'Hey, Jules.'

I stand up and she hesitates in front of me for a second, as if deciding whether to kiss me or not. She decides not to, instead sits, tucking her hands under her legs. I join her.

'That your niece?' she asks, nodding towards the fence.

'The one practically in the elephant enclosure? That's Iris all right. She's mad about animals. Has all kinds of odd pets at home – an ant farm, a wormery, a log covered in woodlice, and a snail collection. Her mum makes her keep her weird menagerie in the shed.'

Arietty laughs, a surprisingly deep, contagious ripple.

'I was exactly the same at that age. Slightly different mini-beasts though. Stick insects, katydids, and spiders. Used to drive Mum wild.'

'Stick insects? Where did you grow up exactly?'

'Port of Spain.'

I look at her blankly. I don't like to admit I've never heard of Port of Spain.

'Trinidad! It's the capital.'

'And how did you end up here?' I ask, curious.

'In the zoo or in Ireland?'

'Both.'

'My stepdad's Irish. Me and Mum moved here when I was thirteen. And I ended up in the zoo because I couldn't hack it as a teacher. The kids were fine but I couldn't bear the parents. They were all so self-deluded about their little angels. And I wasn't mad on some of the other teachers either. They weren't much fun really, very institutionalized. So after a year of it I left, went travelling for a while, ended up working in an elephant sanctuary in Sri Lanka. When I came back to Dublin, I applied to the zoo and I've been here ever since.' She shrugs. 'My grandaddy, he was a zookeeper in Trinidad – big cats though, not elephants – so I guess it's in the blood.'

Wow, I think, that's quite a story. I look at her, dying to hear more, but just then Iris waves up at me.

'Hi, Auntie Jules. I'm still here.'

'I see you, Iris, don't worry.'

Iris notices Arietty and smiles at her shyly.

'Cute kid,' Arietty says. 'Seven?'

'Eight. Sorry she had to tag along, my sister's working this weekend and I'm on babysitting duty today.'

'Where's her daddy? Does she have one?'

I'm a little startled by the directness of the question.

'Sorry,' Arietty says, swatting a wasp away from her face. 'Was that a bit rude? I tend to just wade in sometimes. You can see why the parents weren't exactly impressed.' She puts on a firm teachery voice: 'No sorry, your Johnny isn't a genius, in fact I think he may be low-spectrum autistic.' She sighs. 'You can imagine how that went down.'

I can feel my eyebrows lift. 'You actually said that?'

She grins. 'I was being kind that day.' She stands up and brushes down her bum. 'Would Iris like to see behind the scenes? She can feed one of the girls if she likes.'

'Are you serious? She'd love that. Are you sure it's OK?'

She gives a click of her tongue.

'I checked ahead and the other keepers don't mind, they're pretty easy-going.'

'Thanks, Arietty. She's a good kid and it would mean a

lot to her.' I give her a hug. As soon as my arms are around her, I can feel her body stiffen and I pull away quickly, a little embarrassed.

''s OK,' she murmurs, clearly taken aback. 'This way.'

She jumps down the steps, and takes a sharp left.

'Iris,' I call over the heads of the other children.

She looks up and her little face falls.

'Can't we stay a bit longer?' she asks loudly. 'Please?'

'Arietty has something to show you.'

Iris slopes towards me reluctantly, shoulders hunched. When she's beside me I crouch down and whisper in her ear.

'How would you like to feed one of the elephants?'

Her eyes goggle. 'Yes! Yes! Yes! This is the best day ever.'

We catch up with Arietty and Iris walks beside her, her little legs practically running to keep up with Arietty's long strides. I watch her striding on ahead, hoping she'll tell me more about her background later.

'What do elephants eat, Arietty?' Iris asks excitedly, like a little dog yapping at her master's heels. 'Can I touch them? How heavy are they? Do they really sleep standing up?'

Arietty turns her head, winks at me and then asks Iris, 'Which question would you like me to answer first?'

'Can I touch them?' Obviously the foremost thing in her mind.

'We'll see. If the girls don't mind, yes, you can touch their trunks.'

Iris squeals. 'This is the best day ever in my whole entire life.'

Arietty just laughs. She leads us through a wooden gate that says 'Staff Only', and in through a door at the back of the huge elephant house which is the size of an aeroplane hanger. She says hi to two men in zoo uniforms, who both give a friendly smile to me and Iris as we walk past, and then she shows us into a long room with a stainless-steel sink and countertop, like an industrial kitchen. It smells a little musky, like a stable. There's a large whiteboard against one wall and a large black dustbin sitting underneath it.

'This is where we prepare the feed,' Arietty says.

Iris tucks her hand into mine and I smile down at her. She's looking around, eyes wide as Frisbees, taking everything in. As Arietty grabs a bucket and fills it with carrots and what look like huge pony nuts from the dustbin, I read the board. It lists each elephant's name, weight and temperature, along with lots of other handwritten messages like 'We need more shovels!' and 'I hate pigeons!'

Iris pulls my arm and says in a low voice, 'Will you ask her what the glitter's for?' There are three pots of different coloured glitter sitting on the draining board of the sink.

Arietty, hearing Iris's question, turns around.

'Ah, the glitter. Well spotted, Iris. Sometimes we have to test the elephants' poo to check they're healthy. So we need to know whose poo is whose, so we put different coloured glitter in their food. That way we can tell which dung belongs to which elephant.'

Iris starts giggling. 'Glittery poo? That's really funny.'

Arietty joins in, chuckling away. 'I know. But it works.'

Iris squeezes my hand. 'Isn't it funny, Auntie Jules?'

I squeeze back and nod, smiling. 'Very.'

Arietty leads us out of the room, past enormous chunky metal cages and left down a dusty roadway.

'Is this the way to the elephants?' Iris whispers up at me.

'I think so,' I say.

Arietty is striding towards hefty black gates, as high as a double decker bus. She stops at the gates and says loudly, 'Here, girls. Here, girls,' and then gives a high pitched 'Souk, souk, souk, souk.'

Within seconds two enormous elephants are marching towards us, surprisingly gracefully for such bulky creatures. Iris's mouth falls open as the first one reaches the gate and she tilts her head backwards to take in the full bulk of the animal. They are both massive, and much wilder-looking this close up, with long fluttery eyelashes, hairy backs, and hoary old lady bristles on their trunks. I can hear their loud, horsey breath, smell their musky scent.

'They're so big,' Iris says, stepping back several times and pulling me with her. Then she buries herself in my side.

'Don't be nervous,' Arietty says kindly. 'They won't hurt you. Not intentionally anyway. This old girl is Beatrix. She's the matriarch, which means she rules the roost.'

'Is the other big one male?' I ask.

'No. That's Beatrix's little sister, Enid.' She reaches through the bars and pats the biggest animal's flank. 'The cows, the females, all live together with the babies, remember? I told you all this outside the shop, Jules.'

I smart a little at the rebuke but Arietty seems oblivious.

'The bulls live either alone or in bachelor groups,' she continues, taking her hand back out and directing her information at Iris, who is paying careful attention. 'One of the babies is a bull, Kai, but as soon as he reaches puberty he'll be sent away to another zoo.'

'Sounds like a good plan,' I say, only half joking.

Arietty gives a laugh. 'It certainly works for elephants.'

Beatrix sticks her trunk through the bars and runs the pointed end of it over Arietty's hand. Arietty strokes the smoother skin of the trunk's underbelly. She asks, 'Would you like to stroke her trunk, Iris?' her focus still firmly fixed on Beatrix.

Iris inches forward nervously, gulping several times.

Arietty takes a carrot from the bucket at her feet and hands it to Iris. 'Give her this,' she says. 'Aim it towards the tip of her trunk.'

Iris gingerly holds it out towards the end of Beatrix's trunk, which is bright pink with grey splodges, like a pig's snout. The elephant whips it out of her hand, grasping the carrot between

111

the protruding 'finger' and the base of her trunk, and Iris giggles away delightedly.

'Did you see that?' she squeals. 'She took it off me. Can I do it again?'

'Sure.' Arietty hands her another carrot and Iris feeds Beatrix again, this time putting her other hand out to touch the top of the trunk.

'It feels so weird,' Iris says in wonder. 'Hard. I thought it would be like leather. But it's more like stone or something. What's the stuff that grows under the sea, Auntie Jules? It's pink and white and fish live in it. I saw it in that programme about the sea in Australia.' Iris watches a huge amount of nature programmes.

'Coral?' I suggest.

She nods. 'Yes. It's like coral. All rough and bitty.'

Then Iris feeds the other elephant, Enid, who gives her an ear-blasting trunk hoot for her trouble, sending Iris jumping back in fright, her hands over her ears.

Arietty laughs. 'She's saying thank you. Loud, isn't it? Oh, and here comes trouble.'

Arietty points at the two darker-coloured babies who are running towards us, making excited-sounding hooting and squeaking noises.

'The one with the small tusks is Kai, he's five; and the other's Nina. They love company and Kai's incredibly nosey, loves getting his trunk into everyone's business.'

Arietty lets Iris feed the whole family, until all the carrots and nuts are gone. 'We have to say goodbye now, girls,' Arietty tells the adult elephants, showing them the empty bucket, and giving Beatrix's ear a quick rub through the bars.

'Ready to go, pet?' I look over at Iris. Her little lips are pressed together, her eyes are glistening and I can tell she's trying not to cry.

'What is it?' I crouch down and hold her head between my hands.

'This is the best day ever, ever, ever and I don't want it to end. What if I forget what Beatrix and Enid and Nina and Kai look like?'

I stand up and take out my phone. 'If it's OK with Arietty, I'll take some photos of you and the elephants. And we can come back and visit. Soon, I promise. And maybe they'll have a toy elephant in the gift shop. If they do, would you like one?'

She beams at me.

'Yes, please! Thanks, Auntie Jules. You're the best.'

'Iris looks wiped out,' Arietty says at lunchtime. We're sitting outside one of the restaurants, eating chips. Iris has finished eating, not that she had much, and is now resting her head on her folded arms and watching the peacocks, which are thankfully keeping their distance. Her new fluffy toy elephant is standing on the table beside her. She's already named it Beatrix.

I stroke Iris's head. 'Too much excitement for one day, eh, pet? Thanks for arranging feeding the elephants and everything, Arietty, it was incredible. You officially have the best job in the world.'

Arietty picks up a chip and studies it for a second before deciding not to eat it and putting it back in the carton.

'Not the most glamorous though,' she says. 'Plus I always come home stinking of elephant. It gets right into my pores. Just as well I'm single.' She snorts and stares at one of the peacocks who has whipped his tail out like a Spanish lady flicking open her fan, and is strutting around, parading all his glory to the world. 'Most people think it's a pretty weird job for a girl, but I love it,' she continues. 'Elephants are far less complicated than people. More forgiving too. Take Beatrix for example. She was in a zoo in Russia before she came here, and was very badly treated from what we can make out. But she's still able to trust people. But enough about work, what about finding willing victims to share our dress then? Have you had any ideas?' She smiles at me brightly, obviously keen to change the subject.

'Yes,' I say. 'I thought we could put an ad on Gumtree and eBay, and also create a blog, in case people wanted to see more photos of the dress and ask questions before they commit to anything. I'd stick a notice up in Shoestring, but Pandora might not like it.' I don't add, 'Or might nip our plan in the bud.'

Arietty's nose wrinkles. 'Pandora? Who's that? Weird name.'

I try not to laugh. Arietty isn't exactly common. 'My sister. She runs the shop. You met her actually, yesterday. The tall woman with the dark bob. She can be a bit difficult sometimes. You have sisters?'

She nods. 'Half-sisters. Twins. Lucie and Amanda. They're OK. A bit spoilt though. Still in school.'

Iris interrupts. 'Can I go over there, Auntie Jules? I want to show Beatrix the sheep.' She points at the City Farm.

'Yes,' I say. 'But stay where I can see you.'

Arietty chuckles away to herself.

'What?' I ask, intrigued.

'Worst section in the zoo. No one ever wants to work there.'

'Why?'

She gawks at me. 'Are you serious? Looking after domestic farm animals, when you could be hanging out with Beatrix and Enid, or the rhinos, or the big cats?'

I laugh. 'I see your point. So back to the dress. Tell me about this school reunion. They can't all be complete bitches.'

'Yes, they can, and they are. When I emailed the organizer to tell her I was going – stupid cow called Sasha Davenport – her reply was she'd heard I was working in the zoo and asked if I was shovelling animal shit.'

I wince. 'Nice. But you do muck out the elephant enclosure, Arietty. And that's some pretty big poo. I saw it, remember. Glittering footballs of the stuff. Surprisingly unsmelly however.'

She laughs and slaps my arm, a little harder than necessary.

'Ow!' I rub my skin.

She looks completely unrepentant. She tosses her head and says, 'We don't call it mucking out, we call it round-ups. And elephants are veggies which helps with the smell. The big cats, now their poo yangs. You know something Jules, for a human, you're kind of OK.'

I flick a chip at her. 'From you, I take that as a compliment.'

Chapter 10

'Thanks, Dad, I owe you one.' Pandora pats Dad's shoulder just before ten on Monday morning.

Dad looks decidedly uncomfortable. 'I understand how to work the till, but what if someone wants fashion tips or something. What will I tell them?'

'You'll be fine. Just tell them they look great in anything they try on.'

'Pandora!' I stare at her. We're all sitting at the table in the staff-room at Shoestring. Dad has been pulled in to hold the fort while Pandora, Bird and I have what Bird described as 'a little talk'. They only sprung it on me a few minutes ago – very sneaky.

'What?' my sister demands.

'Our customers trust us,' I say. 'You always say we should tell them the truth – if something doesn't look great, bring them a similar outfit that will suit them better.'

'But Dad can't do that,' Pandora says. 'He's a man for goodness' sake. And he's colour-blind.'

'Only red and green,' Dad points out mildly. It never bothers him, unless his clients want their wooden play sets painted, and then he just gets Bird or Pandora to help him pick the right shade. 'Girls, get on with your meeting, I'm sure I'll be fine. If I have any problems, I'll holler. And I promise not to lie to the customers, OK, Jules?'

'Thank you,' I say.

Pandora is staring at me.

116

'What's your problem?' I ask.

'Who runs this shop exactly?'

'Bird.'

'Don't be smart, Julia. You know what I mean. Yes, Bird's the owner, but I run this shop, not you.' She turns to Bird. 'See, she's taking over already. I knew this was a bad idea.'

'I know it's Monday morning, but do stop squabbling, girls,' Bird says. 'Greg, open up, there's a good chap, it's almost ten. Chop, chop.'

'Try not to kill each other at your pow-wow, girls,' Dad says as he gets up and walks out of the staffroom.

As soon as he's gone, Bird knocks on the tabletop with her knuckles.

'Settle down,' she says. 'I'd like to call this meeting to order.'

I chuckle but Bird darts me a look and I stop.

'Now, Pandora,' Bird continues, 'do you have a copy of Julia's contract?'

'Contract?' I say, sitting up.

'Yes, darling. We're going to have a little chat about the terms and conditions of your employment and then you're going to sign it.'

Pandora takes a sheet of paper out of the plastic folder in her handbag, and slides it across the table towards me. Then she hands me a pen, sits back in her chair and crosses her arms.

'Just sign it, Julia. It's all very straightforward and I have work to do.' Pandora's in a right mood this morning.

'Best to read it first, darling,' Bird says, ignoring Pandora. 'And if you have any questions, ask away.' She gets up, flicks on the kettle and prepares the cafetière.

I start reading.

Contract of employment between Julia Schuster and Shoestring Trading Company, under the management of Pandora Schuster. Owner Bird Schuster.

Julia Schuster will work 40 hours a week for the total sum of €400.

I lift my head.

'Ten euro an hour? That's very low. I was on fourteen at Baroque.'

'It's all we can afford, darling,' Bird says.

'You'd better read on,' Pandora says.

As Julia Schuster owes €1,470 to Greg Schuster, €700 to Bird Schuster and €140 to Pandora Schuster . . .

I stare at Pandora.

'I don't owe you a penny.'

'You destroyed my silk skirt. Have you any idea how much Erdem costs?'

'But you bought it here, secondhand.'

'Which is why I'm only charging you what I paid for it. Count yourself lucky I'm not charging you full retail price. Would you like to discuss how it got so stained? The watery pink streaks that the dry cleaner can't shift, Jules, are they red wine or Red Bull? Do share.'

I wince. 'It's fine, I'll pay for it,' I say quickly, feeling Bird's eyes on me. Then I continue reading.

. . . €300 of her wages will be distributed to her debtors every week until the money is paid back in full.

'Three hundred?' I say. 'That's outrageous. How can I live on a hundred euro a week? That was your idea, wasn't it, Pandora?'

Bird gives me a tight-lipped smile. 'Mine actually. Coffee, darling?' she asks me.

'No!' I snap.

She looks at me sharply.

'Thank you,' I add.

She pours herself another mug, a strong one from the smell wafting around the room.

'But Bird,' I protest, 'that means after tax and stuff I'll have no money to—'

'Spend on drink,' Pandora cuts in.

I scowl at her. What is her problem? Is this pick on Jules day or something?

'Pandora, please.' Bird puts her mug down on the table and slips into a chair beside me. 'Julia, we are a little concerned about your lifestyle at the moment. Which is why we've added certain additional conditions.' She picks up the paper, and pops on her reading glasses which are on a chain around her neck.

'Where had you got to? Ah yes.' She starts reading aloud. 'Julia's duties will include changing the window display weekly and dressing the shop mannequins daily.'

'Daily?'

'Yes, my dear. Always best to keep busy, don't you think? And you are rather good at styling them.' She reads more. 'She will also take charge of all the interior displays and the redesign of the shop's interior.'

I glance at Pandora. She's chewing her lip. She doesn't look happy.

'Redesign?' I ask. 'Why? What's wrong with the interior?'

Pandora sighs deeply. 'Jules,' she says, 'have you any idea how close we are to going under right now?'

I shake my head. 'I knew things weren't great but no, I guess not.'

'Clearly,' she says, then adds, 'I had a meeting with the bank on Friday and unless we do something drastic, Shoestring won't be here this time next month. They're breathing down my neck and to be honest, I'm pretty desperate. We need to attract new customers in, and fast. Dad's offered to help, build new shelving, whatever we ask him to do, but clothes are my thing, not

119

interiors. We want you to come up with something eye-catching, something to bring people in. What exactly, is up to you.

'The Monkstown Book Festival is the weekend after next which will bring some new footfall to the street I hope. But we need to attract their attention. So next Sunday I'm going to close the shop – it's all yours for the day, so you can do your worst.'

I stare at her, the edges of my lips twitching into a shocked smile.

'Are you serious, Pandora? I can redesign the shop? Any way I like? You trust me to do that? What if I wreck the place or get paint on some of the clothes or something?'

Pandora's back stiffens. 'You listen to me, Julia,' she says in a serious tone, 'and you listen good. If Shoestring goes down, this family is in trouble. Not just me, but Bird, and Dad and even Iris. We're behind on the mortgage and the bank is looking to claw their investment back. Shoestring was bought on the back of Sorrento House, if the shop fails we're all homeless, understand? This is your one chance to redeem yourself; don't fuck with Sorrento House, we need that house, got it?'

Bird gulps loudly and I don't think it's Pandora's language that's bothering her. She has a strained look on her face and her eyes are glistening. I know how much she loves that house; how much we all love that house. And Pandora's right, we do need it – it's the glue that keep us together. This is all getting a bit too serious for my liking. They can't honestly expect me to help save the shop.

'I understand,' I say meekly. 'But I'm not sure what I can do.'

Bird pats my hand. 'You can do your best, Boolie,' she says. 'That's all any of us can do right now. Why do you think your father has been working flat-out the past few months? He's working all hours God sends him but it's still not enough. If it wasn't for the café, we wouldn't still be open. Sadly, it's only a small part of the shop.'

'Why don't you make it bigger then?' I say. 'Or open it in the evenings?'

'We did consider making it bigger but . . .' She looks at Pandora. 'Why did we decide against that, darling? There was a reason, wasn't there?'

'We couldn't find any other space for the hat and bag stand,' Pandora reminds her. 'And it's wedding season, so we can't get rid of the hats. So few shops do them these days, it brings people in.'

My mind starts whirring. 'But if I could design a way of displaying them that doesn't take up so much floor space, we could expand the café, yes?'

'I suppose so,' Pandora says slowly.

'This is all sounding super,' Bird says. 'I know you girls can work together just fabulously. But there's one more tiny condition we need to cover, Boolie, before we start making plans.' She lifts up the paper and reads out loud again. 'If Julia comes into work either drunk or hungover, her position will have to be reconsidered.'

'That's hardly fair,' I protest. 'I'd never come in drunk. Hungover, maybe, but never drunk.'

But Bird puts her hand up and continues. 'I haven't finished, darling. And Julia must attend Dr Rowebally on Wednesday the thirteenth of September for a full check up.' She puts the paper back down on the table. 'I'm going to toddle along with you, darling, in case you forget to mention anything. Like the empty bottle collection in your tree house, for example. And that's it. Ready to sign, darling, or do you have any questions?' She smiles at me brightly.

I begged Dad to come back at twelve and take me out for an early lunch. I couldn't bear being in the shop a moment longer than I had to with that backstabbing, sanctimonious witch, Pandora. Because of Pandora, Bird thinks I have some sort of drink problem. My darling sister only went and told her about the industrial estate incident and she didn't stop there, oh no. She climbed into my tree house and took down all the wine and vodka empties I'd been saving for the bottle bank. She said Iris had told her about my cool bottle collection – she often climbs up to play – and asked could she have one too. Pandora had no right to search my tree house like that. How dare she? I'm sitting across the table from Dad in the Purty Kitchen, my blood still boiling. 'Why do I have to go to see Sheila? They can't make me.' Sheila, Dr Rowebally, has been our family doctor for as long as I can remember but I haven't had to visit her in years.

'We're all worried about you, Boolie,' he says. 'Ending up abandoned in the middle of nowhere at night is no joke. Anything could have happened. And it's just a precaution. To check everything's hunky-dory.'

'You don't think I have a drink problem, do you, Dad? You like the odd pint, you understand.'

'Jules, you're twenty-four and you have every right to go out and enjoy yourself, but when it starts affecting your health and your judgement . . .' He shrugs.

'There's nothing wrong with my judgement. It's not my fault some taxi drivers are pigs. And it's not affecting my health. I'm perfectly fine.'

'What about the blackouts?'

'They're not blackouts, I just fall asleep sometimes, that's all.'

'And the concussion you got at, well, you know . . .'

'It's OK, you can say it, Ed and Lainey's engagement announcement. I wasn't drunk. I fainted. It was shock.'

'And the time you fell over and cut your leg and had to get stitches? Was that shock too? And the time the pint glass went through your foot?'

'It was hardly my fault someone dropped a pint glass on my foot.'

'Jules, the cut was on your sole.'

'OK, I stood on a pint glass. What is this, an interrogation?'

'No, Jules,' he says gently. 'An intervention. Unless you calm down a little, you're going to kill yourself.'

I snort. 'Don't be so melodramatic, Dad.'

'I'm serious, Jules. I've been doing some reading. Fifty per cent of head injuries are due to binge drinking and a third of all fatal road—'

I put my hands in the air. 'Dad, stop, please! I get it. And if it keeps you all happy I'll see Sheila, OK?'

He looks relieved. 'Thank you, Jules, that's all we're asking.'

When I get back to the shop, Bird is behind the desk.

'Where's Pandora?' I ask.

'Visiting a client,' she says. 'Feeling a little better now?'

I nod. 'Is it all right if I go off the floor for a few hours, Bird? I want to visit a few shops in town, have a look at their interiors, get some ideas. Brown Thomas, Avoca, and maybe Urban Outfitters. And some of the little cafés around Temple Bar.'

'That's a super idea, Boolie. And I'm sorry we gave you such a hard time this morning, but best to get everything out in the open.'

'Thanks, Bird. There's just one more thing. Is there any way you could give me an advance on my wages?'

Her eyes meet mine and I know the answer before she opens her mouth. 'No darling, I'm sorry. It's just not possible. But I can give you your train fare.'

My heart sinks. 'Just thought I'd ask.'

The man holds the handle bars and lifts my bike off the ground with one tattooed hand. 'Titanium,' he says. 'Nice. How old?'

'Two years. I bought it here.'

He scratches his nose and sniffs. 'Did you? Cool. You've kept it in good nick. Are you sure you want to do this? It's worth a lot more than I can give you for it.' I run my fingers over the frame.

'I have to, I'm afraid. But I still need to get around. I was hoping I could trade it in for a cheaper bike and you could give me the difference. I need three hundred euro.'

'Do you now, cheeky monkey?'

'Please?' I beg him. 'You're my last hope. And as soon as I have the money, I'll come back in and buy the most expensive bike in the shop, I promise.'

He laughs and shakes his head. 'Luckily for you I'm in a good mood today,' he says. 'You've got a deal.'

Chapter 11

'Julia Schuster?' Dr Sheila Rowebally looks up from her appointments sheet, sweeps the waiting room with her eyes and then spots me. As our eyes meet, despite knowing I shouldn't be here, that Bird's concern is ridiculous, I feel nervous.

'There you are, Julia,' she says. 'And Beulah. I believe you'd like to come in with Julia.'

'Please. Is that all right?' Bird asks.

'If it's OK with Julia.'

Sheila looks at me and I nod.

'Good,' Sheila says. 'This way, please.' She heads out the door swiftly without waiting for us to stand up.

I follow Bird out of the waiting room and down the corridor towards Sheila's consultation room, smiling to myself. Bird rarely goes by her real name and it used to crack me up as a child when anyone used it; still does pretty much.

The blue vinyl floor squeaks under my Converse, and the whole place smells of bleach mixed with the lilies from the reception desk, and I can get the metallic odour of fresh blood, although I'm sure I must be imagining it. The place has been painted since I was last here, a warm cream replacing the egg-yolk yellow, but it still smells funny.

Sheila's door is open and she's already sitting down as we walk in. She looks up and gestures at the chairs pulled in front of the examination table. I sit down as Bird closes the door behind us and takes another chair close beside me. I still have butterflies in my stomach; anything medical always makes me a bit on edge.

'So what can I do you for?' Sheila smiles at us both brightly.

Bird comes straight to the point. 'I'm concerned about Julia's health, Sheila. Since coming home from New Zealand in December, she's been under a lot of stress.'

Sheila looks at me carefully. 'That right, Julia?'

'I suppose so,' I say. 'But I feel perfectly fine.'

Sheila sits back in her chair and presses the tips of her fingers together. 'So why are you here then exactly, if you feel fine?'

'I'll come straight to the point. We're all a bit worried about Julia's drinking,' Bird says, her cheeks flaring up. 'Her family I mean.'

I stare down at my hands. This is so embarrassing. For everyone – for Sheila, for Bird, not to mention me. And it's completely ridiculous. I should never have agreed to come here in the first place.

'Look,' I say, 'I'm not an alcoholic or anything. I just like the odd drink at the weekends, is that so bad?'

Sheila looks at me carefully. 'Your grandmother wouldn't drag you here for no reason, Julia. If Beulah's concerned, let's not discount what she's saying, yes? First I need to get an understanding of your drinking pattern. Tell me about your average week.' She takes a pen and a notepad off her desk. 'Monday. Do you drink on a Monday?'

'No, never.' I stop for a second. 'Unless there's a party on or something. But that wouldn't be usual.'

'Good. Tuesday?'

'Not normally.'

'Wednesday?'

I can feel Bird's eyes on me.

'Sometimes,' I say reluctantly. 'I might have a glass of wine in front of the telly.'

'Beulah, is there anything you'd like to add?' Sheila asks.

Bird is staring at me pointedly. 'Julia, darling, you must tell Sheila the truth.'

'OK, maybe two glasses.'

Bird is still looking at me.

'Never more than a bottle,' I say, trying to keep my voice even and in control. And it's not a lie, not really. Mostly I do keep to the one bottle, at least every second or third night anyway.

Sheila makes a few notes.

'Thursday?' she continues.

'Depends if I'm going out or not. If I'm out I'll have a few drinks.'

'How many?'

'Maybe three or four.'

'Glasses of wine?'

'Maybe. Or vodka and cranberry.' I get the feeling Jager bombs or double vodka and Red Bulls would not be the right answer.

'Good. And Friday?'

Somehow I was hoping we wouldn't get to the weekend. 'I tend to go out most Friday and Saturdays, yes.'

'And how many drinks would you have?'

I shrug. Does she really expect me to remember? 'A few.'

'More than six?'

'It depends on the night.'

'On average would you have more than six drinks on both Friday and Saturday night, Julia?'

She sounds stern so I answer immediately.

'Yes,' I say, my voice creeping a notch higher than normal. I cough, trying to compose myself. Is this all really necessary?

'And finally, Sunday?'

'I rarely go out on a Sunday.'

Bird makes a little noise at the back of her throat.

'Maybe once every couple of weeks,' I say.

'And how many drinks on a Sunday?'

'Three or four.' That doesn't sound great so I amend it quickly. 'More like two actually.'

'And would the week you've just outlined be the general weekly pattern for the last nine months or so since you came home from New Zealand?'

'I guess it would.'

She pauses. 'And in New Zealand?'

'It was similar.' I'm no fool, there's no way I'm admitting I partied much harder when I was away.

'And are you worried about anything in particular at the moment, Julia?' she continues. 'Anything causing you stress or anxiety?'

'Not really,' I mumble. I mean, really, where do I start? We could be here all day and I just want to get out of this place.

Bird intervenes. 'Julia broke up with her boyfriend in December. And he's getting married to her best friend in October. '

'Ex-best friend,' I say. I'm about to add 'Stupid cow' but I stop myself.

A dark look flickers across Sheila's face and while lowering her head and scribbling in her notebook, she murmurs something under her breath which sounds suspiciously like 'Bloody men'. She lifts her head and I look at her, but the moment has passed and her face is unreadable now. I don't know much about Sheila, but I do know her husband, a medical sales rep, recently ran off with a receptionist from another GP clinic. I overheard Bird discussing it with someone on the phone, probably Daphne.

'That must have been difficult for you,' Sheila says. 'And are you working, Julia?'

I nod. 'Yes, in Shoestring. With Bird and Pandora.'

She looks at Bird and smiles. 'Good. Plenty of family support.'

I'm not quite sure what Sheila meant by that; is she implying that I'm some sort of charity case that needs looking after and can only get work in the family business? But I let it go. I don't want to be here a second longer than necessary. Then Sheila studies her notebook for a few moments and makes some marks with her pen.

'Back to your drinking,' she says. 'Julia, at present you are averaging twenty-four units a week, maybe more if you're drinking a lot of wine; an average glass of wine is one and a half units. For women we recommend not more than fourteen units, spread out over the week, and certainly not all over one weekend, which can have all sorts of health risks. Beulah is right to be concerned.' She meets my eye. 'Do you understand what binge drinking can do to you? Damage to your liver, to your whole system in fact; not to mention the risk of alcohol-related accidents. And let's get this straight, binge drinking is problem drinking, Julia. And it *is* an addiction.'

I nod. 'Look, I'm not stupid. I know it's not good for me. And I'm really not addicted or anything. I can give up drinking whenever I want to. I just like going out, having a laugh, simple as that. I don't *need* to drink.'

'That's very good to hear, Julia,' Sheila says. 'I'm just going to ask you a few more questions before I check your blood pressure and do a few more tests.'

I start to relax into my chair a little.

'Have you ever had an accident while drunk?' she says, her pen poised above her notebook again.

Hang on, I thought the interrogation was over. I sit up straighter in my chair.

'I stood on some glass once,' I say, 'but it wasn't my fault.'

'Have you ever missed an appointment or work because of a hangover?'

'Once maybe.'

'Do you ever drink alone?'

'Not really.'

I can feel Bird's eyes on me again.

'Sometimes,' I say slowly. 'But not very often.'

'Do you think about alcohol and wonder when you'll get the chance to drink again?'

I hesitate. I know yes is the wrong answer so I say, 'Not really, no.'

'Have you ever done something you've regretted because of alcohol?'

'Like what?'

'Have you ever done something you wouldn't have done if you were sober, or had a bad argument with someone while drunk?'

This is getting far too personal. Of course I have, hasn't everyone?

'No,' I say firmly. 'Absolutely not.'

'Have you ever found yourself in debt because of the amount you spend on alcohol?'

There's an uncomfortable silence.

'Well, Julia?' Sheila presses.

I can hardly say no with Bird sitting beside me.

'Sometimes I borrow money, yes. But it's for going out, not drink. Taxis, food, festival tickets, that kind of thing. And clothes. It's not for drink.'

'I see.' Sheila doesn't sound convinced. 'Just two more to go. Have you ever lied about your alcohol intake to friends or family members?'

'Never.'

I can hear Bird shifting in her seat, but I ignore her.

'And finally, do you react badly when people suggest you might have a drink problem?'

'NO!' That came out a bit stronger than I'd intended. 'I mean, no.'

Sheila puts down her pen and looks at me. 'Julia, thank you for being so honest with me.'

Right at that second, I feel about an inch tall.

'Now,' she adds, 'after we do some tests, I'd like to discuss the possibility of counselling. Would you be open to that?'

'Yes, she most certainly would,' Bird answers for me.

'Beulah, please,' Sheila says. 'It must be Julia's decision.' She gives me a gentle smile. 'Julia, I think talking to someone would really help. I believe you have an alcohol habit and I wouldn't like to see it get any worse. Will you consider it? You may be using alcohol to deal with stressful things in your life. A counsellor could help you find other ways of coping. And I'd like you to try cutting down on your drinking immediately for health reasons. Can you do that?'

'No problem. But I really don't need counselling, Sheila, honestly. I'm fine. I'll stop drinking completely if it makes everyone happy.'

Bird's face lifts and right that second I realize how concerned she's been about me lately, which makes me feel horribly guilty. She has enough on her plate at the moment without fretting about me.

I turn towards her. 'I'm sorry for worrying you, Bird. I'll stay in for the next few weeks and no drinking, OK? I promise.' Even if I did want to, I wouldn't be able to afford it anyway.

'Thank you, darling.' Bird pats my hand.

Sheila rubs her eyes and puts her notebook down. She gives me a warm smile. 'That's a good start, Julia,' she says. 'But if you need help at any stage, if you change your mind about the counselling, or if you find cutting down harder than you anticipated, you will contact me, yes?'

I nod eagerly. 'Of course.'

'How did it go this afternoon, Boolie?' Dad asks after dinner, while we're all still sitting around the table, apart from Iris. Pandora said she could watch *The Simpsons* as a special treat.

'Fine. It was all just a misunderstanding really. I know you're all concerned about me, but you have no reason to be, honest.

I'm going on a healthy-living kick for a while. No going out and no drinking.'

'You? Healthy living?' Pandora makes a little noise, halfway between a snort and a chuckle. I look at her and she's smiling away to herself.

'What's so funny? I ask her.

'Nothing,' she says.

'Good for you, Boolie,' Dad says quickly, ignoring Pandora. 'We're all proud of you, pet. And we're all here to support you, aren't we?' He looks at Pandora pointedly.

'Of course,' she says. 'And if means no more three a.m. wake-up calls and mercy dashes, I'm all for healthy living.'

'Pandora!' Bird isn't amused. 'Let's not dwell on the past. Your sister is doing her best to change.'

'You're right. I'm sorry.' Pandora smiles at me encouragingly. 'It's great, Jules, honestly. I don't mean to be off. I'm just tired. Busy day. Oh and by the way, while you guys were seeing Sheila, that beautiful-looking girl came in with the deposit for the Farenze. Unusual name – Arietty Pilgrim. Sorry, Jules, I know you were mad about that dress. But you're going to have to let it go.'

I try not to look too delighted. Arietty timed part one of our plan to perfection.

'There'll be other dresses. At least it's going to a good home.'

Pandora looks at me suspiciously. 'You're taking it very well.'

I shrug. 'It's only a frock.'

'Very sensible, Boolie,' Dad says. 'And by the way, who owns the mountain bike in the hall I nearly fell over earlier? And where's *your* bike?'

'I sold it,' I say simply. 'That's my new one.'

Dad frowns. 'It looks a bit battered. Are you sure it's road worthy? And why did you sell your old one?'

'I owed a friend some money and I wanted to pay back all my debts, start afresh,' I say. 'Now my only outstanding loans are to you guys.'

He smiles at me. 'You really have turned a corner, haven't you, pet? I'm proud of you, sorting out your finances like that.'

'Hang on a sec,' Pandora says. Unlike Dad, she doesn't look happy. 'Why didn't you pay me back first? Or Bird, or Dad?'

'You're family,' I say.

'So we don't count, is that it?' Pandora sits back in her seat and gives a disgusted huff.

'Pandora, who's minding Iris tonight while you and Bird are off warbling with the Proddy choir?' I ask. 'Dad's at his book club. Which leaves who exactly?'

I look Pandora square in the eye. 'You just presumed I'd do it, didn't you? Now, I could charge you for all the hours of child-minding, but I'm not going to do that. Because I love Iris and because we're *family*.' I smile smugly.

She scowls back at me. She knows I've won.

'How would you like to go cycling, Iris?' We're sitting in front of the telly but *Come Dine with Me* has just come on and it's just not the same without a glass of wine in my hand. I need something to take my mind off the 'Just one glass, who's going to know' thoughts that are creeping into my brain.

'Cool! Thanks, Auntie Jules. Right now you mean?'

I give it one more try. 'Just Jules, remember? And yes, right now. Go and get your helmet.'

'But you don't always wear one, Auntie Jules.'

OK, I give up. Auntie Jules it is. 'I'm a grown up. And until you're eighteen you helmet up, understand?'

She nods. 'Fine, I'll wear it.'

'Good girl.'

She finds her helmet, plonks it on her head and then we go outside to fetch her bike from the shed.

'Wait for me here, Iris, OK?' I say, leaving her at the top of the path as I go back inside the house to grab my own bike. I've just closed the front door behind me when I see Iris whizzing down the paving stones on her small pink bike, over the pavement and towards the road.

I scream, 'Iris!', drop my bike on the ground and sprint down the path towards her.

Thankfully I see someone has already grabbed her handlebars and dragged her to a stop. I reach her and realize with a start that it's Jamie. I look at him for a split second before turning my attention to Iris.

'You all right, Iris?' I say, my heart still pounding in my chest. 'I told you to wait. You could have got knocked down. You gave me such a fright.'

'Sorry, Auntie Jules,' she replies. 'I forgot to use the brakes.' She looks so shaken I soften.

'Next time wait for me, OK? Promise me?'

'I promise,' she says solemnly.

I turn back to Jamie. 'Thanks. That could have been nasty.' My cheeks flare up instantly, remembering my garbled message and the fact that he'd never returned my call.

'Any time,' he says. He looks a little distant, his eyes not fully focusing on mine.

And then I can't stand it any longer, I have to know, so I blurt out, 'I rang you, left a message. Why didn't you ring back?'

He blows the air out of his mouth. 'It's complicated, Jules. I don't want to go into it right now.' He gives a little nod in Iris's direction. 'Things are a bit up in the air at the moment . . .' he tails off.

'Can we go cycling now, Auntie Jules?' Iris is getting impatient. 'Please? It's already a bit dark.'

She's right, the light is fading fast. We shouldn't really be out at all without lights. We'll have to stay in the cul de sac, under the street lamps.

'I have to go, Jamie,' I say.

'I'll ring you,' he says.

'Where have I heard that one before?' I ask him. 'Don't

bother.' Then I turn towards Iris. 'Stay here, Iris. With your brakes on this time, OK? I need to fetch my bike. Don't move an inch.' And with that I turn away from Jamie and march back up the path, towards the house. I can feel his eyes on my back but I don't turn around. By the time I do, he's disappeared.

'Are you all right, Auntie Jules?' Iris asks when I walk back, wheeling my bike. 'You look sad? Are you still cross with me?'

'No, pet, I'm fine. Let's have a quick cycle and then I'll make you some hot chocolate and we can watch some telly.'

'With marshmallows?' she asks eagerly.

'With marshmallows.'

She beams at me. 'You're the best auntie in the whole wide world.'

I smile back at her. At least someone appreciates me.

Chapter 12

'Excuse me, I'd like a second opinion on this outfit.' I look up slowly from my copy of *Wallpaper* magazine the following afternoon. Pandora nearly had a knicker attack when she caught me reading at the till earlier until I explained that I was looking for inspiration for the Shoestring refit, which is partly true. But I'm mainly flicking through the stylish interior pages 'cause I'm feeling a bit glandy and in no mood for tidying the rails or dealing with customers.

The white-haired woman standing in front of me is appallingly dressed in a white shirt that cuts her generous hips at just the wrong place, black trousers that are skimming her ankles, grey socks and brown lace-up shoes. Do we really sell clothes like that? We must do.

I step away from the desk and take a better look.

Shaking my head I say 'It's not great, I'm afraid. Completely wrong for your body shape. It makes you look frumpy and you have a great waist. You should show it off more, nip the shirt in with a belt. But the trousers, no, they really do nothing for you.'

'I meant this outfit.' The woman holds up the hanger she was clutching. She looks at me, her eyebrows raised.

Oops. 'I'm so sorry,' I murmur.

But she looks more amused than annoyed. Her brown eyes are dancing beneath her slightly bushy eyebrows.

'Do I really look that awful?' She stares down at her clothes, her gaze stopping at her shoes. She wiggles a foot. 'These old things are hardly fashionable I know, but they're very comfortable. And I've had these trousers for years, I suppose they are due for retirement. But at my age, it's difficult to know what to wear.' She looks at me again. 'You seem an honest kind of girl, what should I be wearing, so I don't look so appalling? Would this suit me?'

She nods at the two piece she's holding up, a shapeless, flowery blue and white shirt with a very full matching skirt.

I shake my head. 'Absolutely not. The print looks like a duvet cover and the skirt's going to balloon over your hips.'

She sighs. 'Ah yes, my hips. Always my downfall.'

'You just have to be clever, dress for your figure,' I say. 'Why don't I pick out something that might suit you better? Is there anything in particular you need an outfit for?'

She smiles. 'Yes, actually. My wedding anniversary. Forty years with the same wonderful man.'

I whistle. 'Impressive. Now are we thinking vibrant and sexy, or classic and demure?'

She gives a hearty laugh. 'Vibrant and sexy sounds perfect.'

In the end I spend forty minutes dressing Mrs Bloomfield. By the time I've finished she's asked me to call her Hester.

'You really do have a gift for this, Julia,' Hester says at the till as I start ringing up what she's decided to take. 'I hate to think what my husband will say when he sees the credit card bill.' Her eyes twinkle. 'I haven't had as much fun shopping in years. But you will write down the outfits you've suggested, won't you, dear? I'll only go and muddle them up otherwise and wear the purple jacket and trousers together or something.'

I'd found a wonderfully rich purple velvet jacket and trousers for her, which worn together make Hester look like a plum, but separately look fantastic.

'I think we can do one better than that.' I rummage in the large drawer under the till until I locate the digital camera Pandora uses to take snaps of new stock for the Shoestring website.

'Bingo.' I pull it out. 'If you have a few minutes, I'll take a pic of the dummy in each of the outfits, Hester. Then I'll email you the pics and you'll have a record of them at home. How about that?'

'I have a few minutes all right but . . .' Hester hesitates. 'We don't have a printer at home I'm afraid. But I suppose I could look at them on the screen.'

'There's only a black and white one in the office, but we do have a colour one at home,' I say. 'How about I print them out for you this evening and you can collect them tomorrow. How does that sound?'

Hester smiles at me. 'Perfect. You really are a little gem, Julia. I'm going to recommend you to all the girls in my bridge club. Thank you so much for all your assistance. I feel like a new woman.'

I smile back at her. 'It's a pleasure.'

While I get to work on arranging the clothes for the photographs, I realize suddenly that it's true. Making Hester look and feel great was fun. First up, I dress the dummy in the purple trousers, teamed with a cream silk shirt, and a long, purple silk scarf shot through with a swirling green leaf pattern.

'Outfit number one,' I tell Hester, taking a photograph and checking it on the screen of the digital camera before moving on.

Outfit two is a khaki shirt dress, nipped in at the waist with a rather stunning thick, brown leather belt to emphasize Hester's surprisingly neat middle. Three is a very flattering, black scoop-necked Prada top to be worn under the purple jacket, with smart black straight-legged trousers, teamed with black suede wedges to add length to her legs. And four is a simple yet elegant red Issa dress – her wedding anniversary outfit – to be worn with kitten-heeled cream Chanel shoes with a tiny, red tie-bow decoration, a bargain at only a hundred euro (in any other shop they'd be five times that).

Afterwards, I carefully wrap Hester's 'new' clothes in pink Shoestring tissue paper.

'Need some help?' Pandora appears at my shoulder. 'Are these all for the same customer?'

'Yes.' I pop the tissue parcel containing the purple suit in a brown paper bag with Shoestring hand-stamped on it in raspberry ink (one of my more menial tasks). 'Hester went on a much-deserved splurge. Ruby wedding anniversary no less. And she's going to look fabulous.'

Hester smiles at me, and then at Pandora. 'I haven't bought clothes for such a long time – could never find anything to suit me. But Julia was so helpful. She even offered to go through my wardrobe at home, weed out things that have been lurking there for years and show me what goes with what, give me a complete makeover. Said I could drop any of the better pieces in here, might even make some money from them. Such a clever girl. I'd never have thought of that.'

'Did she?' Pandora looks at me. 'Jules, you really are full of surprises these days.'

We finish packing Hester's three Shoestring bags and I see her out.

'Don't forget to collect your photos tomorrow,' I say as Hester toddles happily out of the door, arms weighed down by her new clothes.

'I won't. See you then.'

As soon as Hester's gone Pandora plays with the till and brings up the total of the last sale.

She whistles under her breath. 'Just under five hundred euro. Julia Schuster, I may have underestimated you. When you're on the ball, you're hot.' She smiles. 'A few more customers like this a week, and we're laughing. And I like the way you're thinking. Personal styling for Shoestring clients, you may have something there.' She thinks for a second. 'But having you off-site might prove difficult staffing-wise. In-store styling sessions might work though. Are you really willing to give it a go?'

I hesitate. Pandora is making it all sound a bit serious, and a bit too much like hard work. I was only offering to help Hester out because she was so nice. Imagine if I got stuck for hours with some old stick, or even worse, someone like Sissy Arbuckle.

I say quickly, 'I'd better get on with the refit first, Pandora.'

She nods. 'Probably best. But that customer mentioned photos. And I saw you taking pictures of the dummy. What was all that about?'

I explain what I'd offered to do for Hester.

Pandora cocks her head, considering this for a moment. 'Where did you get that idea? You really are on fire today. Must be all the healthy living.'

I roll my eyes at her. 'Stop with all the healthy-living digs, OK? It's already getting boring.'

She smiles. 'Sorry, couldn't resist.'

'Anyway the photo thing just came to me,' I say. 'People do it for shoes, don't they? Put a photo of the shoes on the box so they can find them quickly. Hester asked me to write down the styling suggestions for her new clothes, and taking photos just seemed quicker and easier.'

'It's a fantastic idea, and very original. Personalized styling, complete with bespoke photos. We could call it Shoestring Style Snap.' Pandora jumps behind the desk, grabs the queries book and a pen and starts scribbling down some notes.

My stomach rumbles loudly. I couldn't find my watch this morning so I have no idea what time it is. 'Pandora?'

She looks up and smiles. 'Yep, you should have gone on lunch twenty minutes ago. But don't worry, you can take your full half-hour. You're in my good books today. In fact, take an extra ten minutes if you like.'

'Thanks, Pandora.' Ten minutes may not sound like much, but it's a big deal for Pandora the control freak who has our breaks practically stopwatched.

'Enjoy.' She waves her fingers at me and gets back to scribbling.

When I walk into the staffroom, Jamie is sitting on the sofa, his feet up on a chair, drawing some odd-looking diagrams of boxes linked with lines on a foolscap pad. What is it with everyone and notebooks today?

Our eyes connect and it's like a rain cloud has drifted over his face. His eyes darken and his jaw hardens.

'Julia,' he says a little stiffly. 'Seen Bird?'

'She's not due in until three.'

He puts his Converse on the floor. 'Thought she said two. I'll come back.'

I look at the kitchen clock. 'She'll be here in ten minutes. You may as well wait. I'll make you some tea if you like.' I'm feeling in a generous mood after my success with Hester.

He seems unsure for a second, then says, 'OK.'

I click on the kettle, thinking. I feel bad about yesterday. He did stop Iris careering into the road and I may have been a bit sharp with him. I turn around.

'About yesterday—'

But simultaneously he says, 'About last night—'

We both stop and I smile a little and say, 'You go first, Jamie.'

He shrugs. 'Just wanted to apologize I guess. I should have rung you back.' He puts his pad down on the sofa and runs his hands through his hair, making it stick up a bit. 'I'm all over the place at the moment, Jules. Losing my job was . . . well, it was shit to be honest. A real kick in the teeth.'

'Losing your job? Daphne said you left.'

'Yeah, before I was pushed. They let five of us go. There just isn't the work at the moment and I was only on a short-term contract. Once the last Pot of Gold cartoon was finished, the work dried up.'

'But Bird told me one of your animations won an Irish Film Award.'

'I know. But no one wanted to invest in our new project, so the lads have gone back to making ads until they can find some funding. But it could take a couple of years. And besides, I want to work on my own ideas.'

'For animated films?'

'Just one, singular. *Bold Tales for Wee Ones*. Irish legends told by this incredibly obnoxious, Father Jack-type character called Sean O'Ti. *Children of Lir*, *The Salmon of Knowledge*, all those kind of stories, but with a really nasty, dark twist.'

'For children?'

'Sure. And adults. Have you heard of *Granny O'Grimm*?'

'Irish cartoon, won an Oscar, right?'

'Yep. Best short animated. *Bold Tales* will be along those lines, but with even darker, almost Gothic animation, using some Celtic, *The Book of Kells*-type styling and motifs.'

'Sounds amazing. How far along are you?'

'I've almost finished *How Cúchulainn Got His Name*. The giant hound is kind of cool. Getting his fur right was a nightmare . . . ' Talking about his work, the dark cloud lifts and he looks almost happy.

'I'd love to see it,' I say when he's finished.

He shrugs again. 'Hopefully it'll be in the cinema one day.'

I expect him to add, 'Call over later and I'll show you what I've done so far.' He used to get a real buzz out of showing me his work. But – nothing, he just looks away. I'm lost for words for a moment, so I busy myself making tea.

'Milk and sugar?' I ask, hoping my voice sounds normal, and not as hurt and confused as I feel.

He nods. 'Both. Two sugars, thanks.'

I hand over his mug, put my own on the table, twist a chair around to face him and sit down.

'So how's the Shoestring website coming along?' I ask, keeping the conversation neutral and wishing I'd never offered him tea in the first place. I blow into my mug and then take a sip.

'It's pretty much done. Just have to add some graphics. Then

I'm starting work on the loyalty cards. I've almost finished designing the database. Should get the prototype up and running next week and after a couple of tests it'll be good to go. Just need to sort out the final details with Bird.'

'Loyalty cards? For Shoestring customers?'

'Here.' He opens his rucksack and hands me a Tiffany-blue plastic card with Shoestring written across it in cursive dark-pink script, and our slogan 'Designer clothes at Shoestring prices' underneath, complete with the website details. 'What do you think?' he asks.

'Looks great. How will it work?' I hand it back to him.

'Customers will sign up at the till for a card, you'll take all their details – the usual, name, address, email, that kind of thing – and I'll input all the data into the computer. It's a pretty basic system. The customers collect points every time they buy something in the shop and you'll have access to all their personal details so you can target your marketing more efficiently.'

I give a fake yawn.

He laughs. 'Jules! Loyalty cards are fascinating.'

'Really? Why?'

'Knowing exactly what someone has bought? All their shopping patterns?'

I look at him. 'Since when have you been interested in shopping patterns, Mr Animation Guru?'

He grins. 'OK, you got me there.' He lowers his voice. 'But I was doing some research for Bird and Pandora on other cards. I hacked into some of the Irish retail databases and it was pretty interesting. The amount of stuff they collect. I'm telling you, criminal profiling has nothing on some of the big supermarkets. If you analyse the data, put it into profiling programmes, you can tell all kinds of things: what age customers are, if they have children or not, if they're single or married, if they have a cat or a dog. Honestly, it's amazing.'

143

I roll my eyes. 'Only if you're a stalker, Jamie. Do you know how weird that all sounds?'

He sighs. 'I know. And don't breathe a word to Bird or Pandora. They'd freak out if they knew how I've been doing my research. I told them it was all legit.'

'I'm not sure about Pandora, but I don't think Bird would give a hoot as long as she can save the shop.'

'Save?' He looks genuinely concerned. 'That doesn't sound good.'

'It's not something they'd like broadcast. Keep it to yourself but the shop's in trouble. And unless we can get the sales up, drastically, we might lose Sorrento House too.'

'I'm sorry, Jules. I had no idea.'

'How would you?' I check the wall clock. 'Look, I'm supposed to be working on this refit for Pandora. Do you mind if I flick though a couple of interior mags while I talk to you? I need to finish my mood board before my meeting with Dad this evening.'

'Go right ahead,' he says.

I pull it out from behind the sofa and study it proudly. It's looking pretty impressive. I have the colours sorted – the woodwork will stay as it is, a neutral 'sail' white, but I'm hoping to add eye-catching splashes of dark pink and sunny yellow to the mirror frames and the desk, and maybe some zesty green or turquoise. I've used the colour of a ripe watermelon, and a photograph of an Indian woman in a pink, green and yellow sari I've pulled out of an old copy of *National Geographic* as my colour inspirations.

I've pinned the pictures, along with some jewel-coloured silks to the mood board – I'm hoping Pandora will let me replace the grey changing-room curtains with something more vibrant; I've sourced fantastically cheap, dark-pink velvet sofas in Ikea, and I want to put them in the middle of the floor, back to back, to make a luxurious sitting area for trying on shoes, or for hubbies and boyfriends to lounge on while waiting for their other halves. I just need to add a few more finishing touches before I unleash the whole scheme on Pandora. I've already shown Bird my ideas, and she loves them.

Jamie is studying the board. 'Bit pink for me, Jules, but I like the general look. Very hip. Are you really going to work during your break? It's not like you. Usually lunch is for catching up on zeds, yeah?'

I smile at him. 'People change, Jamie. Didn't you know?'

'I guess they do.' His eyes seem softer.

Something occurs to me. 'Jamie, do you know anything about blogs?'

'Yeah, why? Don't tell me you have one, Jules?' He chuckles away to himself.

'I do actually,' I say, slightly miffed. 'And I was hoping to make the background look a bit more interesting. It's plain white at the moment.'

'The skin.'

'Sorry?'

'The background's called the skin.'

'Oh, OK, well I'd really appreciate some help with it. If you're free this evening . . .' I tail off. Please say yes, I will him with my eyes.

His eyes shift away from mine and rest on the mood board. 'Sorry, Jules, no can do. I'm working on *Bold Tales* every night, you know how it is.'

'Sure,' I say, feeling disappointed and embarrassed. Jamie clearly doesn't want to spend a second more than necessary in my company. I'm obviously coming over far too manic and needy. No wonder he's running a mile.

'But if you give me the blog address I can have a look at home,' he adds.

'Don't put yourself out, I know you're busy.' I grab my magazines from where I've left them in an overflowing heap in the

145

corner of the table. 'I'm busy too; in fact I'd better stop chatting and get to work. You know how it is, Jamie.'

He looks at me for a second, a strange expression on his face and then just nods. 'Fine.' Then he picks up his notebook and buries his head in it again. 'That's just fine.'

'Is there any way we can keep the grey curtains? They cost a fortune,' Pandora says later that day, just after the shop's closed. We're sitting in the staffroom, talking about my ideas for the shop revamp. Dad, Bird and Iris have all joined us.

I did have my heart set on new hot-pink ones, and normally compromise isn't one of my strong points, but Pandora is being rather nice to me today and she does have a point.

'What if we edge them with pink?' I suggest. 'It would be a nice contrast to the grey and it would brighten them up a bit. A dusky, tea-rose pink might work the best.'

Pandora smiles at me. She looks relieved. 'Sounds like a plan. Happy with that, Bird?'

Bird shrugs. 'Whatever you think, darling.'

'And not much point asking me about curtains or colour schemes.' Dad grins.

I jot it down in my notebook. Find pink silk for curtain edgings. 'Good, I'll start looking for the right fabric. And the gang in Mrs Stitch have already said they'll help out with any of the soft furnishings. I rang them this morning.'

'Excellent, Jules,' Pandora says encouragingly. 'Good thinking.'

I smile back at her. 'So on to the paintwork. I'd suggest keeping the neutral off-white of the shelves and the floor, but injecting a few shots of vibrant colour to make the interior dynamic, but at the same time restful. We've already touched on the curtains, but I thought we could also paint the mirror frames in jewel colours, add some sweeps of voile—'

'What's voile, Auntie Jules?' Iris asks.

'A light, see-through material,' I explain. 'Like net. I thought we could hang some on either side of the door, in similar colours. It would move in the breeze and make the doorway more eye catching.'

Dad smiles. 'Nice idea, Jules. But what about shelving? Do you need me to build anything?'

I point at a sketch I've drawn, attached to the left of the board. 'Just one unit, Dad, to replace the rails down the middle of the floor. The new design has half rails all along the bottom, for shirts and skirts, instead of full rails.' I point at the relevant part of the sketch. 'Covered by a solid piece of chipboard, which will be the new area for the shoes. And then I'd like you to build an open frame of Perspex boxes on top for shoes and hats – I've sourced some from a shop-fitting company and I've put two dozen on hold just in case. As long as the boxes are see-through, we can stack them to the ceiling and it won't block off the light. And I thought we could put hooks here and here,' I point at either end of the stand. 'For bags. Of course the more valuable ones could be placed in the Perspex boxes. But the main point of this unit is to clear some space for the café to expand into the area that the existing shoe and hat stand currently holds.' I look at Dad. 'What do you think?'

He whistles. 'It's a lot of work for one day, pet, but if I pull in some help it should be just about feasible.'

'Bird?' I ask. 'What about you? Do you like the design?'

She smiles. 'I think it's very clever indeed, Boolie. Such a smart cookie.' She pats my hand. 'You have my blessing.'

'Pandora?' I look at my sister. It's impossible to read her blank face. It's Pandora I'm worried about; the plan is pretty radical.

Pandora leans forward, planting her elbows on the table. 'Perspex boxes?' She considers this and then sits up straight again. 'Pure genius. I should have thought of it myself. Go for it, sis.'

Bird claps her hands together. 'That's settled then. Now tell us about these elephants you're planning to make for the entrance, darling, and then let's get home. How about a takeaway for tea to celebrate the new plan?' It's Bird's night to cook and she's always looking for ways to get off the hook.

Iris claps her hands together. 'Yeah! Can we have curry, Bird?'

Bird smiles. 'In honour of what Boolie tells me are Asian elephants, generally found in India, then yes, my darling, we most certainly can.'

That evening, after dinner, I print out Hester's photographs in the living room. I'm just clicking into our Farenze dress blog to check for messages or comments, when Bird walks through the door.

'There you are, darling,' she says. 'Pandora just told us about your styling idea. You're full of clever thoughts these days.'

'I wouldn't get too carried away, it may never come to anything, and I have the shop revamp to work on first, remember?'

She pulls up a chair beside mine. 'I'm very proud of you, Boolie. You've really applied yourself this week. Even Pandora's impressed. I'm so glad the two of you are working so well together. It means a lot to me and to your father.'

I'm filled with a warm feeling. It's not often I make Bird and Dad happy. And I guess the frozen lake of emotion between Pandora and me does seem to be gradually thawing.

Then Bird's eyes rest on the screen.

'The Shoestring Club,' she reads out loud. 'What's that? Something to do with the shop?'

Join The Shoestring Club
Faith Farenze on a Shoestring

Wanted: Two girls to time-share a one of a kind
Faith Farenze dress, in dark-pink silk chiffon.
Guaranteed to make you look drop-dead gorgeous.
An instant self-confidence boost.

All enquiries to theshoestringclub@irmail.com

Blood pumps into my cheeks. I hadn't realized I'd left the blog up on the screen. Before I get a chance to click out of the page, Bird's eyes have scanned the rest of the text, and are resting on the photograph of the chiffon dress, on one of the Shoestring mannequins.

'That dress looks very familiar. Isn't it the Farenze Pandora has on hold in the office for one of our customers?' She stares at me. 'Julia, what's going on? Out with it. Tell me you're not doing something stupid, darling. Something illegal.'

I laugh. 'No, of course not. I was going to tell you, it's just been so busy and . . .' I tail off, fishing frantically for a good excuse, but coming up with exactly nothing.

'Continue,' Bird says.

I guess I'll just have to tell her the truth, much as it pains me. 'I bought a share in the Faith Farenze dress,' I say, my voice quivering a little with nerves. 'The one from the shop.'

'A share? What are you talking about?'

'Me and Arietty, the girl who has the dress on hold, can't afford to buy it on our own so we came up with a plan. We've each put in three hundred euro, and now we're looking for two more girls . . .' Bird is staring at me. As soon as I see the expression on her face, I stop instantly.

149

'Where did you get the three hundred euro?' she asks, her eyes narrowing. I stare at the computer screen, wishing the blog would disappear in front of my eyes. In fact . . . I put a hand out to switch off the computer, but Bird stops me by swatting it away.

'Answer me, Julia.'

'My bike,' I say in a tiny voice. 'I used the money I got for my bike.'

'You blatantly lied to me, and to your father? Is that correct?'

My cheeks flare up again. 'I'm so sorry. But I have to wear the dress, Bird. Just once. And then I'll sell my share instantly, I promise. And give you all back your money.'

She rubs her hands over her eyes and sighs deeply. 'Don't you see, Julia? It's not about the money. It's about trust. And why do you need this ruddy dress so much?'

'For Ed and Lainey's wedding. I have to look amazing. I won't stay long, honestly. I just want to show everyone that I don't care, that I'm over him. It's important.' I pause. 'But it's unlikely to happen now. Our blog's been up for days, and no one has contacted us or left a message. We've put ads up on Gumtree and ebay and Buy and Sell; no one's interested in sharing the dress with us. It's a stupid idea.'

Bird's face softens. 'Actually I think it's rather inspired. But I do wish you hadn't lied to all of us.' She stops for a moment, looks at the blog. 'What's that?' She points at the bottom of the screen.

A message has just popped up.

She reads it out loud. 'Please send more details of the dress – size, length, cost etc. May be interested. Alex.' She looks at me. 'You might just be in business.'

'If we can find another taker in three days,' I point out glumly. 'Pandora has given Arietty until Monday to pay the full amount, otherwise the dress goes back into stock.' I stare at her. 'Hang on, does this mean you're not going to tell Pandora about the money?'

A smile plays over Bird's lips. 'I have a suggestion. Has Pandora shown any interest in the dress?'

'I caught her trying it on once, yes. But she's just as broke as I am. Plus she said she had nothing to wear it to.'

'To wear it to, or to wear it *for*?'

'I don't understand.'

'As you keep so kindly pointing out to everyone who will listen, your sister rarely goes out. And she's unlikely to meet anyone under sixty through the choir.'

I smile. 'A creaky old sexagenarian might be right up her street.'

'Less of the creaky, thank you. No, she needs to meet someone her own age. Someone who will accept her for who she is. You've never had any problem meeting men, darling.'

'The wrong kind of men,' I splutter. 'Look at Ed, he ran off with my best friend.'

She smiles tightly. 'The less said about that boy the better. I want you to bring Pandora out, introduce her to some people her own age. There must be some decent young men out there, they can't all be losers, surely?'

I smile wryly. 'You'd be surprised, Bird.'

She laughs, then says, 'If you find Pandora someone to wear the dress for, I'll keep your little secret to myself. And I'll pay for Pandora's share in the Farenze.'

My mouth falls open. I stare at her. She's smiling and her eyes are sparkling.

'Are you serious, Bird?'

'But of course, darling. I never joke about love. Or money. Especially money.'

Chapter 13

I'm pacing my room, willing Pandora to go out. It's been a really full-on week and now that it's finally Friday night all I feel like doing is collapsing in front of the telly with a drink. I spotted an open bottle of white in the fridge earlier and I'm gagging for a sip. I know I'm not supposed to be drinking at all, but one glass to celebrate the end of the week is hardly a big deal.

Dad's out with Bird at a choir social. Pandora's supposed to be going too, leaving Iris with me, but for some reason my sister seems to be lingering in the kitchen like a bad smell. I look at my watch; it's nearly nine, Iris is already in bed, so what the hell is Pandora doing exactly? The social will be almost over by now.

I walk down the stairs and fling open the kitchen door. Pandora looks up at me from the kitchen table. She's dressed to go out, as dressed up as she normally gets anyway. She's still in her black work trousers, but has exchanged her neat white shirt for a surprisingly low-cut black top with flamenco ruffles on the ends of the short sleeves. There's a slash of crimson on her lips and she's even pinned the sides of her hair up with sparkly red clips.

'What do you think?' she says.

'Of your outfit?'

'No, this one.' She points down at a page of the magazine. A model is wearing raspberry-pink, chunky-knit woollen tights in an Aran pattern with a matching pink leotard and pink hair. Very OTT, but the tights are fab.

I scrunch up my face. 'Not sure you'd get away with the leo-tard. You might give the old lads in the choir heart attacks.'

'I'm talking about the tights. And not for me, for the shop. They're by a young Irish designer called Maeve Fabien. Reason-ably priced too considering they're hand-knitted.'

'You're taking in new stock?'

'I'm thinking about it. There are gaps in our own stock – T-shirt basics, tights, corsetry, accessories. If we're going to offer a full styling service it makes sense. Means we could support up and coming designers too.' She frowns a little. 'But maybe it's too ambitious? Do you think we should play it safe, stick to what we know, or experiment a bit?'

I sit down at the table and study Pandora's face. She seems seri-ous. 'You're really looking for my opinion?' I can't help but smile.

She puts one elbow on the table and rests her head in her hand. 'Why is that so amusing?'

'Because you think I'm a fuckwit.'

She sighs. 'No, I don't.'

'OK then, a waste of space.'

She's quiet for a second. Then she says, 'Fine, I admit that sometimes your lack of appliance drives me crazy.'

I grin. 'Appliance? You mean like a washing machine?'

'You know exactly what I mean, stop being smart. You don't apply yourself. You bounce from one job to the next, and then get fed up or bored, and go travelling.'

'I'm here now,' I point out. 'And in case you haven't noticed, I've been working my ass off in your stupid shop. You wouldn't want to be thin-skinned in this house.'

'Yes, I agree, you've had a good week, but it's all so up in the air with you. Next week you might decide to jack it all in and go and be, oh I don't know, an elephant keeper, like that friend of yours Iris keeps banging on about. Did Iris give you the el-ephant picture she drew for her by the way?'

'Yes.' Oops, where did I put it?

Taking in my face she says, 'You haven't gone and lost it, have you?'

Iris drew this amazing picture for Arietty to say thank you – Beatrix, Enid, Nina and Kai, all playing in the waterpool, Iris herself standing behind them with a big banana grin on her face, holding Arietty's hand. She worked on it every day in her after-school club. On the back she wrote:

From Iris Schuster, age 8. I want to work in the zoo like you one day, Arieti. I love you. XXXXX

She made me promise to pass it on to Arietty. Then it comes to me: it's in the living room, on the desk beside the computer. Phew.

'Of course not,' I say indignantly.

'Good. And thanks for taking Iris to the zoo,' she adds, her face softening a little. 'She had a ball.'

'Anytime. And I know you're not all that keen on her having a dog but—'

'Not this again. Jules, no! Understand? N-O spells no. Absolutely not. I have enough problems without a puppy chewing up the place and weeing on everything.'

'What about a cat? We could visit the Animal Shelter—'

'Drop it, Jules. No animals, full stop.' She sits back in her chair and scrunches up her shoulders, groaning a little. 'God, I'm so tired.'

'I thought you were supposed to be going out.'

'Don't think I'll bother now. Might just go to bed.'

'You'll never meet anyone that way.'

She frowns. 'Meet anyone? What are you on about? Who says I want to meet someone? I'm quite happy on my own, thanks very much. What's up with you tonight? First you try and foist a stray dog on me, now a man. It's the hen thing, isn't it? That's what's got you all angsty.'

154

I stare at her. 'What hen thing?'

'Don't act the innocent, Lainey's hen. It's tonight isn't it?'

I go pale and her face colours a little. 'Shit, Jules, I'm sorry. I shouldn't have said anything.'

'How do *you* know about it?'

'Lainey's big mouth aunt's in the choir. Marie. She's been boasting about it for weeks.'

'But Marie's in her fifties. Why would she be going?'

'They're having some sort of posh dinner tonight in Dublin for all the Anderson aunts and old family friends, then Lainey and her sisters are heading off to some spa in Wicklow for the weekend. I'm really sorry, Jules. I know it must be hard on you.'

Pandora looks at me, and I hate seeing the pity in her eyes.

I feel a bit teary, but I'm trying to keep it together. 'It's fine,' I say. 'We're not exactly friends any more.'

'Are you sure you're all right, Jules? Is there anything—'

'I'm just great.' I get up, grab the first glass I see, one of Iris's favourite pink glass tumblers from the draining board, walk towards the fridge and pull it open so hard that the bottles in the door clink together. I pull out the white wine.

'What are you doing?' Pandora says. 'I thought you were off the booze.'

I swing around. 'I said I'd cut down, OK? And I haven't had a drink all week, which in my book *is* cutting down. But right now I fancy a single solitary glass of wine. Please don't go blabbing about it to Bird or Dad. They'll only start going on at me again.'

'Because they're concerned about you, Jules.'

'I'm fine, honestly. So no one needs to worry a dot. I just need a bit of time on my own. I'm sure you understand.' And with that I walk out of the kitchen.

A few minutes later there's a knock on the front door. If Pandora has summoned Bird or Dad home to deal with me, I'll quite literally kill her. And there's no way I'm working in Shoestring if— But then I stop. It can't be Bird or Dad, they have their own keys.

I hear voices in the hallway, Pandora has obviously let someone in. I open the living-room door just in time to catch her say in a low voice, 'Go easy on her, Jamie. It's Lainey's hen tonight and—'

'Thank you, Pandora,' I cut in. 'Don't you have somewhere to be?'

'I don't think I'll bother now, can't raise the energy.' She yawns deeply. 'Night, Jamie. See you in the morning, Jules. Take it easy on the wine, OK?'

I ignore her.

As she climbs the stairs I stay fixed to the spot, staring at Jamie, not knowing quite what to say or if I'm pleased to see him or not.

He's standing there, just as awkwardly, shifting his weight from foot to foot. There's a laptop cradled in his arms.

'Hi, Jules,' he says after a few long seconds. 'Look, I'm sorry about the other day.' He pauses and gives a nervous smile. 'I seem to spend my time apologizing to you. Anyway, I'm happy to help you design a new skin. And I thought you might like to see some of the *Bold Tales* animation I've been working on.'

I'm still annoyed with him from our last encounter, and I don't *want* to smile back at him, but my mouth has other ideas.

'I'd like that,' I hear myself say. 'Come on in.'

He follows me into the living room and then looks around. 'Is there a plug? I'm pretty low on battery.'

I point at the wall behind the computer and he settles himself on the office chair, then hands me Iris's elephant picture before putting his laptop down on the wood.

He grins. 'Cute. This what you spend your evenings doing, Jules? Sketching elephants?'

'It's Iris's, you goon.' As he sets up his computer, I tell him about our trip and about Arietty. 'She's gorgeous too, even looked stunning in her zoo uniform. I could introduce you guys if you like.'

Jamie gives me a funny look. 'I don't think so, Jules.' He focuses his attention on the laptop screen. 'There's something I need to talk to you about.' His voice wobbles a little. 'This thing happened in Galway. Sorry, "thing" is the wrong word.' He sighs and runs his hands through his hair. 'It's just so hard . . .' he stops.

I pull over a chair. 'Take your time, Jamie. I'm not going anywhere.' When we were teenagers and Jamie had something important or more often, upsetting, to tell me, it always took him ages to get the words out.

After a long pause he says, 'There was this girl, she was really special.'

And as soon he says it I have a strange sensation, like my guts are being twisted. It can't be jealousy can it? We haven't been close for years and we've never been *that* close.

He continues 'But she . . .'

While he starts talking again, about how he met this girl, I try to focus on something else, willing the tension I'm feeling to ease. I stare out of the window, into the darkness of the garden, fixing my eyes on the tree house. I notice the rope ladder is looking a bit worn, probably needs to be replaced.

'Hang on, can you see that?' I jump up and point at a flicker of light. It's coming from inside my tree house.

'What?' He gets up and joins me at the window.

I point. 'Up there.' I press my face against the glass, cup my hand over my eyes and peer out. There it goes again, a bright pinprick of red.

'What is it?' I ask him. 'Can you see? Just inside the window.'

'You don't have a candle lit up there, do you?'

'No. Why? You think it's a flame?' My stomach lurches. Not my tree house, please no.

'I supposed we'd better check . . .' Jamie begins, but I'm already out of the door. Seconds later I'm standing under the oak tree, completely panicked. I sniff the air, and right enough it smells a little smoky, but I don't see any flames. I grab the end of the rope ladder and start to climb, cursing myself for not allowing Dad to build a proper fixed ladder years ago. I always liked being able to pull up the rope ladder, it stopped Pandora or the adults having access to my own secret world while I was up there.

The small wooden door is open, which is strange, I'm always careful to close it. I left it open once years ago and when I next climbed up two startled magpies flew at me, hitting my face with their surprisingly strong wings; I've never forgotten it. Their beady eyes starred in my nightmares for months to come.

The smell of smoke is stronger now, but it's not wood burning . . . it's tobacco. I bend over a little and walk inside.

'Hey, Jules, fancy meeting you here.'

I jump backwards so hard I almost fall off the platform. 'Jesus, Ed, what the hell?'

Sprawled on the cushions at the back of my tree house is Edmund Powers. He pulls hard on his rollie, making the cigarette paper crackle and the red tip flame.

I stare at him in the gloom. Emotion ripples through me – anger, pain, regret, longing – for several seconds I'm so overcome I can't speak. Eventually I manage to squeeze out, 'I thought this place was on fire.'

He starts singing a snippet of an old Bruce Springsteen song. 'Hey babe, I'm on fire,' his voice low and husky.

'What are you doing here?' I demand.

'Waiting for that muppet Jamie to leave so we can talk. Brought some supplies.' He holds up a bottle of vodka, a carton of cranberry and a tube of white plastic cups – which for a second reminds me of Beatrix's trunk – and gives me one of his easy grins.

I narrow my eyes. 'How do you know Jamie's here? Have you been spying on me?'

He picks a bit of stray tobacco out of his mouth, then grins at me, ignoring the question. 'God, Jules, you look great. Let me get a better look at you.'

He reaches over, pulls the glass off the storm lantern and lights the wick of the candle. I study Ed's face, flickering in the candlelight. I'd almost forgotten how ridiculously handsome he is. The blond shaggy hair and those impossibly full lips. My insides rearrange themselves and I feel that old familiar tingle.

'Jules! Jules, you up there?' Jamie calls from underneath the tree.

Shit, that's all I need.

'Stay right there,' I hiss at Ed. He goes to get up but I point my finger at him. 'I'm serious. You move and I'll tell Lainey.'

'Tell her what?' he says, all innocent. 'I haven't done anything. Yet.' He lingers over the last word.

I swear I can feel my organs pump out extra hormones.

'You're not funny,' I whisper. 'Just shush.'

'Are you talking to me, Jules?' Jamie asks. 'Is everything OK? What was the light?'

I stick my head out and look down at him. 'It must have been, um, a firefly or something. Nothing to worry about.'

Behind me I hear Ed chuckling away to himself. 'A firefly? In Ireland? If he believes that he's even more stupid than I thought.'

'Shut up,' I hiss at Ed.

'What did you say?' Jamie stares up at me, bewildered.

'Sorry, um, I was just—'

Suddenly, I can feel the heat of Ed's body behind me, smell Allure mixed with fresh tobacco smoke.

'She was talking to me, mate,' Ed says, holding onto the top of the door frame and sticking his head out. The outside light is on, illuminating Jamie. Even from up here I can see the disgust on his face.

There is complete silence for a moment as the boys' eyes lock.

159

Ed adds easily, 'We're meeting for one final goodbye shag.'

I'm so flabbergasted that for a second I can't speak. Finally I splutter, 'We absolutely are not! I'm sorry, Jamie, I got up here and he was—'

But Jamie is already walking back towards our house at speed.

'Jamie!' I yell. It's lucky Pandora's bedroom is on the far side of the house or she'd be straight out, wondering what all the commotion is.

'You fucking idiot,' I tell Ed, before turning around to climb back down the rope ladder. But he flicks his cigarette onto the grass and grabs both my arms. I try to shake him off. 'Let go, Ed.'

'No.'

'What do you mean, no? Get the hell out of my tree house. Go home to Lainey.'

'That's what I wanted to talk to you about. I think I may have made a mistake.'

My whole world shifts for a second, sending me into a tailspin. This is Ed all over, coming out with sweeping statements that make my mind reel. Does he want me back, is that what he's saying?

'Ed, you can't come out with things like that when I'm swinging around on a rope ladder.'

'Come back up then.'

I'm terrified of what he might say. Is he playing with me? Is he serious? It's impossible to know with Ed. 'No, Jamie's—'

'Not good enough for someone like you. Never has been. Just get back up here, we need to talk. I'm freaking out about all this wedding stuff. I mean I love Lainey and everything—'

I come crashing back down to earth, like a broken lift. Of course he doesn't want me back.

I twist my head just in time to see Jamie's face, staring through the living-room window, his laptop tucked under his arm. I'm not sure if he can see me properly, but I can see him. His hair has flopped over his face so it's hard to read his expression, but from the slope of his shoulders he doesn't look happy. And then he disappears.

And the way things are, the way he feels about Ed Powers in particular, I doubt if he'll ever be back again, unless I talk to him, convince him Ed was joking and that we didn't have some sort of sick pre-arranged rendezvous. I have a choice, Jamie's friendship versus Ed's what . . . guilt? Pre-wedding jitters?

At that moment, I see my mistake, the mistake I've made all along, allowing my hormones to dictate my actions. I lost Jamie once, and I'm not going to let that happen again without a fight. He's worth dozens of Eds. I can cope with being single, but being alone, without a friend in the world, I can't deal with. Right now I *need* Jamie's friendship. A lot more than I need Ed messing with my head.

'At least I think I do,' Ed adds slowly. 'Love her I mean. But maybe I don't. Maybe it's not love at all, maybe it's . . .'

And that pushes me right over the edge. I want him to shut up, to stop talking, stop me feeling so hopeful one second, desolate the next. I was right, Ed is *poison*. I face the tree again and bite down hard on one of his hands.

He pulls it away, yelping. 'Shit, Jules. What are you like? That hurt.'

I scramble down the rope ladder and run towards the front of the house.

'Come on, Jules,' I can hear Ed shout behind me. 'You know you want to talk to me.'

I spin around. 'And what about your email, Ed? You told me to keep away from you.'

'I can explain. And speaking of—'

But I run away from his cajoling voice. And then I spot Jamie, walking quickly towards his house.

'Jamie!'

He stops for a second, so I know he heard me, but he doesn't turn around.

'Jamie, wait up.'

By the time I've reached him, he's sitting on his front step, hugging his laptop to his chest, tapping his feet on the ground.

'Well?' he says, his eyes flat.

I sit down beside him, catching my breath from the run.

'I don't know what he was doing up there,' I say. 'Honestly. I haven't spoken to him in months.'

Jamie is silent.

'Say something,' I beg.

He shrugs. 'There's nothing to say. But you know he's getting married in a few weeks, right? To your best friend?'

I wince. 'Ex-best friend.'

'What are you playing at, Jules?'

I stare at him. 'You don't believe me, do you? You seriously think I'd have anything to do with that slimeball now?' I give a wry laugh. 'I thought you knew me better than that.'

'I used to, but then you changed. Pushed me away.'

I don't know quite what to say to that. He's right, after Ed and Jamie's fight, I pretty much dumped Jamie instantly. I chose Ed over our years of friendship. I take a deep breath. 'I know I hurt you, Jamie, but it was a long time ago. Can't we forget about it, just move on? I could really do with a friend right now.'

He stares down at his feet, making them do a funny little heels-together-toes-together dance.

'Look,' I continue, 'I'm here now, aren't I? Ed Powers can go to hell.'

The front door opens behind us. Daphne Clear smiles down at us, a little too knowingly for my liking. 'There you are, Jamie. And hi Jules, how nice to see you. What are you two doing lingering on the doorstep, come in, come in. I'd love to hear what you've been up to, Jules,' she continues, in her bouncy voice.

'Bird is so delighted with your work in Shoestring. I believe you're making life-size elephants tomorrow.'

I smile. 'Maybe not life-size, Daphne, but big all right. They're for either side of the door. To celebrate Asha Bhandari's visit.'

Daphne clicks her tongue against her teeth. 'Thank you for reminding me. I must book tickets for my book club. Would you like to come along, Jamie, Jules?'

'No thanks, Mum,' he says politely. 'Not really my kind of thing.'

I pretend to consider this for a moment. 'Busy that night I'm afraid.'

Jamie and I swap an amused look.

'Of course you are, poppets. Now, who'd like a nice cup of tea? I've got the kettle on and I'd love a good old chin wag.'

I feel suddenly exhausted. I don't know if it's the week catching up with me or Daphne's dogged good spirits. I give a huge yawn.

'Sorry, Daphne,' I say. 'I'm going to have to call it a night. Bird and Pandora are slave drivers and I'm wrecked. Work tomorrow.'

'I understand.' She smiles at me kindly. 'Don't be a stranger, you hear. I know Jamie missed you while he was in Galway, didn't you, dear? He was always asking after you.'

Jamie sighs. 'Yes, Mum. Now can you stop embarrassing me, please?'

Daphne is unperturbed. 'I'll leave the two of you at it then.'

Once she's back inside I say, 'Look, I'd better get going. Busy day tomorrow. Elephants to build, you know how it is. But are we OK, Jamie?'

He tilts his head and looks at me for a second. 'Yes. We're OK.'

I walk back towards my house, smiling to myself. Jamie offered to see me home, but I told him to stay put. I pull out my door key and hesitate. I hope Ed's had the intelligence to put out the lamp and his last cigarette or else the tree house really might burn down. I sigh, put my key back in my pocket, and walk around the side to check.

But I wish I hadn't. Ed is still there, sitting on the platform, legs dangling down, smoking and swigging from a plastic cup.

'Wondered when you'd be back.' He pats the wood beside him. 'Room for a little one.'

I feel even more exhausted now. 'Go home, Ed.'

'Just one drink, then I'll get out of your face, I swear. I'm really here to apologize, yeah. And I have news.' He stops for a second. 'About Noel. And I don't fancy broadcasting it to the whole neighbourhood. Stop being so feckin' stubborn.'

I stand there, seething. I *have* to know what Noel said, I have to. Ed knows he's won, I can practically hear the self-congratulatory chuckles from down here. Without another word, I climb slowly up the ladder. Just before I reach the top he grabs both my arms and swings me out, over the ground.

'Ed!' For a second I almost believe he really would drop me, but then he laughs and pulls me back in.

'You should have seen your face, Jules.' He pulls a scared expression but stops when he sees I'm not amused.

'Jesus, you're a bundle of laughs these days,' he says, 'what's happened to you?'

'Just get in.' I point at the door, hoping he'll smack his stupid head on the low frame.

He sprawls out on the cushions and, the way he's half sitting, half lying, my eyes are drawn to his crotch. I whip them away quickly, my cheeks hot.

'You joining me?' He pats the mattress beside him.

I ignore him, sitting down under the window on the wooden floor with my back against the wall. It's a little uncomfortable but I don't care.

'Spit it out,' I snap. 'About Noel Hegarty.'

'You read his letter, yeah? He's really sorry. And he's been a bit less grumpy lately, so the counselling's obviously working.'

'And that's it?' I stare at him. 'That's all you have to say about Noel? That he's in a better mood?'

He runs his hands through his hair, stalling.

'Well, yeah. I suppose,' he says eventually.

'Ed, that's pathetic. He's just getting away with it. Don't you care?'

''Course I care. But what do you want me to do? He's said sorry, he's getting counselling. It's best to put the whole thing behind you. Move on.'

I sigh. Maybe Ed's right, maybe I should just forget about the whole damn thing.

'Let it go,' he says gently. 'It's for the best.' He sits up a bit on the cushions. 'Anyway, enough about work. How are you doing?'

I glare at him. 'What are you playing at? You can't just appear out of the blue like this and expect me to be happy to see you. You're supposed to be getting married in a few weeks, remember?'

'Ah, yes, the wedding.' Even in the murkiness, I can see his eyes shift around nervously. 'I have no idea how it got to this point. One minute I'm having a laugh with Lainey, the next minute we're engaged and she's set a date.'

'Having a laugh? Is that what they call affairs these days?'

'Don't start. You were away, we had an understanding. You were hardly a vestal virgin yourself. All those foreign blokes.'

I colour. If he only knew the truth, that I'd been lying about my non-existent, far-flung boyfriends all along in an effort to keep him interested. I could hardly come clean now. Yes, I'd kissed the odd Kiwi at a party, but that was it. I hated the fact that Ed seemed incapable of being on his own, even for a few weeks. Suggesting that we saw other people while I was travelling, but only on a casual basis, nothing serious, wasn't my idea; ironically it had been Lainey's.

165

'You have to give Ed a long leash,' she'd said. 'Guys like that need to feel free. If you want to keep him, you have to stop being so clingy. He's like a tiger, likes a good chase.'

'Yes, we agreed we could see other people on a casual basis, have flings,' I tell him. 'But I didn't mean with my best friend. And getting engaged is hardly a fling, is it?'

'Na.' He takes out his tobacco pouch and starts rolling another cigarette. 'Getting engaged is serious shit.' He pauses. 'I don't think I'm ready for all this. Marriage and everything. I'm only twenty-five.'

'You asked her, Romeo.'

'I was drunk.' He puts the finished cigarette down on the wooden floor and pulls the bottle of vodka towards him. Expensive stuff too: Grey Goose. 'Speaking of which,' he adds. 'Have a drink. Might calm you down a bit.'

'Calm *me* down? You shouldn't be here. Especially not with me.' I fold my arms across my chest.

'Oh and I have something for you. Thought you might be running low on good tunes.' He hands me a CD in a see-through plastic pouch.

I take it off him and turn it over in my hands. Ed always burns the best CDs – new bands he's discovered, old favourites, a smattering of cheesy disco tunes, even the odd comedy song to make me laugh.

'Some mellow stuff in there and some new stuff I think you'll like.' He smiles gently. 'Guess it's my way of saying sorry. I never meant to hurt you. Me and Lainey . . .' He shrugs. 'It just snuck up on us, you understand.'

I can feel tears building up behind my eyes and I steel myself not to cry. 'No, I don't. Why don't you explain why of all the women in the world, you chose to hook up with my best friend?'

He picks up the cigarette and, after holding it in his hands for a few seconds, changes his mind and puts it back into the tobacco pouch. His eyes reach mine. 'She's good for me. All that family stuff. I didn't have any of that when I was a kid, you know that.'

I'd only met Ed's mum once, Diane. We bumped into her accidently on Grafton Street one Christmas – and she wasn't exactly friendly. Slim, dyed-blonde hair, pinched face, carefully dressed in an expensive-looking, white cashmere coat. She was beautiful, but there was a hardness about her, a deadness behind her eyes. Ed's dad had run off to Portugal with a hotel receptionist when Diane was in her late thirties and she'd made a career of extracting as much money as she could out of the man's lawyers. Bitter wouldn't even cover it.

'Lainey's straightforward, nothing bothers her,' he continues, oblivious to the effect his words are having on me. 'I don't have to guess how she feels, she just tells me. We never fight. It's easy.'

'Easy?' I snort. 'It sounds like a slow death. What about passion and excitement? There has to be some sort of spark or what's the point? And you used to complain that Lainey was the least ambitious girl you'd ever met.'

He shrugs again. 'She knows who she is and she's happy with that. She likes being an accountant and she wants to get married and start a family, nothing wrong with that.'

'A family? Jesus, would you listen to yourself? You sound middle-aged.'

'We all have to grow up sometime, Jules, even you.' He blows his breath out in a whoosh. 'Look, it wouldn't have worked out between us, not in the long run. We would have killed each other. We're no good together, maybe we're too alike.'

And then I realize what's been bothering me so much over the last few months. It's not just being dumped by Ed, or even Ed and Lainey hooking up; it's the fact that I couldn't tame him. He wouldn't change for me.

Of course I wanted a proper boyfriend, someone to look out for me, care about me, adore me – being on time would have been a start, he always turned up at least half an hour late when-ever we met – but he came up short every time. But for Lainey he transformed into a proper, reliable partner almost overnight. Which means he loves Lainey more than he ever loved me. And that, more than anything, rips my heart out of my chest.

I start crying, huge tears rolling down my cheeks. Suddenly I feel a huge wave of emotion and before I can stop it I hear myself say, 'I can change. I can be more like Lainey. And I want kids too, not right now, but eventually.'

'You shouldn't have to change, Jules. That's the whole point. You're perfect as you are. We're just not perfect together. Come here to me.' He reaches out and pulls me towards him, my bum sliding across the wood until I'm just in front of him.

He fixes me a strong drink and hands it to me. I rest my back against his chest and he wraps his arms around me from behind, making soothing 'shushing' noises and stroking my hair. I can feel his chest moving up and down as he breathes in and out, the warmth of his fingers on my scalp. I close my eyes and breathe in his familiar smell. Then I open my eyes, bring the plastic cup to my lips and take a long slug.

'I'm so sorry,' he says softly. 'I really miss you.'

I give another sob. 'I miss you too. So goddamn much.'

Twisting his body he leans forward and kisses me on the cheek, and then gently on the lips. For a second we sit there in suspended animation before he slides down on the cushions, taking me with him. I know I should push him away, tell him to stop, but it feels so comfortable, so familiar, *so good*, that I kiss him right back.

Chapter 14

'Morning, Jules,' Pandora says as I walk into Shoestring the following day. 'Look, I'm sorry for coming down so hard on you
last night. I found the wine bottle in the living room when I was
looking for Iris's shoes earlier. Practically still full. You really
did have only the one glass. I'm proud of you, Boolie. And I'm
sorry I didn't give you enough credit.'

'Thanks, and sorry I'm late.'

'Only ten minutes, I'll let you off.'

She smiles at me and I feel as low as a slug. Plus, there's a
sharp pain behind my right eye like a little man is chipping at
my optic nerves with a pickaxe, and my tongue's like sand-
paper. Normally I'd have rung in sick, but I really need to work
on my elephants for the doorway today.

'You OK, Jules?' Pandora looks at me carefully. 'Your eyes
are bloodshot and your glands look a bit puffy. Maybe you're
coming down with something.'

'I don't feel great,' I say.

'Maybe you should go home.'

I shake my head. 'I'll survive. I need to make a start on the
elephants.'

'If you're sure.'

I nod. 'I'm positive.' I feel disgusted with myself for all
manner of reasons. At least in work I'll be busy and I won't get
the chance to think too much.

Pandora smiles at me. 'Great. I can't wait to see them. And

I found this wonderful voile at the curtain exchange for the entrance, not the exact colour of the swatches you gave me, but pretty close and . . .'

I nod, pretending to listen, my mind miles away.

Ed and I managed to finish the Grey Goose last night, a fact I'm not proud of. But it was hardly my fault, he kept filling up my plastic cup. However, I'm starting to think that maybe Sheila is on to something, maybe I am using alcohol as a crutch, but there's no way I could have dealt with Ed sober. Who knows what I might have said? No, the drink was a necessary evil. I try to push Sheila's concerns to the back of my mind. But kissing Ed, now that *was* wrong. The problem is, during the few hours we spent together I began to forget how much I hated him. We laughed and flirted and drank, and it felt good. Like coming home. Now it's the morning after, I don't feel so hot. I'm hungover, stressed and very, very guilty.

I know Ed and Lainey both betrayed me, but what I did was unforgivable. Ed made me swear I wouldn't tell a soul about spending time together or the kiss, but I can't stop thinking about it. Yes, it was only one short, if furious, kiss – I put a halt to things before they went any further – but surely it meant something to him? I'm so confused my head hurts from thinking about it.

'What do you think, Jules?' Pandora asks. 'Cushions or no cushions?'

I look at her. I have no idea what she's talking about. But Pandora has a thing about cushions, she even has them on her bed.

'Cushions,' I say firmly.

'Perfect,' Pandora says smiling. 'Cushions it is.'

By my coffee break I'm starting to feel a little better, mainly due to the painkillers Pandora pressed into my hand earlier. She's convinced I'm fighting something off and is being terrifically nice to me, making me feel even more guilty. So I've been hiding at the back of the shop floor, working on the chicken-wire frames for my elephants. I open the door a crack and check there's no one in the staffroom before walking in and flopping down on the sofa. I take out my iPhone. OK, I know it's a long shot and I'm probably being stupid, but after last night . . . I scan my messages. Nothing from Ed. But there is one from Jamie.

Working on a new skin for you. Can we meet up later? What are you doing this eve? X J

I press my head into the back of the sofa, hugely relieved he still wants to be friends after all the shenanigans last night. I know he said we were OK, but when it comes to our friendship he seems to be blowing hot and cold at the moment. What am I doing tonight? I'd say there's every chance I'll be sitting at home on my tod, obsessing about Ed and the kiss. I certainly don't want to face Jamie in person yet. He's bound to guess something's up. And if he does guess he's unlikely to speak to me again. A risk I'm not prepared to take, not when I've just got him back.

Sorry Jamie, I have to work on my elephants for the shop tonight. Thanks for all your work on the skin so far. Shop closed tomorrow for revamp – all hands on deck. I'll catch up with you during the week. J X

No problem, good luck with the revamp! he texts back. I lie down on the sofa and close my eyes, willing the throbbing to disappear and my dark thoughts to lift.

'Wakey, wakey,' Bird says, flinging open my curtains on Sunday morning. 'Revamp day. Ready for some hard work, Boolie?'

I groan and open my eyes, shielding them against the light with my hand. 'Ten more minutes, Bird.'

'Then you'll have to cycle. I'm leaving in five minutes sharp. Up to you, darling.' She peers down at me. 'Glands any better?'

'A bit.' The monster headache has finally gone. Shame I couldn't sleep a wink last night, my mind churning like a food mixer. And when I did finally drift off, I had a horribly vivid nightmare – Iris lying on the pavement, her head smashed open like a pumpkin. I was standing over her and then blood started pouring from my palms and merging with the pool of her own blood. Terrifying. And that's just the one I remember. No wonder I feel so drained this morning. As soon as Bird's out of the room, I check my phone for messages. Nothing. But I do have an email. Ed? I sit up and quickly click on it.

From: Alex Cinnamon
To: Shoestring Club

Re: Faith Farenze dress
Sunday 17th September

Dear Shoestring Club,

Thank you for sending on details of the dress. It sounds perfect. I would like to purchase one share at €300. Will you accept a personal cheque? My other half says I should ask for a contract with full terms and conditions and your contact details to secure my share (sorry!), is that OK? He's afraid it's one of those Nigerian *give me your bank details and I'll deposit all my money in it* scams.

Let me know who to make the cheque out to and your address. I look forward to the first handover dinner, and even more to my 'turn' with the dress! It looks heavenly and I've always dreamed of wearing a Farenze!

It's our wedding anniversary in December – the 15th – and my husband wants to take me out somewhere special, all being well. He won't say where, but apparently it's très swish. I do hope the dress is available around then.

Kind regards,
Alex Cinnamon

My God, it worked. A complete stranger – Alex – is going to give us €300, and she doesn't need the dress until December, which is perfect. I feel a sudden surge of positivity. For a second I'm almost happy. I check my watch. Ten to ten. Too early to ring Arietty? What the hell.

'Hi, Jules.' Arietty sounds wide awake and pleased to hear from me, even on a Sunday morning.

'It worked!' I say excitedly. 'I got an email this morning from someone called Alex Cinnamon. She wants to buy a share.'

'That's fantastic news. One down, one to go.'

'Ah, I was going to talk to you about that. I think I've found girl number four, only it's a bit complicated. I'll need to explain in person.'

Arietty gives an excited squeal. 'Really? You mean this is actually going to happen? That's fantastic! What are you up to right now? We should celebrate, have brunch in your café or something.'

'I'm working I'm afraid. I have a pair of three-foot elephant frames to cover in papier mâché. And the shop's closed today, including the café. Dad's fitting some new shelving.'

'Why don't I give you a hand? And then we could have lunch in Avoca, yes? It's just down the road.'

'Are you sure? It's a messy business, the wallpaper paste gets everywhere.'

'Who cares?' She gives a rumbling laugh. 'And how else can I be sure you'll get the tusks right this time? And complications? Ha! My whole life is one big complication.'

'I know what you mean. And in that case, I'd love some help.' I click off my phone, smiling to myself. Things are finally looking up – I'm one step closer to being the proud part-owner of the Farenze. And then I remember why I want the dress in the first place and the smile quickly drops off my face.

I lie back and think about Ed. He hasn't contacted me since Friday night and I don't know why I ever thought he would. He's getting married in just under a month, Jules, I tell myself firmly. And he doesn't care about you. He told you himself, he's in love with Lainey. You have to stop all this stupid obsessing and forget about him. It's not rational.

Bird marches back into my room. 'Up! We're wasting precious time. We didn't close the shop for you to malinger in bed all day. Now, young lady!'

I'm kneeling on a flattened cardboard box, slapping strips of newspaper soaked in wallpaper paste onto my first elephant, when I hear a voice behind me.

'Reporting for duty, sir.'

I swing around. Arietty is standing there, grinning, in old denims, frayed at the knees, and a blue sweatshirt that looks at least two sizes too big, still managing to look amazing.

I stand up and brush my hair back off my face with the heel of my hand as my fingers are horribly sticky.

'Hi, Arietty,' I say. 'Now, are you positive you want to do this? Look at the state of me.' I hold up my gooey hands.

She grins. 'Yes. You can tell me all the dress news while we work.'

'In that case . . .' I hand her another flattened box and point at an elephant's rear end. 'You start at his bum and work your way forwards. I've put the first layer down, which is the tricky bit. We just need to build up the body with two or three more layers, then spray it with a thick layer of grey paint. That'll have to be done first thing tomorrow morning, after the newspaper has had a chance to dry. And then I'll add eyes and maybe decorate their necks with bows or something to brighten them up.'

Arietty scowls. 'Bows? That will look stupid.'

I laugh. 'Don't hold back, Arietty.'

'Sorry. But bows? You've seen my elephants up close and personal, Jules. Could you really imagine Beatrix with a red ribbon around her neck, like a Christmas present?'

I shake my head. 'What about a bright rug on their backs? Would that work? I could use the material left over from the curtains.'

'It would be better. Although it's still a bit circus-like. They used to dress them up in enormous red jackets and pill hats in the olden days. In fact, Dublin Zoo was still running elephant rides until the 1950s. I just think elephants deserve our respect. The only thing on their backs in the wild is dust or sand. They spray it on their skin to keep themselves cool.'

'I just want to make them eye catching. I'll think of something. I could always surround each of them with a ring of glittery poos.'

Arietty stares at me. 'That would be weird.'

I smile. 'I'm joking.'

'How are you getting on, Jules?' Pandora walks towards us, then spots Arietty.

'Hello, again,' Pandora says to her. 'I wasn't expecting you till tomorrow. I'm afraid we're not open today. But if you really need your Farenze dress I'm sure we can make an exception.'

'That won't be necessary,' Arietty says politely. 'I can wait. Tomorrow is good.'

Pandora doesn't move. She looks from Arietty to me and then back again.

Arietty smiles. 'You're wondering what I'm doing here then, yes?'

Pandora's cheeks colour. 'Sorry, I don't mean to be nosey.'

175

'I'm helping Jules get the elephants right,' Arietty says unperturbed.

'Of course, you work with them, don't you?' Now that Pandora has her answer, she relaxes a little. 'Iris was very taken with you, won't stop talking about you in fact. Did you get the picture she drew for you?'

Oops, I knew there was something I meant to bring with me today.

'Arietty is going to collect it later,' I pipe up. 'The drawing Iris did for you, of the elephants. Remember I told you about it?' I give Arietty a please play along look.

'No, you didn't,' Arietty says. She's obviously a lot better at reading elephants than people. 'I would have remembered. But I look forward to seeing it. Nice to meet you again, Pandora. Iris is very sweet by the way, smart too, but you really should get her a proper pet. Insects are fascinating, but they don't give much back, not the way mammals do.'

Pandora opens her mouth to say something, but then closes it again. 'Thank you for that advice,' she says stiffly, glaring at me. I'm sure she thinks I put Arietty up to it. 'We'll see.' And with that Pandora marches off.

I laugh into my hand.

Arietty looks at me. 'Was it something I said?'

'Not at all. But I think our Shoestring Club handover dinners have just got a whole heap more interesting.'

Realization dawns over Arietty's face. 'Are you saying Pandora has bought the final share?'

I click my tongue against my teeth. 'My granny, Bird, has put up the money on Pandora's behalf, on one condition. That we find Pandora something, or more precisely, *someone*, to wear it for.'

Arietty grins. 'Are you serious? She's pretty, that shouldn't be a problem, should it?'

My eyebrows soar. 'The fussiest woman in the universe when it comes to men? I would have to say it's a challenge.'

'There must be loads of single men out there who would happily date Pandora. Look, I bet he's single. Let's ask him if he'd like to meet her.' She points down the street at a man walking towards us.

As he gets closer I realize with a start that it's Jamie. I wince with guilt. He's obviously come looking for me. Maybe he knows something about me and Ed. At least Arietty's lunacy might distract him.

I say, 'Go on, ask him, I dare you,' then dive behind the elephant. I crouch down and peer through the gap between the trunk and the mouth.

Arietty steps out a little, blocking Jamie's path. She's a good two inches taller than he is.

'Hello,' she says.

'Um, hello,' he answers nervously.

'Are you single?'

He looks around him. I'm sure he thinks it's a wind up, that someone is videoing him for You Tube.

'Yes,' he says suspiciously. 'Why? Is this some sort of marketing thing?'

'No. Would you like to meet someone? A girl I mean. But you have to be single. And solvent,' she adds firmly. 'Her name is Pandora Schuster and she owns this lovely shop.' She waves her hand at the shop window. 'She's smart and funny and a great business woman. What do you think? Would you like an introduction?'

'Jules?' Jamie says loudly, whipping his head around. 'Is this your idea of a joke? It's not funny. Where are you hiding?'

Arietty puts her hands on her hips. 'Jules! You might have told me you knew the guy. Come out right this second.'

I step out from behind the elephant, chuckling away to myself. 'You should have seen your face, Jamie Clear. Priceless.' I turn to Arietty. 'Sorry, Arietty, I couldn't resist. This is Jamie, an old friend of mine. Jamie, meet Arietty. She's kindly helping me slap soggy paper onto this fellow.' I nod at the elephant.

Jamie smiles. 'Seems the Schusters have dragged in anyone willing to do their dirty work. Your dad asked me to help him build some new shelving, Jules.'

I feel a wave of relief. Makes sense.

'And does Pandora know you're trying to solicit boyfriends for her on the street?' he asks me.

''Course not. But we do need to find her someone. Fast. There's this dress you see . . .' I fill him in on the potted details.

Afterwards, he whistles. 'All that work just for one dress? It must be some frock.'

'It is,' Arietty says. 'And wouldn't you even consider dating Pandora?'

He guffaws and I join in. Soon we're both falling around the place, holding our stomachs.

'It's not that funny.' Arietty looks annoyed.

'I'm sorry,' I manage, breathless from laughing so much. 'But honestly, they'd be like the odd couple. Pandora's into cheesy karaoke music, she sings in a choir, she's anal about timekeeping, likes her men wearing suits. And Jamie—'

'Would rather shoot himself than go near a karaoke bar,' he puts in helpfully. 'And does not own a tie, let alone a suit. Jules is right. Sorry, Arietty, it would be a disaster. You'll just have to keep accosting innocent guys on the street. But there must be easier ways of finding single men. You should try the bike shop down the road, or I know, Monkstown Aquatic Centre. I did some work for them on their website and loyalty cards a few years back, it was always teeming with lads buying tropical fish. The owners call the big tropical tanks bachelor tanks; apparently they're the first thing to go once a guy gets married. That and the pool table.'

My ears prick up. 'Did you say loyalty cards?'

He shrugs. 'Yeah, why?'

'Do you still run their database?'

'No, but if something's on a computer, I can find it, Jules, you know that. Not that I would of course,' he adds for Arietty's benefit.

I stare at him. 'Jamie Clear, I think our prayers have been answered. And don't worry, it's nothing illegal. I'm not after bank details or medical info or whether they have a criminal record.' I pause. 'Although . . .'

Jamie winces. 'No way, José. Hacking into police files? Are you trying to get me put away?'

I smile. 'OK, we'll stick to loyalty cards. Pulling information off those isn't illegal is it?'

'It's a bit of a grey area to be honest.' He still looks a bit uneasy.

'I'm just looking for mobile numbers, Jamie. Or email addresses. Of single men between the ages of say twenty-five and thirty-five who live in the area. Once I have them, I just have to work out what to do with them.'

There's a rap on the window and all three of us jump. It's Dad. He gestures at Jamie to go inside.

Jamie salutes him. 'Better run, ladies. Duty calls.'

'Will you help us?' I ask him, my hands pressed together. 'Please?'

He sighs. 'It's a big ask. But OK, you're on. But you have to keep where you got their details to yourself. Blame one of the supermarkets or something.'

I punch the air. 'Yes!'

Once Jamie's disappeared inside, I grab Arietty's arm and make her do a little Irish jig with me singing, 'Faith Farenze here we come, diddly, diddly, diddly, do,' over and over again before we both collapse on the pavement, breathless with giggles.

'You're crazy, woman,' Arietty says, still grinning from ear to ear. 'Luckily, I like mad people.'

'Takes one to know one I guess.' I smile back at her, realizing I haven't once thought about Ed since she arrived. 'And thanks for coming over this morning, Arietty. You must have better things to do on a Sunday.'

She shrugs. 'No. Not really.'

Our eyes meet and I see a sadness in them. She looks away.

'Broke up with someone recently,' she says, blowing the air out of her mouth. 'We used to spend every Sunday together. Never get involved with a reptile guy, Jules. They're as cold blooded as the snakes they're so obsessed with.'

'And my best friend is marrying my ex and I think I still have feelings for him,' I say in a rush, surprising myself. It's not something I've admitted to anyone, even Pandora. But unlike Pandora, I don't think Arietty will make me analyse my emotions, or tell me I'm wrong to feel this way, so it feels safe to say it out loud. 'That's why I want the dress,' I continue. 'To wear at the wedding. To show everyone I'm completely over him. And to get some sort of closure.'

She nods sagely. 'Hard, isn't it? They get under your skin, then bang, everything changes. And getting over them is a killer.'

'No kidding.'

'Stupid feckers,' she adds.

I laugh. 'Too right.' I pull a piece of gooey paper out of the bucket and slap it onto my elephant's rear. 'That's what I think of Ed bloody Powers.'

She cocks her head. 'That's his name?'

'Yes.'

'Stupid name. Ed.'

I chuckle. 'And yours?'

'Howie Dixon.'

'That's even worse.'

'I know. And this is for you, Howie.' She whips a piece onto her elephant's behind, her eyes sparkling.

'Let's cover their asses in paper and then knock off for chocolate cake, yes?' she suggests.

I grin. 'You're a girl after my own bruised heart, Arietty Pilgrim.'

Chapter 15

Jamie is as good as his word. On Tuesday morning he arrives at Shoestring with a sheaf of paper in his hand and, after looking around him surreptitiously, hands it to me at the till. He needn't have bothered, the place is deathly quiet. The shop looks amazing after the refit – the pops of colour add a freshness to the floor, and the wafting voile curtains and the elephants flanking the doorway should be enticing new customers in, but unfortunately none of our hard work seems to have made any difference to footfall. Even the café's quiet.

I look at the top sheet, a spreadsheet, the cells filled with men's names, dates of birth, email addresses, snail mail addresses, and marital status. I run my eye down the list – he's pulled out the single ones and put an asterix beside the ones that live locally. Result!

I give him a huge grin. 'You're amazing, Jamie. This is perfect. Don't suppose any of them supplied photos?'

He smiles back. 'You could always send Arietty off to doorstep them. She seems pretty shameless.'

I say nothing for a second, considering this.

Jamie shifts his weight from foot to foot. 'I'm kidding. Promise me there'll be no stalking.'

''Course not. It would take far too long. I hadn't realized there'd be so many of them.'

'Jules, half of the men on those sheets probably have a girlfriend. And the other half could be axe murderers for all you know. The only thing they all have in common is fish.'

181

I bite the inside of my lip. He has a point. And suddenly I remember what Arietty said about that reptile keeper in the zoo, Howie. I'm sure fish lovers are just as cold blooded. Why couldn't Jamie have worked for a pet shop? That's what we need. Nice, normal, outdoorsy men with Labradors.

'I've changed my mind. Can you find me dog owners instead? In fact, if you could narrow it down by breed—'

'Jules! What do you want me to do? Hack into every loyalty card database out there?'

I tilt my head. 'Could you?'

'No! It would take for ever. You're a desperate one for changing your mind. Look, you're going about this all the wrong way. First you need to know exactly what you're looking for. The parameters. That way you can narrow down your search.'

I ponder this for a moment, then nod. 'Makes sense.'

'And what are you going to do with all these eligible men once you've found them?'

I grimace. 'I'm not sure to be honest. But basically I want to get them all together in one place, maybe with a karaoke machine; then introduce them to Pandora and hope some misguided fool bites. Some kind of party I guess.'

'As long as there's free food and beer, you won't have a problem getting them in the door. What about a barbeque?'

My nose wrinkles automatically. 'Not Pandora's kind of thing. And where would we have it? In the shop?'

He shrugs. 'Sure. Why not? Move the chairs and tables back in the café and you'd have plenty of floor space. I was in the park last weekend and they had a games day – giant Snakes and Ladders and Twister, things like that – it was for kids, but I would have loved to join in. Maybe you could have a Shoestring games night for big kids – what about all those great 80s games? – Pac-Man, Tetris, Space Invaders, Stretch Armstrong competitions, Rubik's Cube speed trials – I'd go. And yes, a karaoke machine if you must.'

I sigh theatrically. 'Jamie Clear, at times you are deranged—'

'Hey!' he protests.

I put up my hand. 'Whoa there, I haven't finished. Other times you are truly inspired.' I beam at him. 'I can honestly say I would never, ever, have thought of a games night for kidadults, but throw in a karaoke machine and plenty of drink and it might just work.' I rub my head on his shoulder and make happy cat noises. 'Mew, mew, mew.' He laughs heartily and tries to push me away.

'There you are, darling.' Bird catches me and I quickly straighten up. 'And the lovely Jamie.' She smiles beatifically at him. 'I'm so delighted you two are getting on so well. I can't tell you how much it means—'

I cut her off mid-flow. 'Jamie had a great idea for a shop event, Bird. Once the book festival's over and Pandora's not so stressed, I'll run it by her.'

'Probably best to wait all right. I think she was expecting a big uplift in sales on account of the refit over the weekend, but it's quieter than ever. Let's hope it picks up.' She flashes me a smile, but I can see the anxiety behind her eyes. She flicks her hand in front of her face, as if swatting away a fly.

'But anyway,' she adds, 'an event sounds lovely. And maybe you and Jamie could work on it together. You really do make such a wonderful team.' Her eyebrows lift. 'Should Daphne and I start looking for hats?'

Jamie's cheeks flare. He's clearly mortified at the very idea.

I glare at her. 'Don't you have work to do?'

She laughs and waves her fingers at us. 'Toodle pip, lovebirds.'

'Sorry about that,' I say as soon as she's pottered off.

'She doesn't mean any harm.' He pauses for a minute, looking at me, an expression I can't read on his face. I think he's about to add something else, but then he stops. I know his own mum is bad, but she's nowhere near as direct as Bird. It's clearly bothering him more than I thought.

'You OK?' I ask.

'Yeah, yeah. Look, I have to talk to Pandora about some images for the website, but email me exactly what you're looking for, men-wise, and I'll see what I can do.'

'I think she's in the office, doing the accounts. And thank you, thank you, thank you.'

I throw my arms around him, and kiss him on the cheek. 'You rock, Jamie Clear, you know that?'

His face zings red again and his eyes lower. I draw away. Maybe that was a little too much. I don't want to scare him off with over-zealous hugs, not when things are back on track.

'Catch you later, Jules,' he says, walking towards the staff-room, a smile flickering on his lips.

I work on my list of man musts all afternoon, adding things and then changing my mind and crossing them out. This is my list so far:

A Man for Pandora

Must be single
Must be between 25 and 38

Thirty-eight sounds ancient to me, but Pandora's always liked older men. I suspect her Parisian fling was with one of her French fashion lecturers. Pandora has never revealed his identity, even to Dad or Bird. Iris's skin is olive, Pandora's is creamy white, so it would make sense that Iris is half French. Personally I think Iris has a right to know who her father is, but there's no talking to Pandora sometimes.

Must have a job
Must have some interest in music — boring classical stuff if possible

Must like going to the cinema or watching films

Pandora spends any free time she has flopped on the sofa in front of the latest DVDs – she loves movies and boxed sets.

Must be an animal lover

I add this more for Iris's benefit than Pandora's. Besides, every-one knows guys who like animals can't be all bad. Then I think about Arietty. She LOVES animals, and she's more than a bit odd, so I cross this out. Then I change my mind and add it back in. Arietty may be odd, but she seems to have a good heart. Besides, in this case, odd is good – you'd have to be a bit left of centre to fall for Pandora. Then I think, I'm being too fussy, and strike it out again.

Must live in south county Dublin

This one I leave in. Pandora loves the area, says she never wants to move. And with Shoestring and Iris's school and everything, a boyfriend in Meath or even Howth might prove difficult in the long term.

And these are just the deal breakers. I cross off the remaining items on the list – smart dresser, Church of Ireland, likes kids, into healthy eating, keen on hill walking – because a.) they're desirable but less important, b.) they may be hard to unearth, even for Jamie, and c.) there's a good chance the list will have no one on it if I include the finer details.

But it does make me realize (a little smugly I admit) how well I know Pandora when it comes to her romantic needs, and then it also occurs to me that she clearly isn't as self-aware. Take Gav for example, her last boyfriend. He lasted all of two months. Worked part-time delivering pizzas while he worked on his music – navel-gazing singer/songwriter stuff that was so

185

depressing I'm not surprised nobody wanted to listen to it, let alone sign him. He also had a charming habit of ignoring Iris's existence, insisting he and Pandora did things together, just the two of them. In the end he had the cheek to dump my sister – who was way too good for him in the first place – saying she wasn't 'cool' enough for him. Pandora was distraught.

I email my edited list to Jamie and cross my fingers. I'd really like to find someone decent for Pandora, and yes, the dress is part of it, but not all. She deserves to meet someone decent for a change, and Iris deserves a kind stepdad who could take her to the zoo when Pandora's working.

Pandora's a bit of a workaholic, but if she had someone to drag her away from the shop at weekends and in the evenings, she might not be so devoted to Shoestring. At the moment it's almost as if she and the shop are umbilically joined, and it's not healthy.

I've just started tagging some new stock, when I hear some-one marching towards the cash desk, their heels clicking on the wooden floorboards. I lift my head and my stomach instantly tightens. It's Lainey and, from the scowl on her face, it looks like she's on the warpath. I'm not exactly thrilled to see her either. I fold my arms across my chest and wait for her to halt in front of the desk, my heart hammering. Just before she reaches me, Ed's candlelit face flashes in front of my eyes and I can feel my cheeks blush guiltily.

'I want to talk to you,' she says without preamble. She's wearing a neat black suit that I know must have cost a fortune, but with sensible mid-heel courts and a fitted white shirt un-derneath, it says nothing about who she is. Even an interesting necklace or a funky belt would have livened it up a bit.

'Stop judging my clothes,' she snaps perceptively. 'I've just come from work. I couldn't concentrate this morning and it's all your fault.'

'My fault? Why is it my fault?'

She pokes me in the upper chest with a finger. 'Where exactly was Ed on Friday night?'

Blood pumps into my face, much as I try to stop it. I slap her hand away.

'How would I know?' I splutter.

'Tony spotted him on Sorrento Road.'

'Tony who?'

'You know, Tony Kenny. Chloe's boyfriend. Apparently Ed walked into Sorrento Grove at about eight fifty.'

'Thought he was a teacher, not a private investigator,' I say, stalling for time. From the dark expression on her face, Ed has certainly confessed to something.

'Ed went in your gates. Tony said he waited for a few minutes opposite the house but there was no sign of him coming back out. So admit it, he was in your house.'

'So you were having him followed.'

'No! Ed was supposed to be meeting Tony and some other friends for drinks in Finnegan's. Tony lives in Dalkey, he was walking towards the village and he thought they could walk down together. It was a coincidence. I want to know what happened. I have a right. He's my fiancé.'

I give a hollow laugh. 'Lainey, I owe you exactly nothing. And if you want to know what Ed was up to while you were at your precious hen party, why don't you ask him.'

'I did. He said he was sitting in Finnegan's waiting for the lads when he had a sudden pang of guilt and decided to check how you were getting on. He said he was only at your place for about ten minutes, then went to the pub. But Tony says he never appeared in Finnegan's. They rang him a couple of times but his phone was off. So I'm asking you again, what happened?'

I stand there, staring at her. Does she honestly expect me to fill in the pieces of the jigsaw puzzle?

'And again I'm telling you to ask your bloody fiancé.' I'm so angry with Lainey at this stage I could spit. How dare she rub all this fiancé business in my face. Does she have any idea how much it hurts? 'You know something? Yes, he was with me on Friday night,' I continue, enraged and suddenly wanting to hurt her back. 'And that's all I have to say on the matter. You have some nerve coming here, grilling me like this. It's not my fault Ed won't tell you the truth.'

'The truth?' Her face pales. 'What do you mean?'

'I'm not saying another word.'

She grabs my arm.

'Tell me,' she practically shrieks. 'You slept with him, didn't you?'

I shake off her hand. 'Lower your voice. Our customers are not interested in your amateur dramatics.' I come out from behind the till and walk quickly outside. Lainey follows me. I take a few steps away from the front door and swing around. 'And frankly, Lainey, that's none of your goddamn business.'

Her face crumples like a ball of tin foil, her eyes filling with angry tears. 'You bitch! You're disgusting. I bet you lured him to your house, filled him full of drink, and then threw yourself at him.'

I give a wry laugh. Now she's gone too far. 'Excuse me, Lainey high horse Anderson, Ed appeared at my place, not the other way around. With a bottle of vodka, a carton of cranberry juice and plastic cups I may add. It was clearly premeditated and I was pretty shocked to see him. And everything that happened after that is between me and Ed. But he sure as hell wasn't feeling *guilty* by the end of the evening. In fact I believe he rather enjoyed himself.'

Lainey's hand shoots up and slaps me across the face. Then she instantly bursts into tears.

'Jesus, Lainey. That hurt.' I rub my stinging cheek. I look at her. She's a mess, her carefully applied mascara streaming down her face, her nose running. I start to feel a little sorry for her. She's never been good under stress and even I know weddings are hell to organize. I soften a little.

'I'm sorry, I shouldn't have said that,' I say. 'Look, if it puts your mind at rest, of course I didn't sleep with him, OK? I wouldn't do that. We just talked.' I don't mention the kiss. Right now I just want to calm her down and get rid of her so I can ring Ed and ask him what the hell he's playing at, landing me in it like this.

'You hate me, don't you?' She gives a loud sniff and wipes her face on her shirt sleeve.

I consider this for a moment. 'Yes,' I say honestly.

She looks crestfallen. 'I thought it would all blow over, that you'd be annoyed with me for a few weeks, then we could be friends again.' She stares down at her sleeve, then starts playing with the small cuff button, twisting it in her fingers.

I stare at her. 'Did you honestly believe that?'

She nods wordlessly.

I sigh. 'Lainey, I came back from New Zealand to spend Christmas with Ed. He broke up with me on the way home from the airport. I cried for three whole days on your shoulder. You said it was for the best, that we'd both changed too much for it to work out, remember?'

She nods again. 'Which was true.'

I don't agree with her, but I let it go. 'In March you asked me how I'd feel if Ed was seeing someone else. And what did I say?'

'That you'd be fine.'

'No, I said it would kill me, but I'd survive.'

She gives me a tiny smile. 'I thought that was just the usual Schuster exaggeration.'

'Lainey, I didn't expect that someone else to be my best friend. You'd been seeing Ed behind my back for months at that stage. Months!'

Lainey straightens up a little. 'Ed wanted to break up with you in person, he said it was only right. We didn't sleep together until after Christmas out of respect for you.'

I look at her. '*Respect*? You don't get it, do you? I *loved* Ed. We were together for five years. All that time you were just waiting in the wings, hoping eventually he'd notice you. Every time we went out for dinner or to the cinema, up you'd pop, asking was it OK to play gooseberry, when all along you were just waiting to stab me in the back like Brutus.'

Her face falls. 'It wasn't like that. Yes, I've always liked Ed, but we only fell in love while you were in New Zealand. We never meant to hurt you.'

I look her in the eye. 'But why didn't you have the guts to tell me the minute it happened?'

She refuses to meet my gaze, stares down at the ground. 'Because I know you, Jules.'

'What's that supposed to mean?' I demand.

She lifts her eyes. 'You're so territorial. You'd have warned me to keep away from him.'

'Too right. He was my boyfriend for God's sake. What, you think I should have said, "Go right ahead, help yourself. He's only the love of my life. Rip my heart out why don't you?"'

She winces. 'No. But you guys were always arguing. And you both had so many flings,' she falters, 'I just thought . . . that it wasn't serious.'

'I lived for Ed. You of all people know that.'

'You didn't really,' she says, her voice rising a notch. 'If you really cared about him you wouldn't have gone away so much. Ed needs stability, and he needs to be the centre of someone's universe. He was never the centre of yours, Jules, not properly. You've always kept part of yourself back, even with me. Maybe it's a survival mechanism, I don't know.'

I'm about to strongly disagree with her when I stop and think about this for a second. Maybe I do keep something back, but doesn't everyone?

'I couldn't have told you, Jules, honestly,' she continues. 'You would have made me choose between you and Ed. I couldn't bear that. You both mean the world to me.'

I meet her eye. 'Tell me the truth. If you had told me, and I had made you choose between us – me or Ed – who would you have picked?'

She pulls her eyes away, saying nothing. But from the guilty look on her face, I already know the answer.

I sigh, feeling numb and hollow inside. I'd always suspected it, but knowing for a fact that Lainey blatantly chose Ed over me, and doesn't even have the decency to deny it to my face, it's too much to absorb right now. But in her shoes, what would I have done? I like to think I'd have chosen my best friend over a boy, any boy, but maybe not. Where Ed's concerned, my judgement has always been poor.

'That's what I thought,' I say. 'Lainey, I'll be at your wedding, my head held high. I will watch you and Ed exchange your vows, I will sit and eat your wedding breakfast and make polite conversation about how beautiful you look. I will pretend to smile during the speeches when Ed says how much he loves you, and your dad says how perfect you are for each other. And once the meal is over I'll stand up, make my excuses and leave. And from that moment on, I want nothing more to do with you or Ed Powers. That chapter of all our lives will be firmly closed. Do you understand?'

'You're coming?' Her face lifts.

My heart sinks. She hasn't been listening to a word I've said, or maybe she just doesn't care. 'Yes. And after your wedding, you will both be dead to me.'

She laughs nervously. 'You're being melodramatic again.'

'I'm serious, Lainey. Tell me you understand.'

She nods, her eyes filling with tears again. 'Yes, I get it.'

I shrug, blowing out my breath in a whoosh. 'Then there's nothing more to say I guess.'

'Jules?' She looks at me, a funny expression on her face. 'Don't ruin everything. I know he's nervous about the wedding. Please don't talk him out of it or take him away from me, not now. We both know you can. If you really do still love him, let him go. And for the record, I'm sorry.' And with that she turns away quickly and powers down the street, leaving me staring at her back.

I know I should run after her, tell her she's wrong, that it's her he loves, not me. That if she really feels that his heart isn't in it, she shouldn't be marrying him at all. That Ed isn't good enough for her, never will be. But I can't. It's too hard to articulate and I don't have the energy. So instead I stand there, watching my best friend walk out of my life for good.

That night, after telling Pandora and Bird I'm exhausted and going to bed early, I sneak a bottle of wine up the stairs and into my bedroom. I close the door firmly behind me, pull my chair over to the window and sit there, staring out at the tree house, my mind whirring, bottle by my feet. I know I shouldn't be drinking, but it's an emergency. I can't stop thinking about Lainey and Ed, Ed and Lainey, plus, as I was reminded of him earlier, Noel feckin' Hegarty, and it's doing my head in. I need something to numb the pain.

Straight after Lainey's visit to the shop, I rang Ed in a temper, couldn't wait to give him a piece of my mind for landing me in it with his beloved fiancée, but it went straight to messages. Then I rang his work number, again no answer. Finally I tried Clara's line, but she said he was out of the office and to try his mobile.

'How are you holding up?' she then asked kindly. 'I know the wedding's soon.'

'I'm fine,' I lied. 'Keeping busy.'

'Good for you. Look, about the other night, did you get home OK? I'm so sorry I had to run off like that; babysitter hates me being too late, you know how it is.'

'Actually, Clara, I don't know if Ed said anything but—' I was about to tell her about Noel, not caring what Ed thought right at that second, when I heard Noel's voice in the background, barking an order directly at Clara. My insides tumbled and I felt sick.

'Sorry, better run,' Clara said in a small voice. And then the phone cut out. I considered ringing her back, but then thought against it. I didn't want to put her in an awkward position and in retrospect it's probably best to keep it to myself, to try and forget about the whole bloody Noel thing.

After a moment, ignoring the voice of reason in my head telling me not to, I pull my iPhone out of my pocket again and click into Ed's Facebook page. I still haven't de-friended him. Even though I've certainly meant to, something has always held me back. It just seems so final, the last nail in the coffin. Lainey doesn't have a page, says it's not for her, she has issues with the privacy risks, which in the circumstances is probably just as well. One less page I can stalk.

I flick through Ed's photo albums and find recent pictures of himself and Lainey. Ed's arm is flung easily across Lainey's shoulders and both are beaming at the camera, in the background the Eiffel Tower is stark black against the sunny blue sky. Tears sting my eyes and I blink them back.

I reach down and look at the label on the bottle of wine. A Chablis from Burgundy. Of course it had to be bloody French, but it was one of the few screw-top bottles to hand. I open it, take a swig, then go back to torturing myself with Ed and Lainey's smiley, happy holiday snaps.

Chapter 16

By Thursday evening I'm exhausted. Shoestring was hopping today and we had minor press excitement when a film crew from RTÉ swooped on the shop to film Asha Bhandari standing in our window for the six o'clock news. She'd spotted the papier mâché elephants while she was walking back to the hotel from her Monkstown Book Festival reading, came in to have a look around, and ended up buying a red cashmere cardigan from Bird.

Asha adored our elephant window. Clapped her hands together and gave a shriek of delight as soon as she realized the whole tableau was based on her book cover.

'How adorable,' she'd said in her distinctive, rich voice. 'I must put a photo up on my website. Sophie, would you mind?' She waved her hand at a girl in a very short skirt who was lingering behind her, watching everything.

The girl looked at her a little blankly.

Asha smiled at her. 'Take a photograph of the window, would you please?'

Asha leaned towards me and Bird. 'Such posh twits, some of these PR girls. Sweet though.'

I thought it was a little unfair, Sophie seemed nice, but Bird chuckled. 'Can I offer you some coffee? It's nice and strong.'

'Why thank you,' Asha said. 'That sounds wonderful. And won't you join me? I'd love to hear all about Monkstown. No one seems to be able to tell me much about the area's past.'

Bird's face lit up. She knows a lot of local history and loves an audience.

While Bird and Asha had a good old chin wag in the coffee shop, Sophie rang RTÉ, told them about the window and set up an interview. Luckily the news crew were in the area and agreed to do a short piece. Not such a twit after all.

Forty minutes later, Bird, Pandora and I are watching the filming from the sidelines. Pandora is jumpy with excitement.

'RTÉ,' she keeps saying. 'The shop's going to be on national television. I knew that elephant window was a great idea.'

I give a cough.

'Well done, Jules,' she adds quickly. 'You put a lot of work into it and this telly thing is a real coup for Shoestring. I checked the till receipts earlier; things are looking up. Maybe we're finally turning a corner.'

The sound man from the film crew shushes us and we listen to Asha talk about the role elephants play in her book.

'When I was a little girl in Siju,' she says, 'our neighbour was a mahout. Used to allow me and my sisters to visit his elephants whenever we wished. To this day, I've always loved the animals, so majestic. In my novel, the main character, Alisha, a widow with useless sons, knows that she is dying. She decides to make an epic journey from Calcutta to the Garo Hills on the back of her elephant, Jasmin, to visit her beloved sister and to die in the tiny village where she grew up helping her father, also a mahout like my neighbour. And to allow Jasmin to die among her own elephant family.'

Afterwards, Bird says, 'What's Asha's book called again? Sounds fascinating. Must get it for your father.' Bird will only read history and biographies, says real life is a lot more interesting than fiction.

'*The Journey*,' I tell her, wondering if Arietty likes novels. If she does, I'm sure she'd love Asha's book too.

'I'm definitely going to read it,' Pandora says.

Bird and I exchange a look. Pandora already has a row of books as long as her arm beside her bed that she's bought but still hasn't got around to reading yet. She and Dad are the bookworms in the family, and it seems to have rubbed off on Iris too.

I watch the cameraman taking a few final shots of Asha and then something occurs to me. 'We should get our own photo of Asha in the window before she climbs out, Pandora. For the website. And why don't you get her to sign the wall behind the till? Like you see in restaurants sometimes. We can hang her photo over the signature. Our own wall of fame. I'm sure that Sissy creature would do it for you too, she's such an attention seeker.'

Pandora looks at me. 'Clever idea, Jules. I like it. And I appreciate everything you've done to make the shop look so great.'

'Thank you.' I smile at her. It looks like I'm on a Shoestring roll.

Pandora's in such a good mood that even though I'm supposed to be covering the shop until eight this evening – Thursday is late night opening – she gives me the evening off. Dad has offered to mind Iris, so she's going to cover the shop herself, with Lenka's help if it gets busy. So I've called a Shoestring Club meeting with Arietty and asked Jamie to tag along to explain his new man list. It will help keep my mind off Lainey and, more critically, Ed.

I'm still livid with him, I've been ringing his mobile several times an hour, but still no reply. And since Lainey's visit, I keep looking up from the till, expecting to see her glaring at me, after finding out about the kiss. I wouldn't put it past Ed to come clean; he has an evil streak sometimes and he might use it to upset her or slap her down. And *this* is the man I'm holding a torch for? Really? I'm deranged. Dad and Iris have taken over the living room to watch *The Simpsons* (they're both huge fans), so we convene in the kitchen.

As soon as we are sitting, Jamie pulls a plastic folder out of his bag and slaps it down on the table.

'Right, girls,' he says. 'I've taken Jules's list into consideration and this is the best you're going to get. Single men in the right age bracket, who live locally, and who have downloaded music or rented movies in the last month.'

I smile at him and then at Arietty. 'And I spoke to Pandora this afternoon. She's agreed in theory to a mother and son night on Friday next.'

They both gawk at me.

'A mother and son night?' Jamie asks. 'Are you serious?'

I chuckle. 'I know, it's a bit left of centre, but Pandora swallowed it, and that's all that matters. Hester gave me the idea. She's one of our new regulars. She was chatting to me about her son, Declan. She was in a bit of a state. Apparently he was sharing the family home with his ex-wife but she decided she wanted rid of him, so she changed the locks and the alarm code. Locked him out of his own house. So now he's staying with his mother.'

'God love the man,' Jamie murmurs.

'Anyway,' I continue, 'Hester said she wished he'd go out more, that his social life was terrible and what with work and taking his daughter every weekend, he'd never meet anyone. So as you can imagine, my mind went into overdrive and I told her we were thinking of having some sort of evening for customers in the shop, with things for the guys to do while the women shopped, and she was all for it and asked could we make it mothers and sons so her Declan wouldn't feel out of place. Said she'd invite all her Mothers' Union and bridge friends, that loads of them had sons. So that's basically our cover.'

Jamie doesn't look convinced. 'And Pandora really swallowed it?'

I nod enthusiastically. 'I got Hester to talk her round. She's pretty persuasive.'

Jamie gulps. 'Hope Mum doesn't get it into her head—'

I laugh, no wonder he's looking rather uncomfortable. 'She's way ahead of you. Once Bird rang her, Daphne was already picking out her dress. Irish mammies and their sons, it's a shopping match made in heaven. Your idea, Jamie, 80s gaming night for boys, complete with free beer and food.'

He swears under his breath. 'I don't remember saying anything about mothers.'

Arietty grins. 'The place is going to be crawling with single men and older ladies. I love it. It'll be like *Cougar Town*.'

I pretend to gag. 'Euw, please. Hester's about sixty.'

'And that's my mother you're talking about,' Jamie reminds her.

'It happens,' Arietty says simply. 'Although they shouldn't call the women cougars. Real cougars reach sexual maturity at two, not when they're older. And the females are far more interested in eating than mating. Most of them only live six or eight years in the wild. Using the term is nonsense, an insult to the animal kingdom.'

Jamie and I exchange an amused look.

'Quite right, Arietty,' I say, trying not to smile. 'And it looks like with Hester's help, and Jamie's list, all systems are go. If Pandora doesn't score, there's something seriously wrong with her. You might find someone too, Jamie.' I wiggle my eyebrows at him. 'You'd make some old dear a fabulous toy boy.'

He just glares at me.

'You too, Arietty,' I add. 'Once Pandora's taken her pick, the hand-selected single men of south county Dublin are all yours. It'll be like shooting fish in a barrel.'

She wrinkles up her nose. 'No thanks. No offence, Jamie, but most men are complete eejits. My stepdad's all right, but my own dad was a complete waster. Ran off with one of Mum's friends when I was seven. Na, I'm better off on my own.'

I don't know what to say to that and Jamie looks taken aback and a bit uncomfortable, so I keep my mouth shut and flick through Jamie's list, focusing on some of the details. After a few seconds I look up at him.

'This is amazing, Jamie. How on earth—'

He puts both his hands up. 'Don't ask. Honestly. You don't want to know. But I've marked the ten most likely candidates on the final sheet with the movies they've rented and music they've bought. But for God's sake, burn this list after you've studied it and not a word to Pandora or Bird, or my mum will hear about it and probably throw me out on my ear.'

Arietty flicks through the list, her eyes getting wider and wider. 'You can pull this kind off information off the internet? That's terrifying.'

Jamie shrugs. 'It's all there if you know where to look.'

Arietty is staring at Jamie. He goes to take the pages out of her hands. 'I'll happily take it back if you're uncomfortable—'

'No!' I snatch the pages away from Arietty and hold them against my chest. 'Don't you dare. We really appreciate all your work, don't we, Arietty?'

She's still looking at him rather suspiciously. 'I suppose. As long as we don't all get arrested.'

'We won't,' I say firmly. 'Now let's get down to business.' I put the pages back down on the table and flick to the final sheet.

'Number one in Jamie's top ten is Simon Patterson. He's twenty-eight and here are his most recent rentals: *Saw, The Evil Dead, House of 1,000 Corpses*.'

Arietty sits back in her chair and folds her arms stiffly. 'Too violent.'

'And Pandora likes action adventure films,' I put in. 'Not horror.'

'What music is this Simon guy into?' she asks.

I read out the list. 'White Zombie, Goatsnake and Hellhammer.'

Arietty lifts her eyebrows. 'See what I mean?'

I cross out his name. 'Moving swiftly on to number two.

Bryan McAllister, twenty-six. *The Matrix, The Fifth Element*, and *The Empire Strikes Back*. Sounds more like it. Also rented three *Top Gear* boxed sets last weekend.'

She wrinkles up her face. 'Top Gear? Too boring. And three sets over one weekend? Doesn't the man have a life?' Arietty unclips her hair, twists it in both her hands, and then clips it up again. 'Bet he likes Phil Collins too. Next!'

'Lee Devaney. Thirty-one. *Indiana Jones and the Temple of Doom*—'

Jamie clears his throat and we both look at him.

'Yes?' I say.

'For feck's sake, you'll be here all night. Just throw them all in a room with the Mothers' Union sons and let Pandora pick one for herself. What if they're renting films for someone else? What if the card's in their name but their sister or brother is using it?'

I glare at him. 'It's *your* list.'

'And as I keep saying, it's not reliable,' he says. 'You're wasting your time, and it's a beautiful evening. I for one would much rather be sitting outside Finnegan's. It's probably the last night we'll be able to do it all year. Anyone for a pint?'

'I'm driving,' Arietty says, 'but I'll join you for a Coke.'

My heart gives a little hop, then I remember I'm not supposed to be drinking and I've already broken that promise this week as it is. But Jamie's right, it's such a nice evening and I'll kill for a drink. I'll just have the one, then I'll Coke it, like Arietty.

'How many are on your list in total?' I ask.

'Over three hundred.'

I whistle. 'I get your point. Finnegan's it is.' Then I smile at him, feeling stupidly excited. It's only the local.

'Who the hell?' I hear Pandora muttering as she swings open the door. She stares at me. 'Jules, it's nearly one. What are you playing at? Where are your keys? You're lucky it's me and not Bird or Dad.'

'Sorry.' I hiccup loudly, then put my hand over my mouth. 'Oops, sorry.' Then I hiccup again and collapse into giggles.

'Have you been drinking?'

'Noooooooooo.' I can't stop giggling.

Pandora isn't amused. 'You promised Bird.'

''s Jamie's fault. He kept buying me pints.' More hiccups.

'Oh for God's sake, just come inside and go to bed. You're supposed to be working in the morning.'

'Work, smirk.' I go to pat her arm, but miss and end up lurching forwards and whacking my hand off the door frame. It should hurt but strangely it doesn't, just throbs a little dully. 'Oww!' I rub it.

'Shush,' she hisses.

I walk inside, trying not to wobble too much. Pandora wraps her arms around her body and shivers, then closes the front door behind us. 'You'll wake Iris and Bird.' Dad's such a heavy sleeper nothing would wake him. 'Although I've a good mind to make Bird come down here and see the state you're in.'

'Please don't. It won't happen again. I promise. I'll be a really, really, really good girl. No more booze. Cross my heart and hope to die, stick a needle in—'

She cuts me off. 'Fine. But one more relapse and I'm going to have to tell her. Understand?'

'You're the best sis in the whole entire universe.' I go to hug her but she steps away and I end up stumbling into the hall table and sending the keys rattling in the bowl.

We both stand still for a second, listening, but no one stirs.

Pandora sighs. 'I'd better help you up the stairs. Don't want any more drink accidents in this house.'

'Thanks, Panda Bear.' I try resting my head against her shoulder, but instead manage to fall against her side, almost sending her flying. 'I looove you.'

She just shakes her head. 'Jules, I love you too. But boy, do you stink of booze. Better sleep it off now. Come on, sis, I'll help you.'

She puts her arm around my waist. I trip over my own feet. 'Easy now,' she says. 'What am I going to do with you, Boolie?'

Chapter 17

Pandora stands at the door of Shoestring and stares at the dozens of unaccompanied men streaming into the shop. They're heading straight towards the outside courtyard where Klaudia and Lenka are flipping burgers. Pandora wasn't keen at first, said the clothes would stink of barbequed meat for days, but Bird managed to persuade her; she's very partial to burgers. Bird hasn't said anything yet, but I think she's sussed the whole event is a ruse.

'Jules, this is supposed to be a mother and son night,' Pandora says. 'Where are all the mothers exactly?' She stares at me and I can feel my cheeks heating up.

'Cooee, Julia!' Hester is weaving her way through the crowd, followed by a sheepish looking man in a dark-blue shirt and jeans. This must be her son, Declan. She may just have saved my skin.

Hester stands in front of us, beaming. 'Lovely to see you, darlings. Isn't this a super idea?' She turns to the man. 'This is Julia, Declan, the one I've been telling you about. And her sister, Pandora. She's single too, aren't you, Julia?'

'Um, yes.' My face starts to burn again.

Declan looks equally mortified. He sticks out his hand politely.

'Hiya, Julia, Pandora. Sorry about my mother. Ignore her.'

We take turns to shake his hand while Hester tut-tuts. 'Don't be silly, Declan, you have to be proactive about these things.

Now I'm sure you two young people will have lots to talk about. I need Pandora's style advice, urgently.' With that she grabs Pandora's arm and drags her away.

Declan and I stand there, staring at each other. He's in his late-thirties, tall, at least six foot, with warm hazel eyes and dark-brown hair, receding a little at the temples. But I feel exactly . . . nada. Not a zing in sight.

'So your mum dragged you along to find a date?' I say, then give a laugh. 'I guess she's not the kind of person you say no to.'

He smiles, but it doesn't reach his eyes which look flat and tired. 'No kidding. She insisted I meet you. No offence, but what age are you – twenty?'

'Twenty-four.'

He sucks his teeth. 'Twenty-four, right. And look at you.' He waves his hand up and down.

I check I haven't done something stupid like tuck my skirt into my knickers, but no, all seems fine, my white cotton dress is still intact and I haven't caught the amazingly soft Rick Owens leather jacket on anything yet. Pandora only let me borrow it after swearing on the Farenze (still hanging on the hold rail in the office) I'd take care of it. She also made me swear I wouldn't drink and make an eejit of myself this evening. Charming.

He sighs deeply. 'Way out of my league.'

'Thanks,' I say, rather delighted with myself. For a thirty-something divorcee with kids, he isn't bad. I look at him again, trying to focus on the good bits, the lovely eyes complete with the George Clooney crinkles at the edges, the strong, square chin; but no, still nothing. Maybe if I was Pandora's age – twenty-nine – and starting to worry about being left on the shelf I'd give him a go, screw my eyes tightly shut when I was snogging him or something, but I'm not that desperate, not yet.

Hang on a sec. I look him up and down again. She likes clean cut men, maybe he'd do for Pandora.

'Would you like to meet someone?' I ask him, cutting straight to the chase.

He grimaces. 'Absolutely not. I'm only here because Mum insisted. I'm all over the place at the moment. What with my marriage combusting and everything I'm—' He stops abruptly, then sighs. 'I'm sorry, I don't even know you. It's just so—' He gulps and tears spring to his eyes. 'Forgive me. I'd better go.' He goes to walk towards the door but I put my hand on his arm.

'I'm always having inappropriate meltdowns. It's good to see I'm not the only basket case in Dublin.' I smile reassuringly at him.

He nods and smiles back. 'Thanks. I think.'

'Stay for a bit,' I say. 'Have something to eat. Or what about a beer? Will you join me?'

'Sure. Why not?' he agrees.

I know I promised Pandora, but I feel sorry for Declan, he seems nice and it can't be easy being touted about by your mother like a secondhand car she's trying to flog, however well meaning. And one drink is hardly a big deal.

We weave our way towards the table laden with a new designer beer called Cirus, sponsored by the local off licence (more sweet talking from Pandora), grab two long-necked bottles and clink them together.

'Cheers,' I say, taking a glug. It's actually pretty good and I take another, then another mouthful.

'Thirsty?' Declan lifts an eyebrow.

'Too right.' I grab two more bottles from the table and then we head towards the wall, away from the men crowded around the old-fashioned, coffee-table-style Pac-Man console we'd rented for the night, and the Stretch Armstrong dolls I'd found on the internet.

'Great idea for an event, an 80s gaming night,' Declan says as we watch two burly looking Polish guys pull a doll's arms into a thin rubbery worm. They've already tried chatting up Klaudia and Lenka unsuccessfully; both have Irish boyfriends, claim they're much more romantic than their Eastern European counterparts, which makes me seriously worry about Slovakian men.

'Thanks, but Pandora's not going to be too pleased unless we start selling some clothes.' There are some older women checking out the rails, probably Hester's friends, but no one seems to have made it to the cash desk as I can't see anyone holding a Shoestring bag.

I scan the crowd for my sister. She's outside the changing rooms, talking to Hester and two other ladies. Damn, she's supposed to be chatting to all the single men, not fraternizing with the old folk. And where are Arietty and Jamie? They promised they'd be here to give me moral support. Daphne has cried off sick, much to Jamie's relief.

'Look,' Declan says, 'you don't need to talk to me, honestly. I'm OK here on my own. I'll finish my beer then slip away,'

'It's fine, truly.' I'm quite enjoying standing here, watching the action, sipping my second Cirus which is going down rather nicely. 'It'll keep Hester off your back. And you can't leave now, you'll miss the karaoke.'

He puts a hand over his face. 'Don't let my mother near it, I beg you. She's dangerous with a microphone.'

I laugh. 'Wait till you hear my sister, dangerous doesn't cover it.'

Jamie arrives just after eight, but there's still no sign of Arietty. I'm standing to one side of the karaoke machine, watching Pandora set it up. There's already a crowd building in front of the screen, Hester and some of her friends, a gang of Polish lads in tight white T-shirts, and two Italian students I met earlier at the drinks table. The Irish men are predictably enough still hovering around the food and beer and playing the arcade games.

'Where were you?' I ask Jamie a little crossly.

'The Shoestring website crashed. But don't say anything to

Pandora or Bird, it's back up now and I don't want to worry them.' He looks around. 'Where's Arietty?'

I smile knowingly.

He frowns. 'Jules! It's not like that.'

'Of course not. Why on earth would you be interested in a beautiful, funny, single girl like Arietty?'

He ignores me. Declan appears beside me, hands me another beer.

'Thanks, Dec.' We're on nickname terms now. He's actually a lovely guy: architect, devoted to his daughter, Rachel. He told me about the whole marriage breakup thing and it's pretty tragic. His ex-wife sounds like a right cow. After watching *Eat, Pray, Love,* she decided she wanted to 'find herself', signed up for some yoga classes and was soon doing rather more than downward-facing dog with her male yoga teacher.

Declan and I clink bottles. 'Bottoms up,' I say, and take a long sip. ''s really good grog.'

I wipe my mouth with the back of my hand. 'Oh and this is my friend, Jamie.' Then I hiccup and giggle. 'Sorry. It's the bubbles.'

'Hi, Jamie,' Declan says and holds out his hand. 'Nice to meet you. I'm Declan.'

'Hi.' Jamie shakes it but he doesn't look amused. He rounds on me as soon as he's let go of Declan's palm. 'Jules, how much have you had to drink?'

I hiccup again. 'Oops. Lighten up, it's a party.'

'You're supposed to be working.' He lowers his voice. 'Finding a man for Pandora, remember?'

'Panda bear, smanda bear. It's fine. There are dozens of single men in here, she's bound to meet someone.'

Declan looks at me. 'Pandora's single?'

I nod. 'Single as a bull elephant.'

'Excuse me?' He looks confused.

I laugh. 'Where's Arietty when you need her? Male elephants are loners. But the more sociable ones do join bachelor herds sometimes. The others wander lonely as a cloud, that floats on high o'er vales and hills.'

'What are you on about?' Jamie asks.

'Wordsworth.' It was one of Mum's favourites. She used to recite poetry in the car. Sounds odd I know, but we got so used to it that it seemed completely normal.

Jamie shakes his head, but Declan smiles at me.

'A poetry fan, eh?' Declan says. 'Would never have guessed.'

We're distracted by Pandora on the microphone.

'Testing, testing, one, two, three,' she says, sounding rather serious.

'Panda in the house,' I shout. 'Whoo, whoo!' I punch my closed fist in the air and then stagger sideways a little, bumping into Jamie.

'Are you sure you're OK, Jules?' He leans towards my ear and asks me in a low voice, 'And why are you hanging out with that old guy?'

'Dec's not old. And I'm absolutely perfect thank you very much. Get yourself a beer, you seem very tense.'

'I'd like to welcome you all to our very first mother and son night at Shoestring,' Pandora says.

Most of the men look at each other in confusion. It's hardly how it was pitched to them. But luckily no one says anything.

'Would anyone like to kick off the karaoke?' Pandora asks.

Hester waves her hand in the air. 'I will, dear. My son and I will do a duet. Come along, Declan.' She shuffles through the crowd towards us.

Declan swears under his breath. He looks around for an escape exit, but Hester's too quick for him. Within seconds she's standing in front of him. 'There you are, pet. Don't make your old mother drag you to the microphone.'

Declan hands me his bottle. 'Better get this over with quickly. Pray for me.' I laugh.

As they set up their song with Pandora, Jamie grabs my bottle of beer and slugs it down.

'Hey! You'll get my cooties,' I say. 'And what has you in such a bad mood? Missing Arietty, is that it?'

'Jules, you really—' But he's interrupted by the opening bars of 'Something Stupid Like I Love You'.

'I like this one,' I say. 'Poor Declan. He looks mortified, doesn't he?'

Jamie says nothing. He really is in a grump this evening.

Hester starts singing, her voice warbling a little like an opera singer. She turns towards Declan, a look of pure love on her face.

'So sweet,' I say, my eyes glued to Hester and Declan.

Again, Jamie says nothing.

Then Declan starts to join in, his voice surprisingly strong and Sinatra-smooth. Everyone starts cheering and clapping like it's the *X Factor*.

'He's amazing,' I say.

Jamie shrugs. 'I guess.'

When the song ends, Pandora claps enthusiastically and immediately sets up another song.

'Fantastic, Hester,' she says. 'And do you know this one?' The opening bars of 'I've Got You, Babe' ring out.

Hester smiles. 'No, but I'm sure Declan does. I'm sorry, I didn't introduce you two properly earlier. Declan this is Pandora; Pandora, Declan, my son.'

Pandora and Declan smile at each other and once again Declan sticks out his hand for Pandora to shake.

'Why don't you join him instead, dear?' Hester adds. 'He loves a good sing-song.'

Declan rolls his eyes at Pandora and she laughs.

'You really don't have to,' Declan tells her.

'No, I'd be happy to,' Pandora says. 'When they hear how bad I am, it'll encourage other people to give it a go. I'll set the song up again.'

Jamie digs me in the ribs. 'Hear that. Your man likes singing. He's ideal for Pandora. Where did you get him? He looks too old for my list.'

'The lady he was just singing with, Hester, she's one of our customers. Declan is her son.'

'Single?'

'Separated. But still pretty cut up about it.'

'You sure?' He gestures at Declan. Pandora has just started singing and Declan is smiling at her, clearly impressed. She does have a beautiful voice, clear and bell-like. When it comes to Declan's line, he sings the lyrics as if he truly means every word and Pandora is the centre of his universe. Pandora starts to blush – and it takes a lot to make my sister pink up. Jamie's right, it certainly looks like some sort of spark has been ignited.

Arietty appears beside us in her work boots and zoo uniform, reeking of elephant. 'I'm so sorry, Beatrix was having a really bad day and I couldn't leave until she settled. Did it work? Has Pandora found anyone yet?'

'Apparently so. Look!' I point at Pandora and grin.

I shoo Pandora out the door at nine. She wants to stay and help tidy up, but Declan has invited her to join him for a bite to eat and I'm trying to persuade her to accept. They've been chatting away like old friends in-between their multiple karaoke stints – together and solo – and she seems to genuinely like him. Dad is at home with Iris, so she doesn't have to worry about rushing back.

'Are you positive it's OK to run off, Jules?' she says, lingering in the doorway and peering at the boxes of empty beer bottles Declan and Jamie have lifted towards the front of the shop.

'Yes. Dec seems like a really nice bloke. Have fun.' I wiggle my eyebrows at her.

'It's not like that,' she insists. 'He just wants to say thank you for the karaoke and everything. See, not all karaoke fans are complete nerds, Jules.' She brushes her hair off her face and smiles at me. Her hair is a mess, most of her red lipstick has worn off and she's kicked off her heels in favour of ballet flats, but I haven't seen her looking happier or prettier in a long time.

'Enjoy yourself, sis,' I say. 'You deserve it.'

'Thanks, Jules. But I feel bad leaving you to tidy up.'

'Get out of here,' I say and swat my hand at her. Then I wave at Declan who is waiting patiently in a taxi at the far side of the road. Hester left earlier, delighted with 'her' matchmaking. If she only knew!

I go back inside and start clearing the bottles from the Pac-Man console. I've gifted the Stretch Armstrongs to the Polish lads, who were thrilled, said pulling the arms was a lot more fun than lifting weights.

'I'd better get going,' Arietty says. 'Sorry I can't stay and help. I want to get into work early. I'm worried about Beatrix.'

'Me too,' Jamie says.

I grin at him. 'You're worried about an elephant?'

'What? No! I mean I have to work tomorrow, and tonight in fact. I need to sort out the errant Shoestring website before people start trying to order things.'

I pretend to sob into my hands. 'I'm being abandoned. Tragic. So tragic. But looking on the bright side, there's a good chance our plan worked. Plus we now have a partner in crime – Hester. I bet she could convince Declan to take Pandora to a fancy dinner or something. Mwah-ha-ha-ha.' I give an evil laugh and rub my hands together. 'Our plan for world domination is coming together nicely.'

'What plan?' Bird says, appearing at my side with a mop in her hand. 'And I want words with you, Jules. In private if you don't mind.' She looks sharply at Jamie and Arietty.

'Sorry folks,' I wave my fingers at them. 'Granny Shu has spoken. Talk to you both tomorrow.'

'Would you mind if I had a quick look at your computer system while I'm here, Bird?' Jamie asks. 'There's a glitch I'm trying to sort out. Might be a network problem. Nothing to worry about, but I'd like to get it sorted before tomorrow morning.'

She nods. 'Of course, Jamie.'

Once Jamie has disappeared into the office and Arietty has left, I ask Bird, 'So Granny Shu, what's eating you?' grinning to myself at my Seussian rhyme.

Her eyes are flinty. 'Are you drunk, young lady?'

'No! 'Course not. I had a couple of beers with my old mate, Dec. Just to keep him company you understand. And hey, isn't it cool? Declan and Pandora I mean. Aren't they just the most adorable couple? Did you catch their version of 'Summer Nights'? Declan's *wella, wella, wella, uh* bit was hilarious.'

But her expression hasn't changed. 'I was watching you. You had at least six bottles of beer. And you promised, Julia.'

My cheeks flare up. Damn it. I hadn't realized Bird was spying on me. 'It was a party. The beer was there and I—'

'Plus you were supposed to be working, not pouring beer down your gullet. I'm not impressed. In fact I have a good mind to drag you back to Sheila.'

'I had a blip, as I said, the beer was there—'

Bird cuts me off. 'You keep saying that – the beer was there – but you can't drink just because the opportunity arises. You have to learn to abstain sometimes. You say you don't have a drinking problem, darling, but at this stage you need to prove it by keeping away from alcohol. I thought that's what we'd agreed.'

'I'm sorry, with all the karaoke and meeting Declan and everything, I got carried away. He kept fetching me drinks and I didn't want to be rude. I was only keeping him company, honestly. I didn't *need* a drink.' I say this a little louder than I'd intended.

'Then why are your eyes shifting all over the shop, darling?' she asks.

'They're not.' I meet her gaze and hold it. 'I just fancied a beer, that's all. And I'm not drunk, honestly.'

'That's also worrying. After six beers, you should be.'

'Bird, please. You're blowing this all out of proportion. I'm working hard aren't I? I haven't been late for ages. And I'm getting on well with Pandora.'

She sighs. 'I suppose. OK, Julia, I'll give you one more chance, but blow it and you're straight back to Sheila, understand?'

I feel a hiccup coming on so I swallow it down and turn it into a cough instead. 'Yes, I do, honestly.'

She studies my face. 'I have to tell you, darling, I'm not one hundred per cent convinced. Don't make a fool out of me.' Finally she hands me the mop. 'The floor's horribly sticky from all the beer spills. And as part of your penance, you can wash it.'

Chapter 18

After a few days of a hawk-eyed Bird following me around at work and at home – making sure I'm not up to any mischief, banishing open wine bottles from the fridge and forcing Dad to finally cancel Mum's wine club subscription – things start to settle down, until Wednesday morning when Pandora puts the shop phone down in a complete flap.

'Jules, help! Declan's just asked me to a charity ball. On Saturday night. And I have nothing to wear.'

I smile at her, as all the pieces start clicking into place. I try not to look too smug as I say, 'Remember that Farenze dress, Pandora? I have something to tell you . . .'

Once Pandora got over the initial shock, she took the dress time-sharing idea surprisingly well, especially now it means she has something to wear for the charity ball. Hester and her husband were supposed to be going, but Hester's arthritis is acting up apparently, so she gifted her tickets to Declan and insisted he invited Pandora along as his guest. Good old Hester. Clearly on the same wavelength as Bird and Daphne – matchmaking schemers the lot of them. Compared to them, I'm a rank amateur.

Bird and Daphne are off to a flower-arranging talk on Saturday night with the Mothers' Union (thrilling stuff), and Dad's at a poetry reading with one of his book clubs, so I'm on babysitting duty while Pandora turns Cinderella.

'Make sure Iris is in bed by eight,' Pandora tells me as she lingers in the hallway of Sorrento House, checking her hair in the age-spotted mirror. She's rolled it into a chignon and dotted it with sparkly silver clips, standing out like diamonds against her black locks. She pulls at the waist of the Farenze. 'Are you sure I look OK?' she asks nervously.

'Stop fretting. You're going to knock him dead, sis, honest.'

She asked me for some styling advice on Friday, and I borrowed a thick silver Lara Bohinc clench belt from the shop which emphasizes her neat waist, and teamed it with a vintage 1920s beaded bolero (another shop find), silver peep-toe shoes and an orange clutch bag to give the outfit a colour pop. She looks stunning.

'Like a princess, Mummy,' Iris adds. She can't take her eyes off Pandora. 'Would you like to wear my tiara?'

'That's so sweet, darling.' Pandora tickles her under the chin. 'But I'd hate to lose it.'

'I wouldn't mind. It's only a pretend one.' Iris dashes upstairs, holding up her nightie so she doesn't trip.

I laugh. 'Guess you're wearing a plastic tiara then.'

Pandora smiles. 'I'll pop it in my bag in the taxi. Speaking of which, I think I hear a car outside.' Her eyes twinkle. 'God, I'm so nervous. I haven't been on a date in yonks. Not with someone I actually like.'

'So you like Declan, huh?' I grin.

'Yes,' she says simply. 'And don't go saying anything stupid when he gets here, OK? Promise me.'

'As if. I'm hurt, truly hurt.'

'Then why are you smiling?'

I laugh and give her a hug, breathing in a mix of Chanel No. 5 and hair spray. 'Have a ball, Cinderella.'

'I'll try.'

There's a knock on the front door and I draw away. 'Must be Declan. I'll get it if you like.'

Pandora takes a deep breath. 'Thanks, Jules.'

Declan is standing there, looking equally nervous. I beam at him. 'You scrub up well. Black tie suits you.'

His tuxedo is perfectly cut, accentuating his wide shoulders and his shoes are so shiny and unscuffed they're clearly brand new.

'Hi, Jules.' He kisses me on the cheek. 'Good to see you. Is Pandora ready?'

'She certainly is. Come on in.' I stand back to let him step into the hall and as soon as he sees Pandora, he whistles.

'That dress is beautiful, Pandora. You look . . .' he sighs. 'I don't know how to describe it.'

'Like a princess,' Iris pipes up helpfully from halfway down the stairs. She runs down the remaining steps, slips a small hand into Pandora's and then presses herself against her mum's side. She's a little shy with strangers. Especially men. I'm surprised she's taken to Arietty so easily. Once I finally remembered to give Iris's picture to her, Arietty rang Iris on my mobile to say thank you, then brought it into work with her to show the other keepers and the elephants. It's now in pride of place on the no-ticeboard in the 'elephant kitchen' and Iris is thrilled to pieces. Arietty has promised to arrange another zoo visit for Iris soon. Animals and children seem to be Arietty's thing.

Declan smiles at her. 'And you must be Iris. Your mum has told me lots about you. I have a daughter a little bit older than you.'

'What's her name?' Iris asks.

'Rachel. She's ten.'

Iris's eyes light up. She loves 'big girls'. 'That's so cool. Can I meet her? You're mummy's new boyfriend, aren't you? So me and Rachel are kind of like sisters. I've always wanted a big sister.'

Pandora blushes deeply. 'Sorry, Declan, Iris gets a little car-ried away sometimes.'

But Declan doesn't look bothered. In fact, he's beaming at Iris. 'And Rach has always wanted a little sister. You could say it's a match made in heaven. And yes, of course you can meet her. How about next weekend? If that's OK with your mum.' He looks at Pandora.

She nods silently. But for some reason her eyes are flicking around the room and she looks upset.

'Do you mind if I borrow Pandora for just a second?' I ask Declan. 'I need to fix her belt.'

'Sure. I'll tell the taxi to wait.' As Declan walks back outside, I ask Iris to go upstairs and pick a bedtime story for me to read to her. As soon as we're alone, I drag Pandora into the kitchen by the arm.

'What's wrong?' I say in a low voice.

She bites her lip, her eyes filling up. 'Things like this don't happen to me. Declan's too perfect. He must be hiding something. Maybe he has a criminal record.'

I snort. 'A criminal record? With Hester as a mum? I highly doubt it – she'd kill him. Look, stop worrying. I know neither of us have had the best luck with men so far, but maybe Declan is one of the good guys. Give him a chance.'

'You're right. I'm being ridiculous.' She takes another deep breath and presses her fingers against the bottom of her eye sockets to mop up the stray tears that are threatening to smudge her mascara. 'I'm ready.'

We walk back out into the hall, where Iris is chattering away to Declan about her trip to the zoo, a well-loved copy of *The Cat in the Hat* in one hand (it used to be Pandora's, then mine), a plastic tiara in the other.

'Does Rachel like the zoo?' she asks.

'She loves the zoo,' he says firmly. 'She's mad about animals.'

'Does she have a pet?'

'Yes. Sammy. He's a Labrador.'

'What colour?'

'Light brown.'

Iris looks like she's died and gone to heaven. 'Mummy, Rachel has a dog! Oh, and here.' She passes Pandora the tiara.

Pandora places it carefully on her head. 'Thank you, pet. My outfit is now complete.'

Iris looks ecstatic. She claps her hands together and squeals, 'Mummy, now you're Princess Pandora.'

Declan chuckles. 'Are you ready now, Princess Pandora?' He offers her his arm.

She nods. 'Yes. I do believe, I am.' She looks at me and mouths, 'Thank you.'

I kiss my fingers and blow them at her, feeling a little teary myself, like a proud mum waving her daughter off to a graduation ball.

As they walk out the door, arm in arm, Iris leans in towards me. 'Do you think they'll get married, Auntie Jules? Me and Rachel could be bridesmaids. I could wear my tiara.'

I laugh a little. No point in throwing cold water over her Disney-coloured dreams. 'You could. Now, bed young lady. You heard your mum. I'll come up and read you that story in a minute.'

She pouts. 'You always let me stay up late. You promised I could play my Wii, remember?'

'All right. You can have twenty minutes and then it's bed with no moaning, understand?' I'm such a pushover.

She grins. 'Cool! Thanks, Auntie Jules.'

She runs into the living room and I follow her in. By the time I get there, she's already waving her white Wii wand at the television screen.

'It's not working Auntie Jules. Can you fix it?'

I chew my lip. When it comes to electronics, I'm a hopeless case. Pandora is Inspector Gadget in our house, always knows how to unfreeze the Sky box or fix the Wii. I take the wand off Iris, take the batteries out, put them back in again and try once more to get the ball to roll down the bowling lane. No joy.

'Sorry, pet. You could watch some telly,' I suggest, but from the wobble of her lips, she's not impressed.

She flops down on the sofa, her head bowed. 'I really wanted to beat you.'

'I know, but your mum can fix it in the morning. We can have a game tomorrow.'

'You don't get up before lunch, Auntie Jules, and I have a party in the afternoon. And Mum's always too tired to play with me.'

Sadly she's right on all counts. I blow out all my breath and sit down beside her on the sofa. Then I have a sudden brainwave. Jamie! Surely fixing a Wii console would be a walk in the park for a computer guru? I pull out my mobile and punch in his number.

'Are you ringing Mum?' Iris asks hopefully.

I shake my head and press my finger against my lips. 'Hey, Jamie. We have a bowling emergency.' I explain the situation and he promises to come straight over. When I tell Iris she jumps on my knee and gives me a big bath-fresh hug.

'You're the best, Auntie Jules.' She stays there and looks up at me. 'Is Jamie your boyfriend?'

I laugh. 'Not likely. He's my friend.'

She looks puzzled. 'Can boys and girls be friends? When they're big I mean?'

'Of course.'

'Mummy doesn't have any. Friends who are boys I mean. She just has Rowie. And you.'

'We're not friends, we're sisters.'

'Sisters can be friends too. I'm going to be friends with Rachel. Declan said.'

I stroke her hair. She hasn't even met the girl and already she's making plans. Her face drops a little and her eyes widen. 'But what if she doesn't like me? Rachel I mean.'

I kiss the top of her head. 'What are you talking about?

What's not to like? You're my niece, and I'm fabulous. So that makes you fabulous too. It's genetic.'

She grins. 'Mummy doesn't say you're fabulous, she says you're a mess. I heard her talking to Bird in the kitchen earlier.'

'Did you now?' I look at Iris, and she gazes back at me innocently. I try to keep my irritation in check, it's not her fault that Pandora has such a big mouth. She shouldn't be discussing me in front of Iris, in fact she shouldn't be discussing me at all. I thought we were getting on OK for a change, but she's clearly been sniping behind my back. Thanks a lot, Pandora. Next time you can bloody well style yourself and mind your own daughter for a change.

Iris is looking at me. 'Are you cross with me, Auntie Jules? You look cross.'

'No, pet, not with you.'

The doorbell rings and I lift Iris off my knee to answer it, grateful for the distraction. I pull open the door and Jamie gives me a warm smile.

'Hey, Jules. Looking good.'

I'm wearing cut-off denim shorts, red tights, an ancient Blondie T-shirt and one of Bird's old cashmere cardigans that has a hole in the left elbow.

'Are you deranged?' I ask him.

He just chuckles. 'Where's this misbehaving Wii then?'

'Follow me.' I lead him into the living room and point at the offending machine.

'I'll leave you to it. Fancy a drink?'

'Sure, I'll have a coffee if it's going.'

'Coffee?' I look at him. 'It's Saturday night. I'll get you a beer.'

'Honestly, I'm fine.' There's a strange expression on his face and I can't quite read it.

'What's going on?' I ask. 'Why do you look so guilty?'

'I don't.'

'I'm not going to argue with you. I'll be in the kitchen if you're looking for me. Fixing you a beer.' I can feel his eyes follow me out of the room, but I just keep walking. He's behaving very oddly. I'm grateful for the excuse to have a drink. I need one to calm my jittery nerves. I can't let go of the fact that Pandora and Bird think I'm a mess. I'm doing my best. What do they bloody expect? An overnight transformation? I may as well prove them right.

A few minutes later, I'm trying to open a bottle of white plonk. The pantry where the drink is kept has a shiny new padlock on the door, Bird's idea no doubt, which is completely laughable. I'm too amused to be insulted. There's no beer in the fridge but luckily I'd spotted a bottle right at the back of the kitchen cupboard a few days ago. From the dull sheen on the glass and the ripped label it looks like it's been there forever, but it will do. It's lodged between my thighs, and I'm attempting to pull the stubborn cork out with a useless corkscrew when Jamie walks in.

'Did you get the Wii working?' I ask him.

He nods. 'Just had to reload the game. Iris is happily bowling away now.'

'Thanks.' I hand him the wine bottle. 'Here, you try. Bloody thing's stuck. Sorry, we're out of beer.'

He takes the bottle off me and plonks it down on the table, the opener sticking out of the top like a flag on Mount Everest.

'I don't want a drink,' he says. 'A coffee will do me grand.'

'But it's Saturday night.'

'So you said.' He looks at me, his eyebrows raised.

'OK, what's going on here, have I missed something? You're being really weird.'

He points at the table. 'Sit down.'

'No. I'm perfectly happy standing. Spit it out.' I park my bum against the kitchen counter and cross my arms.

He sighs and runs his hands through his hair. 'I was checking the computer at the till the other night and I overheard Bird talking to you about your drinking.'

221

I snort and then start to laugh. 'Not you as well. Jamie, I'm twenty-four, not fifty. I'm entitled to a few drinks every now and then. And I'm not listening to a lecture on drinking from you of all people.'

'What do you mean?'

'Hello, beer boy. Entered any drinking competitions lately? Oh, and sorry, what about that Mr Iron Stomach thing? I seem to remember you managed to down a pint of cooking oil plus a whole bottle of ketchup before you brought it all back up again. No, hang on, it was the goo from the inside of a cow's eye that made you vomit, wasn't it? Daphne told Bird the whole sordid story.'

'That was a college thing. Look, I've been thinking about it and Bird has a point. You do drink a lot.'

'That's nonsense and you know it, Jamie. And right now I'm going to have some evil alcohol. If you're not going to join me, you can get out.'

I go to pick up the wine bottle but he gets there first. He reefs the cork out, flings the opener onto the table with a clatter, strides past me and starts to pour the whole bottle down the sink.

'Jamie, stop!' I try to grab it off him but it's no use, he holds me away with one arm.

I thump his back, hard.

'Jesus, Jules, that hurt.'

'It was meant to. What are you doing? That's such a waste.'

'Why are you so upset? It's only cheap supermarket plonk. And from the smell of it, I think it's corked.'

'You have no right—'

'To look after you? I have every right. Don't you get it? I care about you, Jules. And Bird's right about your drinking. You need to stop.'

'What is it with you people? I like the odd drink, well big deal. I wish the lot of you would just leave me alone, Jamie. In fact, I'd like you to go now.'

'What?'

'You heard me. Get out.'

'You're not being rational. I'm not going anywhere until you calm down.'

'Calm down?' I say, my voice sounding a little hysterical even to my ears. 'I was perfectly calm until you barged your way in here and poured good wine down the sink. Most visitors bring drink, they don't get rid of it. Ed brought vodka—'As soon as it's out I regret it, but too late now.

Jamie's eyes flicker. 'When? Recently?'

Yikes, now I've done it. But I'm too angry to care.

'The night he appeared in my tree house,' I say. 'Grey Goose and a bottle of cranberry. He even thought to bring plastic cups.'

Jamie stares at me for a moment, then his face hardens. 'He was still there when you went back home from my place, wasn't he?'

I jut out my chin. 'Yes. And we drank ourselves stupid. Perfectly normal weekend behaviour. When did *you* get so boring?'

He picks up the empty bottle and shoves it roughly into the swing bin. 'Needing to get wasted all the time isn't normal, Jules. That night we went to Finnegan's with Arietty, you threw all your drinks down like it was some sort of race, then when we left the pub you nearly got knocked down. You walked straight out into the road, remember? Luckily that jeep saw you and swerved away in time.'

I have no idea what he's talking about so I keep my mouth shut.

'And then I had to practically carry you the whole way up the hill,' he continues. 'I'm sorry, Jules, it's gone too far. I'm going to ask Bird to find you an addiction counsellor.'

My eyes prick with tears. How dare he? 'You do that and I will never speak to you again. Do you understand me? Never!'

He sighs. 'I can't talk to you any more. I have to go. And for God's sake, please don't drink while you're minding Iris.'

'Get out,' I say coldly.

He looks at me, his eyes dark. 'Jules—'

'Just go.'

'I'm going.' He turns his back to me and marches out the door. As soon as I'm sure he's left, I start to cry hot, angry tears. I wipe them away with the back of my hand and walk into the living room.

'Bed, Iris. Right this second, no complaints.'

'But Auntie Jules. I'm in the middle of bowling.'

'Don't argue with me, Iris, I'm not in the mood.'

The edges of her mouth start wobbling. 'Sorry.'

I feel bad for snapping at her, she doesn't deserve it. She switches off the console and stands on her tippy toes to kiss me.

'Night, Auntie Jules. Your eyes are a bit red. Are you OK?'

If only she knew. 'I'm just tired, pet. And sorry for snapping at you.'

She nods. 'Mummy gets tired a lot. I'm sorry for annoying you.'

'You didn't, honestly.' I give her the best smile I can manage. 'Sleep well, Iris. Have good dreams.'

'Thanks, Auntie Jules. Love you.'

'Love you to the moon,' I say, quoting one of her favourite books.

'And back,' she adds with a giggle.

As soon as she's toddled up the stairs, I find Dad's toolbox, grab a screwdriver and start unscrewing the bolt mechanism on the pantry door. I don't care what anyone says, it's perfectly normal to fancy a drink on a Saturday night. Jamie Clear can go to hell.

Chapter 19

I tap my glass with my fork. 'I now call the very first Shoestring Club handover dinner to order.'

Arietty giggles and Pandora rolls her eyes. We're sitting in the Shoestring Café booth, which is tucked away at the back, beside the courtyard. Dad built it into an awkward space using reclaimed Victorian old church pews, and the wooden seats and backs are scattered with heaps of feather-filled cushions (Pandora's idea). It's always been my favourite spot, it's like a cocoon.

Pandora brought the Farenze with her and it's now hanging safely in the office. It's Arietty's turn to wear it next – at her school reunion – and Pandora didn't want it picking up any food smells during dinner.

The café is doing surprisingly well. It's only been open for evening meals since the refit, but most of the tables are full and it's barely 7 p.m. From looking at the reservation book, by eight it will be jammers. Klaudia, Lenka and Draza are doing an amazing job; there are delicious smells wafting from the open kitchen. I don't know how they prepare such amazing food in such a small space but they seem to be managing admirably.

Bird is delighted with the whole café enterprise and has already offered Klaudia a large chunk of every evening's takings, which has made her a little less sullen. However I had to laugh when Klaudia pressed her lips together after Bird told her – I was at the counter at the time – and said 'Good. We deserve a cut. We work hard. Me and my mother, not so much Lenka.'

I sink back against the cushions and smile. 'I don't know about you, Arietty, but I'm dying to hear all about Pandora's ball. She refused to go into details this week, said she wanted to save it for tonight. So go on then, put me out of my misery, sis.'

Pandora straightens the cutlery in front of her. 'Not much to tell really. It was in the Four Seasons Hotel which is pretty swish. I didn't recognize a soul, but Declan knew lots of people there, family friends, and the crowd we sat with were pretty nice. Doctors most of them, Hester's husband is an obstetrician.'

'What was the ball in aid of?' Arietty asks.

'Parnell Maternity Hospital. Buying new equipment for premature babies.'

'What about the dress?' I say, cutting to the chase. 'Did anyone comment on it?'

Pandora smiles broadly, and then laughs. 'Yes, actually. Several women spotted the designer and one even asked if she could buy it off me.'

'What did you say?'

'No, of course. But I must admit I was tempted. And it's so easy to dance in, you don't spend half the night hoiking it up your chest, worried you're going to flash a nipple, like with strapless dresses. Plus Declan didn't stop complimenting me all night.'

I smile. 'Did you get a goodnight kiss?'

Pandora blushes. 'Jules! I'm not telling you that.'

'You did, didn't you? When are you seeing him again?'

Pandora rolls some breadcrumbs under her finger. 'That's none of your beeswax either.' She looks up and can't help breaking into a smile. 'But if you must know, he's taking me out tomorrow night. To the theatre. Some sort of Munster Rugby play but it sounds fun.'

I lift my eyebrows. 'The theatre. La, di, da. How civilized.' Then I notice my notebook on the table in front of me. 'Shoot, I meant to take notes for our blog.'

'What blog?' Pandora stares at me a little suspiciously.

I haven't mentioned the blog to Pandora yet; I wasn't sure what her reaction would be. But she's in such a good mood this evening I think I'll chance it.

'It's called The Shoestring Club,' I say. 'We set it up to find co-owners for the dress. That's how we found Alex. She's our fourth time-share partner. I started telling you about her in the shop one day but we got distracted by a customer. Anyway a quarter of the dress belongs to a girl called Alex Cinnamon who found us on the internet via the blog. She lives in Wicklow. She can't be here tonight, so she suggested we chart the progress of the dress on the blog. Where it was worn, pics of the dress at the event, that kind of thing.'

Pandora's brow wrinkles. 'It sounds a bit odd. What do you think, Arietty? In fact, I must apologize for my sister, she hasn't let you get a word in edgeways yet.'

Arietty shrugs. 'I don't mind. And I'm not one for writing, but I like the idea of pictures. Like an online scrapbook.'

'Fantastic idea,' I say. 'We could show all the different ways to style a dress, using the Farenze as an example. Starting with your ensemble, Pandora. Classic yet chic. Did Declan take any photos of you?'

'Yes,' she admits. 'Lots. On his iPhone, but I'm not sure they'd be good enough quality—'

'They'll be perfect,' I say. 'Jamie said the blog's getting a surprising amount of traffic for something so new. But we need to start adding more content. He suggested putting up some details of who we all are. He said it didn't have to be too personal, just our likes and dislikes or something like that.'

As soon as I say the word traffic, Pandora's ears prick up and she looks at me. 'Can we link the blog to the Shoestring website?'

I smile. She never misses a business opportunity. ''Course we can, sis.'

The Shoestring Club Blog
Four girls, one remarkable dress

Our members:
Julia (Jules) – works in Shoestring Designer Swop Shop, Monkstown Crescent, Dublin.
Likes: travelling, clothes, style and art magazines, old 1980s movies like *Pretty in Pink* and *The Breakfast Club*, tree houses, cycling, parties.
Dislikes: ironing, karaoke, sheep-like slaves to fashion, velour tracksuits, motorists who don't respect cyclists, swallowing flies, spiders – especially large black woolly ones – Daddy Long Legs, moths (all flying insects in fact), fake tan (especially the smell), fake friends.

Arietty – works with animals.
Likes: elephants, big cats (tigers, lions and snow leopards; not so much cheetahs or pumas), reading in bed, silence, sunflowers, putting together flat-pack furniture.
Dislikes: celery, farm animals, any events you have to get dressed up for, flying, people asking her where she's from.

Pandora – runs Shoestring (see Jules's entry).
Likes: movies, boxed sets – especially anything medical or political dramas, pillow fights with her daughter, reading her daughter stories, singing, karaoke, fashion, vintage clothes, especially anything by Chanel, Prada or Farenze, ladybirds, good manners.
Dislikes: working on a Sunday, lazy people, being tired, bad manners, getting wool in your mouth, seeing sound booms in movies.

Alex – looks after one husband and three dogs.
Likes: cake, animals – especially dogs, her husband Markham (he should be first in fact!), charm bracelets, open fires, reading cookery books and testing out new recipes.
Dislikes: anyone who is cruel to animals, blood sports, cold callers, mushrooms, when her internet connection goes down, crowds.

• • •

We are delighted to announce that our Faith Farenze dress has had its first outing – to the October Ball in aid of the Parnell Maternity Hospital. It was worn by Pandora and she has reported back many compliments on the dress.

It was styled with a silver Lara Bohinc belt, silver peep-toe courts, a cream beaded shrug, and a hot orange bag.

The Farenze will next be worn to Arietty's school reunion on Saturday 20th October. Stay tuned for more details on that!

And for more outstanding dresses and once-worn designer and vintage pieces visit Shoestring, Monkstown Crescent, Dublin or visit our website: www.shoestring.irlie

• • •

Shoestring Scrapbook
For photos of Pandora in the Farenze, click here.

• • •

Comments:
Pandora, you look amazing! I can't wait to wear the dress myself.
Best, Alex xxx

Loving the way you've accessorized the dress, Shoestring Club. Keep the style tips coming.
Dublin Fashionista

Chapter 20

At lunchtime the following Saturday I'm sitting in the staffroom at Shoestring, flicking through the latest Italian *Vogue* when my mobile pings. Thinking it's probably Arietty – I'm styling her in the shop before her reunion this evening – I finish the page before checking it. But when I do it's not Arietty at all, it's Ed.

Can I ring you Jules? it reads

A ripple of irritation runs up and down my spine. Bloody nerve. I've been trying to contact him for weeks.

'Go feck yourself, Ed Powers,' I mutter under my breath, my fingers typing in

Absolutely not.

Seconds later my phone starts ringing. I check the number – yep, Ed. I throw it onto the table where it vibrates around on the wood like a breakdancer. I let it ring out, but then it starts up again. I turn the ringer onto silence and thrust it into the back pocket of my jeans, determined to ignore it. But it fizzes against my buttock, reminding me. I pull it out again and switch it off. I sit there fuming for a few minutes before Lenka walks in the door.

'Ed is on shop phone for you. Says is urgent. He have nerve, yes? Will I tell him go to hell?'

I nod. 'Please do, thanks, Lenka.' She's clearly up to date on my Ed woes. Must have been Bird or Pandora. Probably Bird. She loves telling anyone who will listen what an idiot he is.

Lenka comes back a few minutes later. 'He say unless you speak to him, he arrive at shop. He say if you not talk to him then, he camp in shop until you do.'

'For Feck's sake.' I stand up, practically spitting with anger, and follow Lenka to the door.

'Sorry, Lenka,' I say as I march towards the phone. 'I didn't mean to snap at you.'

She shrugs. 'Men. Drive you crazy, yes?'

'Too right,' I say.

She lingers for a second, clearly interested in what I'm about to say to Ed, but I stand there, looking at her and eventually she takes the hint and bounces off towards the coffee shop, her white-blonde ponytail swinging behind her.

'What do you want?' I hiss into the mouthpiece.

Annoyingly Ed just chuckles. 'Is that any way to speak to your old buddy?'

'Buddy my ass. Why didn't you answer any of my calls?'

'Lainey made me promise never to speak to you again.'

'She threatened me too. Told me to keep away from you or else.'

He laughs again. 'Threatened you? Lainey? I highly doubt it. Cried you into submission more like. She told me she visited the shop. Brave for Lainey.'

'Brave? Your darling fiancée slapped me, Ed. Did she tell you that?'

There's silence for a second. 'No,' he says. 'I'm sorry, OK. I should never have put you in that position and I really want to make it up to you. What are you doing tonight?'

I snort. 'Has Lainey finally called off the private detective who she's had stalking you then? Or has she had some sort of tracking device implanted under your skin? Look, I've had enough of this. You're marrying Lainey in just over a week; until then, keep away from me, understand? As I told Lainey, I'll make a brief appearance at your wedding, but after that I want nothing to do with either of you, get it?'

'Please, Jules,' he says. 'I just want to say goodbye properly.'

'No. I mean it. I'm sorry, but I have to go. There's a customer waiting for me. I'll see you at the wedding.'

I put down the phone and blow out my breath. That's it, I managed to stand my ground and it's finally over. I thought I'd feel pleased, but instead I feel empty and desperately lonely.

After I've managed to get the last stragglers out of the shop, I lock up and flop down on the sofa facing the door to wait for Arietty. At twenty past six I'm starting to get worried, but then I see someone through the glass, waving in at me. For a second I almost don't recognize her, it's the first time I've seen Arietty wearing any kind of make up, and her hair is pulled back off her face in a simple top bun, decorated with tiny white flowers. She looks amazing. I unlock the door.

'About time,' she says, scowling at me.

I ignore the tone, knowing she's a bundle of nerves, and hold the door open for her. She walks in, staggering a little in her gold strappy sandals, and stands in the middle of the shop floor, fuming, battered red rucksack on her back. She's wearing jeans and her sensible navy jacket with her heels.

I lock the door behind us and then ask, 'What's wrong?'

'That stupid hairdresser and make-up girl. I said simple, not this.' She stars her hands around her face and waves them a little frantically. Her nails are a lush dark red.

'What are you talking about? You look gorgeous. OK, maybe the white flowers around your bun are a bit too much, but the rest is spot on.'

She blinks several times in quick succession and I realize why her eyes look so flirty – fake corner lashes.

'And I love the eyelashes,' I add. 'Très va va voom. I can't wait to get you into the Farenze and see the final effect.'

Arietty's eyes begin to water. 'That's just it. I look like I've made too much effort. It's not what I'd planned, Jules, I just wanted to look pretty, show the girls in my year that I've made something of myself. I didn't want to go in the first place, and I certainly don't now. This isn't me, everyone's going to laugh.'

I take her hands, lead her to the sofa and make her sit down. 'Arietty,' I say, after giving her a few seconds to collect herself and blink away the tears. I hope her lash glue is waterproof. 'No one's going to laugh at you. Listen to me – we can tone it down a little if you like, banish the flowers and the smoky eye make up, take off the nail polish, give you a pair of flatties instead of heels. I'd planned to pop a leather jacket over your shoulders to make the Farenze look less dressy anyway. Does that sound all right?'

'Yes, but what about the lashes? They feel really weird.' She screws her eyes shut and then opens them again.

'You won't notice them after a while. I had a full spider set glued on once, yours are only babies. And they suit you.' I pat her on the hand. 'Let's get cracking. We don't have long to lick you into shape. I ordered you a taxi for seven.'

She sighs and then nods. 'I guess I've shelled out enough money already for this damn reunion. And I do want to give the dress an outing. OK, do your worst.'

I tackle the nails first. Luckily Bird keeps a full nail kit in the staffroom. She's very particular about her nails. As I hold Arietty's fingers and dab a cotton-wool ball soaked in remover over the blood red polish, I notice her hand is shaking.

'How are the nerves holding up?' I ask gently.

She sighs. 'I won't be able to eat a thing. I have a frog in my throat and butterflies in my stomach. But if I can get through the dinner and the speeches I'll be happy.'

'Why are you putting yourself through this, Arietty? I don't understand. It's just a school reunion.'

'Where did you go to school?'

'St John's in Blackrock,' I tell her.

'Mixed, yes? And big. Lots of different kids, yeah?'

I shrug. 'I guess so.'

'And did you like it?'

'I didn't hate it. It was OK. The other kids were pretty nice. And the art teacher was lovely.'

'Well, I went to Loreto Monkstown and I hated it. Really hated it. I was practically the only black girl in the whole school. And I started midway through second year which was a disaster. Everyone had their own friends by then. In third year we did this play with some of the boys from CBC Monkstown and one of them asked me out – a guy called Martin Craig, Craiger they used to call him – and I made the mistake of saying yes. From then on some of the girls made my life hell.'

'Why?' I stop dabbing at her nails and look up. Arietty's eyes are dark and sad.

'There was this one girl, Sasha Davenport, really fancied herself.'

'She's the one organizing the reunion isn't she?' I ask. 'The one who slagged you about mucking out the elephants.'

'That's right.'

'She sounds awful.'

'She's a nightmare. Beautiful though. Long blonde hair, big blue eyes, skinny, huge boobs. A real D4. All fake tan, UGG boots, and ironed hair. Anyway, Sasha had her eye on Craiger. So when she found out we were together, she started telling everyone I was a slut. Then I started getting all these anonymous text messages calling me names and saying I was dead. I broke up with him after that, couldn't take it any more, but the texts didn't stop. And they started to get pretty nasty, telling me to go back to Africa, stuff like that.'

I suck in my breath. Teenage girls can be evil. 'You told someone, right?'

She nods. 'Mum. Who told my stepdad, Jeremy. He was raging and stormed into the school, demanding to see the head, saying he'd sue them for racism. Jeremy's white but he's a lot more sensitive about things like that than me or Mum are. The head managed to calm him down, said he'd implement an anti-bullying policy immediately and come down hard on whoever was behind the messages. The texts stopped, but nothing ever happened to Sasha, even though they were all sent from her mobile. She claimed it wasn't her, that someone must have stolen her mobile and sent them.

Then her dad got involved, said he'd pull all his funding from the new gym extension if the head didn't stop harassing his darling daughter. Mum had to physically stop Jeremy from going over to Mr Davenport's house and confronting him. It was horrible.'

'That's unbelievable,' I say. 'Why didn't they move you to a different school or something?'

She shrugs. 'That's a good question. I don't really know. I guess Lucie and Amanda were really happy there and they didn't want to pull us all out or split us up.'

I sigh. 'And I guess if she's organizing it, Sasha will be taking centre stage tonight.'

Arietty nods solemnly. 'Yes. I want to look her in the eye, stand my ground, show her she hasn't won. If I can eyeball down mad elephants, I can sure as hell deal with Sasha Davenport.' Her eyes are flinty and I can tell she's serious.

'That's the spirit.' I give her a gentle smile. 'Arietty, would you like me to go with you? I could sit in the hotel lobby if you like, give you some moral support.'

She shakes her head. 'That's very kind, Jules, but I'll be fine, honestly. Thanks for the offer, I appreciate it.' She stops for a second. 'Are we friends now? I mean proper friends, not just Shoestring Club friends?'

Man, is she direct. 'Yes,' I say, meaning it. 'I could do with a friend right now, someone I can trust.'

She nods and gives a shy smile. 'Me too,' she says. 'That Lainey is one stupid girl.'

'Thanks.' Then I hold both her hands in mine. 'Now if we're going to make you belle of the ball, we'd better get cracking.'

Half an hour later I make Arietty pose while I take photos with the shop camera. She's in good spirits, nervous, but excited too. I think she secretly knows how stunning she looks, even if she refuses to admit it. She was right about toning down the make up, with her perfect bone structure and dramatic eyes, less is definitely more. I've taken the flowers out of her bun, which makes it look a lot more contemporary, and her nails are now a delicate shade of coral pink. I've thrown the dove-grey Rick Owens jacket over her shoulders – it only came in two weeks ago, but as soon as I spotted it, I knew it would be perfect – and I've knotted a soft black leather belt around her waist, and borrowed some Pretty Ballerina zebra-print pumps from the shop to replace the sandals. Even in the low heels, she'll still tower over most women at the reunion. She looks unbelievable.

'Head up a little, Arietty,' I say, looking through the view-finder. 'Twist your body away from me a bit, throw your hand on your hip, that's it, perfecto.' I snap away. Then I drop to one knee. 'Now arch your back and look down at me. Give me a kind of haughty, proud look. Excellent.' I keep shooting, capturing Arietty in lots of different poses. Surprisingly she seems to quite like the attention, and I've always enjoyed being behind the camera, so we mess around until we hear Arietty's taxi pull up outside.

'I'll leave your rucksack in the staffroom and you can collect it tomorrow,' I say, giving her hug. 'Have a brilliant time. Remember to keep your head up. No stooping, OK?'

'Yes, yes, stop nagging me,' she says. But she's smiling. Then the smile drops off her face. 'I hope I'm not overdressed.' She bites her lip.

'Now you're just fishing for compliments, Miss Supermodel.'
I unlock the shop door and the ruddy-faced driver steps out
of his cab and bustles around to the passenger door to open
it. I asked for their smartest taxi and the sleek black Mercedes
certainly does the trick. As soon as the driver sees Arietty he
gives a low whistle.

I squeeze her shoulder. 'Told you. Now knock them all dead.
You're worth millions of a Sasha Davenport, remember that.'

Cycling home my heart feels light. It was fun styling Arietty and
my life is starting to look a little more positive now that I have a
friend to replace Jamie. I've never found it easy to make friends
and I only realize now how adrift I've felt having no one to confide in. The whole business with Jamie is niggling at me and I'm
still livid with him for treating me like a full-blown alcho. But at
least he had the decency not to say anything to Bird.

As it's a clear evening I take the longer route, turning left
towards Sandycove beach, past the James Joyce Tower. I stop
for a second at the 40 Foot Bathing Place, watching the sea, still
sitting on my bike, my hand resting on the wall. It's white with
sea horses, waves crashing against the rocks. I wince as I spot
two men walking gingerly down the concrete steps into the sea,
their big bellies hanging over their flappy swimming shorts.
They're brave. There's a nip in the air and I shiver and then
start cycling home.

By the time I cycle through the gates, it's already dark. Bird's
car isn't in the driveway and neither is Dad's van, they must
both be out. But Pandora's Golf is there all right.

I open the door, wheel my bike inside and rest it against the
wall.

'You can't leave it there.' Pandora is standing in front of me,
frowning. 'I'm not painting over the scuffs and oil marks yet
again, Jules. You never think, do you?'

I look at her. 'What has you in such a grump?'

237

'I'm not in a grump.'

I rest my tongue on my upper lip and give a laugh. 'Yeah, right. Declan stand you up, did he?'

'Shut up, Jules. You're not funny.' Pandora looks almost in tears. Oops, clearly something is going on.

'What happened?' I ask, softening my tone. 'Please don't tell me you guys broke up? I've booked him for next Saturday, remember? And that would make things very awkward.' I've asked him to accompany me to the wedding – just the church bit – to keep everyone guessing. The wedding breakfast I'll have to brave on my own. It was Pandora's idea originally and he does look amazing in a tux.

'No, we haven't broken up. And yes, it's in his diary. But I don't want to talk about it any more.'

'Come on, sis. Maybe I can help.'

She gives a wry laugh. 'As if.'

'Hey, that's a bit unfair.'

'Sorry, you're right.' She picks at a hangnail and then sighs. 'He's having dinner with his ex-wife. Just the two of them. He says it's the only way he can get her to talk to him in a civil manner. But she's booked The Rosewood, Jules. No one books The Rosewood for civil chats.'

She's right. It's mega expensive, with comfy booths, intimate lighting, and a churchload of candles. It's notorious for hosting foreign rock stars who want to dine incognito, and people having affairs.

'He didn't book it though, did he?' I say, trying to cushion the blow.

'No, and he swears he's not interested in her any more, but they were married for ten years, it has to count for something.'

'I'm sure it'll all be fine, he's mad about you.'

'Thanks. And I'm sorry for being short with you. But you do need to move your bike.' She gives a deep, jaw cracking yawn. 'I'm going to bed now, I'll see you in the morning.'

'It's only eight.'

'I know, sad isn't it? I'm exhausted. I'll read for a while if I can't sleep. See you in the morning, Jules.' She kisses me on the cheek.

'Sleep well,' I say. 'And try not to worry.'

As she climbs the stairs, I open the front door and take my bike back outside. I check my pocket for my keys, shut the door behind me, grab the handlebars and scoot around the side of the house. But as I reach the oak tree, I stop suddenly. There's a familiar dot of light in the tree-house window. My stomach lurches. Not again.

Chapter 21

For a few long minutes I stand underneath the tree house. Unless Jamie's taken up smoking which is highly unlikely, it's Ed. My head is telling me to dump my bike and get the hell out of there – run inside, shut the door tight and wait for Ed to go away. But my heart is telling me something completely different. Because even after everything he's done – ignoring me for weeks, hitching his wagon to my best friend behind my back, telling me I was wrong for him all the time, that it's Lainey he wants, not me – there's still a tiny part of me that craves his love and attention. I know it's not logical, and I know it's self-destructive, but I can't deny the hold he has over me. I know I should just walk away, but Ed is my fatal attraction.

While I'm dithering about what to do, he appears at the tree-house door.

'Thought I heard something. Don't just stand there, Jules, come on up. Toast my last week of freedom.' He waves a glass in the air. This time it's real, not plastic.

'Keep your voice down,' I hiss up at him. 'You'll wake Pandora and Iris.'

He laughs. 'Come on, even your boring sister can't go to bed this early.'

I feel my skin prickle. I know Pandora is a bit of an old granny at times, but boring is unfair.

'Her new boyfriend's tiring her out,' I say in her defence.

'Boyfriend?' He sounds genuinely surprised.

'Yes, Declan. He's mad about her, thinks she's amazing.'

'Some sort of accountant is he? He'd need to be to find Pandora exciting.'

'Don't be so snide. He's an architect if you must know.'

He laughs. 'I hope it works out for her and they have lots of carefully designed children together. Look, quit procrastinating and get up here, woman.'

I stand my ground. 'No.'

'Jules, stop being stubborn. You know you want to.'

'Just go. Lainey would have a hissy fit if she knew you were here.'

'She's not going to find out, is she? I made sure I wasn't being followed this time. Come on, one drink isn't going to kill you. And I promise I'll behave. Or I could sing to you if you like.' He starts singing the chorus of 'Lucky', an old Jason Mraz song he always used to sing to me. It's about being in love with your best friend.

'Stop! Pandora will hear you.'

He continues singing, even louder.

'Ed! I'm warning you.'

But he doesn't stop. So I abandon my bike, pick up a stick and chuck it at him.

He bats it away with his hand. 'Temper, temper.' Then he starts singing again.

'Fine,' I snap. 'If you shut your mouth, I'll come up. Satisfied?'

He stops instantly and grins. 'Very.'

I step over one of Bird's leaf piles – she's been raking her precious grass again – and climb up the ladder. He holds out his hand at the top and pulls me onto the tree-house platform. For a couple of seconds we stand there, staring at each other, Ed still holding my hand, his skin warm against mine, before I shake my hand away, duck my head and walk inside.

He's lit the storm lantern and some of the tealight holders. The air smells strange, slightly salty and acidic, then I spot a greasy brown bag.

I swing around and stare at him. 'Have you been eating chips up here? It stinks.'

He just shrugs. 'I was hungry.' He flops down on the mattress and pats it. 'I've kept a place for you.'

I linger for a minute, the logical part of my brain begging me not to, the emotional, needy part trying to win me over. Needy wins and I sit down beside him. 'No funny business, OK?' I say.

He chuckles. ''Course not, Jules. I'm practically a married man, remember? Just wanted to say goodbye properly. Once Lainey has that ring on my finger, my footloose days are over. She'll probably have me filling out time sheets to account for my every step.'

'And she'd be right not to trust you.'

He pouts. 'Ouch! That's most unfair.'

'Really? So she'd be delighted to know exactly where you are at this exact moment, would she? How about I tell her?' I pull out my mobile.

He just smiles at me. 'You wouldn't do that to me, Jules. You're a big softie underneath it all.' He picks up the open bottle of champagne and pours me a glass. He holds it towards me.

I hesitate. I know I shouldn't take it, especially after Bird's recent tirade. But I can already feel the bubbles breaking over my tongue and the sweet surge of alcohol in my system. I don't just need a drink, I *want* a drink so badly it hurts. Just one glass, I tell myself, taking it out of his hand. Besides, it's medicinal, it will make talking to Ed easier.

'Champagne?' I say. 'My, we have gone up in the world. Don't mind if I do.' I take a long swig, downing half the glass in one go, then splutter and cough a little as bubbles race up my nose.

He pats me on the back and then tops up my glass again. 'Watch those bubbles, Jules, they're lethal.'

I lie back against the cushions and relax as the familiar rush makes my insides tingle.

I tip my glass against his. 'To your impending marriage and my impending . . .' I pause, not knowing quite what to say. I don't have a huge amount to look forward to at the moment, so I just let the end of the sentence hang.

'Kiss,' Ed says gently, and moves towards me.

I put my hand up and push him away.

'Ed! You promised.'

'Oh, come on, Jules, it doesn't mean anything. It's just a kiss. No one will ever know.'

'I'll know. How can I stand there watching you take your wedding vows, promising to be faithful to Lainey for the rest of your life, when I know it's all a lie?'

'It'll be different once we're actually married. And I will do my best to be faithful.'

I stare at him. 'Do your best? That's pathetic.'

He shrugs. 'I'm just being honest. What happens if Lainey balloons after having kids, or goes off sex or something?'

'Then you'll just have to deal with it. Not go off and find some slapper who is happy to overlook the fact that you're wearing a wedding band.'

He gives a dry laugh. 'You're such a romantic, Jules. Everyone has affairs, it's part of life. And stop being so high and mighty. You didn't push me away a few weeks ago, did you? I seem to remember we had a rather passionate snog.'

I can feel my cheeks flame. 'That was a mistake. You don't deserve Lainey. She's devoted to you. We may not be close any more, but I still care about her. I have a good mind to tell her exactly what you've just said.'

His eyebrows arch. 'Why? She knows what I'm like but, unlike you, she accepts me for what I am. She seems happy enough to turn a blind eye when she wants to. And she's hardly a saint herself is she? Coming on to her best friend's guy?'

My back stiffens. I know he's right, but I can't stand his smug, self-satisfied expression any more. Suddenly the scales fall off

243

my eyes. Ed Powers is a pig. I can't believe I've wasted so much time thinking about him, worrying about him, loving him. Because that's exactly what it was – a waste. I've been such a fool. I grab the champagne bottle and take a long swig, then another, until eventually the whole bottle is empty. Then, feeling a little queasy, I stand up.

'I'll see you at the wedding, Ed. Not before and certainly not after. We're finished. I have no idea what I ever saw in you.'

I step towards the door, duck under and turn around at the top of the platform to climb back down the rope ladder. He follows me and grabs my arm.

'Don't go, Jules. I'm sorry, I know I'm a bit of a cynic when it comes to marriage. But I'm just trying to be realistic. Plus I'm freaking out and it's the only way I can cope with the whole concept of getting hitched. Stay, please. For old times' sake.'

'Ed, this is getting boring. Please let go of my arm.' I try to pull it away but he's holding tight. I push my free hand against him, but it unbalances me. I stumble and feel myself falling backwards.

'Jules!'

For a split second I hear Ed shouting and then – nothing.

I open my eyes and wince as bright light hits my pupils. My head feels like it's been thumped with a sledge hammer. I swallow down some vomit, my eyes watering from the burning acidic taste in my throat. My arms are heavy, I try to move them but they seem to be pinned down. There's some sort of mask over my mouth and I shake my head a little to dislodge it, but it makes my neck hurt so I stop.

'Thank God,' I hear a voice say. 'She's awake.' It sounds remarkably like Pandora.

A strange woman in a paramedic's uniform removes the mask and says, 'Take it easy now, and try not to move. You had a nasty fall. We're taking you to St Vincent's Hospital.'

'Fall?' For a second I don't understand. Then it all comes back to me in a rush. The tree house. I slipped off the platform. I gasp and try to sit up again, making my whole body hurt.

Pandora appears, leaning over me, her face pale. 'You're all right, Boolie, lie back now, take it easy. Everything's going to be fine.'

'What's wrong with me?' I say. 'Am I broken?'

She gives a breathy laugh. 'No, Boolie, you're not broken. You got knocked out but the ambulance crew think it's just bad concussion. You had a lucky escape, fell on one of Bird's leaf piles. But I have to ask, were you drinking? Your eyes look a bit unfocused and your breath smells funny.'

I give a tiny nod and whisper, 'Yes. Champagne.'

'And what were you doing up there with Ed Powers?'

'I'm sorry, she needs to rest now,' the paramedic says, putting her hand on Pandora's arm. 'And you must put on your seatbelt.'

'Sorry,' Pandora says, and then I hear a loud click. Pandora must have buckled herself back into her seat.

The woman pats my shoulder kindly. 'Nearly there now.'

I lie still and think about what Pandora's just said. What *was* I doing in the tree house with Ed? My first and correct instinct was to tell him to go to hell. And if it hadn't been for Bird's leaves who knows what might have happened. Why did I down all that champagne? To stop Ed's words hurting me? To numb the pain? The disappointment of wasting so much time and energy on him? Or simply because I just wanted a drink? Because that would be the saddest answer of all. My eyes well up again and I blink away the tears.

I hear Pandora's voice say, 'Don't cry, sweetie. I'm here and I won't leave your side, I promise.'

Which only makes me cry even harder.

Several hours later, after a doctor has checked me thoroughly in the A and E and I've finally been allocated a bed; I'm in a hospital ward in one of those flappy at the back hospital gowns, still feeling a bit groggy. I can't make out if it's the concussion or the lingering after-effects of the champagne. Probably both. Pandora's sitting beside my bed, flicking through a magazine. Every so often a nurse comes to take my temperature and check my pupils, but apart from that we're left pretty much alone.

I'm the only person under sixty on the ward and the woman beside me has been snoring away ever since I climbed into the bed. Now and again she stops, and I look over, worried she's stopped breathing, but then off she goes again, like the local fog horn.

The first question Pandora asked as soon I'd been popped into bed and the nurses had left was about Ed. My eyes had filled with tears and I felt so overwhelmed by stupidity and regret that I couldn't even speak, so she let me be for a while.

But now she puts down her magazine and asks, 'What on earth were you doing in the tree house, Boolie? And why was Ed there too? Talk to me, please.'

I shrug, which makes my neck hurt a little and my head throb. Tears spring to my eyes again.

'Sorry, Jules, I don't mean to upset you. We can talk about it later if you're still not ready.'

I sigh. She's been very patient and she deserves an explanation. She asked me several times in the A and E and I brushed her off then too.

'He called over to say goodbye before the wedding,' I say. 'Brought some champagne.'

She stared at me. 'I thought you hated him.'

'It's complicated. We were together for a long time. I guess part of me still loves him.' I stop for a second. Actually that's not true. Right now, I have no feelings for him whatsoever. Suddenly I feel lighter than I have in months. 'Loved,' I correct myself. 'Definitely past tense. And where is he anyway? What happened after I fell?'

'Ed knocked on the door so loudly it woke up Iris and made her cry. I went outside and found you lying there on the leaves, unconscious. I got such a fright, Jules. Then I found your pulse and figured you'd been knocked out. Ed had already called an ambulance, so he waited with me while it came. I asked him what the two of you were playing at but he was being pretty evasive. Said he just had to talk to you. As soon as he heard the sirens he left pretty abruptly. Said he was sorry but he couldn't stay. Had to get back to Lainey. Stupid fecker.'

I think about this for a second. 'He didn't wait to see what the ambulance crew had to say?'

'Nope.'

'You're right, he is a little fecker.'

'And then the ambulance arrived and you woke up when we were driving through Blackrock.'

'What about Iris? Did you leave her on her own?'

'No. Jamie heard the ambulance sirens and ran over. Must have just missed Ed. Poor guy nearly passed out himself when he saw you, went so pale. He wanted to go with you, but I asked him to stay with Iris instead.'

'That was decent of him. I can't believe Ed ran off like that.' I bite my lip. After everything I've done, it's Jamie who has my back, not Ed. It's always been Jamie. I've made such a mess of things. But it's too late now. My eyes water.

'Oh, Boolie, don't. Ed is not worth it.'

I laugh through my tears. 'I know!'

She pats my hand and leaves it there for a few minutes before pulling it away. She looks around and sighs. 'This place is so depressing.' We both hate anything to do with hospitals.

'What do you expect?' I ask. 'Pink walls? Dance music? And, hello, you're supposed to be the one cheering me up, not the other way around.'

She looks contrite. 'I know, I'm sorry. I'm just tired.' On cue, she gives an almighty yawn.

I glance at my watch. 'I'm not surprised. It's nearly midnight. You should get back to Iris. I'm fine on my own, honestly.'

She shakes her head. 'Bird and Dad have it all under control. They'll both be in first thing in the morning. One night sleeping in a chair isn't going to kill me. Dad used to do it all the time,' she adds softly. 'But you probably don't remember.'

I stare at her. It's not something we mention in our family, ever. She's talking about when Mum was really sick and we were all staying in Bird's house. Dad moved the old squishy armchair from the living room up to Mum's bedroom and stayed there most nights, his legs stretched out in front of him, a rug thrown over his body. Bird tried to make him sleep in his own bed, get some proper rest, but he refused. Like Pandora, he said one night sleeping in a chair wasn't going to kill him. Towards the very end he stopped for some reason.

'Yes, I do remember,' I say in an equally soft voice. 'I was nine, Pandora. I remember everything. Mum dying, Dad going all funny, you trying to take Mum's place.'

She looks upset. 'No, I wasn't. I was just trying to look after you and Dad.'

'I didn't mean it in a bad way,' I say gently. 'But you must admit you did smother me a bit. You even made me sleep in your bed with you.'

She stares at me. 'That was because of your nightmares. You didn't have so many horrible dreams in with me.'

'Was I really that bad?'

'Yes.' She strokes the side of my head. 'You used to wake up screaming and ranting about all kinds of weird stuff.'

'You've never told me that before. Ranting about what?'

She sighs. 'It doesn't matter. Forget about it.'

'I want to know,' I say stubbornly. 'Please? It's important.'

'I don't see how it can be. It was such a long time ago.'

I want to tell her – about how I still wake up in the middle of the night sometimes, heart pounding, howling on the inside, having learnt long ago not to attract attention by screaming out loud. But I can't. I bite the inside of my lip instead.

She studies my face, her eyes soft and kind. 'You still get them, don't you, Boolie?'

I nod and then lower my gaze and stare at my hands which are twisting in my lap.

Pandora sighs. 'Are they very dark?'

My head still dropped, I nod again.

'About your hands being covered in blood?' she whispers.

Tears drip down onto the hospital blanket and I wipe them away with my fingers.

'Sometimes,' I say, remembering the recent dream triggered by Iris's near miss.

'Come here.' She puts her arms around me and holds me tight against her chest. I can smell her orange blossom perfume, feel the slightly scratchiness of her jumper against my cheek.

'I'm so sorry, Boolie. You should have said something. I can't believe you've had to go through it on your own all these years.'

We stay like that for ages, until finally she draws away. She pushes my curls off my face.

'Do you think it has something to do with Mum's death?' she asks. 'It must have frightened you so much. You were so young and seeing her so sick like that . . .' she breaks off, pauses. I can see it's hard for her to find the words. She swallows, looks out of the window for a second, and then back into the room.

'It changes you, doesn't it?' she says eventually. 'I tried to get Dad to find you someone to talk to about the night-mares, someone professional, but he said you'd grow out of it. But if you're still having them, years later . . .' she tails off again. 'I should have tried Bird instead. Dad was all over the place.'

She pauses. 'Boolie, I have to ask you, and please don't shout me down. When you drink, heavily I mean, do you still have nightmares? Or do they go away? Is that why you do it?'

It's not something I've ever consciously thought about. Yes, it makes it easier to get to sleep, but it doesn't banish the images from my head. In fact sometimes it makes them worse and I wake up in the middle of the night in a cold sweat, my heart thumping out of my chest, and I can't get back to sleep again for hours. I'm not comfortable talking about this any more, so I stare out of the window myself, hoping she'll get the message and change the subject.

But Pandora's not one for giving up.

'Boolie?' she says.

And then again, 'Boolie?'

I swing my eyes back towards her. 'That's not why I drink,' I say, answering her question.

'Then it could be your genes.'

'What are you talking about?'

'Grandpa Schuster was an alcoholic.'

I stare at her. 'What? Are you sure?'

'Yes. I overheard Dad and Bird discussing it one evening. It was just before Bird made you visit Sheila. Dad was begging her to tell Sheila but Bird refused, said it was irrelevant and she wouldn't have all that dragged up again. I went straight in, confronted them about it, told Bird that Dad was right. But then Bird talked us both around, you know how persuasive she can be sometimes.'

She sighs. 'But I'm sorry, I should have said something earlier, you had a right to know and this family has far too many secrets already. He died from liver failure and alcohol poisoning, went on an almighty bender after a rugby match and never came out of the hospital after it.'

'Not a heart attack?'

'No. But that's what Bird told everyone. I think she was ashamed at the truth. It was hardly her fault, but I think she blames herself for not being able to help him.' I try to take this in. I'd always been told that my grandpa, Derek Schuster, died of a heart attack when he was thirty-eight. I've seen photographs of him – he was a bit overweight, but he had a lovely wide smile and twinkling sky-blue eyes.

'Which is why Bird is so worried about my drinking,' I say.

'I'd say so.' Pandora looks at me. 'Boolie, do you think it's time to talk to someone about it? I know you don't drink every day, but you can't keep having accidents like this. And I read in the paper the other day that eighty per cent of rape cases involve alcohol. Imagine if something like that happened to you? I'd never forgive myself.'

My face crumples and before I know what's happening I'm crying into my hands.

Pandora looks shocked. 'What did I say? You're scaring me. What's wrong?'

'That night you collected me in the industrial estate, this guy,' I gulp, but try to continue. 'This guy attacked me. In the beer garden at Dicey Reilly's.'

'Jesus! Why didn't you say something?'

'I couldn't. I was drunk and confused. And you were so annoyed with me. You told me to shut up and get in the car.'

'I'm so sorry.' Pandora's eyes well up. 'I had no idea. But nothing happened, did it? He didn't . . . you know.'

'No. But only 'cos someone came out and distracted him. I kneed him in the balls and ran away.'

'Thank Christ for that. Oh, Boolie, what am I going to do with you?' She hugs me again, tight. 'You're shaking,' she says, rubbing my back in circles through the thin cotton of the hospital gown. 'It's going to be OK, darling. Don't you worry. And I'll never let anything like that happen to you again, I swear to God.'

She sighs deeply and pulls away a little. 'Is there anything else you need to tell me? Anything else you're keeping to yourself?'

Mum's face flashes in front of my eyes. Her waxy, peaceful,

just-dead face. But when I open my mouth, nothing comes out. I can't. Not yet.

'Sometimes I need a drink so badly my hands shake,' I say instead. And then I start crying again.

Chapter 22

'You must be Julia. I'm Anne Crampton.' A tall woman looks down at me, smiling warmly. She's wearing a neat navy trouser suit, her long brown hair is streaked with silver and she speaks English with a slight accent, Norwegian maybe or Swedish. I've been sitting in the waiting area outside her consultation rooms for ten minutes trying to focus on a magazine, jittery with nerves.

'Yes, Jules,' I say, putting down the magazine and standing up. She offers me her hand and I shake it, her palm warm and firm against mine.

'Jules, good. Please come in.' She waves her hand towards the open doorway and I follow her through. The room smells clean and slightly lemony from the scented candle burning on the mantelpiece. It's early in the year for a fire, but it's burning away in the black Victorian fireplace. I look around for one of those leather chaises longues that shrinks' offices in movies always seem to have, but there's only two chocolate-brown armchairs opposite each other in front of the fireplace. A glass coffee table sits in-between, and there's a tidy wooden roll-top desk against one of the cream walls with two watercolours hanging above it: one of Dalkey Island, the other of Dun Laoghaire Pier.

'Please, take a seat.' She gestures at one of the chairs. My eye catches the large man-sized box of tissues on the table.

I sit down, cross my legs and jiggle my foot nervously. Anne takes a notepad and pen off her desk and takes a seat opposite me.

'Why don't you start by telling me why you're here today?' she says, her voice calm and soothing. 'I believe you had an accident, is that correct?'

I look at her, wondering what else Sheila's referral notes said, but her gaze seems even and non-judgemental.

I nod and take a deep breath. 'I fell out of a tree last Saturday night. Well, a tree house actually. I'd had some champagne and I lost my footing. I was lucky – I landed on a pile of leaves. Knocked myself out though. Was in hospital for two days with bad concussion.'

'Gosh, you poor thing.' She jots something down in the notebook, then asks, 'And how are you feeling now?'

'OK. I have a bit of a headache still, but the doctor said that's normal.'

'It is. And you say you lost your footing. How is your balance normally?'

'Good. I cycle a lot, you have to have pretty good balance to deal with the traffic in Dublin. But I've had quite a lot of accidents recently.'

She doesn't look up from her pad, her pen still poised. 'Any of them also drink related?'

I can feel my cheeks blush. I know there's no point being here unless I tell the truth. 'Most of them I guess.' I tell her about stepping on the glass and about what happened in Dicey Reilly's, an edited version which doesn't include the phone call to Ed, or the fact that I know Noel. I'm not ready to talk about Ed yet, not by a long way. By the end of the Dicey story I'm crying.

She pushes the box of tissues towards me. I was hoping I wouldn't need them quite so soon. I dab at my eyes and blow my nose.

'Sorry,' I murmur. 'You must think I'm an awful eejit.'

'Nothing to be sorry about. And no, I don't think you're an eejit, not at all. That's a terrible thing to happen to anyone. I'm not surprised it still upsets you. No one has the right to treat you like that, but unfortunately there will always be people out there who will take advantage of certain situations.' She sits back in her seat and steeples her fingers, but she doesn't say anything else, which is unnerving. For a few long seconds I don't say anything either. But me being me I have to fill the vacuum.

'And then there are the nightmares,' I say out of the blue, surprising myself. 'Is it normal to have the same kind of nightmare for years and years? Pandora thinks it's weird. She's my sister.'

'A lot of people have recurring dreams,' Anne says. 'Would you like to tell me about yours?'

I focus on the fire for a second. The flame's small and tidy, flickering evenly. Must be gas. Mum refused to have gas fires in our old house, said it was cheating. Plus she loved the smell of peat briquettes and wood burning. It was Pandora's job to take out the ash and clean the fireplace afterwards; she used to let me help her sometimes. I loved brushing the hearth with the tiny fire brush, pretending to be Cinderella.

Anne's voice cuts into my memories. 'Jules? Your dreams?'

I look at her, then down at my hands. Her eyes are so intense and I think I'll find it easier to talk if I'm not looking directly at her.

'The setting changes,' I say in a low voice, staring at the fire again. 'It's sometimes the corridor at my old school, or the hall at home, or a church for some reason, which is weird because I don't go very often, just at Christmas really. I'm usually alone and suddenly my hands start to feel funny. I look down and they're bleeding and it starts dripping all over the ground and within a few seconds I'm standing in a pool of my own blood. Then I wake up. Recently I had one where my niece was dead on the pavement after some sort of accident or something. I was standing over her and my hands were pouring blood onto her broken body.'

I can hear Anne make a tiny tut-tutting noise with her tongue.

'Poor Jules. Very strong imagery going on there – all that blood – it must be frightening.'

I nod and gnaw at my lip, willing myself not to cry.

'What do you think it means?' She cocks her head. 'Have you any idea?'

I shrug. I do have an idea but don't think I can find the words to vocalize it.

Anne tries another tack. 'When did these dreams begin?'

'When I was nine,' I say slowly.

'Was there anything going on in your life at that time? Anything out of the ordinary?'

And then I start crying again. I can't help myself, the tears pour down my cheeks and I wipe them away with my fingers. Anne passes me the box of tissues again and I pull out several and mop up my face.

'I'm so sorry,' I whisper.

'It's fine, honestly. I'm here to listen, that's my job. Lots of people cry when they're talking to me, most in fact. Hence the tissues.' She pats my hand. 'Take your time, Jules. Most clients find the first meeting the hardest if that's any consolation. It does get easier, I promise. Today, I'm just getting to know you, finding out how I can help you. That's all. It's not a test. And if you want to stop right now, that's not a problem.'

'Thanks.' I sniff, then blow my nose again and sigh. 'I'm not used to talking about myself, not like this. My family . . .' I pause. 'We don't talk about the past much. My dad says we should look forwards, not backwards.'

'Sometimes we need to look at the past a little to help us move forwards,' Anne says gently. 'However difficult or painful it might be. Coming to terms with things that have happened in the past helps us find out who we are, and, more importantly, who we want to be. And I know we haven't gone there yet, but you are worried about your drinking, yes?'

'Yes,' I say softly, my cheeks hot again. 'It's not fun any more.

And I do stupid things when I'm drunk, I see that now. I think it's probably better to stop for a while, until I don't *need* to drink.'

'And do you? Need to drink, I mean?'

'When I'm talking to new people, yes. It helps with the nerves. Or when I'm feeling a bit down and want to blot everything out. It just makes everything easier. Takes the edge off.'

'And do you find yourself thinking about having a drink often, say during work for example?'

'Yes,' I admit.

Anne makes some more notes. Then she looks up again. 'You said you drink sometimes to blot everything out, Jules. Blot out what exactly? Do you know?'

I press my lips together. What *did* I mean? I think about this for a minute.

'Painful feelings I guess,' I reply. 'Feelings of inadequacy. Of things not going right. I broke up with my boyfriend last Christmas; he was seeing my best friend behind my back, so that hurt, a lot. I miss them both. I guess I'm quite lonely sometimes.' Tears spring to my eyes again but I blink them away.

'You mentioned your family, Jules. Are you close to your family?'

I nod. 'Yes. We all live together – me, Dad, Bird, that's my granny, my sister, and her little girl, Iris. She's eight.'

'Busy household.'

'It can be, but it seems to work. Myself and Pandora have a bit of a love-hate relationship, but we've been getting on a bit better since we started working together.'

Anne tilts her head. 'Pandora? Unusual name.'

I give a small smile. 'My mum was obsessed by Greek legends. Used to read them to us at bedtime.'

She smiles. 'Of course. Pandora's box. You didn't mention your mum. Does she live elsewhere?'

'She passed away when I was nine. Cancer.'

'Ah, I see. I'm sorry, that must have been hard.' Anne glances down at her notes again and then adds something.

I nod, the tears starting to flow again and before I know what's happening I hear myself say, 'She died on my birthday, May the third. I snuck in early that morning, desperately wanting to see her. Everyone else was still in bed but I couldn't sleep. Her door was always open a crack so I peeked round it and she was awake. She spotted me and told me to come in but be very quiet so I didn't wake anyone else.' I stop for a second and take a few deep breaths.

'And then she told me to climb into the bed beside her. I wasn't usually allowed to do this, Dad said we couldn't 'cause her body was weak and it would hurt her too much. She put her arm around me and I snuggled in to her. She smelt a bit funny but I didn't mind.' My eyes well up again and there's a lump forming in my throat but I make myself continue.

'I stayed there for ages. She told me about her own ninth birthday. She got a bike and she fell off it and scraped both her knees. Bird put this purple stuff on them and in all the birthday party photos she had bright purple knees under her white lace party dress.' I pause again and stare at the fire for a moment before adding, 'And then she said she was sorry that she hadn't had time to make proper memory boxes for me and Pandora, that she'd never thought everything would happen so quickly. I told her it was OK, that even without one I'd never forget her. And then she told me that Pandora would look after me, and Dad and Bird, that she was so sad she wasn't going to be around to watch me grow up, but, but . . .' Now I'm crying so much I really do have to stop.

Anne pats my hand. 'It's OK, Jules,' she says softly. 'You cry as much as you need.'

I soak up my tears with a tissue and wait for a few minutes, taking deep breaths and trying to compose myself. The memory is still so vivid. I can see Mum's pale, drawn face in front of my eyes, remember every word she'd said to me that morning:

'You're so lucky you have a sister, Boolie. I always hated being an only child. Be good to each other, won't you? And is there anything you want to ask me, anything at all?' She was speaking slowly, straining to get the words out, her breath puffy and laboured. But I wanted to talk to her so much, I pretended not to notice.

'Yes, are you really going to die, Mummy? No one will tell me.'

She looked so sad, she didn't have to say anything. I knew the answer was yes.

'When?' I asked.

She blinked slowly then lifted a hand, slowly, so slowly and stroked my hair lovingly.

'Soon, Boolie,' she said softly. 'Too soon. I'm afraid I really am most awfully sick.'

And then I started crying and she just held me. I could hear her breath catching in her chest a little and it scared me, but I stayed there, squeezing her tight against me.

'Don't go, Mummy, I love you. I want you to stay.'

'I don't want to leave you, darling, believe me. But you have to let me go. Please, Boolie?'

'Will you go to heaven, Mummy?'

'I do hope so.'

'Do you hurt a lot?'

'Yes. Remember that time you had flu, Boolie, and you had to stay in bed for a whole week? It's like that but much, much worse.'

'Will you feel better in heaven?'

'Yes.'

'Then you can go to heaven, Mummy. But I'll miss you. Will you sing to me now? "Three Little Swallows"?'

'Of course, my darling.' Then she started to sing, her voice frail and wispy, but still beautiful.

'Three little swallows said we must fly. Summer is over and

winter's nigh. Cold winds are blowing so we must fly, we must all fly . . . over . . . the sea.'

And she sang to me over and over again, until her breath went raspy and wheezy, and her throat started to make rattling noises.

'I'll have to stop now, Boolie,' she whispered. 'Can you go and get your daddy? I need . . . can't . . .' she stopped talking and her eyelids flickered and then shut.

'But I didn't want to leave her,' I tell Anne, as I come back to the present. 'Her breath went really funny for a few seconds then stopped altogether. I got out of the bed and stood beside her, studying her face. It had changed, it seemed softer, all her skin was resting gently on her bones and her jaw wasn't tense any more. I think I knew she'd gone, but she looked so peaceful that I wasn't scared.

'I stayed there for ages. But gradually I started to realize what I'd done and I felt sick. Dad was always telling me and Pandora not to tire her out, that she didn't have the strength to talk for more than a few minutes at a time. But I'd kept her talking for ages. I'd even got into the bed with her, made her sing to me. I'd worn her out; I'd killed her. So I ran out of the room and back into my own and pretended to be asleep.' I pause, remembering the horrific, searing, all-encompassing guilt I'd felt.

Anne is looking at me intently. Finally she says, 'And then?'

'A bit later, I don't know how long exactly, it can't have been long but it felt like hours, I heard Dad shouting Mum's name, Kirsten, and then howling 'No!' and then crying really loudly. That's when I knew he'd found her and it was true, she really was dead.'

I stare at the fire again, watching the flames dance in their even, regular way. 'I know she would have died anyway, but I shortened her life, maybe by days. Because of me she never got to say goodbye to Dad and Pandora and Bird properly. I was selfish, wanted her all to myself.'

For some reason the tears have stopped now and I say this calmly. I've never told anyone before, not like this, and it shocks me.

Eventually Anne says, 'You were nine, Jules. And it was your birthday, of course you wanted to talk to her. You most certainly did not kill her. She died in the arms of someone she loved deeply. And you gave her permission to go and you told her you loved her and would never forget her. You did everything right. Do you understand?'

I nod, but I don't believe her. She's just saying that to make me feel better.

Anne looks at me, her eyes soft and kind. 'I know you don't believe me, not yet. But you will. Have you spoken to your family about this? Pandora or your dad?'

I shake my head.

'No one?'

'Just my friend, Jamie. But that was years ago, when we were teenagers, and we've never discussed it since.'

'So you've been carrying this on your own all these years?'

'Yes.'

'Jules,' Anne says gently, taking my hand in hers. 'You've been through an awful lot. It can't have been easy telling me about your mum, and I appreciate your honesty. You've made an amazing start and over the weeks—'

'Weeks?' I interrupt. 'You mean there's more?'

'Of course. We're just beginning our journey together. Now we've talked a little about your past, we can build on that and talk about the present and the future.'

I sit back in my chair, feeling overwhelmed and exhausted. 'I don't know if I can do this every week. I'm knackered.'

She smiles softly. 'Talking about yourself takes a lot out of you all right. Be gentle with yourself. Take some time off today to treat yourself kindly. A bath maybe, read a book, but most of all, rest. And before I see you next week I'd like you to consider talking to your family about what happened. Can you do that?'

'I'm not sure I'm ready.'

'I understand. Take as much time as you need. But it may not be as difficult as you expect. You were nine, Jules, please keep remembering that. You did nothing wrong. No, scratch that; as I said before, you did everything right.'

'Thank you.' And for the first time in months, I feel calm. Wiped out, yes, but also strangely hopeful.

Chapter 23

That evening Pandora rings my mobile, waking me up. 'Where are you, Jules? It's nearly seven, Arietty will be here any minute.'

I swear under my breath. Bird collected me from Anne's offices at one and dropped me home afterwards. I was so drained I just about managed half a bowl of soup (Bird insisted) before crawling into bed, where I've been ever since, sound asleep.

'There's steak on tonight,' Pandora says. 'Want me to get an order in before all the good pieces go? You know what Klaudia's like – hates waste. Buys twenty steaks and once they're gone, they're gone.' She puts on Klaudia's strongly accented voice. 'You 'vant steak? You come early next time. You late, no steak.'

I laugh. 'Please, I'm starving and I'd kill for a steak. Tell her to put an enormous one aside for me and I'll jump on my bike right now.'

There's a weighted pause. 'Are you sure you should be cycling, Jules? You're supposed to be taking it easy.'

'Stop being such a worry wart, I'll be fine.'

'There's no major rush. Why don't you get the DART? Please? Humour me. I'm sure Arietty won't mind waiting a few minutes.'

I sigh. She's right. The doctor at St Vincent's told me to stay off my bike for another week at least, or until my headaches have stopped.

So I compromise. I cycle to the train station, lock my bike in the cycle rack and DART it to Monkstown. On the train, I gaze

out of the window, thinking about what Anne said about talking to my family about Mum. I know she's right and part of me
wants to get it off my chest once and for all, whatever the con-
sequences, but it terrifies me. Maybe I could start with Pandora.
But not tonight, it's Arietty's Farenze handover dinner and I
don't want to steal her thunder.

Arietty had rung my mobile several times on Sunday, the
morning after her reunion do, but I was still in the hospital
and my phone had run out of battery by that stage. By the time
Pandora had brought in my charger and I'd had a chance to ring
Arietty back, it was Sunday evening and from her frosty tone, I
think she was a bit annoyed I'd taken so long to reply. But when
I told her why she was contrite.

'You poor thing,' she'd said. 'I had concussion once when
Nina accidently headbutted me. It was horrid. Saw stars for
days. And the headaches. Yuck! How are you feeling? Rotten?'

'Pretty bruised and sore. But I was lucky I didn't break anything.' I told her the full story, including the bit about Ed being
there; it felt good to talk to someone. And she didn't ask me
what the hell I was playing at with Ed, like Pandora had; she
didn't tut-tut and sigh in a stomach-clenching manner like Bird;
she didn't even get all hot and bothered about what might have
happened if the leaves hadn't been there, like Dad; she just said,
'You're right, you were very lucky. But I'm sorry you didn't
take Ed with you. I wish it had been his head you landed on,
not those leaves. Appearing at your house like that uninvited.
Stupid man.

'So please tell me you're completely over that creature now,
Jules,' she added succinctly. 'And finally see him for the snake
that he is.' I think Arietty has always understood more about my
poisonous attraction for Ed then anyone else, even though she's
never met him.

'Completely.'

'Hallelujah! Now I'm not going to tell you a thing about the reunion until our dinner on Friday night. You will be out of hospital by then, won't you?'

'Yes, absolutely, I'm looking forward to it. They're keeping me in one or two more nights for observation, then I'll be home.'

I could almost hear the shiver in her voice. 'I hate hospitals, they give me the heebie-jeebies, but I'll come and visit if you're desperate.'

I laughed. 'Friday's good. But I'll be expecting the full gory reunion details, so don't disappoint me.'

She chuckled. 'I won't. And I'll ring you tomorrow, see how you're doing. Don't get too bored.' And with that she was gone.

Arietty was as good as her word – she rang me twice a day, during her lunch break and every evening at around seven. She made me laugh, telling me about clever things her elephants had done and gossip about the other keepers.

Every time I put down the phone to her I smiled to myself. Over the week I became even more fond of Arietty. No, she didn't have an expensive bouquet delivered to my house, like Ed. Guilt flowers, Bird called them. She told the rather shocked delivery man that they weren't wanted and that he could keep them – heaven knows what the poor man thought. Arietty didn't rush over with chocolates the minute I finally got home on Wednesday like Daphne either; and nor did she leave a bundle of new fashion magazines on the doorstep on Thursday morning like Jamie, bless him, but she kept me entertained on a daily basis with her regular as clockwork phone calls, and that meant a lot.

Pandora was incredible, visiting every day. Sometimes she chatted about the shop, other times she just sat with me companionably, dealing with emails on her iPhone while I flicked through magazines. It was nice to have the company.

Once I worked out who the magazines on the doorstep were from – a process of elimination – I finally plucked up the courage to ring Jamie to thank him on Thursday evening. My hands shook as I keyed in his number.

'Jamie?'

'Hi, Jules.' He also sounded a bit nervous. 'How are you feeling?' I expected him to say something about Ed – I was positive Bird had told Daphne the whole story by now, and his mum was never one for keeping things to herself – but he didn't.

'OK, and I'm so sorry, Jamie. I've made such a mess of things. You were right about my drinking. It was getting out of hand. I'm seeing someone tomorrow. I'm having my first um, meeting, consultation, shrink visit? Whatever you call it.'

'I'm glad you're getting help, Jules.'

His voice was so kind, so genuine, I found myself saying, 'And I'm sorry about Ed and everything. Being taken in by him. Lying to you. I know it's no excuse but I really did love him. He broke my heart when he went off with Lainey like that and I just couldn't let go. But it's over now, I'm finally moving on to pastures new. Or men new I should say.' I gave a hollow laugh.

Jamie was silent for a moment. Then finally he said, 'He never deserved you, Jules. I'm glad you see that now.' There was a catch in his voice and he quickly added, 'Look, I'm sorry I have to go. But are you still planning on going to that bloody wedding on Saturday?'

'Yes, why?'

'I'm glad you're getting the chance to wear that dress you're so mad about, that's all. Pink isn't it?'

'Yep, I'll be collecting it at our handover dinner in Shoestring tomorrow evening.' The thought of a night out with Arietty and Pandora had been keeping me going all week.

'Enjoy yourselves.'

I put down the phone, thinking how sweet it was of Jamie to remember the dress.

On the train to Shoestring to meet the girls, I'm so lost in thought about Mum and Ed and Lainey and the wedding that I almost miss my stop. Luckily I spot the Monkstown sign while the doors are still open and nip through them just in time.

Walking briskly it only takes me five minutes to get to Shoestring and I pause outside for a moment, looking at the shop window, lit up from behind. It looks fantastic. The elephants are still marching over the silk-covered 'hills'. I smile to myself. They'll have to come out soon, and in a funny way I'll miss them. Pandora said the big ones can stay on either side of the door for now, which is just as well as we'd need a van to shift them. I think I'll ask Bird to take the little ones home in her car for Iris. And Arietty might like one too, even if the tusks are 'wrong'.

While looking in the window I spot Arietty chatting to Pandora at the edge of my favourite booth. I watch for a second as Arietty covers her mouth with her hand and giggles into it, her eyes crinkling with delight. I wonder what Pandora has said that's so funny. For a second I feel a dart of jealousy that they're getting on so well – Arietty's *my* friend, not Pandora's – then I stop myself being so petty. I should be delighted that they like each other. I walk inside, determined to be my best self and not to drag the conversation down this evening with any talk of my accident or my session with Anne. And for the first time in years, I'm going to eat without washing down my dinner with wine.

As I approach the booth, Arietty stands up and gives me a warm hug. She smells sweet, like icing sugar mixed with vanilla. Her strong arms give me one final squeeze, then let go.

'How's the head?' she says, stepping back a little and checking me out. 'Can't see any lumps.'

I smile. 'There was an almighty egg right here.' I touch the back of my skull gingerly. 'But it's gone down now. Still pretty sore though.'

'You poor creature. I'm just going to pee.' Arietty points at the seat beside her. 'Squeeze in there. Then when I get back I'll tell you both all about my horrific ordeal.'

I stare at her quizzically.

She smiles. 'The reunion.'

I laugh. 'Ah, right.'

Arietty skips off, leaving Pandora and me alone. I slip into the booth and shuffle along the seat, so I'm sitting opposite her.

'How are you feeling, Jules?' She slides her hand across the table and touches my hand with her fingertips. 'Bird said the counselling session took a lot out of you.'

I whistle under my breath. 'No kidding, it was pretty intense. The counsellor, Anne, was nice, but boy did I cry. Went through nearly a whole box of tissues.'

She leans towards me, her face sympathetic. Pandora knows I hate crying in front of people. She's exactly the same. 'Cry? Did you tell her about . . . you know, the thing that happened in Dicey Reilly's?'

I nod. 'Yeah. And about the accident, and Mum dying and everything.'

She looks very surprised. 'Wow, really? What was it like, telling a stranger about stuff like that? Was it weird?'

I shrug. 'Actually it was OK. Anne was pretty easy to talk to. She just sat there and listened.'

'Did she give you any advice about the drinking?'

'No, it wasn't like that. And Pandora, I know we've never really talked about it, any of us, but there's something I want to tell you, about Mum and about the day—'

Arietty reappears so I stop abruptly.

'Budge over,' Arietty tells me and I scoot further along the seat.

Pandora's still looking at me, a strange expression on her face.

I mouth 'Later' at her and she gives me a tiny nod then says, 'Let's order, girls. Klaudia put aside three steaks just in case. Do you like steak, Arietty?'

Arietty's eyes narrow and she practically growls at Pandora. 'Do I look like a person who eats animals, Pandora Schuster?'

Pandora blinks in fright. Arietty does look pretty scary. I lift my menu over my mouth to stifle my giggles.

Pandora backtracks. 'No, no of course not. I'm a big animal lover myself.'

I give a little cough and Pandora glares at me.

'Why don't we all have fish?' Pandora suggests instead.

Arietty doesn't look impressed. 'Fish are animals too. They have eyes and brains. OK, not very big ones, but they still think.'

Pandora reads the menu again. 'Goat's cheese and rocket tartlets?' she says, failing to keep the disappointment out of her voice. 'Or are you a vegan?'

Arietty shakes her head. 'No. The tartlets sound good.'

I sigh inwardly. I was really looking forward to a big juicy steak. I put the menu on the table and press my head against the wooden seat back, remembering the bruise only after I've done it.

'Ow,' I say, rubbing my skull.

'You hurting yourself again, Jules?' Pandora says gently. 'Be careful.'

Then she looks around the table. 'So it's three goat's cheese tartlets, yes? Any starters? The chicken liver pâté's delicious, but I guess that's out.' She looks archly at Arietty, who has the good grace to smile back at her.

'Oh, have your bloody steaks,' Arietty says with a little huff, although I think it's a bit put on. 'Just do me a favour and eat them quickly, OK? And please don't order them blue.'

'Excellent.' I sit up straighter, feeling instantly brighter. 'I'll have mine medium-rare with chips and garlic potatoes. I could eat the arse of an elephant I'm so hungry.'

Arietty scrunches up her nose. 'Jules, that's gross.'

I just grin at her.

Once we've all placed our orders with Klaudia, I turn to Arietty. 'So Dr Dolittle, you've kept us in suspense long enough. Reunion story please, full disclosure.'

Arietty smiles. 'No problem. I've been dying to tell you all week but I wanted to wait until we were all together. OK, so the taxi drive was uneventful, but I nearly barfed in the back I was so nervous. I got to the hotel – the Radisson Bleu, which is pretty swish – and I walked in and tried to remember what you told me, Jules, to hold my head up and not to slouch. There was a drinks reception in the bar first, so I headed towards it and I was so nervous my hands were shaking. It was quite dark and everyone was hovering around the bar in groups, it was like being in school again, all the hockey girls together, the prefects, the D4s, the drama club girls, it was terrifying.' She gives a shiver.

'I can imagine,' I murmur.

Arietty continues. 'Luckily I spotted one of the girls from my class who was always fun, Denise. She was chatting to a gang of girls who were pretty much the brains of our year – Ash and Stephanie – nice girls, quiet, tended to keep to themselves. They all looked amazing in these 1950s style dresses, vintage Chanel and Dior apparently. Their make up was perfect, red lips and smoky eyes, and their hair was in fab old-fashioned buns. I honestly didn't recognize any of them. Turns out they'd all hired their dresses in this vintage shop in Blackrock called Cocobelle and the owner had organized a hair and make up artist for them too. They'd had a day of pampering. You could do something like that here, girls.'

Pandora nods. 'That's not a bad idea. Certainly something to consider. And what did they think of the Farenze?'

Arietty beams. 'Swooned over it. And they loved the jacket. I felt like a movie star. I told them all about your shop too.'

'Good woman,' Pandora says.

'And what were the D4s wearing?' I ask, already guessing the answer.

Arietty rolls her eyes. 'Full-length evening dresses slashed to their belly buttons and buckets of orange fake tan, very footballers' wives. It's funny, compared to Denise and her friends, they looked really out of date. But Sasha's dress was pretty spectacular, red silk, slashed across the breasts and at the stomach. The D4s do love their slashes.'

'Who's Sasha?' Pandora asks.

'Sorry, Pandora,' Arietty says, 'she was head girl, and a real bully. But I have to admit she looked amazing. It was a while before I spotted her. I felt someone staring at me so I turned around and there she was.'

Arietty puts on a snide sounding D4 accent. 'She said "If it isn't Little Miss Exotic? If it wasn't for . . . like, you know, your skin, I never would have recognized you."'

I snort. 'Cheeky little minx.'

'She sounds a right cow,' Pandora adds.

'It gets worse, believe me,' Arietty says. 'From the way Sasha was slurring her words, I think she'd already had quite a bit to drink. After drinks, we sat down for dinner. Luckily only the top table was seated so I joined Denise's gang. Then Sasha climbed onto a podium and welcomed us to 'her' reunion and then warned us she had lots of juicy gossip for her after-dinner speech. During dinner we chatted about what we were all up to now. Denise is almost qualified as a doctor which is pretty impressive. When I told them where I worked and what I did they all thought it was cool.'

'Why wouldn't they?' I say. 'It *is* cool.'

She shrugs. 'I think so. But I guess I was nervous of saying anything because of Sasha's reaction. Anyway I spent most of the meal telling them about Beatrix and Enid and the gang.'

Arietty pauses as Klaudia arrives with our food. We decided against starters, the desserts in Shoestring are to die for and we all want to leave room.

I tuck quickly into my steak, practically moaning as I chew the tender meat. After several mouthfuls I realize I'm being very rude.

'Sorry, Arietty,' I say. 'I'm ravenous. Tell us more about Denise and the gang. They sound really nice.'

Arietty shrugs. 'Yeah, they are. But apart from school we don't have much in common. Although at the end of the evening, Denise did suggest starting a Sasha Davenport hate club, meeting every month to stick pins in a wax doll. Sasha's speech was pretty appalling.'

'Go on,' Pandora says eagerly. 'What did she say?'

Arietty shifts around in her seat a little, getting comfortable. 'It all started off innocently enough. But it was clear she'd been laying into the wine at dinner big time. She staggered back onto the podium and thanked the usual people. Then she pulled out this sheet of paper, said it was her gossip list. Admitted she'd spent the previous month googling old girls, checking out their Facebook pages and basically stalking everyone. There was a lot of nervous coughing in the room as you can imagine.'

'OK, Arietty,' I say, 'that's just freaky.'

'I know,' Arietty says. 'And she didn't hold back during her speech. First up she read out a list of people who had sent their regrets. One of them was Em Hardman. She read out her email which said she couldn't come to the reunion 'cause she'd lost a baby recently and wasn't up to socializing. Sasha read out every word, including some really personal stuff that I'm sure was meant just for her.'

Pandora gasps. 'Seriously said that? In front of everyone?'

Arietty nods. 'Yep. But believe me, it gets worse. Sasha spotted Denise and waved. She said, "I found a lovely picture of you on the Dublin LGBTQ Pride march last year, Denise." Then she explained that *LGBTQ* stands for lesbian, gay, bisexual, transgender and questioning. And she flashed up a picture on this big tv screen of Denise in a curly pink wig, holding a placard saying, "Out and Proud". Denise was mortified at first, but then everyone started clapping and cheering and yelling, "Good for you, Denise" and I think she was quite touched. But Sasha didn't look too pleased. I'm sure she thought we'd all be shocked.

'Then a video clip started playing on the screen. This time it was me, talking to some children at the zoo. The sound wasn't great so you couldn't hear what I was saying, but during the clip Beatrix squirts me with water from her trunk and I get drenched. It's on the Dublin Zoo website. Apparently it's one of the most popular clips – kids love it.

'So anyway, Sasha said, "Even the elephants think Arietty smells. You see, Arietty spends her day shovelling elephant crap, don't you Arietty?"

'At that stage I'd had enough, so I yelled, "I wish I could shovel some over your head right now, Sasha. You've always been full of shit. And you've always been a bully and you're still a bully."'

'Go, Arietty!' Pandora says, and I give Arietty a big pat on the back.

'What happened then?' I ask, all ears.

'She opened her mouth to say something else but one of her D4 friends grabbed her and dragged her off the stage and out of the room. It was pretty dramatic.'

I stare at Arietty. I've forgotten all about my food. From the way Pandora's staring at her too, mouth open, she's exactly the same.

'No kidding,' I say. 'How long did you stay after that, Arietty?'

'Not long. After dinner, when everything had died down a bit, I tried to make my way towards the door, but loads of girls came up to me and said hi. Said they'd always been in awe of Sasha, but not any more. And every single one of them said how beautiful I looked and how much they loved the elephant video clip. So in the end it wasn't such a bad night after all, I'm glad I went. But I hope I never set eyes on Sasha Davenport again.'

I give a low whistle. 'That's quite a story, Arietty. Well done for sticking up for yourself, I'm proud of you. Now we'd all better tuck in before our food gets cold.'

Pandora looks a little worried.

'What is it, sis?' I ask.

'I'm just trying to figure out how we write that one up on the Shoestring blog.'

I smile. 'I think we'll stick to photographs of Arietty in the Farenze.'

Pandora laughs. 'Probably best.'

'So it's you next, Jules,' Arietty says, picking up her knife and fork and cutting into her tartlet. 'To wear the dress I mean. Pandora hung it up somewhere.'

'In the office,' Pandora says. 'Along with the silver belt and the Rick Owens jacket. It's all safe.'

Arietty is still looking at me. 'You OK about tomorrow?'

My fingers tingle with nerves. I'd almost forgotten. It's D-Day – Ed and Lainey's wedding.

I shrug. 'After your experience, tomorrow will be a doddle.'

Pandora and Arietty both look at me.

'What?' I say. 'It's only a wedding.' But even I know that I'm kidding myself. The steak starts to taste like cardboard in my mouth but I soldier on. At least I'll look stunning and I'll make quite the entrance with Declan on my arm. And that's half the battle.

Chapter 24

'You ready, Jules?' Declan asks. We're sitting in his car on the side of the road opposite St Jude's Church and my hands are shaking like a leaf. My stomach was so tight this morning I couldn't eat a thing. God knows what a glass of champagne would do to me in this state, so it's just as well I'm teetotal these days.

I'm actually rather proud of myself. It's been exactly six and a half days since I last had a drink. I can't deny I've had cravings, like at dinner last night, but I managed to stick to soft drinks instead. And in fact being sober while out wasn't as bad or as scary as I thought it would be. And I didn't miss the hangover this morning, that's for sure.

'One more minute,' I tell him, then stare out of the window at all the familiar faces passing us by – Lainey's aunts, uncles and cousins; mutual friends I haven't seen in a long time; a couple of Lainey's work colleagues in neat pastel-coloured shift dresses. I'm wearing dark glasses and no one's spotted me yet.

No sign of Noel, thank God. I never got around to asking Ed, but after the whole Dicey Reilly business, he couldn't be on the guest list.

'We'd better get inside before the bridal party arrives,' Declan says gently. 'And I think that might be them.' He nods at the Rolls-Royce that is waiting to pull into the church gates.

My stomach lurches. Declan's right. It's now or never. I take a deep breath, open the door and climb out. Declan locks the car and then takes my arm.

'Ready?' He gives me a reassuring smile.

'Ready as I'll ever be.'

We walk up the path together. I fix my eyes on the church doorway, blocking everything to my right and left, concentrating on looking happy and confident. Having Declan to literally lean on makes all the difference. When Pandora first suggested asking him to be my plus one I thought she was crazy.

'And why would he do that exactly?' I asked her.

'Because he's a decent guy and he understands about betrayal and keeping up appearances. Go on, ask him, see what he says.'

So I did. I was expecting him to let me down gently, but Pandora was right. After I explained the background, how I just wanted to show my face, prove that Ed and Lainey hadn't broken me, he said he'd be delighted to be my plus one. There was one small hitch, he had to collect his daughter from a party at four. He explained that things were difficult with his ex-wife at the moment so he had to turn up in person, but he'd happily walk me up the aisle, drive me to the reception and stick around for as long as he could. It was more than I could have hoped for and I'm deeply grateful for the support. He really is one of life's good guys.

Declan holds tight as we walk into the church.

'Bride or groom,' a dark-haired man I don't recognize asks us. He must be one of Lainey's English cousins I've never met.

The other usher I do know. It's Danny.

'Hiya, Jules,' Danny says gently, leaning down to kiss my cheek. He looks inquiringly at Declan but I don't introduce them and Danny doesn't ask.

'Where do you want to sit, babes?' Danny says.

'With Clara if she's here.'

He shakes his head. 'She's been off work all week. Some sort of flu thing.'

'Then Ed's side, please,' I say firmly. I was up all night thinking about the wedding, and where I sit in the church is one thing

I *do* have control over, so I'm going to call the shots. Plus I know sitting there will get up Lainey and her sisters' noses.

And sure enough, as soon as Declan and I sit down halfway up the church on the right-hand side, the whispers start.

'Who's that on Julia's arm?' I hear one of Lainey's deaf aunts say a little too loudly. 'Rather fine-looking chap, isn't he?'

'Shush,' someone tells her, but it's too late. I can feel several sets of eyes gazing at me and Declan, and I bury my head in the wedding missal.

Declan takes my hand in his and squeezes it. I look at him and smile. He said he'd done lots of amateur dramatics in college and was sure he could pull off 'deeply in love and besotted'. And sure enough, his eyes are soft and doe-like, and a goofy smile is playing on his lips.

I squeeze his hand back and chuckle to myself. My stomach is still a riot of nerves, but I'm coping.

But then I spot two figures at the top of the church talking to the clergyman. It's Ed and his best man, his cousin, Harry. Ed looks incredible in a traditional grey morning suit, the sky-blue of his waistcoat making his eyes shine like sapphires. My knees almost buckle.

'You OK?' Declan whispers.

'Talk to me,' I say frantically. 'About anything.'

'You look stunning,' he says. 'Pandora's dress looks amazing on you.'

I don't correct him. I'm delighted for Pandora that he's remembered what she was wearing at the ball.

'It looks better on her,' I say instead. 'She's got the height for it.'

He shrugs. 'It suits you both in different ways. And I love the jacket. And the hair.'

I smile at him. 'You say all the right things.' I'm wearing the same Rick Owens that Arietty wore to her reunion, and, inspired by Arietty's friends, I asked the hairdresser to give me a 1950s-style bun. In mid-height heels – last thing I want to do is to trip today – the silver Bohinc belt (I was humming and hawing about it this morning, but Pandora insisted, said it really finished off the outfit) and the jacket, I feel pretty good. Pandora helped me with my make up, simple eyes and strong ruby-red lips. She also gave me a stirring pep talk.

'You walk into that church with your head held high,' she said. 'Remember you look a million dollars and we're all rooting for you – me and Arietty especially. If you have any wobbles, any at all, run into the loo and ring me immediately, understand? And good luck, Boolie. I love you.'

'I'm not going into battle, Pandora,' I'd said as she squeezed me tight against her chest, as if she'd never see me again. But I appreciated the support.

'The bride is in the house,' Declan says in a low voice. 'Don't look.'

But I can't help it, I swing around and catch a glimpse of Lainey and her sisters just inside the church door. The sisters are fluffing up the skirt of her wedding dress and arranging her puffy veil over her face.

I stare at Lainey. I expected to see her in something classic and elegant – a silk sheath dress and neat veil – not this frothy, over the top creation. Don't get me wrong, it's not horrible by any means, and with all the tulle on the ballerina skirt and the heavy satin train sweeping out behind her, it must have cost a fortune. But the dress swamps her small frame and makes her look quite wide and hippy, when she's actually very petite.

And I hate to admit it, but I smile inwardly. Lainey's sisters, clearly her stylists on this occasion, have done her a disservice. If I'd been in charge – and Lainey always listened to me when it came to clothes – she wouldn't have looked as though she'd been eaten by Disney's Cinderella.

The organist starts playing the wedding march and I set my face into a rictus smile as I watch Lainey's sisters hustle the flower girls in front of them, elbow each other into place and then walk up the aisle slowly, counting out their steps carefully under their breath. Karen's back visibly stiffens as we lock eyes, and I throw her by giving her a wink. She almost walks into one of the flower girls.

It's only when I look towards the chancel and I spot Ed's face, beaming as he watches Lainey walking towards him, that I start withering inside. I can't tear my eyes off him and I can feel my heartbeat quicken. I try to slow it down by taking a few deep yoga breaths and distract myself by clenching and unclenching my calves in time with the music, trying not to think about how happy he looks. Because he looks ecstatic, his eyes are sparkling and he can't stop grinning. And as Lainey takes each step towards him it's as if someone's nailing a tiny shard of glass into my heart. Finally she reaches the top of the aisle and Ed takes her hand. I have to bite inside my cheek, hard, to stop myself crying.

'Jules?' Declan whispers. 'Still all right? You look a bit pale.'

'Hanging in there.' I squeeze his hand. 'Thanks.'

I'm relieved when the clergyman, a surprisingly young-looking man with short dark hair and a friendly, round face, invites us to sing the first hymn – 'All Things Bright and Beautiful' – and I concentrate on singing the words, trying to block out everything else.

Declan's voice soars out – I'd forgotten what a good singer he is – and several people are looking at him, clearly impressed. I catch Lainey's mum checking him out and then, realizing he's with me, she gives me a gentle smile and mouths, 'Hi, Jules.'

She was always a decent woman, kind. It's a pity how everything's worked out. I miss spending time in her kitchen; I miss *her*.

After another hymn, the clergyman says, 'And before we move on to the wedding ceremony itself, this is the part every bride and groom dreads.' He pauses and then continues in a more serious voice, 'If there be anyone present who may show just and lawful cause why this couple should not be legally wed, let him speak now or forever hold his peace.'

Declan squeezes my hand again. He asked me in the car was I going to say anything at the 'forever hold your peace' point of the ceremony. I think he was only joking.

I said, 'What, you mean about Ed and Lainey betraying my trust and being lying, sneaky toads?'

He'd laughed. 'Something like that.'

I'd said no. And I meant it. But by God, right at this second I sure as hell feel like saying something.

And is it my imagination, or can I feel eyes boring into my back? I keep my head up and stare straight in front of me, holding Declan's hand tightly in my own.

And Declan, bless him, leans down and gives the top of my head a tiny kiss. Ha! That will perplex any gossipmongers who are staring at me, just waiting for any sign of longing or regret on my face.

The clergyman says, 'Good, good, that's what I like to hear, silence,' and then launches into the vows.

The vows are hard, I can't deny it. Lainey's voice is quivering so much I can barely hear what's she's saying and she starts crying as soon as Ed belts out his 'I do'. My heart softens a little, she's always been such a marshmallow when it comes to weddings. Then they're pronounced man and wife and everyone claps and cheers. I join in and try to appear genuine.

'It's over now, Jules,' Declan says in a low voice as we stand for the last hymn, 'Love Divine'. 'You put on a good show.'

I give him a smile. 'So did you. Thanks, Declan.'

He brings my hand to his lips and kisses it. 'You're most welcome, my love.'

Walking out of the church is hard. Ed and Lainey are standing at the doorway, holding hands, waiting to greet their guests as Mr and Mrs Powers. Lainey and I always said we'd keep our own names when we got married, but from the clergyman's quip – 'Mr Powers you may now kiss Mrs Powers' – she's obviously changed her mind. Or maybe she was never the girl I thought she was.

Standing there, holding Ed's hand, gazing at him proudly, she looks blissfully happy. Close up she looks glowing, her tasteful make up highlighting her light-brown eyes, her hair in a loose chignon with soft curls around her face. Pity about the dress though.

For a moment I forget how much she's hurt me and I manage to say, 'You look beautiful, Lainey. I hope you'll be very happy together.'

She stares at me. 'Jules. You're here.'

'I promised I'd come, remember? To say goodbye.'

She nods, looking genuinely sad. 'Thanks. It means a lot to me. To us both.' She pulls Ed's arm and he swings around.

'It's Jules,' she adds, her hand still firmly holding his arm.

'Jules,' he says. He seems lost for words and his eyes flicker around nervously. There's an awkward silence.

'We'd better get you out of the cold, darling,' Declan says, putting his arm around me. 'Excuse us.' And we walk away together. It's only when I step into the car, I realize I'm quivering all over. I check my face in my compact mirror. I look a little pale under my foundation, but my hair remains perfect and my red movie-star lips are still in place.

I flip the compact closed and sit back in the seat.

'God I need a drink,' I say. I'm ashamed to say my hands are shaking a little. Sheila warned me about this, but it's happening far more often than I'd like. And I'm slowly beginning to realize just what all the drinking was doing to my system, not to mention my mental health. Every day I'm more and more determined to stay off it.

Declan says nothing for a second and from the way he's staring out of the windscreen I know Pandora's said something to him. He starts the engine and pulls out.

'Did you eat anything this morning?' he asks.

'No, I couldn't face it.'

'You'll feel better once you've eaten.'

Declan grabs two bacon rolls from a deli in Dun Laoghaire. We eat them on the way to the reception and I start to feel much better. We don't say much at first, focusing on eating. We're early and Declan finds a parking space just outside the yacht club and we sit in the car, watching the front door.

'Everyone must be still outside the church,' Declan says. 'Maybe they're doing a group photo or something. But I thought it was best to get you out of there before you keeled over.'

After wiping my mouth and fingers on a napkin I say, 'You were right, I really needed to eat. You've been so sweet to me today, Declan. I wish I could find someone like you.'

He looks at me, a smile on his lips. 'Are you ready for someone like me?'

'What do you mean?'

'Pandora told me a little about the groom. Sounds like you had a pretty tempestuous relationship.'

I think about this for a second. With Ed, all the drama that came with arguing, breaking up and then making up seemed normal, but I guess it's anything but.

'I guess we did,' I say. 'How are you doing for time?'

He glances at his watch. 'Not great. It's already half three I'm afraid. But Rachel's party is only up the road. Dads are expected to be a bit late.'

I laugh. 'If you're sure.'

We watch for a while as guests start to arrive. I spot Danny struggling to get a huge flower arrangement through the door and I make a decision.

'I'll be OK,' I tell Declan. 'Just the drinks reception and the meal to endure now. You've been an absolute angel, but it's time to fly solo.'

'Are you sure?'

I nod. 'Yes.'

'I'll go inside with you,' he says. 'Explain to a few busybodies that I'm a fireman and I have to leave early for my next life-saving shift.'

I grin. 'I dare you to say that.'

He chuckles. 'You're on. Do I look like a hunky fireman?' He sticks his jaw out and sucks in his cheekbones.

'Absolutely.'

And he's as good as his word. He manages to tell two of Lainey's aunts his fabricated story in the bar before kissing me soundly on the lips (I hope Pandora doesn't mind), and saying, 'I love you, babe. Can't wait for tonight, hot stuff,' and leaving me to my fate.

As soon as he's gone one of them asks me, 'Was it hard for you today, pet? I know you were very fond of Ed.' She pats my arm.

I gulp, trying to keep it together. 'It was a bit. But now that I've found Declan . . .' I tail off. 'But please excuse me.' I spot Danny talking to someone on the balcony outside, so I walk quickly through the door before anyone else has the chance to grab me. But as soon as I get there, I wish I hadn't. A whole team of Lainey's batty aunts would be better than this.

Because standing there, bold as brass, is Noel Hegarty.

I can feel blood rushing to my head and whooshing past my ears, and for a second I think I'm going to either vomit or pass out. Then I hear Danny's voice and feel a hand on my arm.

'Jules, Jules, are you OK?'

'Maybe she's coming down with that virus thing Clara has,' I hear Noel say.

Just then one of Lainey's aunts calls Danny from the doorway. 'Danny, where are people to put their presents? Is there a special room?'

'Excuse me a second,' he says and walks off, leaving Noel and me alone.

'Maybe you should sit down, Jules,' Noel says, calm as anything.

I say nothing, just stare at the floor and shake my head. I can't bear to look at the man. How dare he act as if nothing happened between us? I turn to follow Danny inside when Noel grabs my arm. I'm glad I'm wearing a jacket, I couldn't stand his fingers touching my bare skin.

'We're all right, aren't we, Jules?' he says in a low, loaded voice.

What's he talking about? Of course we're not 'all right'. Is he deranged? I shake his hand off, still unable to speak, and run inside. I push through the crowds gathering in the bar and manage to find the toilet. Locking myself in a cubicle, I sit down on the closed seat and lean forward, resting my head in my hands. I'm too shocked and disgusted to cry. And angry, seethingly angry. At Noel for daring to speak to me like that, but most of all at Ed for inviting him. What was he thinking? He promised he'd take care of everything, so what the hell is Noel doing at his bloody wedding? I feel humiliated, betrayed, but, most of all, furious.

I sit up and stare at the closed cubicle door, my blood still pounding through my veins. I can't stay here all day. But I'm in no state to go back outside, not with *him* out there, ready to grab me again. I have to do something, but what?

I pull my mobile out of my bag. I consider ringing Pandora, but then stop myself. There's nothing she can do and talking to her might just make me cry. Arietty too. Jamie? I shake the idea out of my head. I've burnt my bridges there too many times. Then it comes to me, Clara. She's always hated Noel; maybe she'll understand. I know Ed told me to keep it to myself, but right now I'm so hurt and angry I feel like storming his precious radio station, hijacking a studio and broadcasting what happened to the nation.

I find Clara's number and ring it.

'Hello?' She sounds nervous. 'Jules? Aren't you at the wedding?'

'Yes. But it's not going so well. Can you talk?'

'Sure. But I'm supposed to be off with flu. Please don't say anything to Ed or Danny about speaking to me. Or Noel if he's there. Especially Noel.'

'Are you bunking off work?'

She sighs. 'It's complicated. I have a doctor's cert all right, but it's not flu. I've been having panic attacks. The doctor thinks they're stress related, brought on by work.'

'You do put in incredibly long hours, Clara.'

'It's not the hours. It's something that keeps happening, something . . .' she stops abruptly. 'Look, I've already said too much.'

She sounds anxious and upset. Something occurs to me. 'Clara, it doesn't have anything to do with Noel, does it?'

There's silence for a second. 'Has Ed said something to you?'

'No, nothing.' I take a deep breath. It's now or never. 'Clara, Noel attacked me. In Dicey Reilly's. Put his hand up my skirt. I managed to knee him and run away. And now he's here, at the wedding.'

'Oh, Jules. It's all my fault. I should never have left you there in that state, knowing what he's like. I'm so sorry.'

'What he's like? You mean he's done it before?'

'Remember Antonia? The researcher before Mickey? He used to say things to her, how hot she was looking, how she must be a real goer in bed, that kind of thing; then he started sending her porn links, disgusting stuff, then asking had she watched them. She reported him for sexual harassment but he managed to wangle his way out of it. She was moved to another show but he used to follow her into the car park. She was so freaked out she left the station altogether. Well he's started to do the same thing to me. It's more subtle, he's covering his tracks this time; cornering me in the office when no one's around, whispering things at my back. It's revolting. And I can't cope any more. He's never going to stop. I didn't think he was capable of actually attacking anyone, but after what you've said he clearly is. I can't stay there, Jules. I'm going to have to leave the show and maybe the station.'

'Clara, that's appalling. And you can't leave, you're brilliant at your job. Can't you say something to Ed or one of the others? Danny even?'

She gives a dry laugh. 'Ed? I told him what was going on, asked for his help and he told me he'd have a word with Noel. But nothing changed. Ed is Noel's lapdog, Jules. Sorry, but it's true. And Danny's just as bad when it comes to Noel. Thinks the sun shines out of his ass. I'm afraid the close-knit Danny Delaney team is all a sham. Just a bunch of egos all looking to claw their way to the top. It's the biggest show on the whole bloody network and Noel has the powers that be in his pocket. Even if I did report him, they're all so hungry to keep the ratings high, I doubt if they'd do anything about it even if they did believe me.' She sounds so bitter and so unlike the Clara I know that it makes me shiver. 'And frankly I'm not prepared to throw my own career away by being branded as a telltale. I saw what happened to Antonia and it wasn't pleasant. I've worked too hard to be spat out of the system like that. No, I think I'll start looking for a job on another station and until then keep out of the bloody man's way.'

'He can't just get away with it,' I say strongly. 'I'm going to say something to him. Tell him if he doesn't resign and leave you the hell alone I'll tell everyone what happened in Dicey Reilly's.'

'Be careful, Jules. Noel's clever, he knows exactly what to say to get himself out of bad situations. It's probably best just to steer well clear of him.'

'No! That's exactly what he wants me to do. You too. Someone has to stand up to him, Clara. And I don't have as much to lose as you do. I'm going to confront him, right now, before I chicken out.'

'You're amazing, Jules. I really admire you, but please be careful.'

I give a wry laugh. 'Clara, I'm a mess. But he can't get away with this.'

'Ring me later, Jules, OK? But mind yourself. And make sure there are people around when you talk to him, understand?'

'I will, I promise.' I click off the phone and walk out of the cubicle. I check myself out in the mirror and take a deep breath before swinging the door open. I make my way down the corridor, through the bar and back outside again. My palms are sticky with nerves but I steel myself. I'm not doing this for myself alone any more, I'm doing it for Clara and Antonia too, and for all the other girls whose lives and careers Noel might destroy in the future. I focus on how disgusted I feel – Noel, Ed, Danny – they're all the same. I'll need all the anger I can muster to confront Noel. He's still on the balcony, finishing a cigarette. He stubs it out rather aggressively under the sole of his boot and then turns, sees me and smiles. But his eyes are flat.

'Everything OK, Jules?'

I look around. There's a couple lighting cigarettes down the far end of the balcony which makes me feel a little less afraid. For a second, I'm dumbstruck, then his lips curl into a sneer.

'No!' I snap.

'What is it now, Jules? And why the serious face? Go and knock back a few drinks. You're really boring when you're sober. Go on, have a vodka and show us your tits like you used to.'

I blush deeply. Unfortunately he's right. But it only happened once. Ed made me stop, got a bit jealous I think.

'Don't be so crude,' I say. 'And what the hell are you doing here?'

He laughs again. 'Ed invited me. What's it to you?'

OK, now I'm bristling. 'You fucking attacked me, you pig!'

He puts up both his hands. 'Whoa, there, Jules. You can't go around making accusations like that.'

'But it's true.'

'Says who?'

I stare at him. 'You apologized, Noel. I still have the email.'

He shrugs. 'We had a brief affair. I broke up with you. You didn't take it so well, Ed had a word with you, sorted everything out. That's what happened.' He lifts his eyebrows at me. 'I think if you re-read the email you'll see that's all it says. Yeah, I tried it on, big deal, but you can't prove a thing.'

'You bastard! But Ed knows the truth. I want you to resign from the radio station or he'll tell everyone what really happened.'

He snorts. 'You don't get it, do you, Jules? Ed's on my side. I've just recommended him for the producer's job on the *Drive Time Show*. He's not going to jeopardize his career, not for you. And for feck's sake, stop with the long face and the moaning. You and that Clara are just the same. Can't take a joke.'

'Being attacked is not a joke. Neither is being sexually harassed at work.'

'What do you expect? Clara's boobs are massive and she wears those tight tops, what's a guy to do? And you're a right cock-tease yourself. Look like a slut and people will treat you like a slut.'

He has such an ugly expression on his face, tears spring to my eyes. Clara's right, he's a pig and if what he says about Ed is right, he's won.

'And for God's sake stop the flaming waterworks, woman. This is supposed to be a wedding. Our conversation is over. Keep away from me, understand? Jesus wept, *women*. You're psycho, the lot of you.' And with that he walks back inside, leaving me a wet rag of frustration, anger and exhaustion.

I flop down on one of the wooden benches and stare out to sea. It's a beautiful day, crisp and bright. I watch the water for a while, allowing my breath to slow and trying to blink back the tears that are flowing down my face. My make up must be ruined but I don't care. I'm going to wait here until the tears have stopped, then slink home. It hasn't been the wedding experience I was hoping for, but I'm done. With Lainey and most especially with Ed.

Ed put his career over me. Simple as that. And he didn't protect Clara, even when she begged him for his help. What kind of person would behave like that? Not someone I'd ever want to end up with, that's for sure. I am totally, 100 per cent cured of Ed Powers. In fact, I'm starting to feel sorry for Lainey.

'Budge over.' Danny appears beside me a few minutes later. 'I'm being chased by mad Anderson aunts and it's not pretty. I'm dying for a fag.' He slots in beside me and offers me the box of Marlboro Red. 'Want one?'

I shake my head.

Only then does he notice the tears.

'What's up, Jules? Finding today hard, is that it?'

'No. Danny, I quite honestly wouldn't know where to start.'

He pulls on his cigarette. 'Try me.'

I look at him. He seems genuine. And for Danny he seems pretty calm and, more importantly, sober. This may be my only chance. I jump straight in.

'It's Noel,' I say. 'He attacked me, in Dicey Reilly's that night I was out with you all. But he's denying anything happened.'

'Noel? Noel Hegarty? Attacked you?' To my dismay he gives a laugh. 'You're having me on, right? That's a good one.'

Then he sees my face. 'You're not serious, Jules?'

I nod. 'And he's making Clara's life hell. That's why she's off. She doesn't have flu, she's having panic attacks. The poor girl's terrified of having to work with him.'

'They're pretty serious accusations, Jules. Do you have any proof?'

I sigh. 'Not really. He's smart, he's been covering his tracks.'

Danny thinks for a second. 'Hang on, there was something, a few years ago. That girl Antonia said he was sending her dirty pictures or something. We all thought it was a bit of a joke.'

'Being sent porn by your boss isn't very funny, Danny,' I point out.

'Guess not.' He shrugs again. 'But unless you can prove any of it, not much I can do I'm afraid.'

Now my blood is boiling. 'You're all such cowards. Don't you care about Clara? She's going through hell right now.'

He doesn't look pleased. "Course I care about Clara. But Noel's the backbone of the show. Without him—'

'Grow up, Danny. It's a radio show. People are more important.' I go to stand up.

'Jules?' I hear someone calling me from the doorway. 'There you are.' Jamie's standing there looking rather out of place in jeans and a grey hoody.

He walks towards us and thrusts an open laptop and headphones into Danny's hands.

'Listen to the voice clip, mate,' he says. 'It's that Noel guy making a confession. I have a hard copy in case you need it for an employment tribunal or something. Jules is right, I think the dude needs to resign or it might end up all over the internet. You know how these things go. Wouldn't reflect too well on the show, employing a scumbag like that, or on you for that matter.'

I stare at Jamie. 'What? I don't understand.'

'I recorded your conversation with Noel,' Jamie says.

I glare at him, appalled. 'What? How? Have you been following me or something?'

'No! I bugged your dress.'

My mouth falls open. Is he deranged? 'You *what*?'

'Jules, let's just deal with this first, all right?' Jamie says.

He turns to Danny again, leaving me seething beside him. 'Will you listen to it? Please?'

Danny who's being uncharacteristically quiet, nods, sits down with the laptop on his knee, puts the headphones over his ears and presses play on the screen. As he listens his face goes paler and paler, his eyes sparking with anger. A few minutes later he takes off the headphones and looks at me.

'I should have trusted you, Jules, I'm so sorry. You were right. I need a good kick up the ass. Noel's so out of there. I knew he was a bit sexist but his attitude towards women is clearly off the scale. If they don't fire him, I'll walk. Plenty other stations who'd be happy to have me. I'm gutted for you and for Clara, genuinely.'

He hands Jamie back the laptop and then roots in his wallet for a business card. 'Can you send me the voice file? I'll make sure Noel Hegarty never produces another radio show if I can help it. Or goes anywhere near you or Clara ever again, Jules. I promise.'

'Sure.' Jamie takes the card and puts it in his pocket.

'Is there anything else I can do?' Danny asks. 'Anything at all.'

'Ring Clara,' I say. 'She's very upset.'

'Of course. And for you?'

I look at him for a moment. I could tell him about Ed's lack of action after Noel attacked me, how he refused to help Clara, but something stops me. It's certainly not love for Ed. I think it may be residual love for Lainey, or certainly loyalty.

'No,' I say firmly. 'Just look after Clara.'

Danny nods. 'I will. And I really am sorry.'

Jamie holds out his hand. 'Come on, Jules. I think it's time to get out of here.'

I refuse to take his hand, but follow him out reluctantly, feeling faint with relief, but still practically frothing at the mouth with rage. Jamie's been listening to all my private conversations – with Declan, with Clara. He could even hear me pee! I'll kill him!

Chapter 25

As soon as we step off the balcony and into the bar Jamie asks, 'Where is he?' and looks around the wedding party manically.

'Who?' I ask sharply.

'That Noel guy? I want to punch his lights out.'

'You've caused enough trouble already, Jamie. Let's just get out of here.' I spot Ed and Lainey lingering in the main doorway, talking to guests arriving. There's no way out of it, I'll have to speak to them, unless . . .

I look at Jamie. 'How did you get in here?'

'Round the back. Climbed over the railings.'

'Do you think I could get over?'

He shrugs. 'They aren't that high and I could help you.'

'Good. Which way?'

He points down some stairs to the far left of the hallway.

I look at Lainey and Ed one last time. Ed's laughing at something Harry is saying. I watch him for a second but he doesn't turn towards me. But Lainey does. Our eyes lock. I raise my hand and wave at her.

'Jules, don't go,' she calls, breaking away from the group and walking towards me.

'I have to,' I say. 'Have a fab day, Lainey. I mean it.' And before I know what I'm doing I hug her, tightly. She's wearing her favourite Chloe perfume and I sniff it in, trying to remember how things were before Ed came along and ruined everything.

'I'm so sorry, Jules,' she whispers in my ear. 'For everything. I wasn't a good friend to you.'

I draw away and give her a teary smile. 'That doesn't matter now. I hope you and Ed are very happy together, really. Take care of yourself, you hear?'

She nods and smiles back.

'Lainey,' Ed calls her.

And then Ed's eyes rest on mine. And I feel exactly nothing apart from a ripple of disgust and loathing. I think about saying something to him about Clara, calling him a lying, self-serving, heartless pig, but at the end of the day it would only hurt Lainey. Plus it would make me look like a shrew. So I keep my mouth shut. Instead I say, 'Goodbye, Lainey. Enjoy your day.'

'Bye, Jules.' There are tears in her eyes and I turn away before I well up myself.

Then, because I really don't trust myself to go near Ed without saying something, I join Jamie who is waiting for me at the top of the stairs.

'Everything all right?' he asks me as we descend.

'Nothing's all right,' I snap back. 'And I can't believe you were stalking me.'

He holds open a door at the bottom of the stairs for me to walk through.

'I was worried about you,' as we pass through a small empty function room towards the exit.

'I'm perfectly capable of looking after myself thanks very much.' My feet are starting to yang in my heels, so I stop and pull them off.

He's outside now, marching past some dinghies towards the tall perimeter railing.

'I thought you said it was easy to climb,' I shout at his back. 'I'm a midget, remember?'

He stops beside the railings and waits for me. 'There's a gate, OK. Maybe if we wait someone will open it for us.'

'I'm not standing around, Jamie. You'll have to lift me.'

'Fine.' He clasps his hands together to make a foothold and crouches down a little. 'Go on then.'

I put my foot in his hand, but luckily a rather startled-looking woman comes through the gate and holds it open for us.

'Wait here,' Jamie says when we're safely outside. 'I'll get the car.'

'Car? You don't own a car.'

'It's Mum's. And stop being so snappy. It doesn't suit you.'

Minutes later he reappears with Daphne's Fiesta and stretches over to open the passenger door. I climb in, slam the door behind me, cross my arms and stare out of the windscreen, my lips clamped together, my jaw set.

He drives towards Dun Laoghaire main street, then swings a left onto the coast road. Before we get to Dalkey, he slows down and then parks up in front of the sea.

'Why have we stopped?' I ask. 'I'm tired, Jamie, I want to go home. I have nothing to say to you right now.'

'I know you're annoyed with me for bugging you, but—'

'Where is it?' I say, peering down the bodice. 'Take it off right now.'

He reaches down and plucks a small circle the size of a watch battery off my belt. It has four tiny claws and, as it's also silver, it's no wonder I didn't spot it.

'You said it was on my dress,' I say. 'And please tell me you didn't sneak into my bedroom to put it there.'

He smiles. 'I lied. Wanted to keep it in place in case you removed it and then ran off or something stupid. And no, I didn't break into your bedroom.'

I scowl at him. 'You'd better explain how it got there, Jamie Clear. Or I'll do something bad to you.' Right this second, I don't have the energy to come up with a better threat.

'It was when you were having dinner with Arietty and Pandora. The belt was in the office.'

My eyes narrow. 'How did you know that?'

'I may have had a little help.'

'Pandora! I'll kill her too. No wonder she insisted I wore the belt today. Was this whole bugging thing her idea?'

'No, mine. I was just trying to watch your back, Jules. The way you've been drinking lately, I was worried about you, OK? I didn't want you to hurt yourself or get into any trouble.'

'You have some bloody nerve. I had everything under control. I didn't need you interfering. Who do you think you are? James Bond?'

'I don't really care what you think, Jules. I was trying to keep you safe. And it did catch Noel out, remember? So it paid off. And if you can't see that, you're blind and stupid.'

'Would you stop calling me stupid,' I demand.

'When you stop acting like a complete idiot I'll consider it.'

'I don't act like an idiot.'

'Jules, you got drunk and fell out of a tree last week. And you managed to pick the most useless boyfriend in the world. From what that scumbag Noel said, Ed is even more of a slimeball than I always thought possible.'

'I know, Ed's a prick.'

'Sorry?'

'You heard me, he's a prick. With no redeeming qualities whatsoever. I have no idea what I ever saw in him. In fact, even thinking about him makes my skin crawl.'

Jamie sits back in his seat and runs his hands through his hair. 'Finally she sees sense. Jesus, Jules, how long has it taken you? Six years?'

'Something like that. And no, I don't want to talk about it, thank you very much. Or my drinking, OK? It's none of your business.' I turn to face him. 'But one thing I don't understand, Jamie. The bugging and everything – why? Why do you care about me so much? After everything I've done.'

He stares down at the bug and plays with it in his fingers.

'You know why, Jules. You've always known deep down.'

'What are you talking about?'

He lifts his head and stares out at the sea. 'I love you. I always have, ever since we were kids.'

'Don't be daft, Jamie, we're friends. It's never been a love thing, you know that. We used to talk about it, remember? I said kissing you would be like kissing my own brother.'

He looks at me, his eyes intense. 'I was just playing along. I didn't want to scare you off. But I've always been in love with you. I still am.'

'Now you're being stupid. It wouldn't work. You need fire-works, Jamie, passion, drama, excitement. With us it isn't like that. It's too safe, too easy.'

'It is fireworks for me.'

'But I don't think of you that way.'

His face drops so I quickly add, 'I love you as a friend, Jamie. A dear, dear friend, but that's all.'

'Can't you give it a chance? Maybe the sparks will come in time. How will you know if you don't give it a try?'

I shrug. 'I just know.' I shake my head. 'It wouldn't work, I'm sorry. You're too kind.'

He snorts. 'And kind is a bad thing? Jules, most couples don't practically kill each other on a daily basis. What you had with Ed wasn't normal. Look at your mum and dad. They adored each other, were devoted to each other. And they started out as best friends, you told me that.'

'That was different.'

'Why?'

'They were one in a million. And please stop talking about Mum and Dad, OK?'

But he continues on regardless. 'Jules, I remember your mum, she was amazing. And I know she'd want you to be with some-one who adores you, who wants to take care of you, the way your dad always took care of her.'

Now he's stepped over the line. 'Mum didn't need anyone looking after her! She was strong and clever and smart—'

'And she once put water in the car instead of oil, and ruined the engine,' he says gently. 'And she was forever losing her keys and locking herself out of the house. Yes, she was smart, but your dad was the practical one.'

I sigh. He's right. Mum was incredible in so many ways, but practical she was not.

He continues, 'She'd want you to be happy. And she'd want you to find someone who loves you unconditionally, who thinks you're the best thing on the planet.' He pauses for a moment. 'And by the way, you look stunning in that dress. It's beautiful. You're beautiful.'

I bite my lip. Never once in all the time we were together did Ed Powers notice what I was wearing, let alone comment on it. And then I start crying again. Is Jamie right, do we have a chance? I've treated him so badly, not just now but over the years. Yes, I always had an inkling that he had feelings for me, but I blocked it out, refused to acknowledge it. But even now he doesn't know everything.

'I kissed Ed,' I say in a rush. 'That first night in the tree house, the time before the accident. I know it was stupid but he kissed me and I kissed him back.'

Jamie says nothing, just stares at me. Tears roll down my cheeks and I don't bother wiping them away.

'I drank too much vodka and I just wanted to remember the good bits,' I add. 'It was a stupid thing to do and I'm a horrible, horrible person.'

'Your fall,' he asks softly. 'Were you with him then? I never got the full story.'

'Yes. He wanted to talk to me but I'd had enough of him. I was trying to climb down the ladder to get away from him and I lost my footing and fell. He woke Pandora, told her what had happened and then left.'

Jamie looks appalled. 'Hang on, let me get this straight, you were lying unconscious on the ground and he left you?'

I nod and twist my hands together in my lap.

'And you still went to his wedding? Jules, why did you do that to yourself?'

'Because I'm all over the place. I'm such a mess I have to see a shrink now, every week.'

'You're trying to sort yourself out, Jules, that's great. Look, it's perfectly normal. I was seeing someone for a while too.'

'A shrink? Why?'

He gives a small smile. 'A counsellor. Stop calling them shrinks, Jules.'

'You didn't answer my question.'

'I was trying to tell you weeks ago. Lynda, my girlfriend in Galway, well she got pregnant. I wanted her to keep it, begged her to, said I'd marry her, but she had an abortion, in London, wouldn't let me go with her, took her sister instead. It was all pretty harrowing. She shut me out after that, refused to communicate, and to cut a long story short, we broke up.

'A few months later, she was with someone else. I met her in a pub in Salthill, wrapped around this tall blond guy. Anyway, she told me she was sorry about the abortion and everything, but it was all for the best, we weren't meant to be together. I'm still finding it hard to come to terms with it to be honest; it was my baby too. I only got together with her in the first place because she had long curly hair and she reminded me of you.' He smiles sadly. 'Silly I know.'

I take his hand and hold it tight. His skin feels cool against mine. 'I don't know what to say, Jamie. I'm so sorry.'

We sit in silence for a while, staring out at the sea.

'Life's pretty shit sometimes, isn't it?' I say eventually. I put my head on his shoulder.

'Yep,' he says softly. He puts his arm around me. I think about shrugging it off, but I don't. Sitting there, beside Jamie, I feel safe.

Eventually I break the silence. 'I told the counsellor, about killing mum.'

Jamie sighs. 'You didn't kill your mum, Jules.'

'That's what she said. And I have to talk to my family about the whole birthday thing. But they'll hate me.'

'No they won't, it wasn't your fault.'

'But I tired her out, she might have lived a little longer if I wasn't such a blabbermouth.'

'She loved you, Jules. With all her heart. And she died knowing you loved her back. You have to stop blaming yourself. It's gone on far too long.'

I sigh. I know he's right, but I've been blaming myself for so many years it's part of who I am. But maybe old habits can be broken.

'Can we stop talking, Jamie?' I say. 'Can we just stay here for a while? Please?'

He nods. 'Sure, whatever you need, Jules.'

I drop my head onto his chest and as he strokes my hair, I cry my heart out.

After a while the tears dry up and I mop my face with tissues from Daphne's glove compartment.

'Feeling better?' Jamie asks gently.

I nod and give him a half-hearted smile. My eyes sweep his face and then rest on his lips. I've never noticed before but they're surprisingly firm and I begin to wonder what it might be like to kiss them. I let the thought linger for a second. I've known Jamie all my life, for years we were practically joined at the hip. He also knows all my many faults and yet he still loves me. Would loving him back really be all that difficult? Could I really spend my life with someone like Jamie? With Ed it was so simple, just spotting him across a crowded room made my heart beat faster and my body squirm with longing. But look where that got me. It's all so confusing.

Jamie brushes some loose strands of hair back off my face and my skin tingles underneath his touch. Involuntarily I move my cheek towards his hand.

'Jules?' He looks at me in confusion.

'Do that again,' I say softly.

'What, this?' He strokes my cheek gently and again my skin fizzes. This time my breath quickens a little and I swallow, unprepared for the warm feeling that is sweeping through my body.

I look him in the eye. His pupils are dilated and he's breathing quickly. Before I have a chance to analyse what's happening, my lips are moving towards his and we're kissing, softly at first, but within seconds it's strong and passionate and I don't want it to stop. But I have an overwhelming urge to be closer to him, to feel his body pressed against mine, to roam my hands over his bare skin.

I break away for a second.

'Move your seat back,' I say urgently.

He looks concerned. 'Jules, you don't have to do this. I know you don't feel the same way about me as I do about you. It's OK, you don't have to pretend.'

I start to giggle, which turns into full on bubbling laughter. 'Jamie Clear, as strange as it may sound, I think I may fancy the ass off you. Now move the bloody seat so I can ravish you properly, and then shut up and kiss me.'

Chapter 26

The following morning at eleven my mobile rings, waking me up. I open my eyes and reach for it.

'Hello?'

'Sorry, Jules, did I wake you? I know it's early.' It's Danny. For a second I'm completely flummoxed. He's never rung me before. Clara must have given him my number.

'No, no, it's fine. Just give me one second.' I sit up. I expect to feel horrible, but I feel remarkably OK, considering. And I don't remember waking up once during the night, which is a novelty. In fact I feel quite refreshed, borderline chipper. My lips feel a little swollen, but that's not surprising. I touch my finger to them and smile to myself. Jamie. Last night he was concerned that I'd wake up and think I'd made a terrible mistake, but he was wrong.

'Is anything wrong?' I ask. 'Is it Clara?'

'No, no, she's fine. Good in fact. I just wanted to let you know that I had words with Noel. He's agreed to leave RTÉ and find a job in London, something outside the radio sector altogether; finance maybe. He has to let me know where he's living and working, and check in with me once a week.'

'Like a parole officer?'

'Exactly. And if he so much as sneezes at a woman again, so help me God he won't know what's hit him. That way you and Clara won't be dragged though any kind of industrial tribunals or the courts or anything. Clara isn't keen on taking the legal

301

route, wants him out of the country as quickly as possible. Unless *you* want to take him to court?'

'No,' I say. 'I don't think that would achieve anything. But Clara can go back to work now, yes?'

'One hundred per cent. In fact, if I can persuade the powers that be, I'd like her to be my new producer.'

'You'd be lucky to have her.'

He laughs. 'I know. I rang some of my colleagues for advice and they all had nothing but praise, said they'd make her producer in a heartbeat. She's been helping them out with ideas and contacts for years. Sounds like I've been totally underestimating her. I've already talked to her about it, and she's considering it. But I hope she'll say yes.'

'And Ed?'

There's a pause. 'I left the reception early. Clara and I both think he'll do very well on another show. We want to build a new team and I'm going to make sure she gets the chance to pick her own researchers, people she trusts. I know she's hoping to talk to you later, Jules. Put in a good word for me, will you? The show really needs her.'

'The *show*?' I say archly.

'Ah, feck it, you're right, *I* need her. She's amazing.'

So Danny has finally seen through Ed and realized how lucky he is to have Clara. No doubt Ed will put some spin on his move, making it sound like a promotion, but the radio world is very small and people talk. I wonder what will happen to him? I feel sorry for Lainey, she deserves better. But she chose Ed, for better or for worse.

'Don't worry, I will,' I tell Danny. 'You and Clara will make a great team.'

As I click off my mobile, I smile to myself. Strange how things turn out. I'd always thought Danny was a bit of a plonker, but I guess I've called him wrong.

Bird comes into my room. 'You're awake. About time.' She

pulls back my curtains and opens the shutters halfway. Then she sits down on the end of my bed. 'So how was the wedding, Jules? You got in later than I'd expected.'

Jamie had dropped me home. We'd talked, laughed and kissed for hours, catching up on six years of joint memories, both good and bad. Then we'd bought chips in Borzas in Dalkey and sat on the wall overlooking Dalkey Island, talking some more. I started yawning at eleven and Jamie insisted on dropping me home.

'I'm fine, Jamie,' I'd protested.

'Jules, your eyes are drooping and you fell asleep kissing me a few minutes ago.'

'Only because my eyes were closed. I'll keep them open this time.'

He laughed. 'I'll see you tomorrow, Jules.'

'Promise?'

He stroked my cheek and smiled. 'Promise. And the next day, and the day after that. I'm not going anywhere. Not without you anyway.'

'How did it go?' Bird asks again.

'It actually went OK. I didn't disgrace myself and Declan was charming as always.'

Bird smiles. 'I do like Declan and I'm glad you had a plus one. Was it painful my darling, seeing them at the altar, exchanging their vows?'

I shrug. 'A bit. But honestly, I'm all right, Bird. I'll survive. And I can put the whole Ed and Lainey thing behind me now, move on with my life.'

She looks at me curiously. 'You're taking it very well, I must say. Is the counselling helping? What did you talk about exactly, Boolie? I haven't had a chance to ask you yet. Ed obviously?'

'Not really.'

'What then? Family things?'

'Did they like the dress?' Pandora walks into the room, interrupting us.

'Hello, this isn't Grand Central Station,' I say. 'I'm still in my pyjamas. All we need is Dad now.'

Pandora chuckles. 'In fact I think he's on his way up to give you breakfast in bed. Unless the full Irish he's cooking is for Bird. It's not for Iris, she's at a soccer tournament. I hope her team wins this time, she was in a right snot after the last defeat.'

I grab another pillow and put it behind my back. 'Great. I think I'll just stay here all day. Any chance one of you could bring the telly up?'

Bird sniffs. 'I don't believe in watching television in bed, Julia. You know that. Rots the brain.'

Pandora and I swap a look. She rolls her eyes and I giggle.

Dad walks through the door, holding a tray. I get a waft of bacon and my mouth starts watering. 'Thanks, Dad, I'm starving.'

I wolf down the food while the others chat about Iris and her competitive streak.

The atmosphere suddenly changes when Pandora says, 'This reminds me of when Mum was sick. We all used to sit on her bed every evening, to keep her company while she tried to eat something. She called it "Schuster Time".'

Bird pats Pandora's hand and nods. 'That's right. She loved having her family all around her. Jules used to show her little pictures she'd drawn at school and you brushed her hair, very gently.'

Bird looks at Dad. 'They were happy times, weren't they, Greg?'

Dad doesn't respond, not even a nod.

After a moment he says, 'Finished, Jules?'

'Yes, thanks,' I say.

He stands up and takes the tray away. He's about to walk out of the room when I add, 'Stay, Dad. I haven't seen you all week.'

He looks at me. His eyes are sad. 'I need to wash up.'

'Please, Dad?'

He stands there, tray still in his hands.

'Greg, come back and join us.' Bird pats the bed beside her.

He puts the tray on my dressing table and sits down.

No one says anything for a second and it begins to feel awkward so I pipe up, 'Anne's nice.'

'Who's Anne, darling?' Bird asks.

'My counsellor. We talked about all kinds of things. I cried a lot of course, but she said that was normal, everyone bawls apparently, especially at the first session.' My heart is thumping in my chest but I make myself continue. 'She told me I should try talking to all of you, about my birthday and Mum dying and—'

Dad stands up abruptly. 'I'm sorry, I can't do this. I'll be downstairs if you need me.'

'Sit down right now,' Bird says firmly. 'You've been running away from this for years, Greg. The girls need to be able to talk about Kirsten. And we need to listen. It's our duty. So sit. Boolie's trying to tell us something.'

I look at Bird and there's a softness in her eyes I've never seen before. 'Go on, darling,' she says to me.

Pandora reaches over and holds my hand, her skin warm against mine. From the way her mouth is twisted, I can tell she's biting her cheek, trying to stop herself crying.

'Greg?' Bird says, staring at him. 'You want to hear what Boolie has to say, don't you?'

He nods and says, 'Yes, of course,' in a low voice, but he can't meet my eyes.

Pandora squeezes my hand gently. 'Tell us, Boolie.'

I start, my voice shaking with nerves. 'I woke up early that day, nobody was awake. So I went into Mum. I knew I wasn't supposed to, and I wouldn't have woken her up or anything, but her eyes were open and I so wanted to talk to her. She told me all about her own ninth birthday. Then she said that she felt tired and that she wanted to go to heaven, it was time. And I told her if it would make her feel better, she could go. She sang me "Three Little Swallows" and afterwards her breathing went all funny.'

I stop and blink back my tears. 'Then . . . then . . . I hugged her and she . . . she . . .' I'm crying so much I have to stop. After a few moments I add in a tiny voice, 'I tired her out. It was my fault she died.'

'Oh, Boolie,' Pandora says, still holding my hand firmly. 'No it wasn't. She had cancer.'

Tears are rolling down both Bird and Pandora's faces but it's Dad I'm worried about. I look at him. He's hunched over, his face buried in his hands.

'I'm so sorry Dad,' I say. 'I'm so sorry. You should have had more time with her.'

He lifts his head. I expected sparks of anger or at the very least disappointment, but he looks distraught.

'I'm the one who should be sorry,' he says. 'For years I've been beating myself up for not being there when Kirsten took her last breath, but towards the end I just couldn't . . . I had to have some distance . . . it was all too much. I should have been there with her all the time. You and Pandora and Bird, you were the strong ones. I failed you all. Your mum loved you and Pandora with all her being. Towards the end she was really suffering, and I've worried so much that she was in pain when she went. You can't begin to understand how happy I am that you were there with her. It's like a weight being lifted off my shoulders. I'm so sorry it had to be you, pet, and on your birthday too. You gave your mum the most precious gift, your total and absolute love. And I can't believe you've carried this all your life, alone. You're the bravest of all of us, do you understand that? You've carried us all these years with your good humour and yes, your mad antics. I know your mum is still looking out for you both. And she must be so proud of you too.'

Jamie and Anne were right. Dad isn't angry with me and I

didn't ruin everything. Suddenly my heart feels as light and as free as a bird.

'I know we were young,' Pandora tells him. 'But we did understand, Dad. Mum always said what you two had was true love. We knew you were sad because you loved her so much.'

'Thank you,' Dad whispers, giving Pandora a small smile.

'And you certainly didn't fail any of us, Greg,' Bird says gently. 'Pandora's right, what you and Kirsten had was special, you were so close, like two peas in a pod. You couldn't bear the thought of losing her, so you just shut down. But you've been an incredible father to the girls over the years, and I couldn't have asked for a better son-in-law.'

Dad nods, unable to say anything. Since the day Mum died he's never shed a tear, but he's certainly crying now. He wipes his eyes on his sleeve.

'And all these years we thought we were minding you, Boolie,' Bird says thoughtfully. 'But in reality, you were minding us. Funny how life works out, isn't it?'

Bird leans forward, joins the group hug for a moment, then pulls away. 'But we do have a business to run, my darlings. And much as I adore Klaudia she does rather scare the customers. I'll pop in and hold the fort. And there's no rush, girls. Spend some time with your dad first. See you all for family dinner this evening, yes?' She stands up.

'Yes, Bird!' Pandora and I chorus as she leaves the room, and then we both collapse into giggles. I think it's all the emotion, it always gets to us. Dad is seeing Bird out but has promised to come straight back up.

Crying and laughing at the same time, I look at Pandora and she looks back at me.

'Boolie?' she says.

'Yes, sis?'

'I'm sorry I wasn't with you. On your birthday. With mum.'

'Me too,' I say. 'And I'm sorry I didn't go and get you. I should have shared her with you.'

'That's OK. I don't think I would have coped, seeing her die in front of my eyes, it would have upset me too much. There was a reason you were with Mum that morning, Boolie, and not me or Dad. Even Bird was in bits, Mum was her baby. Dad's right, you're stronger than any of us, you were meant to be there. And I'm sorry I haven't always been a good sister to you.'

'Are you kidding?' I say, genuinely taken aback. 'You've always been extraordinary.' I smile. 'Bossy, yes, but extraordinary. And I'm sorry for pushing you away for so many years. It was my loss, I see that now.'

She smiles back at me, her eyes glittering with tears. 'Does that mean we're friends now?'

I nod firmly. 'Of course we're friends, best friends, you're my sister.'

She hugs me and we stay like that for a long, long time.

Epilogue

Two Weeks Later

'A rabbit?' Arietty says. 'Pandora has a rabbit?'

I grin. 'It was Declan's idea. He said Iris needed a pet. Went off and bought a hutch with them and everything. Iris called him Fluffy and he's gorgeous, but Pandora's still not convinced. Keeps going on about having to clean up the poos.'

'At least they're only small. The poos, I mean. And you mentioned Jamie. Why's he coming to our handover dinner? He hardly wants to borrow the dress. Hang on, he's not one of those cross-dressers is he?' She stares at me, eyes wide.

'How would I know?'

Her mouth flickers at the edges.

'What?' I demand.

'Oh come on, you must admit you have been spending rather a lot of time together. And I'm not blind.'

I can feel my cheeks pinking up so I pick up the menu and start studying it. 'He's not eating with us, he's just dropping in for a second. And we're just friends.'

'Do you snog all your friends?'

'It's not like that.'

She grins. 'It's written all over your face. I knew it. Ha! That's brilliant news.'

I put the menu down. 'OK, fine, I'm kissing Jamie. I didn't want to say anything until I knew it was serious.'

'So it's serious?'

'No! Serious is the wrong word. Look, we're together, all right. Now stop interrogating me, you're as bad as Pandora.'

'You two look very cosy.' Just then Pandora slides along the seat towards me and kisses me on the cheek. 'And what were you saying about me?'

Arietty launches straight in. 'Jules is snogging Jamie and she says it's serious.'

Pandora looks smug. 'I know. Jamie told Daphne who told Bird who told me.'

'I hate being the last to know.' Arietty crosses her arms huffily.

'I even told your elephants last week,' I say. 'And they're obviously better at keeping secrets than Jamie Clear.'

Arietty sticks her tongue out at me and I laugh.

'Speaking of which,' I add, 'he'll be here any second.'

'You never answered my question,' Arietty says. 'Why's he coming?'

I smile at her. 'He's been at his old tricks again. Found some sort of Google Earth camera outside Wicklow post office and to cut a long story short, he has a video clip of Alex he wants to show us.'

'How do you know it's Alex?'

'He's carrying a large cardboard box covered with Shoestring bags. I wrapped and posted it myself.'

'Hang on a second, did you just say *he*?' Pandora says. 'Is Alex a boy?'

I smile. 'There's been a slight twist in The Shoestring Club tale . . .'

Acknowledgements

This book would never have made it to publication without the Trojan efforts of Peta Nightingale, my agent, and Thalia Suzuma, my editor, who both showed endless reserves of patience and empathy. Thank you both so much. Thanks also to Trisha Jackson for her support.

Thanks must also go to my family: Mum, Dad, Kate, Emma, Richard. And my own gang at home – Ben, Sam, Amy and Jago.

Martina Devlin, my writer in crime, must get a special mention for always being at the end of the phone when I need her advice (or just a chat).

To my friends Tanya, Nicky and Andrew, and to my dear friends in writing, especially Clare Dowling, Martina Reilly, Marita Conlon McKenna, Judi Curtin and Vanessa O'Loughlin, Ms Inkwell herself, thank you.

Alice Cooper, one of the Elephant Keepers at Dublin Zoo, kindly introduced me to the Asian elephants in her care, for which I'm supremely grateful. Any elephant-related mistakes are of course my own. And Stock Exchange in Dun Laoghaire, one of my favourite places to shop, gave me lots of designer swap shop inspiration.

The lovely David Adamson and Cormac Kinsella, my Pan Macmillan team in Ireland make touring the bookshops such a treat. And huge thanks to all the booksellers who continue to support my books, especially the gang in Eason and Dubray.

311

And finally to you, the reader. This is book ten – ten, imagine! Many of you have been with me throughout my writing journey and I thank you from the bottom of my heart. Here's to another ten!

Much love,
Sarah XXX

P.S. Do write to me – sarah@sarahwebb.ie – I love hearing from readers. Or you can catch me on Facebook: www.facebook.com/sarahwebbauthor or Twitter: @sarahwebbishere

And if you have young teens or tweens in the house, check out my Amy Green series – see www.askamygreen.com for details